Y0-CAX-154

The Evil Genius

Wilkie Collins

THE EVIL GENIUS

by Wilkie Colllins

A Domestic Story

Affectionately Dedicated to
Holman Hunt

BEFORE THE STORY.

Miss Westerfield's Education

1. —The Trial.

THE gentlemen of the jury retired to consider their verdict.

Their foreman was a person doubly distinguished among his colleagues. He had the clearest head, and the readiest tongue. For once the right man was in the right place.

Of the eleven jurymen, four showed their characters on the surface. They were:

The hungry juryman, who wanted his dinner.

The inattentive juryman, who drew pictures on his blotting paper.

The nervous juryman, who suffered from fidgets.

The silent juryman, who decided the verdict.

Of the seven remaining members, one was a little drowsy man who gave no trouble; one was an irritable invalid who served under protest; and five represented that vast majority of the population— easily governed, tranquilly happy—which has no opinion of its own.

The foreman took his place at the head of the table. His colleagues seated themselves on either side of him. Then there fell upon that assembly of men a silence, never known among an assembly of women—the silence which proceeds from a general reluctance to be the person who speaks first.

It was the foreman's duty, under these circumstances, to treat his deliberative brethren as we treat our watches when they stop: he wound the jury up and set them going.

"Gentlemen, " he began, "have you formed any decided opinion on the case—thus far? "

Some of them said "Yes, " and some of them said "No. " The little drowsy man said nothing. The fretful invalid cried, "Go on! " The nervous juryman suddenly rose. His brethren all looked at him, inspired by the same fear of having got an orator among them. He was an essentially polite man; and he hastened to relieve their minds. "Pray don't be alarmed, gentlemen: I am not going to make a speech. I suffer from fidgets. Excuse me if I occasionally change my position. " The hungry juryman (who dined early) looked at his watch. "Half-past four, " he said. "For Heaven's sake cut it short. " He was the fattest person present; and he suggested a subject to the inattentive juryman who drew pictures on his blotting-paper. Deeply interested in the progress of the likeness, his neighbors on either side looked over his shoulders. The little drowsy man woke with a start, and begged pardon of everybody. The fretful invalid said to himself, "Damned fools, all of them! " The patient foreman, biding his time, stated the case.

"The prisoner waiting our verdict, gentlemen, is the Honorable Roderick Westerfield, younger brother of the present Lord Le Basque. He is charged with willfully casting away the British bark *John Jerniman*, under his command, for the purpose of fraudulently obtaining a share of the insurance money; and further of possessing himself of certain Brazilian diamonds, which formed part of the cargo. In plain words, here is a gentleman born in the higher ranks of life accused of being a thief. Before we attempt to arrive at a decision, we shall only be doing him justice if we try to form some general estimate of his character, based on the evidence—and we may fairly begin by inquiring into his relations with the noble family to which he belongs. The evidence, so far, is not altogether creditable to him. Being at the time an officer of the Royal Navy, he appears to have outraged the feelings of his family by marrying a barmaid at a public-house. "

The drowsy juryman, happening to be awake at that moment, surprised the foreman by interposing a statement. "Talking of barmaids, " he said, "I know a curate's daughter. She's in distressed circumstances, poor thing; and she's a barmaid somewhere in the north of England. Curiously enough, the name of the town has escaped my memory. If we had a map of England—" There he was interrupted, cruelly interrupted, by one of his brethren.

"And by what right, " cried the greedy juryman, speaking under the exasperating influence of hunger—"by what right does Mr.

Westerfield's family dare to suppose that a barmaid may not be a perfectly virtuous woman? "

Hearing this, the restless gentleman (in the act of changing his position) was suddenly inspired with interest in the proceedings. "Pardon me for putting myself forward, " he said, with his customary politeness. "Speaking as an abstainer from fermented liquors, I must really protest against these allusions to barmaids. "

"Speaking as a consumer of fermented liquors, " the invalid remarked, "I wish I had a barmaid and a bottle of champagne before me now. "

Superior to interruption, the admirable foreman went on:

"Whatever you may think, gentlemen, of the prisoner's marriage, we have it in evidence that his relatives turned their backs on him from that moment—with the one merciful exception of the head of the family. Lord Le Basque exerted his influence with the Admiralty, and obtained for his brother (then out of employment) an appointment to a ship. All the witnesses agree that Mr. Westerfield thoroughly understood his profession. If he could have controlled himself, he might have risen to high rank in the Navy. His temper was his ruin. He quarreled with one of his superior officers—"

"Under strong provocation, " said a member of the jury.

"Under strong provocation, " the foreman admitted. "But provocation is not an excuse, judged by the rules of discipline. The prisoner challenged the officer on duty to fight a duel, at the first opportunity, on shore; and, receiving a contemptuous refusal, struck him on the quarter-deck. As a matter of course, Mr. Westerfield was tried by court-martial, and was dismissed the service. Lord Le Basque's patience was not exhausted yet. The Merchant Service offered a last chance to the prisoner of retrieving his position, to some extent at least. He was fit for the sea, and fit for nothing else. At my lord's earnest request the owners of the *John Jerniman*, trading between Liverpool and Rio, took Mr. Westerfield on trial as first mate, and, to his credit be it said, he justified his brother's faith in him. In a tempest off the coast of Africa the captain was washed overboard and the first mate succeeded to the command. His seamanship and courage saved the vessel, under circumstances of danger which paralyzed the efforts of the other officers.. He was confirmed, rightly confirmed, in the command of the ship. And, so far, we shall certainly not be wrong if we view his character on the favorable side. "

There the foreman paused, to collect his ideas.

Certain members of the assembly—led by the juryman who wanted his dinner, and supported by his inattentive colleague, then engaged in drawing a ship in a storm, and a captain falling overboard—proposed the acquittal of the prisoner without further consideration. But the fretful invalid cried "Stuff! " and the five jurymen who had no opinions of their own, struck by the admirable brevity with which he expressed his sentiments, sang out in chorus, "Hear! hear! hear! " The silent juryman, hitherto overlooked, now attracted attention. He was a bald-headed person of uncertain age, buttoned up tight in a long frockcoat, and wearing his gloves all through the proceedings. When the chorus of five cheered, he smiled mysteriously. Everybody wondered what that smile meant. The silent juryman kept his opinion to himself. From that moment he began to exercise a furtive influence over the jury. Even the foreman looked at him, on resuming the narrative.

"After a certain term of service, gentlemen, during which we learn nothing to his disadvantage, the prisoner's merits appear to have received their reward. He was presented with a share in the ship which he commanded, in addition to his regular salary as master. With these improved prospects he sailed from Liverpool on his last voyage to Brazil; and no one, his wife included, had the faintest suspicion that he left England under circumstances of serious pecuniary embarrassment. The testimony of his creditors, and of other persons with whom he associated distinctly proves that his leisure hours on shore had been employed in card-playing and in betting on horse races. After an unusually long run of luck, his good fortune seems to have deserted him. He suffered considerable losses, and was at last driven to borrowing at a high rate of interest, without any reasonable prospect of being able to repay the money-lenders into whose hands he had fallen. When he left Rio on the homeward voyage, there is no sort of doubt that he was returning to England to face creditors whom he was unable to pay. There, gentlemen, is a noticeable side to his character which we may call the gambling side, and which (as I think) was too leniently viewed by the judge. "

He evidently intended to add a word or two more. But the disagreeable invalid insisted on being heard.

"In plain English, " he said, "you are for finding the prisoner guilty. "

"In plain English, " the foreman rejoined, "I refuse to answer that question. "

"Why? "

"Because it is no part of my duty to attempt to influence the verdict. "

"You have been trying to influence the verdict, sir, ever since you entered this room. I appeal to all the gentlemen present. "

The patience of the long-suffering foreman failed him at last. "Not another word shall pass my lips, " he said, "until you find the prisoner guilty or not guilty among yourselves—and then I'll tell you if I agree to your verdict. "

He folded his arms, and looked like the image of a man who intended to keep his word.

The hungry juryman laid himself back in his chair, and groaned. The amateur artist, who had thus far found a fund of amusement in his blotting-paper, yawned discontentedly and dropped his pen. The courteous gentleman who suffered from fidgets requested leave to walk up and down the room; and at the first turn he took woke the drowsy little man, and maddened the irritable invalid by the creaking of his boots. The chorus of five, further than ever from arriving at an opinion of their own, looked at the silent juryman. Once more he smiled mysteriously; and once more he offered an explanation of what was passing in his mind—except that he turned his bald head slowly in the direction of the foreman. Was he in sympathy with a man who had promised to be as silent as himself?

In the meantime, nothing was said or done. Helpless silence prevailed in every part of the room.

"Why the devil doesn't somebody begin? " cried the invalid. "Have you all forgotten the evidence? "

This startling question roused the jury to a sense of what was due to their oaths, if not to themselves. Some of them recollected the evidence in one way, and some of them recollected it in another; and each man insisted on doing justice to his own excellent memory, and on stating his own unanswerable view of the case.

The first man who spoke began at the middle of the story told by the witnesses in court. "I am for acquitting the captain, gentlemen; he ordered out the boats, and saved the lives of the crew. " — "And I am for finding him guilty, because the ship struck on a rock in broad daylight, and in moderate weather. " — "I agree with you, sir. The evidence shows that the vessel was steered dangerously near to the land, by direction of the captain, who gave the course. " — "Come, come, gentlemen! let us do the captain justice. The defense declares that he gave the customary course, and that it was not followed when he left the deck. As for his leaving the ship in moderate weather, the evidence proves that he believed he saw signs of a storm brewing. " — "Yes, yes, all very well, but what were the facts? When the loss of the ship was reported, the Brazilian authorities sent men to the wreck, on the chance of saving the cargo; and, days afterward, there the ship was found, just as the captain and the crew had left her. " — "Don't forget, sir, that the diamonds were missing when the salvors examined the wreck. " — "All right, but that's no proof that the captain stole the diamonds; and, before they had saved half the cargo, a storm did come on and break the vessel up; so the poor man was only wrong in the matter of time, after all. " — "Allow me to remind you, gentlemen that the prisoner was deeply in debt, and therefore had an interest in stealing the diamonds. " — "Wait a little, sir. Fair play's a jewel. Who was in charge of the deck when the ship struck? The second mate. And what did the second mate do, when he heard that his owners had decided to prosecute? He committed suicide! Is there no proof of guilt in that act? " — "You are going a little too fast, sir. The coroner's jury declared that the second mate killed himself in a state of temporary insanity. " — "Gently! gently! we have nothing to do with what the coroner's jury said. What did the judge say when he summed up? " — "Bother the judge! He said what they all say: 'Find the prisoner guilty, if you think he did it; and find him not guilty, if you think he didn't. ' And then he went away to his comfortable cup of tea in his private room. And here are we perishing of hunger, and our families dining without us. " — "Speak for yourself, sir, *I* haven't got a family. " — "Consider yourself lucky, sir; *I* have got twelve, and my life is a burden to me, owing to the difficulty of making both ends meet. " —

"Gentlemen! gentlemen! we are wandering again. Is the captain guilty or not? Mr. Foreman, we none of us intended to offend you. Will you tell us what *you* think? "

No; the foreman kept his word. "Decide for yourselves first, " was his only reply.

In this emergency, the member afflicted with fidgets suddenly assumed a position of importance. He started a new idea.

"Suppose we try a show of hands, " he suggested. "Gentlemen who find the prisoner guilty will please hold up their hands. "

Three votes were at once registered in this way, including the vote of the foreman. After a moment of doubt, the chorus of five decided on following the opinion which happened to be the first opinion expressed in point of time. Thereupon, the show of hands for the condemnation of the prisoner rose to eight. Would this result have an effect on the undecided minority of four? In any case, they were invited to declare themselves next. Only three hands were held up. One incomprehensible man abstained from expressing his sentiments even by a sign. Is it necessary to say who that man was? A mysterious change had now presented itself in his appearance, which made him an object of greater interest than ever. His inexplicable smile had vanished. He sat immovable, with closed eyes. Was he meditating profoundly? or was he only asleep? The quick-witted foreman had long since suspected him of being simply the stupidest person present—with just cunning enough to conceal his own dullness by holding his tongue. The jury arrived at no such sensible conclusion. Impressed by the intense solemnity of his countenance, they believed him to be absorbed in reflections of the utmost importance to the verdict. After a heated conference among themselves, they decided on inviting the one independent member present—the member who had taken no part in their proceedings— to declare his opinion in the plainest possible form. "Which way does your view of the verdict incline, sir? Guilty or not guilty? "

The eyes of the silent juryman opened with the slow and solemn dilation of the eyes of an owl. Placed between the alternatives of declaring himself in one word or in two, his taciturn wisdom chose the shortest form of speech. "Guilty, " he answered—and shut his eyes again, as if he had had enough of it already.

An unutterable sense of relief pervaded the meeting. Enmities were forgotten and friendly looks were exchanged. With one accord, the jury rose to return to court. The prisoner's fate was sealed. The verdict was Guilty.

2. — The Sentence.

The low hum of talk among the persons in court ceased when the jury returned to their places. Curiosity now found its center of attraction in the prisoner's wife—who had been present throughout the trial. The question of the moment was: How will she bear the interval of delay which precedes the giving of the verdict?

In the popular phrase, Mrs. Westerfield was a showy woman. Her commanding figure was finely robed in dark colors; her profuse light hair hung over her forehead in little clusters of ringlets; her features, firmly but not delicately shaped, were on a large scale. No outward betrayal of the wife's emotion rewarded the public curiosity: her bold light-gray eyes sustained the general gaze without flinching. To the surprise of the women present, she had brought her two young children with her to the trial. The eldest was a pretty little girl of ten years old; the second child (a boy) sat on his mother's knee. It was generally observed that Mrs. Westerfield took no notice of her eldest child. When she whispered a word from time to time, it was always addressed to her son. She fondled him when he grew restless; but she never looked round to see if the girl at her side was as weary of the proceedings as the boy.

The judge took his seat, and the order was given to bring the prisoner up for judgment.

There was a long pause. The audience—remembering his ghastly face when he first appeared before them—whispered to each other, "He's taken ill"; and the audience proved to be right.

The surgeon of the prison entered the witness-box, and, being duly sworn, made his medical statement.

The prisoner's heart had been diseased for some time past, and the malady had been neglected. He had fainted under the prolonged suspense of waiting for the verdict. The swoon had proved to be of such a serious nature that the witness refused to answer for consequences if a second fainting-fit was produced by the excitement of facing the court and the jury.

Under these circumstances, the verdict was formally recorded, and sentence was deferred. Once more, the spectators looked at the prisoner's wife.

She had risen to leave the court. In the event of an adverse verdict, her husband had asked for a farewell interview; and the governor of the prison, after consultation with the surgeon, had granted the request. It was observed, when she retired, that she held her boy by the hand, and left the girl to follow. A compassionate lady near her offered to take care of the children while she was absent. Mrs. Westerfield answered quietly and coldly: "Thank you—their father wishes to see them. "

The prisoner was dying; nobody could look at him and doubt it.

His eyes opened wearily, when his wife and children approached the bed on which he lay helpless—the wreck of a grandly-made man. He struggled for breath, but he could still speak a word or two at a time. "I don't ask you what the verdict is, " he said to his wife; "I see it in your face. "

Tearless and silent, she waited by her husband's side. He had only noticed her for a moment. All his interest seemed to be centered in his children. The girl stood nearest to him, he looked at her with a faint smile.

The poor child understood him. Crying piteously, she put her arms around his neck and kissed him. "Dear papa, " she said; "come home and let me nurse you. "

The surgeon, watching the father's face, saw a change in him which the other persons present had not observed. The failing heart felt that parting moment, and sank under it. "Take the child away, " the surgeon whispered to the mother. Brandy was near him; he administered it while he spoke, and touched the fluttering pulse. It felt, just felt, the stimulant. He revived for a moment, and looked wistfully for his son. "The boy, " he murmured; "I want my boy. " As his wife brought the child to him, the surgeon whispered to her again. "If you have anything to say to him be quick about it! " She shuddered; she took his cold hand. Her touch seemed to nerve him with new strength; he asked her to stoop over him. "They won't let me write here, " he whispered, "unless they see my letter. " He paused to get his breath again. "Lift up my left arm, " he gasped. "Open the wrist-band. "

She detached the stud which closed the wrist-band of the shirt. On the inner side of the linen there was a line written in red letters—red of the color of blood. She saw these words: *Look in the lining of my trunk.*

"What for? " she asked.

The fading light in his eyes flashed on her a dreadful look of doubt. His lips fell apart in the vain effort to answer. His last sigh fluttered the light ringlets of her hair as she bent over him.

The surgeon pointed to her children. "Take the poor things home, " he said; "they have seen the last of their father. "

Mrs. Westerfield obeyed in silence. She had her own reasons for being in a hurry to get home. Leaving the children under the servant's care, she locked herself up in the dead man's room, and emptied his trunk of the few clothes that had been left in it.

The lining which she was now to examine was of the customary material, and of the usual striped pattern in blue and white. Her fingers were not sufficiently sensitive to feel anything under the surface, when she tried it with her hand. Turning the empty trunk with the inner side of the lid toward the light, she discovered, on one of the blue stripes of the lining, a thin little shining stain which looked like a stain of dried gum. After a moment's consideration, she cut the gummed line with a penknife. Something of a white color appeared through the aperture. She drew out a folded sheet of paper.

It proved to be a letter in her husband's hand-writing. An inclosure dropped to the floor when she opened it, in the shape of a small slip of paper. She picked it up. The morsel of paper presented letters, figures, and crosses arranged in lines, and mingled together in what looked like hopeless confusion.

The Evil Genius

3. — The Letter.

Mrs. Westerfield laid the incomprehensible slip of paper aside, and, in search of an explanation, returned to the letter. Here again she found herself in a state of perplexity. Directed to "Mrs. Roderick Westerfield, " the letter began abruptly, without the customary form of address. Did it mean that her husband was angry with her when he wrote? It meant that he doubted her.

In these terms he expressed himself:

"I write to you before my trial takes place. If the verdict goes in my favor, I shall destroy what I have written. If I am found guilty, I must leave it to you to do what I should otherwise have done for myself.

"The undeserved misfortune that has overtaken me began with the arrival of my ship in the port of Rio. Our second mate (his duty for the day being done) asked leave to go on shore—and never returned. What motive determined him on deserting, I am not able to say. It was my own wish to supply his place by promoting the best seaman on board. My owners' agents overruled me, and appointed a man of their own choosing.

"What nation he belonged to I don't know. The name he gave me was Beljames, and he was reported to be a broken-down gentleman. Whoever he might be, his manner and his talk were captivating. Everybody liked him.

"After the two calamities of the loss of the ship and the disappearance of the diamonds—these last being valued at five thousand pounds—I returned to England by the first opportunity that offered, having Beljames for a companion.

"Shortly after getting back to my house in London, I was privately warned by a good friend that my owners had decided to prosecute me for willfully casting away the ship, and (crueler still) for having stolen the missing diamonds. The second mate, who had been in command of the vessel when she struck on the rock, was similarly charged along with me. Knowing myself to be innocent, I determined, of course, to stand my trial. My wonder was, what Beljames would do. Would he follow my example? or, if he got the chance, would he try to make his escape?

"I might have thought it only friendly to give this person a word of warning, if I had known where to find him. We had separated when the ship reached the port of Falmouth, in Cornwall, and had not met since. I gave him my address in London; but he gave me no address in return.

"On the voyage home, Beljames told me that a legacy had been left to him; being a small freehold house and garden in St. John's Wood, London. His agent, writing to him on the subject, had reported the place to be sadly out of repair, and had advised him to find somebody who would take it off his hands on reasonable terms. This seemed to point to a likelihood of his being still in London, trying to sell his house.

"While my mind was running on these recollections, I was told that a decent elderly woman wanted to see me. She proved to be the landlady of the house in which Beljames lodged; and she brought an alarming message. The man was dying, and desired to see me. I went to him immediately.

"Few words are best, when one has to write about one's own troubles.

"Beljames had heard of the intended prosecution. How he had been made aware of it, death left him no time to tell me. The miserable wretch had poisoned himself—whether in terror of standing his trial, or in remorse of conscience, it is not any business of mine to decide. Most unluckily for me, he first ordered the doctor and the landlady out of the room; and then, when we two were alone, owned that he had purposely altered the course of the ship, and had stolen the diamonds.

"To do him justice, he was eager to save me from suffering for his fault.

"Having eased his mind by confession, he gave me the slip of paper (written in cipher) which you will find inclosed in this. 'There is my note of the place where the diamonds are hidden, ' he said. Among the many ignorant people who know nothing of ciphers, I am one— and I told him so. 'That's how I keep my secret, ' he said; 'write from my dictation, and you shall know what it means. Lift me up first. ' As I did it, he rolled his head to and fro, evidently in pain. But he managed to point to pen, ink, and paper, on a table hard by, on which his doctor had been writing. I left him for a moment, to pull the table nearer to the bed—and in that moment he groaned, and cried out for help. I ran to the room downstairs where the doctor was waiting. When we got back to him he was in convulsions. It was all over with Beljames.

"The lawyers who are to defend me have tried to get Experts, as they call them, to interpret the cipher. The Experts have all failed. They will declare, if they are called as witnesses, that the signs on the paper are not according to any known rules, and are marks made at random, meaning nothing.

"As for any statement, on my part, of the confession made to me, the law refuses to hear it, except from the mouth of a witness. I might prove that the ship's course was changed, contrary to my directions, after I had gone below to rest, if I could find the man who was steering at the time. God only knows where that man is.

"On the other hand, the errors of my past life, and my being in debt, are circumstances dead against me. The lawyers seem to trust almost entirely in a famous counsel, whom they have engaged to defend me. For my own part, I go to my trial with little or no hope.

"If the verdict is guilty, and if you have any regard left for my character, never rest until you have found somebody who can interpret these cursed signs. Do for me, I say, what I cannot do for myself. Recover the diamonds; and, when you restore them, show my owners this letter.

"Kiss the children for me. I wish them, when they are old enough, to read this defense of myself and to know that their father, who loved them dearly, was an innocent man. My good brother will take care of you, for my sake. I have done.

RODERICK WESTERFIELD. "

Mrs. Westerfield took up the cipher once more. She looked at it as if it were a living thing that defied her.

"If I am able to read this gibberish, " she decided, "I know what I'll do with the diamonds! "

4. — The Garret.

One year exactly after the fatal day of the trial, Mrs. Westerfield (secluded in the sanctuary of her bedroom) celebrated her release from the obligation of wearing widow's weeds.

The conventional graduations in the outward expression of grief, which lead from black clothing to gray, formed no part of this afflicted lady's system of mourning. She laid her best blue walking dress and her new bonnet to match on the bed, and admired them to her heart's content. Her discarded garments were left on the floor. "Thank Heaven, I've done with you! " she said — and kicked her rusty mourning out of the way as she advanced to the fireplace to ring the bell.

"Where is my little boy? " she asked, when the landlady entered the room.

"He's down with me in the kitchen, ma'am; I'm teaching him to make a plum cake for himself. He's so happy! I hope you don't want him just now? "

"Not the least in the world. I want you to take care of him while I am away. By-the-by, where's Syd? "

The elder child (the girl) had been christened Sydney, in compliment to one of her father's female relatives. The name was not liked by her mother — who had shortened it to Syd, by way of leaving as little of it as possible. With a look at Mrs. Westerfield which expressed ill-concealed aversion, the landlady answered: "She's up in the lumber-room, poor child. She says you sent her there to be out of the way. "

"Ah, to be sure, I did. "

"There's no fireplace in the garret, ma'am. I'm afraid the little girl must be cold and lonely. "

It was useless to plead for Syd — Mrs. Westerfield was not listening. Her attention was absorbed by her own plump and pretty hands. She took a tiny file from the dressing-table, and put a few finishing touches to her nails. "Send me some hot water, " she said; "I want to dress. "

The Evil Genius

The servant girl who carried the hot water upstairs was new to the ways of the house. After having waited on Mrs. Westerfield, she had been instructed by the kind-hearted landlady to go on to the top floor. "You will find a pretty little girl in the garret, all by herself. Say you are to bring her down to my room, as soon as her mamma has gone out. "

Mrs. Westerfield's habitual neglect of her eldest child was known to every person in the house. Even the new servant had heard of it. Interested by what she saw, on opening the garret door, she stopped on the threshold and looked in.

The lumber in the room consisted of two rotten old trunks, a broken chair, and a dirty volume of sermons of the old-fashioned quarto size. The grimy ceiling, slanting downward to a cracked window, was stained with rain that had found its way through the roof. The faded wall-paper, loosened by damp, was torn away in some places, and bulged loose in others. There were holes in the skirting-board; and from one of them peeped the brightly timid eyes of the child's only living companion in the garret—a mouse, feeding on crumbs which she had saved from her breakfast.

Syd looked up when the mouse darted back into its hole, on the opening of the door. "Lizzie! Lizzie! " she said, gravely, "you ought to have come in without making a noise. You have frightened away my youngest child. "

The good-natured servant burst out laughing. "Have you got a large family, miss? " she inquired, humoring the joke.

Syd failed to see the joke. "Only two more, " she answered as gravely as ever—and lifted up from the floor two miserable dolls, reduced to the last extremity of dirt and dilapidation. "My two eldest, " this strange child resumed, setting up the dolls against one of the empty trunks. "The eldest is a girl, and her name is Syd. The other is a boy, untidy in his clothes, as you see. Their kind mamma forgives them when they are naughty, and buys ponies for them to ride on, and always has something nice for them to eat when they are hungry. Have you got a kind mamma, Lizzie? And are you very fond of her? "

Those innocent allusions to the neglect which was the one sad experience of Syd's young life touched the servant's heart. A bygone time was present to her memory, when she too had been left without a playfellow to keep her company or a fire to warm her, and she had not endured it patiently.

"Oh, my dear, " she said, "your poor little arms are red with cold. Come to me and let me rub them. "

But Syd's bright imagination was a better protection against the cold than all the rubbing that the hands of a merciful woman could offer. "You are very kind, Lizzie, " she answered. "I don't feel the cold when I am playing with my children. I am very careful to give them plenty of exercise, we are going to walk in the Park. "

She gave a hand to each of the dolls, and walked slowly round and round the miserable room, pointing out visionary persons of distinction and objects of interest. "Here's the queen, my dears, in her gilt coach, drawn by six horses. Do you see her scepter poking out of the carriage window? She governs the nation with that. Bow to the queen. And now look at the beautiful bright water. There's the island where the ducks live. Ducks are happy creatures. They have their own way in everything, and they're good to eat when they're dead. At least they used to be good, when we had nice dinners in papa's time. I try to amuse the poor little things, Lizzie. Their papa is dead. I'm obliged to be papa and mamma to them, both in one. Do you feel the cold, my dears? " She shivered as she questioned her imaginary children. "Now we are at home again, " she said, and led the dolls to the empty fireplace. "Roaring fires always in *my* house, " cried the resolute little creature, rubbing her hands cheerfully before the bleak blank grate.

Warm-hearted Lizzie could control herself no longer.

"If the child would only make some complaint, " she burst out, "it wouldn't be so dreadful! Oh, what a shame! what a shame! " she cried, to the astonishment of little Syd. "Come down, my dear, to the nice warm room where your brother is. Oh, your mother? I don't care if your mother sees us; I should like to give your mother a piece of my mind. There! I don't mean to frighten you; I'm one of your bad children—I fly into a passion. You carry the dolls and I'll carry *you*. Oh, how she shivers! Give us a kiss. "

Sympathy which expressed itself in this way was new to Syd. Her eyes opened wide in childish wonder—and suddenly closed again in childish terror, when her good friend the servant passed Mrs. Westerfield's door on the way downstairs. "If mamma bounces out on us, " she whispered, "pretend we don't see her. " The nice warm room received them in safety. Under no stress of circumstances had Mrs. Westerfield ever been known to dress herself in a hurry. A good half-hour more had passed before the house door was heard to bang—and the pleasant landlady, peeping through the window, said: "There she goes. Now, we'll enjoy ourselves! "

5. —The Landlord.

Mrs. Westerfield's destination was the public-house in which she had been once employed as a barmaid. Entering the place without hesitation, she sent in her card to the landlord. He opened the parlor door himself and invited her to walk in.

"You wear well, " he said, admiring her. "Have you come back here to be my barmaid again? "

"Do you think I am reduced to that? " she answered.

"Well, my dear, more unlikely things have happened. They tell me you depend for your income on Lord Le Basque—and his lordship's death was in the newspapers last week. "

"And his lordship's lawyers continue my allowance. "

Having smartly set the landlord right in those words, she had not thought it necessary to add that Lady Le Basque, continuing the allowance at her husband's request, had also notified that it would cease if Mrs. Westerfield married again.

"You're a lucky woman, " the landlord remarked. "Well, I'm glad to see you. What will you take to drink? "

"Nothing, thank you. I want to know if you have heard anything lately of James Bellbridge? "

The landlord was a popular person in his own circle—not accustomed to restrain himself when he saw his way to a joke. "Here's constancy! " he said. "She's sweet on James, after having jilted him twelve years ago! "

Mrs. Westerfield replied with dignity. "I am accustomed to be treated respectfully, " she replied. "I wish you good-morning. "

The easy landlord pressed her back into her chair. "Don't be a fool, " he said; "James is in London—James is staying in my house. What do you think of that? "

Mrs. Westerfield's bold gray eyes expressed eager curiosity and interest. "You don't mean that he is going to be barman here again? "

"No such luck, my dear; he is a gentleman at large, who patronizes my house. "

Mrs. Westerfield went on with her questions.

"Has he left America for good? "

"Not he! James Bellbridge is going back to New York, to open a saloon (as they call it) in partnership with another man. He's in England, he says, on business. It's my belief that he wants money for this new venture on bad security. They're smart people in New York. His only chance of getting his bills discounted is to humbug his relations, down in the country. "

"When does he go to the country? "

"He's there now. "

"When does he come back? "

"You're determined to see him, it appears. He comes back to-morrow. "

"Is he married? "

"Aha! now we're coming to the point. Make your mind easy. Plenty of women have set the trap for him, but he has not walked into it yet. Shall I give him your love? "

"Yes, " she said, coolly. "As much love as you please. "

"Meaning marriage? " the landlord inquired.

"And money, " Mrs. Westerfield added.

"Lord Le Basque's money. "

"Lord Le Basque's money may go to the Devil! "

"Hullo! Your language reminds me of the time when you were a barmaid. You don't mean to say you have had a fortune left you? "

"I do! Will you give a message to James? "

"I'll do anything for a lady with a fortune. "

"Tell him to come and drink tea with his old sweetheart tomorrow, at six o'clock. "

"He won't do it. "

"He will. "

With that difference of opinion, they parted.

6. —The Brute.

To-morrow came—and Mrs. Westerfield's faithful James justified her confidence in him.

"Oh, Jemmy, how glad I am to see you! You dear, dear fellow. I'm yours at last. "

"That depends, my lady, on whether I want you. Let go of my neck. "

The man who entered this protest against imprisonment in the arms of a fine woman, was one of the human beings who are grown to perfection on English soil. He had the fat face, the pink complexion, the hard blue eyes, the scanty yellow hair, the smile with no meaning in it, the tremendous neck and shoulders, the mighty fists and feet, which are seen in complete combination in England only. Men of this breed possess a nervous system without being aware of it; suffer affliction without feeling it; exercise courage without a sense of danger; marry without love; eat and drink without limit; and sink (big as they are), when disease attacks them, without an effort to live.

Mrs. Westerfield released her guest's bull-neck at the word of command. It was impossible not to submit to him—he was so brutal. Impossible not to admire him—he was so big.

"Have you no love left for me? " was all she ventured to say.

He took the reproof good-humoredly. "Love? " he repeated. "Come! I like that—after throwing me over for a man with a handle to his name. Which am I to call you: 'Mrs? ' or 'My Lady'? "

"Call me your own. What is there to laugh at, Jemmy? You used to be fond of me; you would never have gone to America, when I married Westerfield, if I hadn't been dear to you. Oh, if I'm sure of anything, I'm sure of that! You wouldn't bear malice, dear, if you only knew how cruelly I have been disappointed. "

He suddenly showed an interest in what she was saying: the brute became cheery and confidential. "So he made you a bad husband, did he? Up with his fist and knocked you down, I daresay, if the truth was known? "

"You're all in the wrong, dear. He would have been a good husband if I had cared about him. I never cared about anybody but you. It wasn't Westerfield who tempted me to say Yes. "

"That's a lie. "

"No, indeed it isn't. "

"Then why did you marry him? "

"When I married him, Jemmy, there was a prospect—oh, how could I resist it? Think of being one of the Le Basques! Held in honor, to the end of my life, by that noble family, whether my husband lived or died! "

To the barman's ears, this sounded like sheer nonsense. His experience in the public-house suggested an explanation. "I say, my girl, have you been drinking? "

Mrs. Westerfield's first impulse led her to rise and point indignantly to the door. He had only to look at her—and she sat down again a tamed woman. "You don't understand how the chance tempted me, " she answered, gently.

"What chance do you mean? "

"The chance, dear, of being a lord's mother. "

He was still puzzled, but he lowered his tone. The true-born Briton bowed by instinct before the woman who had jilted him, when she presented herself in the character of a lord's mother. "How do you make that out, Maria? " he asked politely.

She drew her chair nearer to him, when he called her by her Christian name for the first time.

"When Westerfield was courting me, " she said, "his brother (my lord) was a bachelor. A lady—if one can call such a creature a lady! —was living under his protection. He told Westerfield he was very fond of her, and he hated the idea of getting married. 'If your wife's first child turns out to be a son, ' he said, 'there is an heir to the title and estates, and I may go on as I am now. ' We were married a month afterward—and when my first child was born it was a girl. I leave you to judge what the disappointment was! My lord (persuaded, as I suspect, by the woman I mentioned just now) ran the risk of waiting another year, and a year afterward, rather than be married. Through all that time, I had no other child or prospect of a child. His lordship was fairly driven into taking a wife. Ah, how I hate her! *Their* first child was a boy—a big, bouncing, healthy brute of a boy! And six months afterward, my poor little fellow was born. Only think of it! And tell me, Jemmy, don't I deserve to be a happy woman, after suffering such a dreadful disappointment as that? Is it true that you're going back to America? "

"Quite true. "

"Take me back with you. "

"With a couple of children? "

"No. Only with one. I can dispose of the other in England. Wait a little before you say No. Do you want money? "

"You couldn't help me, if I did. "

"Marry me, and I can help you to a fortune. "

He eyed her attentively and saw that she was in earnest. "What do you call a fortune? " he asked.

"Five thousand pounds, " she answered.

His eyes opened; his mouth opened; he scratched his head. Even his impenetrable nature proved to be capable of receiving a shock. Five thousand pounds! He asked faintly for "a drop of brandy. "

She had a bottle of brandy ready for him.

"You look quite overcome, " she said.

He was too deeply interested in the restorative influence of the brandy to take any notice of this remark. When he had recovered himself he was not disposed to believe in the five thousand pounds.

"Where's the proof of it? " he said, sternly.

She produced her husband's letter. "Did you read the Trial of Westerfield for casting away his ship? " she asked.

"I heard of it. "

"Will you look at this letter? "

"Is it long? "

"Yes. "

"Then suppose you read it to me. "

He listened with the closest attention while she read. The question of stealing the diamonds (if they could only be found) did not trouble either of them. It was a settled question, by tacit consent on both sides. But the value in money of the precious stones suggested a doubt that still weighed on his mind.

"How do you know they're worth five thousand pounds? " he inquired.

"You dear old stupid! Doesn't Westerfield himself say so in his letter? "

"Read that bit again. "

She read it again: "After the two calamities of the loss of the ship, and the disappearance of the diamonds—these last being valued at five thousand pounds—I returned to England. "

Satisfied so far, he wanted to look at the cipher next. She handed it to him with a stipulation: "Yours, Jemmy, on the day when you marry me. "

He put the slip of paper into his pocket. "Now I've got it, " he said, "suppose I keep it? "

A woman who has been barmaid at a public-house is a woman not easily found at the end of her resources.

"In that case, " she curtly remarked, "I should first call in the police, and then telegraph to my husband's employers in Liverpool. "

He handed the cipher back. "I was joking, " he said.

"So was I, " she answered.

They looked at each other. They were made for each other—and they both felt it. At the same time, James kept his own interests steadily in view. He stated the obvious objection to the cipher. Experts had already tried to interpret the signs, and had failed.

"Quite true, " she added, "but other people may succeed. "

"How are you to find them? "

"Leave me to try. Will you give me a fortnight from to-day? "

"All right. Anything else? "

"One thing more. Get the marriage license at once. "

"Why? "

"To show that you are in earnest. "

He burst out laughing. "It mightn't be much amiss, " he said, "if I took you back with me to America; you're the sort of woman we want in our new saloon. I'll get the license. Good-night. "

As he rose to go, there was a soft knock at the door. A little girl, in a shabby frock, ventured to show herself in the room.

"What do you want here? " her mother asked sharply.

Syd held out a small thin hand, with a letter in it, which represented her only excuse. Mrs. Westerfield read the letter, and crumpled it up in her pocket. "One of your secrets? " James asked. "Anything about the diamonds, for instance? "

"Wait till you are my husband, " she said, "and then you may be as inquisitive as you please. " Her amiable sweetheart's guess had actually hit the mark. During the year that had passed, she too had tried her luck among the Experts, and had failed. Having recently heard of a foreign interpreter of ciphers, she had written to ask his terms. The reply (just received) not only estimated his services at an extravagantly high rate, but asked cautious questions which it was not convenient to answer. Another attempt had been made to discover the mystery of the cipher, and made in vain.

James Bellbridge had his moments of good-humor, and was on those rare occasions easily amused. He eyed the child with condescending curiosity. "Looks half starved, " he said—as if he were considering the case of a stray cat. "Hollo, there! Buy a bit of bread. " He tossed a penny to Syd as she left the room; and took the opportunity of binding his bargain with Syd's mother. "Mind! if I take you to New York, I'm not going to be burdened with both your children. Is that girl the one you leave behind you? "

Mrs. Westerfield smiled sweetly, and answered: "Yes, dear. "

7. —The Cipher.

An advertisement in the newspapers, addressed to persons skilled in the interpretation of ciphers, now represented Mrs. Westerfield's only chance of discovering where the diamonds were hidden. The first answer that she received made some amends for previous disappointment. It offered references to gentlemen, whose names were in themselves a sufficient guarantee. She verified the references nevertheless, and paid a visit to her correspondent on the same day.

His personal appearance was not in his favor—he was old and dirty, infirm and poor. His mean room was littered with shabby books. None of the ordinary courtesies of life seemed to be known to him; he neither wished Mrs. Westerfield good-morning nor asked her to take a seat. When she attempted to enter into explanations relating to her errand, he rudely interrupted her.

"Show me your cipher, " he said; "I don't promise to study it unless I find it worth my while. "

Mrs. Westerfield was alarmed.

"Do you mean that you want a large sum of money? " she asked.

"I mean that I don't waste my time on easy ciphers invented by fools. "

She laid the slip of paper on his desk.

"Waste your time on *that*, " she said satirically, "and see how you like it! "

He examined it—first with his bleared red-rimmed eyes; then with a magnifying-glass. The only expression of opinion that escaped him was indicated by his actions. He shut up his book, and gloated over the signs and characters before him. On a sudden he looked at Mrs. Westerfield. "How did you come by this? " he asked.

"That's no business of yours. "

"In other words, you have reasons of your own for not answering my question? "

"Yes. "

Drawing his own inferences from that reply, he showed his three last-left yellow teeth in a horrid grin. "I understand! " he said, speaking to himself. He looked at the cipher once more, and put another question: "Have you got a copy of this? "

It had not occurred to her to take a copy. He rose and pointed to his empty chair. His opinion of the cipher was, to all appearance, forced to express itself by the discovery that there was no copy.

"Do you know what might happen? " he asked. "The only cipher that has puzzled me for the last ten years might be lost—or stolen—or burned if there was a fire in the house. You deserve to be punished for your carelessness. Make the copy yourself. "

This desirable suggestion (uncivilly as it was expressed) had its effect upon Mrs. Westerfield. Her marriage depended on that precious slip of paper. She was confirmed in her opinion that this very disagreeable man might nevertheless be a man to be trusted.

"Shall you be long in finding out what it means? " she asked when her task was completed.

He carefully compared the copy with the original—and then he replied:

"Days may pass before I can find the clew; I won't attempt it unless you give me a week. "

She pleaded for a shorter interval. He coolly handed back her papers; the original and the copy.

"Try somebody else, " he suggested—and opened his book again. Mrs. Westerfield yielded with the worst possible grace. In granting him the week of delay, she approached the subject of his fee for the second time. "How much will it cost me? " she inquired.

"I'll tell you when I've done. "

"That won't do! I must know the amount first. "

He handed her back her papers for the second time. Mrs. Westerfield's experience of poverty had never been the experience of such independence as this. In sheer bewilderment, she yielded again. He took back the original cipher, and locked it up in his desk. "Call here this day week, " he said—and returned to his book.

"You are not very polite, " she told him, on leaving the room.

"At any rate, " he answered, "I don't interrupt people when they are reading. "

The week passed.

Repeating her visit, Mrs. Westerfield found him still seated at his desk, still surrounded by his books, still careless of the polite attentions that he owed to a lady.

"Well? " she asked, "have you earned your money? "

"I have found the clew. "

"What is it? " she burst out. "Tell me the substance. I can't wait to read. "

He went on impenetrably with what he had to say. "But there are some minor combinations, which I have still to discover to my own satisfaction. I want a few days more. "

She positively refused to comply with this request. "Write down the substance of it, " she repeated, "and tell me what I owe you. "

He handed her back her cipher for the third time.

The woman who could have kept her temper, under such provocation as this, may be found when the mathematician is found who can square the circle, or the inventor who can discover perpetual motion. With a furious look, Mrs. Westerfield expressed her opinion of the philosopher in two words: "You brute! " She failed to produce the slightest impression on him.

"My work, " he proceeded, "must be well done or not done at all. This is Saturday, eleventh of the month. We will say the evening of Wednesday next. "

Mrs. Westerfield sufficiently controlled herself to be able to review her engagements for the coming week. On Thursday, the delay exacted by the marriage license would expire, and the wedding might take place. On Friday, the express train conveyed passengers to Liverpool, to be in time for the departure of the steamer for New York on Saturday morning. Having made these calculations, she asked, with sulky submission, if she was expected to call again on the Wednesday evening.

"No. Leave me your name and address. I will send you the cipher, interpreted, at eight o'clock. "

Mrs. Westerfield laid one of her visiting cards on his desk, and left him.

8. — The Diamonds.

The new week was essentially a week of events.

On the Monday morning, Mrs. Westerfield and her faithful James had their first quarrel. She took the liberty of reminding him that it was time to give notice of the marriage at the church, and to secure berths in the steamer for herself and her son. Instead of answering one way or another, James asked how the Expert was getting on.

"Has your old man found out where the diamonds are? "

"Not yet. "

"Then we'll wait till he does. "

"Do you believe my word? " Mrs. Westerfield asked curtly.

James Bellbridge answered, with Roman brevity, "No. "

This was an insult; Mrs. Westerfield expressed her sense of it. She rose, and pointed to the door. "Go back to America, as soon as you please, " she said; "and find the money you want—if you can. "

As a proof that she was in earnest she took her copy of the cipher out of the bosom of her dress, and threw it into the fire. "The original is safe in my old man's keeping, " she added. "Leave the room. "

James rose with suspicious docility, and walked out, having his own private ends in view.

Half an hour later, Mrs. Westerfield's old man was interrupted over his work by a person of bulky and blackguard appearance, whom he had never seen before.

The stranger introduced himself as a gentleman who was engaged to marry Mrs. Westerfield: he requested (not at all politely) to be permitted to look at the cipher. He was asked if he had brought a written order to that effect, signed by the lady herself. Mr. Bellbridge, resting his fists on the writing-table, answered that he had come to look at the cipher on his own sole responsibility, and that he insisted on seeing it immediately. "Allow me to show you something else first, " was the reply he received to this assertion of his will and pleasure. "Do you know a loaded pistol, sir, when you see it? " The barrel of the pistol approached within three inches of the barman's big head as he leaned over the writing-table. For once in his life he was taken by surprise. It had never occurred to him that a professed interpreter of ciphers might sometimes be trusted with secrets which placed him in a position of danger, and might therefore have wisely taken measures to protect himself. No power of persuasion is comparable to the power possessed by a loaded pistol. James left the room; and expressed his sentiments in language which has not yet found its way into any English Dictionary.

But he had two merits, when his temper was in a state of repose. He knew when he was beaten; and he thoroughly appreciated the value of the diamonds. When Mrs. Westerfield saw him again, on the next day, he appeared with undeniable claims on her mercy. Notice of the marriage had been received at the church; and a cabin had been secured for her on board the steamer.

Her prospects being thus settled, to her own satisfaction, Mrs. Westerfield was at liberty to make her arrangements for the desertion of poor little Syd.

The person on whose assistance she could rely was an unmarried elder sister, distinguished as proprietor of a cheap girls' school in one of the suburbs of London. This lady—known to local fame as Miss Wigger—had already proposed to take Syd into training as a pupil teacher. "I'll force the child on, " Miss Wigger promised, "till she can earn her board and lodging by taking my lowest class. When she gets older she will replace my regular governess, and I shall save the salary. "

With this proposal waiting for a reply, Mrs. Westerfield had only to inform her sister that it was accepted. "Come here, " she wrote, "on Friday next, at any time before two o'clock, and Syd shall be ready for you. P.S. —I am to be married again on Thursday, and start for America with my husband and my boy by next Saturday's steamer. "

The letter was posted; and the mother's anxious mind was, to use her own phrase, relieved of another worry.

As the hour of eight drew near on Wednesday evening, Mrs. Westerfield's anxiety forced her to find relief in action of some kind. She opened the door of her sitting-room and listened on the stairs. It still wanted for a few minutes to eight o'clock, when there was a ring at the house-bell. She ran down to open the door. The servant happened to be in the hall, and answered the bell. The next moment, the door was suddenly closed again.

"Anybody there? " Mrs. Westerfield asked.

"No, ma'am. "

This seemed strange. Had the old wretch deceived her, after all? "Look in the letter-box, " she called out. The servant obeyed, and found a letter. Mrs. Westerfield tore it open, standing on the stairs. It contained half a sheet of common note-paper. The interpretation of the cipher was written on it in these words:

"Remember Number 12, Purbeck Road, St. John's Wood. Go to the summer-house in the back garden. Count to the fourth plank in the floor, reckoning from the side wall on the right as you enter the summer-house. Prize up the plank. Look under the mould and rubbish. Find the diamonds. "

Not a word of explanation accompanied these lines. Neither had the original cipher been returned. The strange old man had earned his money, and had not attended to receive it—had not even sent word where or how it might be paid! Had he delivered his letter himself? He (or his messenger) had gone before the house-door could be opened!

A sudden suspicion of him turned her cold. Had he stolen the diamonds? She was on the point of sending for a cab, and driving it to his lodgings, when James came in, eager to know if the interpretation had arrived.

Keeping her suspicions to herself, she merely informed him that the interpretation was in her hands. He at once asked to see it. She refused to show it to him until he had made her his wife. "Put a chisel in your pocket, when we go to church, to-morrow morning, " was the one hint she gave him. As thoroughly worthy of each other as ever, the betrothed lovers distrusted each other to the last.

At eleven o'clock the next morning they were united in the bonds of wedlock; the landlord and the landlady of the public-house in which they had both served being the only witnesses present. The children were not permitted to see the ceremony. On leaving the church door, the married pair began their honeymoon by driving to St. John's Wood.

A dirty printed notice, in a broken window, announced that the House was To Let; and a sour-tempered woman informed them that they were free to look at the rooms.

The bride was in the best of humors. She set the bridegroom the example of keeping up appearances by examining the dilapidated house first. This done, she said sweetly to the person in charge, "May we look at the garden? "

The woman made a strange answer to this request. "That's curious, " she said.

James interfered for the first time. "What's curious? " he asked roughly.

"Among all the idle people who have come here, at one time or another, to see this house. " the woman said, "only two have wanted to look at the garden. "

James turned on his heel, and made for the summer-house, leaving it to his wife to pursue the subject or not as she pleased. She did pursue the subject.

"I am one of the persons, of course, " she said. "Who is the other? "

"An old man came on Monday. "

The bride's pleasant smile vanished.

"What sort of person was he? " she asked.

The sour-tempered woman became sourer than ever.

"Oh, how can I tell! A brute. There! "

"A brute! " The very words which the new Mrs. Bellbridge had herself used when the Expert had irritated her. With serious misgivings, she, too, turned her steps in the direction of the garden.

James had already followed her instructions and used his chisel. The plank lay loose on the floor. With both his big hands he rapidly cleared away the mould and the rubbish. In a few minutes the hiding-place was laid bare.

They looked into it. They looked at each other. There was the empty hole, telling its own story. The diamonds were gone.

9. —The Mother.

Mrs. Bellbridge eyed her husband, prepared for a furious outbreak of rage. He stood silent, staring stupidly straight before him. The shock that had fallen on his dull brain had stunned it. For the time, he was a big idiot—speechless, harmless, helpless.

She put back the rubbish, and replaced the plank, and picked up the chisel. "Come, James, " she said; "pull yourself together. " It was useless to speak to him. She took his arm and led him out to the cab that was waiting at the door.

The driver, helping him to get in, noticed a piece of paper lying on the front seat. Advertisements, seeking publicity under all possible circumstances, are occasionally sent flying into the open windows of vehicles. The driver was about to throw the paper away, when Mrs. Bellbridge (seeing it on the other side) took it out of his hand. "It isn't print, " she said; "it's writing. " A closer examination showed that the writing was addressed to herself. Her correspondent must have followed her to the church, as well as to the house in St. John's Wood. He distinguished her by the name which she had changed that morning, under the sanction of the clergy and the law.

This was what she read: "Don't trouble yourself, madam, about the diamonds. You have made a mistake—you have employed the wrong man. "

Those words—and no more. Enough, surely, to justify the conclusion that he had stolen the diamonds. Was it worth while to drive to his lodgings? They tried the experiment. The Expert had gone away on business—nobody knew where.

The newspaper came as usual on Friday morning. To Mrs. Bellbridge's amazement it set the question of the theft at rest, on the highest authority. An article appeared, in a conspicuous position, thus expressed:

"Another of the many proofs that truth is stranger than fiction has just occurred at Liverpool. A highly respected firm of shipwreckers in that city received a strange letter at the beginning of the present week. Premising that he had some remarkable circumstances to communicate, the writer of the letter entered abruptly on the narrative which follows: A friend of his—connected with literature— had, it appeared, noticed a lady's visiting card on his desk, and had been reminded by it (in what way it was not necessary to explain) of a criminal case which had excited considerable public interest at the time; viz., the trial of Captain Westerfield for willfully casting away a ship under his command. Never having heard of the trial, the writer, at his friend's suggestion, consulted a file of newspapers— discovered the report—and became aware, for the first time, that a collection of Brazilian diamonds, consigned to the Liverpool firm, was missing from the wrecked vessel when she had been boarded by the salvage party, and had not been found since. Events, which it was impossible for him to mention (seeing that doing so would involve a breach of confidence placed in him in his professional capacity), had revealed to his knowledge a hiding-place in which these same diamonds, in all probability, were concealed. This circumstance had left him no alternative, as an honest man, but to be beforehand with the persons, who (as he believed) contemplated stealing the precious stones. He had, accordingly, taken them under his protection, until they were identified and claimed by the rightful owners. In now appealing to these gentlemen, he stipulated that the claim should be set forth in writing, addressed to him under initials at a post-office in London. If the lost property was identified to his satisfaction, he would meet—at a specified place and on a certain day and hour—a person accredited by the firm and would personally restore the diamonds, without claiming (or consenting to receive) a reward. The conditions being complied with, this remarkable interview took place; the writer of the letter, described as an infirm old man very poorly dressed, fulfilled his engagement, took his receipt, and walked away without even waiting to be thanked. It is only an act of justice to add that the diamonds were afterward counted, and not one of them was missing. "

Miserable, deservedly-miserable married pair. The stolen fortune, on which they had counted, had slipped through their fingers. The berths in the steamer for New York had been taken and paid for. James had married a woman with nothing besides herself to bestow on him, except an incumbrance in the shape of a boy.

Late on the fatal wedding-day his first idea, when he was himself again after the discovery in the summer-house, was to get back his passage-money, to abandon his wife and his stepson, and to escape to America in a French steamer. He went to the office of the English company, and offered the places which he had taken for sale. The season of the year was against him; the passenger-traffic to America was at its lowest ebb, and profits depended upon freights alone.

If he still contemplated deserting his wife, he must also submit to sacrifice his money. The other alternative was (as he expressed it himself) to "have his pennyworth for his penny, and to turn his family to good account in New York. " He had not quite decided what to do when he got home again on the evening of his marriage.

At that critical moment in her life the bride was equal to the demand on her resources.

If she was foolish enough to allow James to act on his natural impulses, there were probably two prospects before her. In one state of his temper, he might knock her down. In another state of his temper, he might leave her behind him. Her only hope of protecting herself, in either case, was to tame the bridegroom. In his absence, she wisely armed herself with the most irresistible fascinations of her sex. Never yet had he seen her dressed as she was dressed when he came home. Never yet had her magnificent eyes looked at him as they looked now. Emotions for which he was not prepared overcame this much injured man; he stared at the bride in helpless surprise. That inestimable moment of weakness was all Mrs. Bellbridge asked for. Bewildered by his own transformation, James found himself reading the newspaper the next morning sentimentally, with his arm round his wife's waist.

By a refinement of cruelty, not one word had been said to prepare little Syd for the dreary change that was now close at hand in her young life. The poor child had seen the preparations for departure, and had tried to imitate her mother in packing up. She had collected her few morsels of darned and ragged clothing, and had gone upstairs to put them into one of the dilapidated old trunks in the garret play ground, when the servant was sent to bring her back to the sitting-room. There, enthroned in an easy-chair, sat a strange lady; and there, hiding behind the chair in undisguised dislike of the visitor, was her little brother Roderick. Syd looked timidly at her mother; and her mother said:

"Here is your aunt. "

The personal appearance of Miss Wigger might have suggested a modest distrust of his own abilities to Lavater, when that self-sufficient man wrote his famous work on Physiognomy. Whatever betrayal of her inner self her face might have presented, in the distant time when she was young, was now completely overlaid by a surface of a flabby fat which, assisted by green spectacles, kept the virtues (or vices) of this woman's nature a profound secret until she opened her lips. When she used her voice, she let out the truth. Nobody could hear her speak, and doubt for a moment that she was an inveterately ill-natured woman.

"Make your curtsey, child! " said Miss Wigger. Nature had so toned her voice as to make it worthy of the terrors of her face. But for her petticoats, it would have been certainly taken for the voice of a man.

The child obeyed, trembling.

"You are to go away with me, " the school-mistress proceeded, "and to be taught to make yourself useful under my roof. "

Syd seemed to be incapable of understanding the fate that was in store for her. She sheltered herself behind her merciless mother. "I'm going away with you, mamma, " she said — "with you and Rick. "

Her mother took her by the shoulders, and pushed her across the room to her aunt.

The child looked at the formidable female creature with the man's voice and the green spectacles.

"You belong to me, " said Miss Wigger, by way of encouragement, "and I have come to take you away. " At those dreadful words, terror shook little Syd from head to foot. She fell on her knees with a cry of misery that might have melted the heart of a savage. "Oh, mamma, mamma, don't leave me behind! What have I done to deserve it? Oh, pray, pray, pray have some pity on me! "

Her mother was as selfish and as cruel a woman as ever lived. But even her hard heart felt faintly the influence of the most intimate and most sacred of all human relationships. Her florid cheeks turned pale. She hesitated.

Miss Wigger marked (through her own green medium) that moment of maternal indecision—and saw that it was time to assert her experience as an instructress of youth.

"Leave it to me, " she said to her sister. "You never did know, and you never will know, how to manage children. "

She advanced. The child threw herself shrieking on the floor. Miss Wigger's long arms caught her up—held her—shook her. "Be quiet, you imp! " It was needless to tell her to be quiet. Syd's little curly head sank on the schoolmistress's shoulder. She was carried into exile without a word or a cry—she had fainted.

10. —The School.

Time's march moves slowly, where weary lives languish in dull places.

Dating from one unkempt and unacknowledged birthday to another, Sydney Westerfield had attained the sixth year of her martyrdom at School. In that long interval no news of her mother, her brother, or her stepfather had reached England; she had received no letter, she had not even heard a report. Without friends, and without prospects, Roderick Westerfield's daughter was, in the saddest sense of the word, alone in the world.

The hands of the ugly old clock in the school-room were approaching the time when the studies of the morning would come to an end. Wearily waiting for their release, the scholars saw an event happen which was a novelty in their domestic experience. The maid-of-all-work audaciously put her head in at the door, and interrupted Miss Wigger conducting the education of the first-class.

"If you please, miss, there's a gentleman—"

Having uttered these introductory words, she was reduced to silence by the tremendous voice of her mistress.

"Haven't I forbidden you to come here in school hours? Go away directly! "

Hardened by a life of drudgery, under conditions of perpetual scolding, the servant stood her ground, and recovered the use of her tongue.

"There's a gentleman in the drawing-room, " she persisted. Miss Wigger tried to interrupt her again. "And here's his card! " she shouted, in a voice that was the louder of the two.

Being a mortal creature, the schoolmistress was accessible to the promptings of curiosity. She snatched the card out of the girl's hand.

Mr. Herbert Linley, Mount Morven, Perthshire. "I don't know this person, " Miss Wigger declared. "You wretch, have you let a thief into the house? "

"A gentleman, if ever I see one yet, " the servant asserted.

"Hold your tongue! Did he ask for me? Do you hear? "

"You told me to hold my tongue. No; he didn't ask for you. "

"Then who did he want to see? "

"It's on his card. "

Miss Wigger referred to the card again, and discovered (faintly traced in pencil) these words: "To see Miss S. W."

The schoolmistress instantly looked at Miss Westerfield. Miss Westerfield rose from her place at the head of her class.

The pupils, astonished at this daring act, all looked at the teacher—their natural enemy, appointed to supply them with undesired information derived from hated books. They saw one of Mother Nature's favorite daughters; designed to be the darling of her family, and the conqueror of hearts among men of all tastes and ages. But Sydney Westerfield had lived for six weary years in the place of earthly torment, kept by Miss Wigger under the name of a school. Every budding beauty, except the unassailable beauty of her eyes and her hair, had been nipped under the frosty superintendence of her maternal aunt. Her cheeks were hollow, her delicate lips were pale; her shabby dress lay flat over her bosom. Observant people, meeting her when she was out walking with the girls, were struck by her darkly gentle eyes, and by the patient sadness of her expression. "What a pity! " they said to each other. "She would be a pretty girl, if she didn't look so wretched and so thin. "

At a loss to understand the audacity of her teacher in rising before the class was dismissed, Miss Wigger began by asserting her authority. She did in two words: "Sit down! "

"I wish to explain, ma'am. "

"Sit down. "

"I beg, Miss Wigger, that you will allow me to explain. "

"Sydney Westerfield, you are setting the worst possible example to your class. I shall see this man myself. *Will* you sit down? "

Pale already, Sydney turned paler still. She obeyed the word of command—to the delight of the girls of her class. It was then within ten minutes of the half hour after twelve—when the pupils were dismissed to the playground while the cloth was laid for dinner. What use would the teacher make of that half hour of freedom?

In the meanwhile Miss Wigger had entered her drawing-room. With the slightest possible inclination of her head, she eyed the stranger through her green spectacles. Even under that disadvantage his appearance spoke for itself. The servant's estimate of him was beyond dispute. Mr. Herbert Linley's good breeding was even capable of suppressing all outward expression of the dismay that he felt, on finding himself face to face with the formidable person who had received him.

"What is your business, if you please? " Miss Wigger began.

Men, animals, and buildings wear out with years, and submit to their hard lot. Time only meets with flat contradiction when he ventures to tell a woman that she is growing old. Herbert Linley had rashly anticipated that the "young lady, " whom it was the object of his visit to see, would prove to be young in the literal sense of the word. When he and Miss Wigger stood face to face, if the door had been set open for him, he would have left the house with the greatest pleasure.

"I have taken the liberty of calling, " he said, "in answer to an advertisement. May I ask"—he paused, and took out a newspaper from the pocket of his overcoat—"If I have the honor of speaking to the lady who is mentioned here? "

He opened the newspaper, and pointed to the advertisement.

Miss Wigger's eyes rested—not on the passage indicated, but on the visitor's glove. It fitted him to such perfection that it suggested the enviable position in life which has gloves made to order. He politely pointed again. Still inaccessible to the newspaper, Miss Wigger turned her spectacles next to the front window of the room, and discovered a handsome carriage waiting at the door. (Money evidently in the pockets of those beautiful trousers, worthy of the gloves!) As patiently as ever, Linley pointed for the third time, and drew Miss Wigger's attention in the right direction at last. She read the advertisement.

"A Young Lady wishes to be employed in the education of a little girl. Possessing but few accomplishments, and having been only a junior teacher at a school, she offers her services on trial, leaving it to her employer to pay whatever salary she may be considered to deserve, if she obtains a permanent engagement. Apply by letter, to S. W., 14, Delta Gardens, N.E. "

"Most impertinent, " said Miss Wigger.

Mr. Linley looked astonished.

"I say, most impertinent! " Miss Wigger repeated.

Mr. Linley attempted to pacify this terrible woman. "It's very stupid of me, " he said; "I am afraid I don't quite understand you. "

"One of my teachers has issued an advertisement, and has referred to My address, without first consulting Me. Have I made myself understood, sir? " She looked at the carriage again, when she called him "sir. "

Not even Linley's capacity for self-restraint could repress the expression of relief, visible in his brightening face, when he discovered that the lady of the advertisement and the lady who terrified him were two different persons.

"Have I made myself understood? " Miss Wigger repeated.

"Perfectly, madam. At the same time, I am afraid I must own that the advertisement has produced a favorable impression on me. "

"I fail entirely to see why, " Miss Wigger remarked.

"There is surely, " Linley repeated, "something straightforward—I might almost say, something innocent—in the manner in which the writer expresses herself. She seems to be singularly modest on the subject of her own attainments, and unusually considerate of the interests of others. I hope you will permit me—? "

Before he could add, "to see the young lady, " the door was opened: a young lady entered the room.

Was she the writer of the advertisement? He felt sure of it, for no better reason than this: the moment he looked at her she interested him. It was an interest new to Linley, in his experience of himself There was nothing to appeal to his admiration (by way of his senses) in the pale, worn young creature who stood near the door, resigned beforehand to whatever reception she might meet with. The poor teacher made him think of his happy young wife at home—of his pretty little girl, the spoiled child of the household. He looked at Sydney Westerfield with a heartfelt compassion which did honor to them both.

"What do you mean by coming here? " Miss Wigger inquired.

She answered gently, but not timidly. The tone in which the mistress had spoken had evidently not shaken her resolution, so far.

"I wish to know, " she said, "if this gentleman desires to see me on the subject of my advertisement? "

"Your advertisement? " Miss Wigger repeated. "Miss Westerfield! how dare you beg for employment in a newspaper, without asking my leave? "

"I only waited to tell you what I had done, till I knew whether my advertisement would be answered or not. "

She spoke as calmly as before, still submitting to the insolent authority of the schoolmistress with a steady fortitude very remarkable in any girl—and especially in a girl whose face revealed a sensitive nature. Linley approached her, and said his few kind words before Miss Wigger could assert herself for the third time.

"I am afraid I have taken a liberty in answering you personally, when I ought to have answered by letter. My only excuse is that I have no time to arrange for an interview, in London, by correspondence. I live in Scotland, and I am obliged to return by the mail to-night. "

He paused. She was looking at him. Did she understand him?

She understood him only too well. For the first time, poor soul, in the miserable years of her school life, she saw eyes that rested on her with the sympathy that is too truly felt to be uttered in words. The admirable resignation which had learned its first hard lesson under her mother's neglect—which had endured, in after-years, the daily persecution that heartless companionship so well knows how to inflict—failed to sustain her, when one kind look from a stranger poured its balm into the girl's sore heart. Her head sank; her wasted figure trembled; a few tears dropped slowly on the bosom of her shabby dress. She tried, desperately tried, to control herself. "I beg your pardon, sir, " was all she could say; "I am not very well. "

Miss Wigger tapped her on the shoulder and pointed to the door. "Are you well enough to see your way out? " she asked.

Linley turned on the wretch with a mind divided between wonder and disgust. "Good God, what has she done to deserve being treated in that way? " he asked.

Miss Wigger's mouth widened; Miss Wigger's forehead developed new wrinkles. To own it plainly, the schoolmistress smiled.

When it is of serious importance to a man to become acquainted with a woman's true nature—say, when he contemplates marriage—his one poor chance of arriving at a right conclusion is to find himself provoked by exasperating circumstances, and to fly into a passion. If the lady flies into a passion on her side, he may rely on it that her faults are more than balanced by her good qualities. If, on the other hand, she exhibits the most admirable self-control, and sets him an example which ought to make him ashamed of himself, he has seen a bad sign, and he will do well to remember it.

Miss Wigger's self-control put Herbert Linley in the wrong, before she took the trouble of noticing what he had said.

"If you were not out of temper, " she replied, "I might have told you that I don't allow my house to be made an office for the engagement of governesses. As it is, I merely remind you that your carriage is at the door. "

He took the only course that was open to him; he took his hat.

Sydney turned away to leave the room. Linley opened the door for her. "Don't be discouraged, " he whispered as she passed him; "you shall hear from me. " Having said this, he made his parting bow to the schoolmistress. Miss Wigger held up a peremptory forefinger, and stopped him on his way out. He waited, wondering what she would do next. She rang the bell.

"You are in the house of a gentlewoman, " Miss Wigger explained. "My servant attends visitors, when they leave me. " A faint smell of soap made itself felt in the room; the maid appeared, wiping her smoking arms on her apron. "Door. I wish you good-morning"— were the last words of Miss Wigger.

Leaving the house, Linley slipped a bribe into the servant's hand. "I am going to write to Miss Westerfield, " he said. "Will you see that she gets my letter? "

"That I will! "

He was surprised by the fervor with which the girl answered him. Absolutely without vanity, he had no suspicion of the value which his winning manner, his kind brown eyes, and his sunny smile had conferred on his little gift of money. A handsome man was an eighth wonder of the world, at Miss Wigger's school.

At the first stationer's shop that he passed, he stopped the carriage and wrote his letter.

"I shall be glad indeed if I can offer you a happier life than the life you are leading now. It rests with you to help me do this. Will you send me the address of your parents, if they are in London, or the name of any friend with whom I can arrange to give you a trial as governess to my little girl? I am waiting your answer in the neighborhood. If any hinderance should prevent you from replying at once, I add the name of the hotel at which I am staying—so that you may telegraph to me, before I leave London to-night. "

The stationer's boy, inspired by a private view of half-a-crown, set off at a run—and returned at a run with a reply.

"I have neither parents nor friends, and I have just been dismissed from my employment at the school. Without references to speak for me, I must not take advantage of your generous offer. Will you help me to bear my disappointment, permitting me to see you, for a few minutes only, at your hotel? Indeed, indeed, sir, I am not forgetful of what I owe to my respect for you, and my respect for myself. I only ask leave to satisfy you that I am not quite unworthy of the interest which you have been pleased to feel in—S. W."

In those sad words, Sydney Westerfield announced that she had completed her education.

THE STORY

FIRST BOOK.

Chapter I.

Mrs. Presty Presents Herself.

NOT far from the source of the famous river, which rises in the mountains between Loch Katrine and Loch Lornond, and divides the Highlands and the Lowlands of Scotland, travelers arrive at the venerable gray walls of Mount Morven; and, after consulting their guide books, ask permission to see the house.

What would be called, in a modern place of residence, the first floor, is reserved for the occupation of the family. The great hall of entrance, and its quaint old fireplace; the ancient rooms on the same level opening out of it, are freely shown to strangers. Cultivated travelers express various opinions relating to the family portraits, and the elaborately carved ceilings. The uninstructed public declines to trouble itself with criticism. It looks up at the towers and the loopholes, the battlements and the rusty old guns, which still bear witness to the perils of past times when the place was a fortress—it enters the gloomy hall, walks through the stone-paved rooms, stares at the faded pictures, and wonders at the lofty chimney-pieces hopelessly out of reach. Sometimes it sits on chairs which are as cold and as hard as iron, or timidly feels the legs of immovable tables which might be legs of elephants so far as size is concerned. When these marvels have been duly admired, and the guide books are shut up, the emancipated tourists, emerging into the light and air, all find the same social problem presented by a visit to Mount Morven: "How can the family live in such a place as that? "

If these strangers on their travels had been permitted to ascend to the first floor, and had been invited (for example) to say good-night to Mrs. Linley's pretty little daughter, they would have seen the stone walls of Kitty's bed-chamber snugly covered with velvet hangings which kept out the cold; they would have trod on a doubly-laid carpet, which set the chilly influences of the pavement beneath it at defiance; they would have looked at a bright little bed, of the last new pattern, worthy of a child's delicious sleep; and they would only have discovered that the room was three hundred years old when they had drawn aside the window curtains, and had revealed the adamantine solidity of the outer walls. Or, if they had been allowed to pursue their investigations a little further, and had found their way next into Mrs. Linley's sitting room, here again a transformation scene would have revealed more modern luxury, presented in the perfection which implies restraint within the limits of good taste. But on this occasion, instead of seeing the head of a lively little child on the pillow, side by side with the head of her doll, they would have encountered an elderly lady of considerable size, fast asleep and snoring in a vast armchair, with a book on her lap. The married men among the tourists would have recognized a mother-in-law, and would have set an excellent example to the rest; that is to say, the example of leaving the room.

The lady composed under the soporific influence of literature was a person of importance in the house—holding rank as Mrs. Linley's mother; and being otherwise noticeable for having married two husbands, and survived them both.

The first of these gentlemen—the Right Honorable Joseph Norman— had been a member of Parliament, and had taken office under Government. Mrs. Linley was his one surviving child. He died at an advanced age; leaving his handsome widow (young enough, as she was always ready to mention, to be his daughter) well provided for, and an object of matrimonial aspiration to single gentlemen who admired size in a woman, set off by money. After hesitating for some little time, Mrs. Norman accepted the proposal of the ugliest and dullest man among the ranks of her admirers. Why she became the wife of Mr. Presty (known in commercial circles as a merchant enriched by the sale of vinegar) she was never able to explain. Why she lamented him, with tears of sincere sorrow, when he died after two years of married life, was a mystery which puzzled her nearest and dearest friends. And why when she indulged (a little too frequently) in recollections of her married life, she persisted in putting obscure Mr. Presty on a level with distinguished Mr. Norman, was a secret which this remarkable woman had never been known to reveal. Presented by their widow with the strictest impartiality to the general view, the characters of these two husbands combined, by force of contrast, the ideal of manly perfection. That is to say, the vices of Mr. Norman were the virtues of Mr. Presty; and the vices of Mr. Presty were the virtues of Mr. Norman.

Returning to the sitting-room after bidding Kitty goodnight, Mrs. Linley discovered the old lady asleep, and saw that the book on her mother's lap was sliding off. Before she could check the downward movement, the book fell on the floor, and Mrs. Presty woke.

"Oh, mamma, I am so sorry! I was just too late to catch it. "

"It doesn't matter, my dear. I daresay I should go to sleep again, if I went on with my novel. "

"Is it really as dull as that? "

"Dull? " Mrs. Presty repeated. "You are evidently not aware of what the new school of novel writing is doing. The new school provides the public with soothing fiction. "

"Are you speaking seriously, mamma? "

"Seriously, Catherine—and gratefully. These new writers are so good to old women. No story to excite our poor nerves; no improper characters to cheat us out of our sympathies, no dramatic situations to frighten us; exquisite management of details (as the reviews say), and a masterly anatomy of human motives which—I know what I mean, my dear, but I can't explain it. "

"I think I understand, mamma. A masterly anatomy of human motives which is in itself a motive of human sleep. No; I won't borrow your novel just now. I don't want to go to sleep; I am thinking of Herbert in London. "

Mrs. Presty consulted her watch.

"Your husband is no longer in London, " she announced; "he has begun his journey home. Give me the railway guide, and I'll tell you when he will be here tomorrow. You may trust me, Catherine, to make no mistakes. Mr. Presty's wonderful knowledge of figures has been of the greatest use to me in later life. Thanks to his instructions, I am the only person in the house who can grapple with the intricacies of our railway system. Your poor father, Mr. Norman, could never understand time-tables and never attempted to conceal his deficiencies. He had none of the vanity (harmless vanity, perhaps) which led poor Mr. Presty to express positive opinions on matters of which he knew nothing, such as pictures and music. What do you want, Malcolm? "

The servant to whom this question was addressed answered: "A telegram, ma'am, for the mistress. "

Mrs. Linley recoiled from the message when the man offered it to her. Not usually a very demonstrative person, the feeling of alarm which had seized on her only expressed itself in a sudden change of color. "An accident! " she said faintly. "An accident on the railway! "

Mrs. Presty opened the telegram.

"If you had been the wife of a Cabinet Minister, " she said to her daughter, "you would have been too well used to telegrams to let them frighten you. Mr. Presty (who received his telegrams at his office) was not quite just to the memory of my first husband. He used to blame Mr. Norman for letting me see his telegrams. But Mr. Presty's nature had all the poetry in which Mr. Norman's nature was deficient. He saw the angelic side of women—and thought telegrams and business, and all that sort of thing, unworthy of our mission. I don't exactly understand what our mission is—"

"Mamma! mamma! is Herbert hurt? "

"Stuff and nonsense! Nobody is hurt; there has been no accident. "

"They why does he telegraph to me? "

Hitherto, Mrs. Presty had only looked at the message. She now read it through attentively to the end. Her face assumed an expression of stern distrust. She shook her head.

"Read it yourself, " she answered; "and remember what I told you, when you trusted your husband to find a governess for my grandchild. I said: 'You do not know men as I do. ' I hope you may not live to repent it. "

Mrs. Linley was too fond of her husband to let this pass. "Why shouldn't I trust him? " she asked. "He was going to London on business—and it was an excellent opportunity. "

Mrs. Presty disposed of this weak defense of her daughter's conduct by waving her hand. "Read your telegram, " she repeated with dignity, "and judge for yourself. "

Mrs. Linley read:

"I have engaged a governess. She will travel in the same train with me. I think I ought to prepare you to receive a person whom you may be surprised to see. She is very young, and very inexperienced; quite unlike the ordinary run of governesses. When you hear how cruelly the poor girl has been used, I am sure you will sympathize with her as I do. "

Mrs. Linley laid down the message, with a smile.

"Poor dear Herbert! " she said tenderly. "After we have been eight years married, is he really afraid that I shall be jealous? Mamma! Why are you looking so serious? "

Mrs. Presty took the telegram from her daughter and read extracts from it with indignant emphasis of voice and manner.

"Travels in the same train with him. Very young, and very inexperienced. And he sympathizes with her. Ha! I know the men, Catherine—I know the men! "

Chapter II.

The Governess Enters.

Mr. Herbert Linley arrived at his own house in the forenoon of the next day. Mrs. Linley, running out to the head of the stairs to meet her husband, saw him approaching her without a traveling companion. "Where is the governess? " she asked—when the first salutes allowed her the opportunity of speaking.

"On her way to bed, poor soul, under the care of the housekeeper, " Linley answered.

"Anything infectious, my dear Herbert? " Mrs. Presty inquired appearing at the breakfast-room door.

Linley addressed his reply to his wife:

"Nothing more serious, Catherine, than want of strength. She was in such a state of fatigue, after our long night journey, that I had to lift her out of the carriage. "

Mrs. Presty listened with an appearance of the deepest interest. "Quite a novelty in the way of a governess, " she said. "May I ask what her name is? "

"Sydney Westerfield. "

Mrs. Presty looked at her daughter and smiled satirically.

Mrs. Linley remonstrated.

"Surely, " she said, "you don't object to the young lady's name! "

"I have no opinion to offer, Catherine. I don't believe in the name. "

"Oh, mamma, do you suspect that it's an assumed name? "

"My dear, I haven't a doubt that it is. May I ask another question? " the old lady continued, turning to Linley. "What references did Miss Westerfield give you? "

49

"No references at all. "

Mrs. Presty rose with the alacrity of a young woman, and hurried to the door. "Follow my example, " she said to her daughter, on her way out. "Lock up your jewel-box. "

Linley drew a deep breath of relief when he was left alone with his wife. "What makes your mother so particularly disagreeable this morning? " he inquired.

"She doesn't approve, dear, of my leaving it to you to choose a governess for Kitty. "

"Where is Kitty? "

"Out on her pony for a ride over the hills. Why did you send a telegram, Herbert, to prepare me for the governess? Did you really think I might be jealous of Miss Westerfield? "

Linley burst out laughing. "No such idea entered my head, " he answered. "It isn't *in* you, my dear, to be jealous. "

Mrs. Linley was not quite satisfied with this view of her character. Her husband's well-intended compliment reminded her that there are occasions when any woman may be jealous, no matter how generous and how gentle she may be. "We won't go quite so far as that, " she said to him, "because—" She stopped, unwilling to dwell too long on a delicate subject. He jocosely finished the sentence for her. "Because we don't know what may happen in the future? " he suggested; making another mistake by making a joke.

Mrs. Linley returned to the subject of the governess.

"I don't at all say what my mother says, " she resumed; "but was it not just a little indiscreet to engage Miss Westerfield without any references? "

"Unless I am utterly mistaken, " Linley replied, "you would have been quite as indiscreet, in my place. If you had seen the horrible woman who persecuted and insulted her—"

His wife interrupted him. "How did all this happen, Herbert? Who first introduced you to Miss Westerfield? "

Linley mentioned the advertisement, and described his interview with the schoolmistress. Having next acknowledged that he had received a visit from Miss Westerfield herself, he repeated all that she had been able to tell him of her father's wasted life and melancholy end. Really interested by this time, Mrs. Linley was eager for more information. Her husband hesitated. "I would rather you heard the rest of it from Miss Westerfield, " he said, "in my absence. "

"Why in your absence? "

"Because she can speak to you more freely, when I am not present. Hear her tell her own story, and then let me know whether you think I have made a mistake. I submit to your decision beforehand, whichever way it may incline. "

Mrs. Linley rewarded him with a kiss. If a married stranger had seen them, at that moment, he would have been reminded of forgotten days—the days of his honeymoon.

"And now, " Linley resumed, "suppose we talk a little about ourselves. I haven't seen any brother yet. Where is Randal? "

"Staying at the farm to look after your interests. We expect him to come back to-day. Ah, Herbert, what do we not all owe to that dear good brother of yours? There is really no end to his kindness. The last of our poor Highland families who have emigrated to America have had their expenses privately paid by Randal. The wife has written to me, and has let out the secret. There is an American newspaper, among the letters that are waiting your brother's return, sent to him as a little mark of attention by these good grateful people. " Having alluded to the neighbors who had left Scotland, Mrs. Linley was reminded of other neighbors who had remained. She was still relating events of local interest, when the clock interrupted her by striking the hour of the nursery dinner. What had become of Kitty? Mrs. Linley rose and rang the bell to make inquiries.

On the point of answering, the servant looked round at the open door behind him. He drew aside, and revealed Kitty, in the corridor, hand in hand with Sydney Westerfield—who timidly hesitated at entering the room. "Here she is mamma, " cried the child. "I think she's afraid of you; help me to pull her in. "

Mrs. Linley advanced to receive the new member of her household, with the irresistible grace and kindness which charmed every stranger who approached her. "Oh, it's all right, " said Kitty. "Syd likes me, and I like Syd. What do you think? She lived in London with a cruel woman who never gave her enough to eat. See what a good girl I am? I'm beginning to feed her already. " Kitty pulled a box of sweetmeats out of her pocket, and handed it to the governess with a tap on the lid, suggestive of an old gentleman offering a pinch of snuff to a friend.

"My dear child, you mustn't speak of Miss Westerfield in that way! Pray excuse her, " said Mrs. Linley, turning to Sydney with a smile; "I am afraid she has been disturbing you in your room. "

Sydney's silent answer touched the mother's heart; she kissed her little friend. "I hope you will let her call me Syd, " she said gently; "it reminds me of a happier time. " Her voice faltered; she could say no more. Kitty explained, with the air of a grown person encouraging a child. "I know all about it, mamma. She means the time when her papa was alive. She lost her papa when she was a little girl like me. I didn't disturb her. I only said, 'My name's Kitty; may I get up on the bed? ' And she was quite willing; and we talked. And I helped her to dress. " Mrs. Linley led Sydney to the sofa, and stopped the flow of her daughter's narrative. The look, the voice, the manner of the governess had already made their simple appeal to her generous nature. When her husband took Kitty's hand to lead her with him out of the room, she whispered as he passed: "You have done quite right; I haven't a doubt of it now! "

Chapter III.

Mrs. Presty Changes Her Mind.

The two ladies were alone.

Widely as the lot in life of one differed from the lot in life of the other, they presented a contrast in personal appearance which was more remarkable still. In the prime of life, tall and fair—the beauty of her delicate complexion and her brilliant blue eyes rivaled by the charm of a figure which had arrived at its mature perfection of development—Mrs. Linley sat side by side with a frail little dark-eyed creature, thin and pale, whose wasted face bore patient witness to the three cruelest privations under which youth can suffer—want of fresh air, want of nourishment, and want of kindness. The gentle mistress of the house wondered sadly if this lost child of misfortune was capable of seeing the brighter prospect before her that promised enjoyment of a happier life to come.

"I was afraid to disturb you while you were resting, " Mrs. Linley said. "Let me hope that my housekeeper has done what I might have done myself, if I had seen you when you arrived. "

"The housekeeper has been all that is good and kind to me, madam. "

"Don't call me 'madam'; it sounds so formal—call me 'Mrs. Linley. ' You must not think of beginning to teach Kitty till you feel stronger and better. I see but too plainly that you have not been happy. Don't think of your past life, or speak of your past life. "

"Forgive me, Mrs. Linley; my past life is my one excuse for having ventured to come into this house. "

"In what way, my dear? "

At the moment when that question was put, the closed curtains which separated the breakfast-room from the library were softly parted in the middle. A keen old face, strongly marked by curiosity and distrust, peeped through—eyed the governess with stern scrutiny—and retired again into hiding.

The introduction of a stranger (without references) into the intimacy of the family circle was, as Mrs. Presty viewed it, a crisis in domestic history. Conscience, with its customary elasticity, adapted itself to the emergency, and Linley's mother-in-law stole information behind the curtain—in Linley's best interests, it is quite needless to say.

The talk of the two ladies went on, without a suspicion on either side that it was overheard by a third person.

Sydney explained herself.

"If I had led a happier life, " she said, "I might have been able to resist Mr. Linley's kindness. I concealed nothing from him. He knew that I had no friends to speak for me; he knew that I had been dismissed from my employment at the school. Oh, Mrs. Linley, everything I said which would have made other people suspicious of me made *him* feel for me! I began to wonder whether he was an angel or a man. If he had not prevented it, I should have fallen on my knees before him. Hard looks and hard words I could have endured patiently, but I had not seen a kind look, I had not heard a kind word, for more years than I can reckon up. That is all I can say for myself; I leave the rest to your mercy. "

"Say my sympathy, " Mrs. Linley answered, "and you need say no more.. But there is one thing I should like to know. You have not spoken to me of your mother. Have you lost both your parents? "

"No. "

"Then you were brought up by your mother? "

"Yes. "

"You surely had some experience of kindness when you were a child? "

A third short answer would have been no very grateful return for Mrs. Linley's kindness. Sydney had no choice but to say plainly what her experience of her mother had been.

"Are there such women in the world! " Mrs. Linley exclaimed. "Where is your mother now? "

"In America—I think. "

"You think? "

"My mother married again, " said Sydney. "She went to America with her husband and my little brother, six years ago. "

"And left you behind? "

"Yes. "

"And has she never written to you; "

"Never. "

This time, Mrs. Linley kept silence; not without an effort. Thinking of Sydney's mother—and for one morbid moment seeing her own little darling in Sydney's place—she was afraid to trust herself to speak while the first impression was vividly present to her mind.

"I will only hope, " she replied, after waiting a little, "that some kind person pitied and helped you when you were deserted. Any change must have been for the better after that. Who took charge of you? "

"My mother's sister took charge of me, an elder sister, who kept a school. The time when I was most unhappy was the time when my aunt began to teach me. 'If you don't want to be beaten, and kept on bread and water, ' she said, 'learn, you ugly little wretch, and be quick about it. "'

"Did she speak in that shameful way to the other girls? "

"Oh, no! I was taken into her school for nothing, and, young as I was, I was expected to earn my food and shelter by being fit to teach the lowest class. The girls hated me. It was such a wretched life that I hardly like to speak of it now. I ran away, and I was caught, and severely punished. When I grew older and wiser, I tried to find some other employment for myself. The elder girls bought penny journals that published stories. They were left about now and then in the bedrooms. I read the stories when I had the chance. Even my ignorance discovered how feeble and foolish they were. They encouraged me to try if I could write a story myself; I couldn't do worse, and I might do better. I sent my manuscript to the editor. It was accepted and printed—but when I wrote and asked him if he would pay me something for it, he refused. Dozens of ladies, he said, wrote stories for him for nothing. It didn't matter what the stories were. Anything would do for his readers, so long as the characters were lords and ladies, and there was plenty of love in it. My next attempt to get away from the school ended in another disappointment. A poor old man, who had once been an actor, used to come to us twice a week, and get a few shillings by teaching the girls to read aloud. He was called 'Professor of English Literature, ' and he taught out of a ragged book of verses which smelled of his pipe. I learned one of the pieces and repeated it to him, and asked if there was any hope of my being able to go on the stage. He was very kind; he told me the truth. 'My dear, you have no dramatic ability; God forbid you should go on the stage. ' I went back again to the penny journals, and tried a new editor. He seemed to have more money than the other one; or perhaps he was kinder. I got ten shillings from him for my story. With that money I made my last attempt—I advertised for a situation as governess. If Mr. Linley had not seen my advertisement, I might have starved in the streets. When my aunt heard of it, she insisted on my begging her pardon before the whole school. Do girls get half maddened by persecution? If they do, I think I must have been one of those girls. I refused to beg pardon; and I was dismissed from my situation without a character. Will you think me very foolish? I shut my eyes again, when I woke in my delicious bed today. I was afraid that the room, and everything in it, was a dream. " She looked round, and started to her feet. "Oh, here's a lady! Shall I go away? "

The curtains hanging over the entrance to the library were opened for the second time. With composure and dignity, the lady who had startled Sydney entered the room.

"Have you been reading in the library? " Mrs. Linley asked. And Mrs. Presty answered: "No, Catherine; I have been listening. "

Mrs. Linley looked at her mother; her lovely complexion reddened with a deep blush.

"Introduce me to Miss Westerfield, " Mrs. Presty proceeded, as coolly as ever.

Mrs. Linley showed some hesitation. What would the governess think of her mother? Perfectly careless of what the governess might think, Mrs. Presty crossed the room and introduced herself.

"Miss Westerfield, I am Mrs. Linley's mother. And I am, in one respect, a remarkable person. When I form an opinion and find it's the opinion of a fool, I am not in the least ashamed to change my mind. I have changed my mind about you. Shake hands. "

Sydney respectfully obeyed.

"Sit down again. " Sydney returned to her chair.

"I had the worst possible opinion of you, " Mrs. Presty resumed, "before I had the pleasure of listening on the other side of the curtain. It has been my good fortune—what's your Christian name? Did I hear it? or have I forgotten it? 'Sydney, ' eh? Very well. I was about to say, Sydney, that it has been my good fortune to be intimately associated, in early life, with two remarkable characters. Husbands of mine, in short, whose influence over me has, I am proud to say, set death and burial at defiance. Between them they have made my mind the mind of a man. I judge for myself. The opinions of others (when they don't happen to agree with mine) I regard as chaff to be scattered to the winds. No, Catherine, I am not wandering. I am pointing out to a young person, who has her way to make in the world, the vast importance, on certain occasions, of possessing an independent mind. If I had been ashamed to listen behind those curtains, there is no injury that my stupid prejudices might not have inflicted on this unfortunate girl. As it is, I have heard her story, and I do her justice. Count on me, Sydney, as your friend, and now get up again. My grandchild (never accustomed to wait for anything since the day when she was born) is waiting dinner for you. She is at this moment shouting for her governess, as King Richard (I am a great reader of Shakespeare) once shouted for his horse. The maid (you will recognize her as a stout person suffering under tight stays) is waiting outside to show you the way to the nursery. *Au revoir.* Stop! I should like to judge the purity of your French accent. Say 'au revoir' to me. Thank you. —Weak in her French, Catherine, " Mrs. Presty pronounced, when the door had closed on the governess; "but what can you expect, poor wretch, after such a life as she has led? Now we are alone, I have a word of advice for your private ear. We have much to anticipate from Miss

Westerfield that is pleasant and encouraging. But I don't conceal it from myself or from you, we have also something to fear. "

"To fear? " Mrs. Linley repeated. "I don't understand you. "

"Never mind, Catherine, whether you understand me or not. I want more information. Tell me what your husband said to you about this young lady? "

Wondering at the demon of curiosity which appeared to possess her mother, Mrs. Linley obeyed. Listening throughout with the closest attention, Mrs. Presty reckoned up the items of information, and pointed the moral to be drawn from them by worldly experience.

"First obstacle in the way of her moral development, her father— tried, found guilty, and dying in prison. Second obstacle, her mother—an unnatural wretch who neglected and deserted her own flesh and blood. Third obstacle, her mother's sister—being her mother over again in an aggravated form. People who only look at the surface of things might ask what we gain by investigating Miss Westerfield's past life. We gain this: we know what to expect of Miss Westerfield in the future. "

"I for one, " Mrs. Linley interposed, "expect everything that is good and true. "

"Say she's naturally an angel, " Mrs. Presty answered; "and I won't contradict you. But do pray hear how my experience looks at it. I remember what a life she has led, and I ask myself if any human creature could have suffered as that girl has suffered without being damaged by it. Among those damnable people—I beg your pardon, my dear; Mr. Norman sometimes used strong language, and it breaks out of me now and then—the good qualities of that unfortunate young person can *not* have always resisted the horrid temptations and contaminations about her. Hundreds of times she must have had deceit forced on her; she must have lied, through ungovernable fear; she must have been left (at a critical time in her life, mind!) with no more warning against the insidious advances of the passions than—than—I'm repeating what Mr. Presty said of a niece of his own, who went to a bad school at Paris; and I don't quite remember what comparisons that eloquent man used when he was excited. But I know what I mean. I like Miss Westerfield; I believe Miss Westerfield will come out well in the end. But I don't forget that she is going to lead a new life here—a life of luxury, my dear; a life of ease and health and happiness—and God only knows what evil seed sown in her, in her past life, may not spring up under new influences. I tell you we must be careful; I tell you we must keep our eyes open. And so much the better for Her. And so much the better for Us. "

Mrs. Presty's wise and wary advice (presented unfavorably, it must be owned, through her inveterately quaint way of expressing herself) failed to produce the right impression on her daughter's mind. Mrs. Linley replied in the tone of a person who was unaffectedly shocked.

"Oh, mamma, I never knew you so unjust before! You can't have heard all that Miss Westerfield said to me. You don't know her, as I know her. So patient, so forgiving, so grateful to Herbert. "

"So grateful to Herbert. " Mrs. Presty looked at her daughter in silent surprise. There could be no doubt about it; Mrs. Linley failed entirely to see any possibilities of future danger in the grateful feeling of her sensitive governess toward her handsome husband. At this exhibition of simplicity, the old lady's last reserves of endurance gave way: she rose to go. "You have an excellent heart, Catherine, " she remarked; "but as for your head—"

"Well, and what of my head? "

"It's always beautifully dressed, my dear, by your maid. " With that parting shot, Mrs. Presty took her departure by way of the library. Almost at the same moment, the door of the breakfast-room was opened. A young man advanced, and shook hands cordially with Mrs. Linley.

Chapter IV.

Randal Receives His Correspondence.

Self-revealed by the family likeness as Herbert's brother, Randal Linley was nevertheless greatly Herbert's inferior in personal appearance. His features were in no way remarkable for manly beauty. In stature, he hardly reached the middle height; and young as he was, either bad habit or physical weakness had so affected the upper part of his figure that he stooped. But with these, and other disadvantages, there was something in his eyes, and in his smile — the outward expression perhaps of all that was modestly noble in his nature — so irresistible in its attractive influence that men, women, and children felt the charm alike. Inside of the house, and outside of the house, everybody was fond of Randal; even Mrs. Presty included.

"Have you seen a new face among us, since you returned? " were his sister-in-law's first words. Randal answered that he had seen Miss Westerfield. The inevitable question followed. What did he think of her? "I'll tell you in a week or two more, " he replied.

"No! tell me at once. "

"I don't like trusting my first impression; I have a bad habit of jumping to conclusions. "

"Jump to a conclusion to please me. Do you think she's pretty? "

Randal smiled and looked away. "Your governess, " he replied, "looks out of health, and (perhaps for that reason) strikes me as being insignificant and ugly. Let us see what our fine air and our easy life here will do for her. In so young a woman as she is, I am prepared for any sort of transformation. We may be all admiring pretty Miss Westerfield before another month is over our heads. — Have any letters come for me while I have been away? "

He went into the library and returned with his letters. "This will amuse Kitty, " he said, handing his sister-in-law the illustrated New York newspaper, to which she had already referred in speaking to her husband.

Mrs. Linley examined the engravings—and turned back again to look once more at an illustration which had interested her. A paragraph on the same page caught her attention. She had hardly glanced at the first words before a cry of alarm escaped her. "Dreadful news for Miss Westerfield! " she exclaimed. "Read it, Randal. "

He read these words:

"The week's list of insolvent traders includes an Englishman named James Bellbridge, formerly connected with a disreputable saloon in this city. Bellbridge is under suspicion of having caused the death of his wife in a fit of delirium tremens. The unfortunate woman had been married, for the first time, to one of the English aristocracy—the Honorable Roderick Westerfield—whose trial for casting away a ship under his command excited considerable interest in London some years since. The melancholy circumstances of the case are complicated by the disappearance, on the day of the murder, of the woman's young son by her first husband. The poor boy is supposed to have run away in terror from his miserable home, and the police are endeavoring to discover some trace of him. It is reported that another child of the first marriage (a daughter) is living in England. But nothing is known about her. "

"Has your governess any relations in England? " Randal asked.

"Only an aunt, who has treated her in the most inhuman manner. "

"Serious news for Miss Westerfield, as you say, " Randal resumed. "And, as I think, serious news for us. Here is a mere girl—a poor friendless creature—absolutely dependent on our protection. What are we to do if anything happens, in the future, to alter our present opinion of her? "

"Nothing of the sort is likely to happen, " Mrs. Linley declared.

"Let us hope not, " Randal said, gravely.

Chapter V.

Randal Writes to New York.

The members of the family at Mount Morven consulted together, before Sydney Westerfield was informed of her brother's disappearance and of her mother's death.

Speaking first, as master of the house, Herbert Linley offered his opinion without hesitation. His impulsive kindness shrank from the prospect of reviving the melancholy recollections associated with Sydney's domestic life. "Why distress the poor child, just as she is beginning to feel happy among us? " he asked. "Give me the newspaper; I shan't feel easy till I have torn it up. "

His wife drew the newspaper out of his reach. "Wait a little, " she said, quietly; "some of us may feel that it is no part of our duty to conceal the truth. "

Mrs. Presty spoke next. To the surprise of the family council, she agreed with her son-in-law.

"Somebody must speak out, " the old lady began; "and I mean to set the example. Telling the truth, " she declared, turning severely to her daughter, "is a more complicated affair than you seem to think. It's a question of morality, of course; but—in family circles, my dear—it's sometimes a question of convenience as well. Is it convenient to upset my granddaughter's governess, just as she is entering on her new duties? Certainly not! Good heavens, what does it matter to my young friend Sydney whether her unnatural mother lives or dies? Herbert, I second your proposal to tear up the paper with the greatest pleasure. "

Herbert, sitting next to Randal, laid his hand affectionately on his brother's shoulder. "Are you on our side? " he asked.

Randal hesitated.

"I feel inclined to agree with you, " he said to Herbert. "It does seem hard to recall Miss Westerfield to the miserable life that she has led, and to do it in the way of all others which must try her fortitude most cruelly. At the same time—"

"Oh, don't spoil what you have said by seeing the other side of the question! " cried his brother "You have already put it admirably; leave it as it is. "

"At the same time, " Randal gently persisted, "I have heard no reasons which satisfy me that we have a right to keep Miss Westerfield in ignorance of what has happened. "

This serious view of the question in debate highly diverted Mrs. Presty. "I do not like that man, " she announced, pointing to Randal; "he always amuses me. Look at him now! He doesn't know which side he is on, himself. "

"He is on my side, " Herbert declared.

"Not he! "

Herbert consulted his brother. "What do you say yourself? "

"I don't know, " Randal answered.

"There! " cried Mrs. Presty. "What did I tell you? "

Randal tried to set his strange reply in the right light. "I only mean, " he explained, "that I want a little time to think. "

Herbert gave up the dispute and appealed to his wife. "You have still got the American newspaper in your hand, " he said. "What do you mean to do with it? "

Quietly and firmly Mrs. Linley answered: "I mean to show it to Miss Westerfield. "

"Against my opinion? Against your mother's opinion? " Herbert asked. "Have we no influence over you? Do as Randal does—take time, my dear, to think. "

She answered this with her customary calmness of manner and sweetness of tone. "I am afraid I must appear obstinate; but it is indeed true that I want no time to think; my duty is too plain to me. "

Her husband and her mother listened to her in astonishment. Too amiable and too happy—and it must be added too indolent—to assert herself in the ordinary emergencies of family life, Mrs. Linley only showed of what metal she was made on the very rare occasions when the latent firmness in her nature was stirred to its innermost depths. The general experience of this sweet-tempered and delightful woman, ranging over long intervals of time, was the only experience which remained in the memories of the persons about her. In bygone days, they had been amazed when her unexpected readiness and firmness of decision presented an exception to a general rule—just as they were amazed now.

Herbert tried a last remonstrance. "Is it possible, Catherine, that you don't see the cruelty of showing that newspaper to Miss Westerfield? "

Even this appeal to Mrs. Linley's sympathies failed to shake her resolution. "You may trust me to be careful, " was all she said in reply; "I shall prepare her as tenderly for the sad news from America, as if she was a daughter of my own. "

Hearing this, Mrs. Presty showed a sudden interest in the proceedings "When do you mean to begin? " she asked.

"At once, mamma. "

Mrs. Presty broke up the meeting on the spot. "Wait till I am out of the way, " she stipulated. "Do you object to Herbert giving me his arm? Distressing scenes are not in his line or in mine. "

Mrs. Linley made no objection. Herbert resigned himself (not at all unwillingly) to circumstances. Arm in arm, he and his wife's mother left the room.

Randal showed no intention of following them; he had given himself time to think. "We are all wrong, Catherine, " he said; "and you alone are right. What can I do to help you? "

She took his hand gratefully. "Always kind! Never thinking of yourself! I will see Miss Westerfield in my own room. Wait here, in case I want you. "

After a much shorter absence than Randal anticipated, Mrs. Linley returned. "Has it been very distressing? " he asked, seeing the traces of tears in her eyes.

"There are noble qualities, " she answered, "in that poor ill-used girl. Her one thought, as soon as she began to understand my motive in speaking to her, was not for herself, but for me. Even you, a man, must have felt the tears in your eyes, if you had heard her promise that I should suffer no further anxiety on her account. 'You shall see no distressing change in me, ' she said, 'when we meet to-morrow. ' All she asked was to be left in her room for the rest of the day. I feel sure of her resolution to control herself; and yet I should like to encourage her if I can. Her chief sorrow (as it seems to me) must be—not for the mother who has so shamefully neglected her—but for the poor little brother, a castaway lost in a strange land. Can we do nothing to relieve her anxiety? "

"I can write, " Randal said, "to a man whom I know in New York; a lawyer in large practice. "

"The very person we want! Write—pray write by today's post. "

The letter was dispatched. It was decided—and wisely decided, as the result proved—to say nothing to Sydney until the answer was received. Randal's correspondent wrote back with as little delay as possible. He had made every inquiry without success. Not a trace of the boy had been found, or (in the opinion of the police) was likely to be found. The one event that had happened, since the appearance of the paragraph in the New York journal, was the confinement of James Bellbridge in an asylum, as a madman under restraint without hope of recovery.

The Evil Genius

Chapter VI.

Sydney Teaches.

Mrs. Presty had not very seriously exaggerated the truth, when she described her much-indulged granddaughter as "a child who had never been accustomed to wait for anything since the day when she was born. "

Governesses in general would have found it no easy matter to produce a favorable impression on Kitty, and to exert the necessary authority in instructing her, at the same time. Spoiled children (whatever moralists may say to the contrary) are companionable and affectionate children, for the most part—except when they encounter the unfortunate persons employed to introduce them to useful knowledge. Mr. and Mrs. Linley (guiltily conscious of having been too fond of their only child to subject her to any sort of discipline) were not very willing to contemplate the prospect before Miss Westerfield on her first establishment in the schoolroom. To their surprise and relief there proved to be no cause for anxiety after all. Without making an attempt to assert her authority, the new governess succeeded nevertheless when older and wiser women would have failed.

The secret of Sydney's triumph over adverse circumstances lay hidden in Sydney herself.

Everything in the ordinary routine of life at Mount Morven was a source of delight and surprise to the unfortunate creature who had passed through six years of cruelty, insult, and privation at her aunt's school. Look where she might, in her new sphere of action, she saw pleasant faces and heard kind words. At meal times, wonderful achievements in the art of cookery appeared on the table which she had not only never tasted, but never even heard of. When she went out walking with her pupil they were free to go where they pleased, without restriction of time—except the time of dinner. To breathe the delicious air, to look at the glorious scenery, were enjoyments so exquisitely exhilarating that, by Sydney's own confession, she became quite light headed with pleasure. She ran races with Kitty—and nobody reproved her. She rested, out of breath, while the stronger child was ready to run on—and no merciless voice cried "None of your laziness; time's up! " Wild flowers that she had never yet seen might be gathered, and no offense was committed. Kitty told her the names of the flowers, and the names of the summer insects that flashed and hummed in the hillside breezes; and was so elated at teaching her governess that her rampant spirits burst out in singing. "Your turn next, " the joyous child cried, when she too was out of breath. "Sing, Sydney—sing! " Alas for Sydney! She had not sung since those happiest days of her childhood, when her good father had told her fairy stories, and taught her songs. They were all forgotten now. "I can't sing, Kitty; I can't sing. " The pupil, hearing this melancholy confession, became governess once more. "Say the words, Syd; and hum the tune after me. " They laughed over the singing lesson, until the echoes of the hills mocked them, and laughed too. Looking into the schoolroom, one day, Mrs. Linley found that the serious business of teaching was not neglected. The lessons went on smoothly, without an obstacle in the way. Kitty was incapable of disappointing her friend and playfellow, who made learning easy with a smile and a kiss. The balance of authority was regulated to perfection in the lives of these two simple creatures. In the schoolroom, the governess taught the child. Out of the schoolroom, the child taught the governess. Division of labor was a principle in perfect working order at Mount Morven—and nobody suspected it! But, as the weeks followed each other, one more remarkable circumstance presented itself which every person in the household was equally quick to observe. The sad Sydney Westerfield whom they all pitied had now become the pretty Sydney Westerfield whom they all admired. It was not merely a change—it was a transformation. Kitty stole the hand-glass from her mother's room, and insisted that her governess should take it and look at herself. "Papa says you're as plump as a partridge; and mamma says you're as fresh as a rose; and Uncle Randal wags his head, and tells them he saw it from the first. I heard it all when they thought I was playing with my doll—and I want to know, you best of nice girls, what you think of your own self? "

"I think, my dear, it's time we went on with our lessons. "

"Wait a little, Syd; I have something else to say. "

"What is it? "

"It's about papa. He goes out walking with us—doesn't he? "

"Yes. "

"He didn't go out walking with me—before you came here. I've been thinking about it; and I'm sure papa likes you. What are you looking in the drawer for? "

"For your lesson books, dear. "

"Yes—but I haven't quite done yet. Papa talks a good deal to you, and you don't talk much to papa. Don't you like him? "

"Oh, Kitty! "

"Then do you like him? "

"How can I help liking him? I owe all my happiness to your papa. "

"Do you like him better than mamma? "

"I should be very ungrateful, if I liked anybody better than your mamma. "

Kitty considered a little, and shook her head. "I don't understand that, " she declared roundly. "What do you mean? "

Sydney cleaned the pupil's slate, and set the pupil's sum—and said nothing.

Kitty placed a suspicious construction of her own on her governess's sudden silence. "Perhaps you don't like my wanting to know so many things, " she suggested. "Or perhaps you meant to puzzle me? "

Sydney sighed, and answered, "I'm puzzled myself. "

Chapter VII.

Sydney Suffers.

In the autumn holiday-time friends in the south, who happened to be visiting Scotland, were invited to stop at Mount Morven on their way to the Highlands; and were accustomed to meet the neighbors of the Linleys at dinner on their arrival. The time for this yearly festival had now come round again; the guests were in the house; and Mr. and Mrs. Linley were occupied in making their arrangements for the dinner-party. With her unfailing consideration for every one about her, Mrs. Linley did not forget Sydney while she was sending out her cards of invitation. "Our table will be full at dinner, " she said to her husband; "Miss Westerfield had better join us in the evening with Kitty. "

"I suppose so, " Linley answered with some hesitation.

"You seem to doubt about it, Herbert. Why? "

"I was only wondering—"

"Wondering about what? "

"Has Miss Westerfield got a gown, Catherine, that will do for a party? "

Linley's wife looked at him as if she doubted the evidence of her own senses. "Fancy a man thinking of that! " she exclaimed. "Herbert, you astonish me. "

He laughed uneasily. "I don't know how I came to think of it— unless it is that she wears the same dress every day. Very neat; but (perhaps I'm wrong) a little shabby too. "

"Upon my word, you pay Miss Westerfield a compliment which you have never paid to me! Wear what I may, you never seem to know how *I* am dressed. "

"I beg your pardon, Catherine, I know that you are always dressed well. "

That little tribute restored him to his place in his wife's estimation. "I may tell you now, " she resumed, with her gentle smile, "that you only remind me of what I had thought of already. My milliner is at work for Miss Westerfield. The new dress must be your gift. "

"Are you joking? "

"I am in earnest. To-morrow is Sydney's birthday; and here is *my* present. " She opened a jeweler's case, and took out a plain gold bracelet. "Suggested by Kitty, " she added, pointing to an inlaid miniature portrait of the child. Herbert read the inscription: *To Sydney Westerfield with Catherine Linley's love.* He gave the bracelet back to his wife in silence; his manner was more serious than usual—he kissed her hand.

The day of the dinner-party marked an epoch in Sydney's life.

For the first time, in all her past experience, she could look in the glass, and see herself prettily dressed, with a gold bracelet on her arm. If we consider how men (in one way) and milliners (in another) profit by it, vanity is surely to be reckoned, not among the vices but among the virtues of the sex. Will any woman, who speaks the truth, hesitate to acknowledge that her first sensations of gratified vanity rank among the most exquisite and most enduring pleasures that she has ever felt? Sydney locked her door, and exhibited herself to herself—in the front view, the side view, and the back view (over the shoulder) with eyes that sparkled and cheeks that glowed in a delicious confusion of pride and astonishment. She practiced bowing to strangers in her new dress; she practiced shaking hands gracefully, with her bracelet well in view. Suddenly she stood still before the glass and became serious and thoughtful. Kind and dear Mr. Linley was in her mind now. While she was asking herself anxiously what he would think of her, Kitty—arrayed in *her* new finery, as vain and as happy as her governess—drummed with both fists outside the door, and announced at the top of her voice that it was time to go downstairs. Sydney's agitation at the prospect of meeting the ladies in the drawing-room added a charm of its own to the flush that her exercises before the glass had left on her face. Shyly following instead of leading her little companion into the room, she presented such a charming appearance of youth and beauty that the ladies paused in their talk to look at her. Some few admired Kitty's governess with generous interest; the greater number doubted Mrs. Linley's prudence in engaging a girl so very pretty and so very young. Little by little, Sydney's manner—simple, modest, shrinking from observation—pleaded in her favor even with the ladies who had been prejudiced against her at the outset. When Mrs. Linley presented her to the guests, the most beautiful woman among them (Mrs. MacEdwin) made room for her on the sofa, and with perfect tact and kindness set the stranger at her ease. When the gentlemen came in from the dinner-table, Sydney was composed enough to admire the brilliant scene, and to wonder again, as she had wondered already, what Mr. Linley would say to her new dress.

Mr. Linley certainly did notice her—at a distance.

He looked at her with a momentary fervor of interest and admiration which made Sydney (so gratefully and so guiltlessly attached to him) tremble with pleasure; he even stepped forward as if to approach her, checked himself, and went back again among his guests. Now, in one part of the room, and now in another, she saw him speaking to them. The one neglected person whom he never even looked at again, was the poor girl to whom his approval was the breath of her life. Had she ever felt so unhappy as she felt now? No, not even at her aunt's school!

Friendly Mrs. MacEdwin touched her arm. "My dear, you are losing your pretty color. Are you overcome by the heat? Shall I take you into the next room? "

Sydney expressed her sincere sense of the lady's kindness. Her commonplace excuse was a true excuse—she had a headache; and she asked leave to retire to her room.

Approaching the door, she found herself face to face with Mr. Linley. He had just been giving directions to one of the servants, and was re-entering the drawing-room. She stopped, trembling and cold; but, in the very intensity of her wretchedness, she found courage enough to speak to him.

"You seem to avoid me, Mr. Linley, " she began, addressing him with ceremonious respect, and keeping her eyes on the ground. "I hope—" she hesitated, and desperately looked at him—"I hope I haven't done anything to offend you? "

In her knowledge of him, up to that miserable evening, he constantly spoke to her with a smile. She had never yet seen him so serious and so inattentive as he was now. His eyes, wandering round the room, rested on Mrs. Linley—brilliant and beautiful, and laughing gayly. Why was he looking at his wife with plain signs of embarrassment in his face? Sydney piteously persisted in repeating her innocent question: "I hope I haven't done anything to offend you? "

He seemed to be still reluctant to notice her—on the one occasion of all others when she was looking her best! But he answered at last.

"My dear child, it is impossible that you should offend me; you have misunderstood and mistaken me. Don't suppose—pray don't suppose that I am changed or can ever be changed toward you. "

He emphasized the kind intention which those words revealed by giving her his hand.

But the next moment he drew back. There was no disguising it, he drew back as if he wished to get away from her. She noticed that his lips were firmly closed and his eyebrows knitted in a frown; he looked like a man who was forcing himself to submit to some hard necessity that he hated or feared.

Sydney left the room in despair.

He had denied in the plainest and kindest terms that he was changed toward her. Was that not enough? It was nothing like enough. The facts were there to speak for themselves: he was an altered man; anxiety, sorrow, remorse—one or the other seemed to have got possession of him. Judging by Mrs. Linley's gayety of manner, his wife could not possibly have been taken into his confidence.

What did it mean? Oh, the useless, hopeless question! And yet, again and again she asked herself: what did it mean?

In bewildered wretchedness she lingered on the way to her room, and stopped at the end of a corridor.

On her right hand, a broad flight of old oak stairs led to the bed-chambers on the second floor of the house. On her left hand, an open door showed the stone steps which descended to the terrace and the garden. The moonlight lay in all its loveliness on the flower-beds and the grass, and tempted her to pause and admire it. A prospect of sleepless misery was the one prospect before her that Sydney could see, if she retired to rest. The cool night air came freshly up the vaulted tunnel in which the steps were set; the moonlit garden offered its solace to the girl's sore heart. No curious women-servants appeared on the stairs that led to the bed-chambers. No inquisitive eyes could look at her from the windows of the ground floor—a solitude abandoned to the curiosity of tourists. Sydney took her hat and cloak from the stand in a recess at the side of the door, and went into the garden.

Chapter VIII.

Mrs. Presty Makes a Discovery.

The dinner-party had come to an end; the neighbors had taken their departure; and the ladies at Mount Morven had retired for the night.

On the way to her room Mrs. Presty knocked at her daughter's door. "I want to speak to you, Catherine. Are you in bed? "

"No, mamma. Come in. "

Robed in a dressing-gown of delicately-mingled white and blue, and luxuriously accommodated on the softest pillows that could be placed in an armchair, Mrs. Linley was meditating on the events of the evening. "This has been the most successful party we have ever given, " she said to her mother. "And did you notice how charmingly pretty Miss Westerfield looked in her new dress? "

"It's about that girl I want to speak to you, " Mrs. Presty answered, severely. "I had a higher opinion of her when she first came here than I have now. "

Mrs. Linley pointed to an open door, communicating with a second and smaller bed-chamber. "Not quite so loud, " she answered, "or you might wake Kitty. What has Miss Westerfield done to forfeit your good opinion? "

Discreet Mrs. Presty asked leave to return to the subject at a future opportunity.

"I will merely allude now, " she said, "to a change for the worse in your governess, which you might have noticed when she left the drawing-room this evening. She had a word or two with Herbert at the door; and she left him looking as black as thunder. "

Mrs. Linley laid herself back on her pillows and burst out laughing. "Black as thunder? Poor little Sydney, what a ridiculous description of her! I beg your pardon, mamma; don't be offended. "

"On the contrary, my dear, I am agreeably surprised. Your poor father—a man of remarkable judgment on most subjects—never thought much of your intelligence. He appears to have been wrong; you have evidently inherited some of my sense of humor. However, that is not what I wanted to say; I am the bearer of good news. When we find it necessary to get rid of Miss Westerfield—"

Mrs. Linley's indignation expressed itself by a look which, for the moment at least, reduced her mother to silence. Always equal to the occasion, however, Mrs. Presty's face assumed an expression of innocent amazement, which would have produced a round of applause on the stage. "What have I said to make you angry? " she inquired. "Surely, my dear, you and your husband are extraordinary people. "

"Do you mean to tell me, mamma, that you have said to Herbert what you said just now to me? "

"Certainly. I mentioned it to Herbert in the course of the evening. He was excessively rude. He said: 'Tell Mrs. MacEdwin to mind her own business—and set her the example yourself. '"

Mrs. Linley returned her mother's look of amazement, without her mother's eye for dramatic effect. "What has Mrs. MacEdwin to do with it? " she asked.

"If you will only let me speak, Catherine, I shall be happy to explain myself. You saw Mrs. MacEdwin talking to me at the party. That good lady's head—a feeble head, as all her friends admit—has been completely turned by Miss Westerfield. 'The first duty of a governess' (this foolish woman said to me) 'is to win the affections of her pupils. My governess has entirely failed to make the children like her. A dreadful temper; I have given her notice to leave my service. Look at that sweet girl and your little granddaughter! I declare I could cry when I see how they understand each other and love each other. ' I quote our charming friend's nonsense, verbatim (as we used to say when we were in Parliament in Mr. Norman's time), for the sake of what it led to. If, by any lucky chance, Miss Westerfield happens to be disengaged in the future, Mrs. MacEdwin's house is open to her—at her own time, and on her own terms. I promised to speak to you on the subject, and I perform my promise. Think over it; I strongly advise you to think over it. "

Even Mrs. Linley's good nature declined to submit to this. "I shall certainly not think over what cannot possibly happen, " she said. "Good-night, mamma. "

"Good-night, Catherine. Your temper doesn't seem to improve as you get older. Perhaps the excitement of the party has been too much for your nerves. Try to get some sleep before Herbert comes up from the smoking-room and disturbs you. "

Mrs. Linley refused even to let this pass unanswered. "Herbert is too considerate to disturb me, when his friends keep him up late, " she said. "On those occasions, as you may see for yourself, he has a bed in his dressing-room. "

Mrs. Presty passed through the dressing-room on her way out. "A very comfortable-looking bed, " she remarked, in a tone intended to reach her daughter's ears. "I wonder Herbert ever leaves it. "

The way to her own bed-chamber led her by the door of Sydney's room. She suddenly stopped; the door was not shut. This was in itself a suspicious circumstance.

Young or old, ladies are not in the habit of sleeping with their bedroom doors ajar. A strict sense of duty led Mrs. Presty to listen outside. No sound like the breathing of a person asleep was to be heard. A strict sense of duty conducted Mrs. Presty next into the room, and even encouraged her to approach the bed on tip-toe. The bed was empty; the clothes had not been disturbed since it had been made in the morning!

The old lady stepped out into the corridor in a state of excitement, which greatly improved her personal appearance. She looked almost young again as she mentally reviewed the list of vices and crimes which a governess might commit, who had retired before eleven o'clock, and was not in her bedroom at twelve. On further reflection, it appeared to be barely possible that Miss Westerfield might be preparing her pupil's exercises for the next day. Mrs. Presty descended to the schoolroom on the first floor.

No. Here again there was nothing to see but an empty room.

Where was Miss Westerfield?

Was it within the limits of probability that she had been bold enough to join the party in the smoking-room? The bare idea was absurd.

In another minute, nevertheless, Mrs. Presty was at the door, listening. The men's voices were loud: they were talking politics. She peeped through the keyhole; the smokers had, beyond all doubt, been left to themselves. If the house had not been full of guests, Mrs. Presty would now have raised an alarm. As things were, the fear of a possible scandal which the family might have reason to regret forced her to act with caution. In the suggestive retirement of her own room, she arrived at a wise and wary decision. Opening her door by a few inches, she placed a chair behind the opening in a position which commanded a view of Sydney's room. Wherever the governess might be, her return to her bed-chamber, before the servants were astir in the morning, was a chance to be counted on. The night-lamp in the corridor was well alight; and a venerable person, animated by a sense of duty, was a person naturally superior to the seductions of sleep. Before taking the final precaution of extinguishing her candle, Mrs. Presty touched up her complexion, and resolutely turned her back on her nightcap. "This is a case in which I must keep up my dignity, " she decided, as she took her place in the chair.

One man in the smoking-room appeared to be thoroughly weary of talking politics. That man was the master of the house.

Randal noticed the worn, preoccupied look in his brother's face, and determined to break up the meeting. The opportunity for which he was waiting occurred in another minute. He was asked as a moderate politician to decide between two guests, both members of Parliament, who were fast drifting into mere contradiction of each other's second-hand opinions. In plain terms, they stated the matter in dispute: "Which of our political parties deserves the confidence of the English people? " In plain terms, on his sides Randal answered: "The party that lowers the taxes. " Those words acted on the discussion like water on a fire. As members of Parliament, the two contending politicians were naturally innocent of the slightest interest in the people or the taxes; they received the new idea submitted to them in helpless silence. Friends who were listening began to laugh. The oldest man present looked at his watch. In five minutes more the lights were out and the smoking-room was deserted.

Linley was the last to retire—fevered by the combined influences of smoke and noise. His mind, oppressed all through the evening, was as ill at ease as ever. Lingering, wakeful and irritable, in the corridor (just as Sydney had lingered before him), he too stopped at the open door and admired the peaceful beauty of the garden.

The sleepy servant, appointed to attend in the smoking room, asked if he should close the door. Linley answered: "Go to bed, and leave it to me. " Still lingering at the top of the steps, he too was tempted by the refreshing coolness of the air. He took the key out of the lock; secured the door after he had passed through it; put the key in his pocket, and went down into the garden.

Chapter IX.

Somebody Attends to the Door.

With slow steps Linley crossed the lawn; his mind gloomily absorbed in thoughts which had never before troubled his easy nature—thoughts heavily laden with a burden of self-reproach.

Arrived at the limits of the lawn, two paths opened before him. One led into a quaintly pretty inclosure, cultivated on the plan of the old gardens at Versailles, and called the French Garden. The other path led to a grassy walk, winding its way capriciously through a thick shrubbery. Careless in what direction he turned his steps, Linley entered the shrubbery, because it happened to be nearest to him.

Except at certain points, where the moonlight found its way through open spaces in the verdure, the grassy path which he was now following wound onward in shadow. How far he had advanced he had not noticed, when he heard a momentary rustling of leaves at some little distance in advance of him. The faint breeze had died away; the movement among the leaves had been no doubt produced by the creeping or the flying of some creature of the night. Looking up, at the moment when he was disturbed by this trifling incident, he noticed a bright patch of moonlight ahead as he advanced to a new turn in the path.

The instant afterward he was startled by the appearance of a figure, emerging into the moonlight from the further end of the shrubbery, and rapidly approaching him. He was near enough to see that it was the figure of a woman. Was it one of the female servants, hurrying back to the house after an interview with a sweetheart? In his black evening dress, he was, in all probability, completely hidden by the deep shadow in which he stood. Would he be less likely to frighten the woman if he called to her than if he allowed her to come close up to him in the dark? He decided on calling to her.

"Who is out so late? " he asked.

A cry of alarm answered him. The figure stood still for a moment, and then turned back as if to escape him by flight.

"Don't be frightened, " he said. "Surely you know my voice? "

The figure stood still again. He showed himself in the moonlight, and discovered—Sydney Westerfield.

"You! " he exclaimed.

She trembled; the words in which she answered him were words in fragments.

"The garden was so quiet and pretty—I thought there would be no harm—please let me go back—I'm afraid I shall be shut out—"

She tried to pass him. "My poor child! " he said, "what is there to be frightened about? I have been tempted out by the lovely night, like you. Take my arm. It is so close in here among the trees. If we go back to the lawn, the air will come to you freely. "

She took his arm; he could feel her heart throbbing against it. Kindly silent, he led her back to the open space. Some garden chairs were placed here and there; he suggested that she should rest for a while.

"I'm afraid I shall be shut out, " she repeated. "Pray let me get back. "

He yielded at once to the wish that she expressed. "You must let me take you back, " he explained. "They are all asleep at the house by this time. No! no! don't be frightened again. I have got the key of the door. The moment I have opened it, you shall go in by yourself. "

She looked at him gratefully. "You are not offended with me now, Mr. Linley, " she said. "You are like your kind self again. "

They ascended the steps which led to the door. Linley took the key from his pocket. It acted perfectly in drawing back the lock; but the door, when he pushed it, resisted him. He put his shoulder against it, and exerted his strength, helped by his weight. The door remained immovable.

Had one of the servants—sitting up later than usual after the party, and not aware that Mr. Linley had gone into the garden—noticed the door, and carefully fastened the bolts on the inner side? That was exactly what had happened.

There was nothing for it but to submit to circumstances. Linley led the way down the steps again. "We are shut out, " he said.

Sydney listened in silent dismay. He seemed to be merely amused; he treated their common misfortune as lightly as if it had been a joke.

"There's nothing so very terrible in our situation, " he reminded her. "The servants' offices will be opened between six and seven o'clock; the weather is perfect; and the summer-house in the French Garden has one easy-chair in it, to my certain knowledge, in which you may rest and sleep. I'm sure you must be tired—let me take you there. "

She drew back, and looked up at the house.

"Can't we make them hear us? " she asked.

"Quite impossible. Besides—" He was about to remind her of the evil construction which might be placed on their appearance together, returning from the garden at an advanced hour of the night; but her innocence pleaded with him to be silent. He only said, "You forget that we all sleep at the top of our old castle. There is no knocker to the door, and no bell that rings upstairs. Come to the summer-house. In an hour or two more we shall see the sun rise. "

She took his arm in silence. They reached the French Garden without another word having passed between them.

The summer-house had been designed, in harmony with the French taste of the last century, from a classical model. It was a rough copy in wood of The Temple of Vesta at Rome. Opening the door for his companion, Linley paused before he followed her in. A girl brought up by a careful mother would have understood and appreciated his hesitation; she would have concealed any feeling of embarrassment that might have troubled her at the moment, and would have asked him to come back and let her know when the rising of the sun began. Neglected by her mother, worse than neglected by her aunt, Sydney's fearless ignorance put a question which would have lowered the poor girl cruelly in the estimation of a stranger. "Are you going to leave me here by myself? " she asked. "Why don't you come in? "

Linley thought of his visit to the school, and remembered the detestable mistress. He excused Sydney; he felt for her. She held the door open for him. Sure of himself, he entered the summer-house.

As a mark of respect on her part, she offered the armchair to him: it was the one comfortable seat in the neglected place. He insisted that she should take it; and, searching the summer-house, found a wooden stool for himself. The small circular room received but little of the dim outer light—they were near each other—they were silent. Sydney burst suddenly into a nervous little laugh.

"Why do you laugh? " he asked good-humoredly.

"It seems so strange, Mr. Linley, for us to be out here. " In the moment when she made that reply her merriment vanished; she looked out sadly, through the open door, at the stillness of the night. "What should I have done, " she wondered, "if I had been shut out of the house by myself? " Her eyes rested on him timidly; there was some thought in her which she shrank from expressing. She only said: "I wish I knew how to be worthy of your kindness. "

Her voice warned him that she was struggling with strong emotion. In one respect, men are all alike; they hate to see a woman in tears. Linley treated her like a child; he smiled, and patted her on the shoulder. "Nonsense! " he said gayly. "There is no merit in being kind to my good little governess. "

She took that comforting hand—it was a harmless impulse that she was unable to resist—she bent over it, and kissed it gratefully. He drew his hand away from her as if the soft touch of her lips had been fire that burned it. "Oh, " she cried, "have I done wrong? "

"No, my dear—no, no. "

There was an embarrassment in his manner, the inevitable result of his fear of himself if he faltered in the resolute exercise of self-restraint, which was perfectly incomprehensible to Sydney. He moved his seat back a little, so as to place himself further away. Something in that action, at that time, shocked and humiliated her. Completely misunderstanding him, she thought he was reminding her of the distance that separated them in social rank. Oh, the shame of it! the shame of it! Would other governesses have taken a liberty with their master? A fit of hysterical sobbing burst its way through her last reserves of self-control; she started to her feet, and ran out of the summer-house.

Alarmed and distressed, he followed her instantly.

She was leaning against the pedestal of a statue in the garden, panting, shuddering, a sight to touch the heart of a far less sensitive man than the man who now approached her. "Sydney! " he said. "Dear little Sydney! " She tried to speak to him in return. Breath and strength failed her together; she lifted her hand, vainly grasping at the broad pedestal behind her; she would have fallen if he had not caught her in his arms. Her head sank faintly backward on his breast. He looked at the poor little tortured face, turned up toward him in the lovely moonlight. Again and again he had honorably restrained himself—he was human; he was a man—in one mad moment it was done, hotly, passionately done—he kissed her.

For the first time in her maiden's life, a man's lips touched her lips. All that had been perplexing and strange, all that had been innocently wonderful to herself in the feeling that bound Sydney to her first friend, was a mystery no more. Love lifted its veil, Nature revealed its secrets, in the one supreme moment of that kiss. She threw her arms around his neck with a low cry of delight—and returned his kiss.

"Sydney, " he whispered, "I love you. "

She heard him in rapturous silence. Her kiss had answered for her.

At that crisis in their lives, they were saved by an accident; a poor little common accident that happens every day. The spring in the bracelet that Sydney wore gave way as she held him to her; the bright trinket fell on the grass at her feet. The man never noticed it. The woman saw her pretty ornament as it dropped from her arm— saw, and remembered Mrs. Linley's gift.

Cold and pale—with horror of herself confessed in the action, simple as it was—she drew back from him in dead silence.

He was astounded. In tones that trembled with agitation, he said to her: "Are you ill? "

"Shameless and wicked, " she answered. "Not ill. " She pointed to the bracelet on the grass. "Take it up; I am not fit to touch it. Look on the inner side. "

He remembered the inscription: "To Sydney Westerfield, with Catherine Linley's love. " His head sank on his breast; he understood her at last. "You despise me, " he said, "and I deserve it. "

"No; I despise myself. I have lived among vile people; and I am vile like them. "

She moved a few steps away with a heavy sigh. "Kitty! " she said to herself. "Poor little Kitty! "

He followed her. "Why are you thinking of the child, " he asked, "at such a time as this? "

She replied without returning or looking round; distrust of herself had inspired her with terror of Linley, from the time when the bracelet had dropped on the grass.

"I can make but one atonement, " she said. "We must see each other no more. I must say good-by to Kitty—I must go. Help me to submit to my hard lot—I must go. "

He set her no example of resignation; he shrank from the prospect that she presented to him.

"Where are you to go if you leave us? " he asked.

"Away from England! The further away from *you* the better for both of us. Help me with your interest; have me sent to the new world in the west, with other emigrants. Give me something to look forward to that is not shame and despair. Let me do something that is innocent and good—I may find a trace of my poor lost brother. Oh, let me go! Let me go! "

Her resolution shamed him. He rose to her level, in spite of himself.

"I dare not tell you that you are wrong, " he said. "I only ask you to wait a little till we are calmer, before you speak of the future again. " He pointed to the summer-house. "Go in, my poor girl. Rest, and compose yourself, while I try to think. "

He left her, and paced up and down the formal walks in the garden. Away from the maddening fascination of her presence, his mind grew clearer. He resisted the temptation to think of her tenderly; he set himself to consider what it would be well to do next.

The moonlight was seen no more. Misty and starless, the dark sky spread its majestic obscurity over the earth. Linley looked wearily toward the eastern heaven. The darkness daunted him; he saw in it the shadow of his own sense of guilt. The gray glimmering of dawn, the songs of birds when the pure light softly climbed the sky, roused and relieved him. With the first radiant rising of the sun he returned to the summer-house.

"Do I disturb you? " he asked, waiting at the door.

"No. "

"Will you come out and speak to me? "

She appeared at the door, waiting to hear what he had to say to her.

"I must ask you to submit to a sacrifice of your own feelings, " he began. "When I kept away from you in the drawing room, last night—when my strange conduct made you fear that you had offended me—I was trying to remember what I owed to my good wife. I have been thinking of her again. We must spare her a discovery too terrible to be endured, while her attention is claimed by the guests who are now in the house. In a week's time they will leave us. Will you consent to keep up appearances? Will you live with us as usual, until we are left by ourselves? "

"It shall be done, Mr. Linley. I only ask one favor of you. My worst enemy is my own miserable wicked heart. Oh, don't you understand me? I am ashamed to look at you! "

He had only to examine his own heart, and to know what she meant. "Say no more, " he answered sadly. "We will keep as much away from each other as we can. "

She shuddered at that open recognition of the guilty love which united them, in spite of their horror of it, and took refuge from him in the summer-house. Not a word more passed between them until the unbarring of doors was heard in the stillness of the morning, and the smoke began to rise from the kitchen chimney. Then he returned, and spoke to her.

"You can get back to the house, " he said. "Go up by the front stairs, and you will not meet the servants at this early hour. If they do see you, you have your cloak on; they will think you have been in the garden earlier than usual. As you pass the upper door, draw back the bolts quietly, and I can let myself in. "

She bent her head in silence. He looked after her as she hastened away from him over the lawn; conscious of admiring her, conscious of more than he dared realize to himself. When she disappeared, he turned back to wait where she had been waiting. With his sense of the duty he owed to his wife penitently present to his mind, the memory of that fatal kiss still left its vivid impression on him. "What a scoundrel I am! " he said to himself as he stood alone in the summer-house, looking at the chair which she had just left.

Chapter X.

Kitty Mentions Her Birthday.

A clever old lady, possessed of the inestimable advantages of worldly experience, must submit nevertheless to the laws of Nature. Time and Sleep together—powerful agents in the small hours of the morning—had got the better of Mrs. Presty's resolution to keep awake. Free from discovery, Sydney ascended the stairs. Free from discovery, Sydney entered her own room.

Half-an-hour later, Linley opened the door of his dressing-room. His wife was still sleeping. His mother-in-law woke two hours later; looked at her watch; and discovered that she had lost her opportunity. Other old women, under similar circumstances, might have felt discouraged. This old woman believed in her own suspicions more devoutly than ever. When the breakfast-bell rang, Sydney found Mrs. Presty in the corridor, waiting to say good morning.

"I wonder what you were doing last night, when you ought to have been in bed? " the old lady began, with a treacherous amiability of manner. "Oh, I am not mistaken! your door was open, my dear, and I looked in. "

"Why did you look in, Mrs. Presty? "

"My young friend, I was naturally anxious about you. I am anxious still. Were you in the house? or out of the house? "

"I was walking in the garden, " Sydney replied.

"Admiring the moonlight? "

"Yes; admiring the moonlight. "

"Alone, of course? " Sydney's friend suggested.

And Sydney took refuge in prevarication. "Why should you doubt it? " she said.

Mrs. Presty wasted no more time in asking questions. She was pleasantly reminded of the words of worldly wisdom which she had addressed to her daughter on the day of Sydney's arrival at Mount Morven. "The good qualities of that unfortunate young creature" (she had said) "can *not* have always resisted the horrid temptations and contaminations about her. Hundreds of times she must have lied through ungovernable fear. " Elevated a little higher than ever in her own estimation, Mrs. Presty took Sydney's arm, and led her down to breakfast with motherly familiarity. Linley met them at the foot of the stairs. His mother-in-law first stole a look at Sydney, and then shook hands with him cordially. "My dear Herbert, how pale you are! That horrid smoking. You look as if you had been up all night. "

Mrs. Linley paid her customary visit to the schoolroom that morning.

The necessary attention to her guests had left little leisure for the exercise of observation at the breakfast-table; the one circumstance which had forced itself on her notice had been the boisterous gayety of her husband. Too essentially honest to practice deception of any kind cleverly, Linley had overacted the part of a man whose mind was entirely at ease. The most unsuspicious woman living, his wife was simply amused "How he does enjoy society! " she thought. "Herbert will be a young man to the end of his life. "

In the best possible spirits—still animated by her successful exertions to entertain her friends—Mrs. Linley opened the schoolroom door briskly. "How are the lessons getting on? " she began—and checked herself with a start, "Kitty! " she exclaimed, "Crying? "

The child ran to her mother with tears in her eyes. "Look at Syd! She sulks; she cries; she won't talk to me—send for the doctor. "

"You tiresome child, I don't want the doctor. I'm not ill. "

"There, mamma! " cried Kitty. "She never scolded me before to-day. "

In other words, here was a complete reversal of the usual order of things in the schoolroom. Patient Sydney was out of temper; gentle Sydney spoke bitterly to the little friend whom she loved. Mrs. Linley drew a chair to the governess's side, and took her hand. The strangely altered girl tore her hand away and burst into a violent fit of crying. Puzzled and frightened, Kitty (to the best of a child's ability) followed her example. Mrs. Linley took her daughter on her knee, and gave Sydney's outbreak of agitation time to subside. There were no feverish appearances in her face, there was no feverish heat in her skin when their hands had touched each other for a moment. In all probability the mischief was nervous mischief, and the outburst of weeping was an hysterical effort at relief.

"I am afraid, my dear, you have had a bad night, " Mrs. Linley said.

"Bad? Worse than bad! "

Sydney stopped; looked at her good mistress and friend in terror; and made a confused effort to explain away what she had just said. As sensibly and kindly self-possessed as ever, Mrs. Linley told her that she only wanted rest and quiet. "Let me take you to my room, " she proposed. "We will have the sofa moved into the balcony, and you will soon go to sleep in the delicious warm air. You may put away your books, Kitty; this is a holiday. Come with me, and be petted and spoiled by the ladies in the morning-room. "

Neither the governess nor the pupil was worthy of the sympathy so frankly offered to them. Still strangely confused, Sydney made commonplace apologies and asked leave to go out and walk in the park. Hearing this, Kitty declared that where her governess went she would go too. Mrs. Linley smoothed her daughter's pretty auburn hair, and said, playfully: "I think I ought to be jealous. " To her surprise, Sydney looked up as if the words had been addressed to herself "You mustn't be fonder, my dear, of your governess, " Mrs. Linley went on, "than you are of your mother. " She kissed the child, and, rising to go, discovered that Sydney had moved to another part of the room. She was standing at the piano, with a page of music in her hand. The page was upside down—and she had placed herself in a position which concealed her face. Slow as Mrs. Linley was to doubt any person (more especially a person who interested her), she left the room with a vague fear of something wrong, and with a conviction that she would do well to consult her husband.

Hearing the door close, Sydney looked round. She and Kitty were alone again; and Kitty was putting away her books without showing any pleasure at the prospect of a holiday.

Sydney took the child fondly in her arms. "Would you be very sorry, " she asked, "if I was obliged to go away, some day, and leave you? " Kitty turned pale with terror at the dreadful prospect which those words presented. "There! there! I am only joking, " Sydney said, shocked at the effect which her attempt to suggest the impending separation had produced. "You shall come with me, darling; we will walk in the park together. "

Kitty's face brightened directly. She proposed extending their walk to the paddock, and feeding the cows. Sydney readily consented. Any amusement was welcome to her which diverted the child's attention from herself.

They had been nearly an hour in the park, and were returning to the house through a clump of trees, when Sydney's companion, running on before her, cried: "Here's papa! " Her first impulse was to draw back behind a tree, in the hope of escaping notice. Linley sent Kitty away to gather a nosegay of daisies, and joined Sydney under the trees.

"I have been looking for you everywhere, " he said. "My wife—"

Sydney interrupted him. "Discovered! " she exclaimed.

"There is nothing that need alarm you, " he replied. "Catherine is too good and too true herself to suspect others easily. She sees a change in you that she doesn't understand—she asks if I have noticed it— and that is all. But her mother has the cunning of the devil. There is a serious reason for controlling yourself. "

He spoke so earnestly that he startled her. "Are you angry with me? " she asked.

"Angry! Does the man live who could be angry with you? "

"It might be better for both of us if you *were* angry with me. I have to control myself; I will try again. Oh, if you only knew what I suffer when Mrs. Linley is kind to me! "

He persisted in trying to rouse her to a sense of the danger that threatened them, while the visitors remained in the house. "In a few days, Sydney, there will be no more need for the deceit that is now forced on us. Till that time comes, remember—Mrs. Presty suspects us. "

Kitty ran back to them with her hands full of daisies before they could say more.

"There is your nosegay, papa. No; I don't want you to thank me—I want to know what present you are going to give me. " Her father's mind was preoccupied; he looked at her absently. The child's sense of her own importance was wounded: she appealed to her governess. "Would you believe it? " she asked. "Papa has forgotten that next Tuesday is my birthday! "

"Very well, Kitty; I must pay the penalty of forgetting. What present would you like to have? "

"I want a doll's perambulator. "

"Ha! In my time we were satisfied with a doll. "

They all three looked round. Another person had suddenly joined in the talk. There was no mistaking the person's voice: Mrs. Presty appeared among the trees, taking a walk in the park. Had she heard what Linley and the governess had said to each other while Kitty was gathering daisies?

"Quite a domestic scene! " the sly old lady remarked. "Papa, looking like a saint in a picture, with flowers in his hand. Papa's spoiled child always wanting something, and always getting it. And papa's governess, so sweetly fresh and pretty that I should certainly fall in love with her, if I had the advantage of being a man. You have no doubt remarked Herbert—I think I hear the bell; shall we go to lunch? —you have no doubt, I say, remarked what curiously opposite styles Catherine and Miss Westerfield present; so charming, and yet such complete contrasts. I wonder whether they occasionally envy each other's good looks? Does my daughter ever regret that she is not Miss Westerfield? And do you, my dear, some times wish you were Mrs. Linley? "

"While we are about it, let me put a third question, " Linley interposed. "Are you ever aware of it yourself, Mrs. Presty, when you are talking nonsense? "

He was angry, and he showed it in that feeble reply. Sydney felt the implied insult offered to her in another way. It roused her to the exercise of self-control as nothing had roused her yet. She ignored Mrs. Presty's irony with a composure worthy of Mrs. Presty herself. "Where is the woman, " she said, "who would *not* wish to be as beautiful as Mrs. Linley—and as good? "

"Thank you, my dear, for a compliment to my daughter: a sincere compliment, no doubt. It comes in very neatly and nicely, " Mrs. Presty acknowledged, "after my son-in-law's little outbreak of temper. My poor Herbert, when will you understand that I mean no harm? I am an essentially humorous person; my wonderful spirits are always carrying me away. I do assure you, Miss Westerfield, I don't know what worry is. My troubles—deaths in the family, and that sort of thing—seem to slip off me in a most remarkable manner. Poor Mr. Norman used to attribute it to my excellent digestion. My second husband would never hear of such an explanation as that. His high ideal of women shrank from allusions to stomachs. He used to speak so nicely (quoting some poet) of the sunshine of my breast. Vague, perhaps, " said Mrs. Presty, modestly looking down at the ample prospect of a personal nature which presented itself below her throat, "but so flattering to one's feelings. There's the luncheon bell again, I declare! I'll run on before and tell them you are coming. Some people might say they wished to be punctual. I am truth itself, and I own I don't like to be helped to the underside of the fish. *Au revoir!* Do you remember, Miss Westerfield, when I asked you to repeat *au revoir* as a specimen of your French? I didn't think much of your accent. Oh, dear me, I didn't think much of your accent! "

Kitty looked after her affluent grandmother with eyes that stared respectfully in ignorant admiration. She pulled her father's coat-tail, and addressed herself gravely to his private ear. "Oh, papa, what noble words grandmamma has! "

Chapter XI.

Linley Asserts His Authority.

On the evening of Monday in the new week, the last of the visitors had left Mount Morven. Mrs. Linley dropped into a chair (in, what Randal called, "the heavenly tranquillity of the deserted drawing-room") and owned that the effort of entertaining her guests had completely worn her out. "It's too absurd, at my time of life, " she said with a faint smile; "but I am really and truly so tired that I must go to bed before dark, as if I was a child again. "

Mrs. Presty—maliciously observant of the governess, sitting silent and apart in a corner—approached her daughter in a hurry; to all appearance with a special object in view. Linley was at no loss to guess what that object might be. "Will you do me a favor, Catherine? " Mrs. Presty began. "I wish to say a word to you in your own room. "

"Oh, mamma, have some mercy on me, and put it off till to-morrow! "

Mrs. Presty reluctantly consented to this proposal, on one condition. "It is understood, " she stipulated "that I am to see you the first thing in the morning? "

Mrs. Linley was ready to accept that condition, or any condition, which promised her a night of uninterrupted repose. She crossed the room to her husband, and took his arm. "In my state of fatigue, Herbert, I shall never get up our steep stairs, unless you help me. "

As they ascended the stairs together, Linley found that his wife had a reason of her own for leaving the drawing-room.

"I am quite weary enough to go to bed, " she explained. "But I wanted to speak to you first. It's about Miss Westerfield. (No, no, we needn't stop on the landing.) Do you know, I think I have found out what has altered our little governess so strangely—I seem to startle you? "

"No. "

"I am only astonished, " Mrs. Linley resumed, "at my own stupidity in not having discovered it before. We must be kinder than ever to the poor girl now; can't you guess why? My dear, how dull you are! Must I remind you that we have had two single men among our visitors? One of them is old and doesn't matter. But the other—I mean Sir George, of course—is young, handsome, and agreeable. I am so sorry for Sydney Westerfield. It's plain to me that she is hopelessly in love with a man who has run through his fortune, and must marry money if he marries at all. I shall speak to Sydney to-morrow; and I hope and trust I shall succeed in winning her confidence. Thank Heaven, here we are at my door at last! I can't say more now; I'm ready to drop. Good-night, dear; you look tired, too. It's a nice thing to have friends, I know; but, oh, what a relief it is sometimes to get rid of them! "

She kissed him, and let him go.

Left by himself, to compare his wife's innocent mistake with the terrible enlightenment that awaited her, Linley's courage failed him. He leaned on the quaintly-carved rail that protected the outer side of the landing, and looked down at the stone hall far below. If the old woodwork (he thought) would only give way under his weight, there would be an escape from the coming catastrophe, found in an instant.

A timely remembrance of Sydney recalled him to himself. For her sake, he was bound to prevent Mrs. Presty's contemplated interview with his wife on the next morning.

Descending the stairs, he met his brother in the corridor on the first floor.

"The very man I want to see, " Randal said. "Tell me, Herbert, what is the matter with that curious old woman? "

"Do you mean Mrs. Presty? "

"Yes. She has just been telling me that our friend Mrs. MacEdwin has taken a fancy to Miss Westerfield, and would be only too glad to deprive us of our pretty governess. "

"Did Mrs. Presty say that in Miss Westerfield's presence? "

"No. Soon after you and Catherine left the room, Miss Westerfield left it too. I daresay I am wrong, for I haven't had time to think of it;

but Mrs. Presty's manner suggested to me that she would be glad to see the poor girl sent out of the house. "

"I am going to speak to her, Randal, on that very subject. Is she still in the drawing-room? "

"Yes. "

"Did she say anything more to you? "

"I didn't give her the chance; I don't like Mrs. Presty. You look worn and worried, Herbert. Is there anything wrong? "

"If there is, my dear fellow, you will hear of it tomorrow. "

So they parted.

Comfortably established in the drawing-room, Mrs. Presty had just opened her favorite newspaper. Her only companion was Linley's black poodle, resting at her feet. On the opening of the door, the dog rose—advanced to caress his master—and looked up in Linley's face. If Mrs. Presty's attention had happened to be turned that way, she might have seen, in the faithful creature's sudden and silent retreat, a warning of her son-in-law's humor at that moment. But she was, or assumed to be, interested in her reading; and she deliberately overlooked Linley's appearance. After waiting a little to attract her attention, he quietly took the newspaper out of her hand.

"What does this mean? " Mrs. Presty asked.

"It means, ma'am, that I have something to say to you. "

"Apparently, something that can't be said with common civility? Be as rude as you please; I am well used to it. "

Linley wisely took no notice of this.

"Since you have lived at Mount Morven, " he proceeded, "I think you have found me, on the whole, an easy man to get on with. At the same time, when I do make up my mind to be master in my own house, I *am* master. "

Mrs. Presty crossed her hands placidly on her lap, and asked: "Master of what? "

"Master of your suspicions of Miss Westerfield. You are free, of course, to think of her and of me as you please. What I forbid is the expression of your thoughts—either by way of hints to my brother, or officious communications with my wife. Don't suppose that I am afraid of the truth. Mrs. Linley shall know more than you think for, and shall know it to-morrow; not from you, but from me. "

Mrs. Presty shook her head compassionately. "My good sir, surely you know me too well to think that I am to be disposed of in that easy way? Must I remind you that your wife's mother has 'the cunning of the devil'? "

Linley recognized his own words. "So you were listening among the trees! " he said.

"Yes; I was listening; and I have only to regret that I didn't hear more. Let us return to our subject. I don't trust my daughter's interests—my much-injured daughter's interests—in your hands. They are not clean hands, Mr. Linley. I have a duty to do; and I shall do it to-morrow. "

"No, Mrs. Presty, you won't do it to-morrow. "

"Who will prevent me? "

"I shall prevent you. "

"In what way, if you please? "

"I don't think it necessary to answer that question. My servants will have their instructions; and I shall see myself that my orders are obeyed. "

"Thank you. I begin to understand; I am to be turned out of the house. Very well. We shall see what my daughter says. "

"You know as well as I do, Mrs. Presty, that if your daughter is forced to choose between us she will decide for her husband. You have the night before you for consideration. I have no more to say. "

The Evil Genius

Among Mrs. Presty's merits, it is only just to reckon a capacity for making up her mind rapidly, under stress of circumstances. Before Linley had opened the door, on his way out, he was called back.

"I am shocked to trouble you again, " Mrs. Presty said, "but I don't propose to interfere with my night's rest by thinking about *you*. My position is perfectly clear to me, without wasting time in consideration. When a man so completely forgets what is due to the weaker sex as to threaten a woman, the woman has no alternative but to submit. You are aware that I had arranged to see my daughter to-morrow morning. I yield to brute force, sir. Tell your wife that I shall not keep my appointment. Are you satisfied? "

"Quite satisfied, " Linley said—and left the room.

His mother-in-law looked after him with a familiar expression of opinion, and a smile of supreme contempt.

"You fool! "

Only two words; and yet there seemed to be some hidden meaning in them—relating perhaps to what might happen on the next day— which gently tickled Mrs. Presty in the region assigned by phrenologists to the sense of self-esteem.

Chapter XII.

Two of Them Sleep Badly.

Waiting for Sydney to come into the bedroom as usual and wish her good-night, Kitty was astonished by the appearance of her grandmother, entering on tiptoe from the corridor, with a small paper parcel in her hand.

"Whisper! " said Mrs. Presty, pointing to the open door of communication with Mrs. Linley's room. "This is your birthday present. You mustn't look at it till you wake to-morrow morning. " She pushed the parcel under the pillow—and, instead of saying good-night, took a chair and sat down.

"May I show my present, " Kitty asked, "when I go to mamma in the morning? "

The present hidden under the paper wrapper was a sixpenny picture-book. Kitty's grandmother disapproved of spending money lavishly on birthday gifts to children. "Show it, of course; and take the greatest care of it, " Mrs. Presty answered gravely. "But tell me one thing, my dear, wouldn't you like to see all your presents early in the morning, like mine? "

Still smarting under the recollection of her interview with her son-in-law, Mrs. Presty had certain ends to gain in putting this idea into the child's head. It was her special object to raise domestic obstacles to a private interview between the husband and wife during the earlier hours of the day. If the gifts, usually presented after the nursery dinner, were produced on this occasion after breakfast, there would be a period of delay before any confidential conversation could take place between Mr. and Mrs. Linley. In this interval Mrs. Presty saw her opportunity of setting Linley's authority at defiance, by rousing the first jealous suspicion in the mind of his wife.

Innocent little Kitty became her grandmother's accomplice on the spot. "I shall ask mamma to let me have my presents at breakfast-time, " she announced.

"And kind mamma will say Yes, " Mrs. Presty chimed in. "We will breakfast early, my precious child. Good-night. "

Kitty was half asleep when her governess entered the room afterward, much later than usual. "I thought you had forgotten me, " she said, yawning and stretching out her plump little arms.

Sydney's heart ached when she thought of the separation that was to come with the next day; her despair forced its way to expression in words.

"I wish I could forget you, " she answered, in reckless wretchedness.

The child was still too drowsy to hear plainly. "What did you say? " she asked. Sydney gently lifted her in the bed, and kissed her again and again. Kitty's sleepy eyes opened in surprise. "How cold your hands are! " she said; "and how often you kiss me. What is it you have come to say to me—good-night or good-by? "

Sydney laid her down again on the pillow, gave her a last kiss, and ran out of the room.

In the corridor she heard Linley's voice on the lower floor. He was asking one of the servants if Miss Westerfield was in the house or in the garden. Her first impulse was to advance to the stairs and to answer his question. In a moment more the remembrance of Mrs. Linley checked her. She went back to her bed-chamber. The presents that she had received, since her arrival at Mount Morven, were all laid out so that they could be easily seen by any person entering the room, after she had left the house. On the sofa lay the pretty new dress which she had worn at the evening party. Other little gifts were arranged on either side of it. The bracelet, resting on the pedestal of a statue close by, kept a morsel of paper in its place—on which she had written a few penitent words of farewell addressed to Mrs. Linley. On the toilet-table three photographic portraits showed themselves among the brushes and combs. She sat down, and looked first at the likenesses of Mrs. Linley and Kitty.

Had she any right to make those dear faces her companions in the future?

She hesitated; her tears dropped on the photographs. "They're as good as spoiled now, " she thought; "they're no longer fit for anybody but me. " She paused, and abruptly took up the third and last photograph—the likeness of Herbert Linley.

Was it an offense, now, even to look at his portrait? No idea of leaving it behind her was in her mind. Her resolution vibrated between two miseries—the misery of preserving her keep-sake after she had parted from him forever, and the misery of destroying it. Resigned to one more sacrifice, she took the card in both hands to tear it up. It would have been scattered in pieces on the floor, but for the chance which had turned the portrait side of the card toward her instead of the back. Her longing eyes stole a last look at him—a frenzy seized her—she pressed her lips to the photograph in a passion of hopeless love. "What does it matter? " she asked herself. "I'm nothing but the ignorant object of his kindness—the poor fool who could see no difference between gratitude and love. Where is the harm of having him with me when I am starving in the streets, or dying in the workhouse? " The fervid spirit in her that had never known a mother's loving discipline, never thrilled to the sympathy of a sister-friend, rose in revolt against the evil destiny which had imbittered her life. Her eyes still rested on the photograph. "Come to my heart, my only friend, and kill me! " As those wild words escaped her, she thrust the card furiously into the bosom of her dress—and threw herself on the floor. There was something in the mad self-abandonment of that action which mocked the innocent despair of her childhood, on the day when her mother left her at the cruel mercy of her aunt.

That night was a night of torment in secret to another person at Mount Morven.

Wandering, in his need of self-isolation, up and down the dreary stone passages in the lower part of the house, Linley counted the hours, inexorably lessening the interval between him and the ordeal of confession to his wife. As yet, he had failed to find the opportunity of addressing to Sydney the only words of encouragement he could allow to pass his lips: he had asked for her earlier in the evening, and nobody could tell him where she was. Still in ignorance of the refuge which she might by bare possibility hope to find in Mrs. MacEdwin's house, Sydney was spared the torturing doubts which now beset Herbert Linley's mind. Would the noble woman whom they had injured allow their atonement to plead for them, and consent to keep their miserable secret? Might they still put their trust in that generous nature a few hours hence? Again and again those questions confronted Linley; and again and again he shrank from attempting to answer them.

Chapter XIII.

Kitty Keeps Her Birthday.

They were all assembled as usual at the breakfast-table.

Preferring the request suggested to her by Mrs. Presty, Kitty had hastened the presentation of the birthday gifts, by getting into her mother's bed in the morning, and exacting her mother's promise before she would consent to get out again. By her own express wish, she was left in ignorance of what the presents would prove to be. "Hide them from me, " said this young epicure in pleasurable sensations, "and make me want to see them until I can bear it no longer. " The gifts had accordingly been collected in an embrasure of one of the windows; and the time had now arrived when Kitty could bear it no longer.

In the procession of the presents, Mrs. Linley led the way.

She had passed behind the screen which had thus far protected the hidden treasures from discovery, and appeared again with a vision of beauty in the shape of a doll. The dress of this wonderful creature exhibited the latest audacities of French fashion. Her head made a bow; her eyes went to sleep and woke again; she had a voice that said two words—more precious than two thousand in the mouth of a mere living creature. Kitty's arms opened and embraced her gift with a scream of ecstasy. That fervent pressure found its way to the right spring. The doll squeaked: "Mamma! "—and creaked—and cried again—and said: "Papa! " Kitty sat down on the floor; her legs would support her no longer. "I think I shall faint, " she said quite seriously.

In the midst of the general laughter, Sydney silently placed a new toy (a pretty little imitation of a jeweler's casket) at Kitty's side, and drew back before the child could look at her. Mrs. Presty was the only person present who noticed her pale face and the trembling of her hands as she made the effort which preserved her composure.

The doll's necklace, bracelets, and watch and chain, riveted Kitty's attention on the casket. Just as she thought of looking round for her dear Syd, her father produced a new outburst of delight by presenting a perambulator worthy of the doll. Her uncle followed with a parasol, devoted to the preservation of the doll's complexion when she went out for an airing. Then there came a pause. Where was the generous grandmother's gift? Nobody remembered it; Mrs. Presty herself discovered the inestimable sixpenny picture-book cast away and forgotten on a distant window-seat. "I have a great mind to keep this, " she said to Kitty, "till you are old enough to value it properly. " In the moment of her absence at the window, Linley's mother-in-law lost the chance of seeing him whisper to Sydney. "Meet me in the shrubbery in half an hour, " he said. She stepped back from him, startled by the proposal. When Mrs. Presty was in the middle of the room again, Linley and the governess were no longer near each other.

Having by this time recovered herself, Kitty got on her legs. "Now, " the spoiled child declared, addressing the company present, "I'm going to play. "

The doll was put into the perambulator, and was wheeled about the room, while Mrs. Linley moved the chairs out of the way, and Randal attended with the open parasol—under orders to "pretend that the sun was shining. " Once more the sixpenny picture-book was neglected. Mrs. Presty picked it up from the floor, determined by this time to hold it in reserve until her ungrateful grandchild reached years of discretion. She put it in the bookcase between Byron's "Don Juan" and Butler's "Lives of the Saints. " In the position which she now occupied, Linley was visible approaching Sydney again. "Your own interests are seriously concerned, " he whispered, "in something that I have to tell you. "

Incapable of hearing what passed between them, Mrs. Presty could see that a secret understanding united her son-in-law and the governess. She looked round cautiously at Mrs. Linley.

Kitty's humor had changed; she was now eager to see the doll's splendid clothes taken off and put on again. "Come and look at it, " she said to Sydney; "I want you to enjoy my birthday as much as I do. " Left by himself, Randal got rid of the parasol by putting it on a table near the door. Mrs. Presty beckoned to him to join her at the further end of the room.

"I want you to do me a favor, " she began.

Glancing at Linley before she proceeded, Mrs. Presty took up a newspaper, and affected to be consulting Randal's opinion on a passage which had attracted her attention. "Your brother is looking our way, " she whispered: "he mustn't suspect that there is a secret between us. "

False pretenses of any kind invariably irritated Randal. "What do you want me to do? " he asked sharply.

The reply only increased his perplexity.

"Observe Miss Westerfield and your brother. Look at them now. "

Randal obeyed.

"What is there to look at? " he inquired.

"Can't you see? "

"I see they are talking to each other. "

"They are talking confidentially; talking so that Mrs. Linley can't hear them. Look again. "

Randal fixed his eyes on Mrs. Presty, with an expression which showed his dislike of that lady a little too plainly. Before he could answer what she had just said to him, his lively little niece hit on a new idea. The sun was shining, the flowers were in their brightest beauty—and the doll had not yet been taken into the garden! Kitty at once led the way out; so completely preoccupied in steering the perambulator in a straight course that she forgot her uncle and the parasol. Only waiting to remind her husband and Sydney that they were wasting the beautiful summer morning indoors, Mrs. Linley followed her daughter—and innocently placed a fatal obstacle in Mrs. Presty's way by leaving the room. Having consulted each other by a look, Linley and the governess went out next. Left alone with Randal, Mrs. Presty's anger, under the complete overthrow of her carefully-laid scheme, set restraint at defiance.

"My daughter's married life is a wreck, " she burst out, pointing theatrically to the door by which Linley and Sydney Westerfield had retired. "And Catherine has the vile creature whom your brother picked up in London to thank for it! Now do you understand me? "

"Less than ever, " Randal answered—"unless you have taken leave of your senses. "

Mrs. Presty recovered the command of her temper.

On that fine morning her daughter might remain in the garden until the luncheon-bell rang. Linley had only to say that he wished to speak with his wife; and the private interview which he had so rudely insisted on as his sole privilege, would assuredly take place. The one chance left of still defeating him on his own ground was to force Randal to interfere by convincing him of his brother's guilt. Moderation of language and composure of manner offered the only hopeful prospect of reaching this end. Mrs. Presty assumed the disguise of patient submission, and used the irresistible influence of good humor and good sense.

"I don't complain, dear Randal, of what you have said to me, " she replied. "My indiscretion has deserved it. I ought to have produced my proofs, and have left it to you to draw the conclusion. Sit down, if you please. I won't detain you for more than a few minutes. "

Randal had not anticipated such moderation as this; he took the chair that was nearest to Mrs. Presty. They were both now sitting with their backs turned to the entrance from the library to the drawing-room.

"I won't trouble you with my own impressions, " Mrs. Presty went on. "I will be careful only to mention what I have seen and heard. If you refuse to believe me, I refer you to the guilty persons themselves. "

She had just got to the end of those introductory words when Mrs. Linley returned, by way of the library, to fetch the forgotten parasol.

Randal insisted on making Mrs. Presty express herself plainly. "You speak of guilty persons, " he said. "Am I to understand that one of those guilty persons is my brother? "

Mrs. Linley advanced a step and took the parasol from the table. Hearing what Randal said, she paused, wondering at the strange allusion to her husband. In the meanwhile, Mrs. Presty answered the question that had been addressed to her.

"Yes, " she said to Randal; "I mean your brother, and your brother's mistress—Sydney Westerfield. "

Mrs. Linley laid the parasol back on the table, and approached them.

She never once looked at her mother; her face, white and rigid, was turned toward Randal. To him, and to him only, she spoke.

"What does my mother's horrible language mean? " she asked.

Mrs. Presty triumphed inwardly; chance had decided in her favor, after all! "Don't you see, " she said to her daughter, "that I am here to answer for myself? "

Mrs. Linley still looked at Randal, and still spoke to him. "It is impossible for me to insist on an explanation from my mother, " she proceeded. "No matter what I may feel, I must remember that she *is* my mother. I ask you again—you who have been listening to her— what does she mean? "

Mrs. Presty's sense of her own importance refused to submit to being passed over in this way.

"However insolently you may behave, Catherine, you will not succeed in provoking me. Your mother is bound to open your eyes to the truth. You have a rival in your husband's affections; and that rival is your governess. Take your own course now; I have no more to say. " With her head high in the air—looking the picture of conscious virtue—the old lady walked out.

At the same moment Randal seized his first opportunity of speaking.

He addressed himself gently and respectfully to his sister-in-law. She refused to hear him. The indignation which Mrs. Presty had roused in her made no allowances, and was blind to all sense of right.

"Don't trouble yourself to account for your silence, " she said, most unjustly. "You were listening to my mother without a word of remonstrance when I came into the room. You are concerned in this vile slander, too. "

Randal considerately refrained from provoking her by attempting to defend himself, while she was incapable of understanding him. "You will be sorry when you find that you have misjudged me, " he said, and sighed, and left her.

She dropped into a chair. If there was any one distinct thought in her at that moment, it was the thought of her husband. She was eager to see him; she longed to say to him: "My love, I don't believe a word of it! " He was not in the garden when she had returned for the parasol; and Sydney was not in the garden. Wondering what had become of her father and her governess, Kitty had asked the nursemaid to look for them. What had happened since? Where had they been found? After some hesitation, Mrs. Linley sent for the nursemaid. She felt the strongest reluctance, when the girl appeared, to approach the very inquiries which she was interested in making.

"Have you found Mr. Linley? " she said—with an effort.

"Yes, ma'am. "

"Where did you find him? "

"In the shrubbery. "

"Did your master say anything? "

"I slipped away, ma'am, before he saw me. "

"Why? "

"Miss Westerfield was in the shrubbery, with my master. I might have been mistaken—" The girl paused, and looked confused.

Mrs. Linley tried to tell her to go on. The words were in her mind; but the capacity of giving expression to them failed her. She impatiently made a sign. The sign was understood.

"I might have been mistaken, " the maid repeated—"but I thought Miss Westerfield was crying. "

Having replied in those terms, she seemed to be anxious to get away. The parasol caught her eye. "Miss Kitty wants this, " she said, "and wonders why you have not gone back to her in the garden. May I take the parasol? "

"Take it. "

The tone of the mistress's voice was completely changed. The servant looked at her with vague misgivings. "Are you not well, ma'am? "

"Quite well. "

The servant withdrew.

Mrs. Linley's chair happened to be near one of the windows, which commanded a view of the drive leading to the main entrance of the house. A carriage had just arrived bringing holiday travelers to visit that part of Mount Morven which was open to strangers. She watched them as they got out, talking and laughing, and looking about them. Still shrinking instinctively from the first doubt of Herbert that had ever entered her mind, she found a refuge from herself in watching the ordinary events of the day. One by one the tourists disappeared under the portico of the front door. The empty carriage was driven away next, to water the horses at the village inn. Solitude was all she could see from the windows; silence, horrible silence, surrounded her out of doors and in. The thoughts from which she recoiled forced their way back into her mind; the narrative of the nursemaid's discovery became a burden on her memory once more. She considered the circumstances. In spite of herself, she considered the circumstances again. Her husband and Sydney Westerfield together in the shrubbery—and Sydney crying. Had Mrs. Presty's abominable suspicion of them reached their ears? or? —No! that second possibility might be estimated at its right value by any other woman; not by Herbert Linley's wife.

She snatched up the newspaper, and fixed her eyes on it in the hope of fixing her mind on it next. Obstinately, desperately, she read without knowing what she was reading. The lines of print were beginning to mingle and grow dim, when she was startled by the sudden opening of the door. She looked round.

Her husband entered the room.

Chapter XIV.

Kitty Feels the Heartache.

Linley advanced a few steps—and stopped.

His wife, hurrying eagerly to meet him, checked herself. It might have been distrust, or it might have been unreasoning fear—she hesitated on the point of approaching him.

"I have something to say, Catherine, which I'm afraid will distress you. "

His voice faltered, his eyes rested on her—then looked away again. He said no more.

He had spoken a few commonplace words—and yet he had said enough. She saw the truth in his eyes, heard the truth in his voice. A fit of trembling seized her. Linley stepped forward, in the fear that she might fall. She instantly controlled herself, and signed to him to keep back. "Don't touch me! " she said. "You come from Miss Westerfield! "

That reproach roused him.

"I own that I come from Miss Westerfield, " he answered. "She addresses a request to you through me. "

"I refuse to grant it. "

"Hear it first. "

"No! "

"Hear it—in your own interest. She asks permission to leave the house, never to return again. While she is still innocent—"

His wife eyed him with a look of unutterable contempt. He submitted to it, but not in silence.

"A man doesn't lie, Catherine, who makes such a confession as I am making now. Miss Westerfield offers the one atonement in her power, while she is still innocent of having wronged you—except in thought. "

"Is that all? " Mrs. Linley asked.

"It rests with you, " he replied, "to say if there is any other sacrifice of herself which will be more acceptable to you. "

"Let me understand first what the sacrifice means. Does Miss Westerfield make any conditions? "

"She has positively forbidden me to make conditions. "

"And goes out into the world, helpless and friendless? "

"Yes. "

Even under the terrible trial that wrung her, the nobility of the woman's nature spoke in her next words.

"Give me time to think of what you have said, " she pleaded. "I have led a happy life; I am not used to suffer as I am suffering now. "

They were both silent. Kitty's voice was audible on the stairs that led to the picture-gallery, disputing with the maid. Neither her father nor her mother heard her.

"Miss Westerfield is innocent of having wronged me, except in thought, " Mrs. Linley resumed. "Do you tell me that on your word of honor? "

"On my word of honor. "

So far his wife was satisfied. "My governess, " she said, "might have deceived me—she has not deceived me. I owe it to her to remember that. She shall go, but not helpless and not friendless. "

Her husband forgot the restraints he had imposed on himself.

"Is there another woman in the world like you! " he exclaimed.

"Many other women, " she answered, firmly. "A vulgar termagant, feeling a sense of injury, finds relief in an outburst of jealousy and a furious quarrel. You have always lived among ladies. Surely you ought to know that a wife in my position, who respects herself, restrains herself. I try to remember what I owe to others as well as what they owe to me. "

She approached the writing table, and took up a pen.

Feeling his position acutely, Linley refrained from openly admiring her generosity. Until he had deserved to be forgiven, he had forfeited the right to express an opinion on her conduct. She misinterpreted his silence. As she understood it, he appreciated an act of self-sacrifice on Miss Westerfield's side—but he had no word of encouragement for an act of self-sacrifice on his wife's side. She threw down the pen, with the first outbreak of anger that had escaped her yet.

"You have spoken for the governess, " she said to him. "I haven't heard yet, sir, what you have to say for yourself. Is it you who tempted her? You know how gratefully she feels toward you—have you perverted her gratitude, and led her blindfold to love? Cruel, cruel, cruel! Defend yourself if you can. "

He made no reply.

"Is it not worth your while to defend yourself? " she burst out, passionately. "Your silence is an insult! "

"My silence is a confession, " he answered, sadly. "*She* may accept your mercy—I may not even hope for it. "

Something in the tone of his voice reminded her of past days—the days of perfect love and perfect confidence, when she had been the one woman in the world to him. Dearly treasured remembrances of her married life filled her heart with tenderness, and dimmed with tears the angry light that had risen in her eyes. There was no pride, no anger, in his wife when she spoke to him now.

"Oh, my husband, has she taken your love from me? "

"Judge for yourself, Catherine, if there is no proof of my love for you in what I have resisted—and no remembrance of all that I owe to you in what I have confessed. "

She ventured a little nearer to him. "Can I believe you? "

"Put me to the test. "

She instantly took him at his word. "When Miss Westerfield has left us, promise not to see her again. "

"I promise. "

"And not even to write to her. "

"I promise. "

She went back to the writing-table. "My heart is easier, " she said, simply. "I can be merciful to her now. "

After writing a few lines, she rose and handed the paper to him. He looked up from it in surprise. "Addressed to Mrs. MacEdwin! " he said.

"Addressed, " she answered, "to the only person I know who feels a true interest in Miss Westerfield. Have you not heard of it? "

"I remember, " he said — and read the lines that followed:

"I recommend Miss Westerfield as a teacher of young children, having had ample proof of her capacity, industry, and good temper while she has been governess to my child. She leaves her situation in my service under circumstances which testify to her sense of duty and her sense of gratitude. "

"Have I said, " she asked, "more than I could honorably and truly say — even after what has happened? "

He could only look at her; no words could have spoken for him as his silence spoke for him at that moment. When she took back the written paper there was pardon in her eyes already.

The last worst trial remained to be undergone; she faced it resolutely. "Tell Miss Westerfield that I wish to see her. "

On the point of leaving the room, Herbert was called back. "If you happen to meet with my mother, " his wife added, "will you ask her to come to me? "

Mrs. Presty knew her daughter's nature; Mrs. Presty had been waiting near at hand, in expectation of the message which she now received.

Tenderly and respectfully, Mrs. Linley addressed herself to her mother. "When we last met, I thought you spoke rashly and cruelly. I know now that there was truth—*some* truth, let me say—in what offended me at the time. If you felt strongly, it was for my sake. I wish to beg your pardon; I was hasty, I was wrong. "

On an occasion when she had first irritated and then surprised him, Randal Linley had said to Mrs. Presty, "You have got a heart, after all! " Her reply to her daughter showed that view of her character to be the right one. "Say no more, my dear, " she answered "*I* was hasty; *I* was wrong. "

The words had barely fallen from her lips, before Herbert returned. He was followed by Sydney Westerfield.

The governess stopped in the middle of the room. Her head sank on her breast; her quick convulsive breathing was the only sound that broke the silence. Mrs. Linley advanced to the place in which Sydney stood. There was something divine in her beauty as she looked at the shrinking girl, and held out her hand.

Sydney fell on her knees. In silence she lifted that generous hand to her lips. In silence, Mrs. Linley raised her—took the writing which testified to her character from the table—and presented it. Linley looked at his wife, looked at the governess. He waited—and still neither the one nor the other uttered a word. It was more than he could endure. He addressed himself to Sydney first.

"Try to thank Mrs. Linley, " he said.

She answered faintly: "I can't speak! "

He appealed to his wife next. "Say a last kind word to her, " he pleaded.

She made an effort, a vain effort to obey him. A gesture of despair answered for her as Sydney had answered: "I can't speak! "

True, nobly true, to the Christian virtue that repents, to the Christian virtue that forgives, those three persons stood together on the brink of separation, and forced their frail humanity to suffer and submit.

In mercy to the woman, Linley summoned the courage to part them. He turned to his wife first.

"I may say, Catherine, that she has your good wishes for happier days to come? "

Mrs. Linley pressed his hand.

He approached Sydney, and gave his wife's message. It was in his heart to add something equally kind on his own part. He could only say what we have all said—how sincerely, how sorrowfully, we all know—the common word, "Good-by! "—the common wish, "God bless you! "

At that last moment the child ran into the room, in search of her mother.

There was a low murmur of horror at the sight of her. That innocent heart, they had all hoped, might have been spared the misery of the parting scene!

She saw that Sydney had her hat and cloak on. "You're dressed to go out, " she said. Sydney turned away to hide her face. It was too late; Kitty had seen the tears. "Oh, my darling, you're not going away! " She looked at her father and mother. "Is she going away? " They were afraid to answer her. With all her little strength, she clasped her beloved friend and play-fellow round the waist. "My own dear, you're not going to leave me! " The dumb misery in Sydney's face struck Linley with horror. He placed Kitty in her mother's arms. The child's piteous cry, "Oh, don't let her go! don't let her go! " followed the governess as she suffered her martyrdom, and went out. Linley's heart ached; he watched her until she was lost to view. "Gone! " he murmured to himself—"gone forever! "

Mrs. Presty heard him, and answered him: —"She'll come back again! "

SECOND BOOK

Chapter XV.

The Doctor.

As the year advanced, the servants at Mount Morven remarked that the weeks seemed to follow each other more slowly than usual. In the higher regions of the house, the same impression was prevalent; but the sense of dullness among the gentlefolks submitted to circumstances in silence.

If the question had been asked in past days: Who is the brightest and happiest member of the family? everybody would have said: Kitty. If the question had been asked at the present time, differences of opinion might have suggested different answers—but the whole household would have refrained without hesitation from mentioning the child's name.

Since Sydney Westerfield's departure Kitty had never held up her head.

Time quieted the child's first vehement outbreak of distress under the loss of the companion whom she had so dearly loved. Delicate management, gently yet resolutely applied, held the faithful little creature in check, when she tried to discover the cause of her governess's banishment from the house. She made no more complaints; she asked no more embarrassing questions—but it was miserably plain to everybody about her that she failed to recover her spirits. She was willing to learn her lessons (but not under another governess) when her mother was able to attend to her: she played with her toys, and went out riding on her pony. But the delightful gayety of other days was gone; the shrill laughter that once rang through the house was heard no more. Kitty had become a quiet child; and, worse still, a child who seemed to be easily tired.

The doctor was consulted.

He was a man skilled in the sound medical practice that learns its lessons without books—bedside practice. His opinion declared that the child's vital power was seriously lowered. "Some cause is at work here, " he said to the mother, "which I don't understand. Can you help me? " Mrs. Linley helped him without hesitation. "My little daughter dearly loved her governess; and her governess has been obliged to leave us. " That was her reply. The doctor wanted to hear no more; he at once advised that Kitty should be taken to the seaside, and that everything which might remind her of the absent friend— books, presents, even articles of clothing likely to revive old associations—should be left at home. A new life, in new air. When pen, ink, and paper were offered to him, that was the doctor's prescription.

Mrs. Linley consulted her husband on the choice of the seaside place to which the child should be removed.

The blank which Sydney's departure left in the life of the household was felt by the master and mistress of Mount Morven—and felt, unhappily, without any open avowal on either side of what was passing in their minds. In this way the governess became a forbidden subject between them; the husband waited for the wife to set the example of approaching it, and the wife waited for the husband. The trial of temper produced by this state of hesitation, and by the secret doubts which it encouraged, led insensibly to a certain estrangement—which Linley in particular was morbidly unwilling to acknowledge. If, when the dinner-hour brought them together, he was silent and dull in his wife's presence, he attributed it to anxiety on the subject of his brother—then absent on a critical business errand in London. If he sometimes left the house the first thing in the morning, and only returned at night, it was because the management of the model farm had become one of his duties, in Randal's absence. Mrs. Linley made no attempt to dispute this view of the altered circumstances in home-life—but she submitted with a mind ill at ease. Secretly fearing that Linley was suffering under Miss Westerfield's absence, she allowed herself to hope that Kitty's father would see a necessity, in his own case, for change of scene, and would accompany them to the seaside.

"Won't you come with us, Herbert? " she suggested, when they had both agreed on the choice of a place.

His temper was in a state of constant irritation. Without meaning it he answered her harmless question sharply.

"How can I go away with you, when we are losing by the farm, and when there is nobody to check the ruinous expenses but myself? "

Mrs. Linley's thoughts naturally turned to Randal's prolonged absence. "What can be keeping him all this time in London? " she said.

Linley's failing patience suffered a severe trial.

"Don't you know, " he broke out, "that I have inherited my poor mother's property in England, saddled with a lawsuit? Have you never heard of delays and disappointments, and quibbles and false pretenses, encountered by unfortunate wretches like me who are obliged to go to law? God only knows when Randal will be free to return, or what bad news he may bring with him when he does come back. "

"You have many anxieties, Herbert; and I ought to have remembered them. "

That gentle answer touched him. He made the best apology in his power: he said his nerves were out of order, and asked her to excuse him if he had spoken roughly. There was no unfriendly feeling on either side; and yet there was something wanting in the reconciliation. Mrs. Linley left her husband, shaken by a conflict of feelings. At one moment she felt angry with him; at another she felt angry with herself.

With the best intentions (as usual) Mrs. Presty made mischief, nevertheless. Observing that her daughter was in tears, and feeling sincerely distressed by the discovery, she was eager to administer consolation. "Make your mind easy, my dear, if you have any doubt about Herbert's movements when he is away from home. I followed him myself the day before yesterday when he went out. A long walk for an old woman—but I can assure you that he does really go to the farm. "

Implicitly trusting her husband—and rightly trusting him—Linley's wife replied by a look which Mrs. Presty received in silent indignation. She summoned her dignity and marched out of the room.

Five minutes afterward, Mrs. Linley received an intimation that her mother was seriously offended, in the form of a little note:

"I find that my maternal interest in your welfare, and my devoted efforts to serve you, are only rewarded with furious looks. The less we see of each other the better. Permit me to thank you for your invitation, and to decline accompanying you when you leave Mount Morven tomorrow. " Mrs. Linley answered the note in person. The next day Kitty's grandmother—ripe for more mischief—altered her mind, and thoroughly enjoyed her journey to the seaside.

Chapter XVI.

The Child.

During the first week there was an improvement in the child's health, which justified the doctor's hopeful anticipations. Mrs. Linley wrote cheerfully to her husband; and the better nature of Mrs. Linley's mother seemed, by some inscrutable process, to thrive morally under the encouraging influences of the sea air. It may be a bold thing to say, but it is surely true that our virtues depend greatly on the state of our health.

During the second week, the reports sent to Mount Morven were less encouraging. The improvement in Kitty was maintained; but it made no further progress.

The lapse of the third week brought with it depressing results. There could be no doubt now that the child was losing ground. Bitterly disappointed, Mrs. Linley wrote to her medical adviser, describing the symptoms, and asking for instructions. The doctor wrote back: "Find out where your supply of drinking water comes from. If from a well, let me know how it is situated. Answer by telegraph. " The reply arrived: "A well near the parish church. " The doctor's advice ran back along the wires: "Come home instantly. "

They returned the same day—and they returned too late.

Kitty's first night at home was wakeful and restless; her little hands felt feverish, and she was tormented by perpetual thirst. The good doctor still spoke hopefully; attributing the symptoms to fatigue after the journey. But, as the days followed each other, his medical visits were paid at shorter intervals. The mother noticed that his pleasant face became grave and anxious, and implored him to tell her the truth. The truth was told in two dreadful words: "Typhoid Fever. "

A day or two later, the doctor spoke privately with Mr. Linley. The child's debilitated condition—that lowered state of the vital power which he had observed when Kitty's case was first submitted to him—placed a terrible obstacle in the way of successful resistance to the advance of the disease. "Say nothing to Mrs. Linley just yet. There is no absolute danger so far, unless delirium sets in. " "Do you think it likely? " Linley asked. The doctor shook his head, and said "God knows. "

On the next evening but one, the fatal symptom showed itself. There was nothing violent in the delirium. Unconscious of past events in the family life, the poor child supposed that her governess was living in the house as usual. She piteously wondered why Sydney remained downstairs in the schoolroom. "Oh, don't keep her away from me! I want Syd! I want Syd! " That was her one cry. When exhaustion silenced her, they hoped that the sad delusion was at an end. No! As the slow fire of the fever flamed up again, the same words were on the child's lips, the same fond hope was in her sinking heart.

The doctor led Mrs. Linley out of the room. "Is this the governess? " he asked.

"Yes! "

"Is she within easy reach? "

"She is employed in the family of a friend of ours, living five miles away from us. "

"Send for her instantly! "

Mrs. Linley looked at him with a wildly-mingled expression of hope and fear. She was not thinking of herself—she was not even thinking, for that one moment, of the child. What would her husband say, if she (who had extorted his promise never to see the governess again) brought Sydney Westerfield back to the house?

The doctor spoke to her more strongly still.

"I don't presume to inquire into your private reasons for hesitating to follow my advice, " he said; "but I am bound to tell you the truth. My poor little patient is in serious danger—every hour of delay is an hour gained by death. Bring that lady to the bedside as fast as your carriage can fetch her, and let us see the result. If Kitty recognizes her governess—there, I tell you plainly, is the one chance of saving the child's life. "

The Evil Genius

Mrs. Linley's resolution flashed on him in her weary eyes—the eyes which, by day and night alike, had known so little rest. She rang for her maid. "Tell your master I want to speak to him. "

The woman answered: "My master has gone out. "

The doctor watched the mother's face. No sign of hesitation appeared in it—the one thought in her mind now was the thought of the child. She called the maid back.

"Order the carriage. "

"At what time do you want it, ma'am? "

"At once! "

Chapter XVII.

The Husband.

Mrs. Linley's first impulse in ordering the carriage was to use it herself. One look at the child reminded her that her freedom of action began and ended at the bedside. More than an hour must elapse before Sydney Westerfield could be brought back to Mount Morven; the bare thought of what might happen in that interval, if she was absent, filled the mother with horror. She wrote to Mrs. MacEdwin, and sent her maid with the letter.

Of the result of this proceeding it was not possible to entertain a doubt.

Sydney's love for Kitty would hesitate at no sacrifice; and Mrs. MacEdwin's conduct had already answered for her. She had received the governess with the utmost kindness, and she had generously and delicately refrained from asking any questions. But one person at Mount Morven thought it necessary to investigate the motives under which she had acted. Mrs. Presty's inquiring mind arrived at discoveries; and Mrs. Presty's sense of duty communicated them to her daughter.

"There can be no sort of doubt, Catherine, that our good friend and neighbor has heard, probably from the servants, of what has happened; and (having her husband to consider—men are so weak!) has drawn her own conclusions. If she trusts our fascinating governess, it's because she knows that Miss Westerfield's affections are left behind her in this house. Does my explanation satisfy you? "

Mrs. Linley said: "Never let me hear it again! "

And Mrs. Presty answered: "How very ungrateful! "

The dreary interval of expectation, after the departure of the carriage, was brightened by a domestic event.

Thinking it possible that Mrs. Presty might know why her husband had left the house, Mrs. Linley sent to ask for information. The message in reply informed her that Linley had received a telegram announcing Randal's return from London. He had gone to the railway station to meet his brother.

Before she went downstairs to welcome Randal, Mrs. Linley paused to consider her situation. The one alternative before her was to acknowledge at the first opportunity that she had assumed the serious responsibility of sending for Sydney Westerfield. For the first time in her life, Catherine Linley found herself planning beforehand what she would say to her husband.

A second message interrupted her, announcing that the two brothers had just arrived. She joined them in the drawing-room.

Linley was sitting in a corner by himself. The dreadful discovery that the child's life (by the doctor's confession) was in danger had completely overwhelmed him: he had never even lifted his head when his wife opened the door. Randal and Mrs. Presty were talking together. The old lady's insatiable curiosity was eager for news from London: she wanted to know how Randal had amused himself when he was not attending to business.

He was grieving for Kitty; and he was looking sadly at his brother. "I don't remember, " he answered, absently. Other women might have discovered that they had chosen their time badly. Mrs. Presty, with the best possible intentions, remonstrated.

"Really, Randal, you must rouse yourself. Surely you can tell us something. Did you meet with any agreeable people, while you were away? "

"I met one person who interested me, " he said, with weary resignation.

Mrs. Presty smiled. "A woman, of course! "

"A man, " Randal answered; "a guest like myself at a club dinner. "

"Who is he? "

"Captain Bennydeck. "

"In the army? "

"No: formerly in the navy. "

"And you and he had a long talk together? "

Randal's tones began to betray irritation. "No, " he said "the Captain went away early. "

Mrs. Presty's vigorous intellect discovered an improbability here. "Then how came you to feel interested in him? " she objected.

Even Randal's patience gave way. "I can't account for it, " he said sharply. "I only know I took a liking to Captain Bennydeck. " He left Mrs. Presty and sat down by his brother. "You know I feel for you, " he said, taking Linley's hand. "Try to hope. "

The bitterness of the father's despair broke out in his answer. "I can bear other troubles, Randal, as well as most men. This affliction revolts me. There's something so horribly unnatural in the child being threatened by death, while the parents (who should die first) are alive and well —" He checked himself. "I had better say no more, I shall only shock you. "

The misery in his face wrung the faithful heart of his wife. She forgot the conciliatory expressions which she had prepared herself to use. "Hope, my dear, as Randal tells you, " she said, "because there *is* hope. "

His face flushed, his dim eyes brightened. "Has the doctor said it? " he asked.

"Yes. "

"Why haven't I been told of it before? "

"When I sent for you, I heard that you had gone out. "

The explanation passed by him unnoticed —perhaps even unheard. "Tell me what the doctor said, " he insisted; "I want it exactly, word for word. "

She obeyed him to the letter.

The sinister change in his face, as the narrative proceeded was observed by both the other persons present, as well as by his wife. She waited for a kind word of encouragement. He only said, coldly: "What have you done? "

Speaking coldly on her side, she answered: "I have sent the carriage to fetch Miss Westerfield. "

There was a pause. Mrs. Presty whispered to Randal: "I knew she would come back again! The Evil Genius of the family—that's what I call Miss Westerfield. The name exactly fits her! "

The idea in Randal's mind was that the name exactly fitted Mrs. Presty. He made no reply; his eyes rested in sympathy on his sister-in-law. She saw, and felt, his kindness at a time when kindness was doubly precious. Her ton es trembled a little as she spoke to her silent husband.

"Don't you approve of what I have done, Herbert? "

His nerves were shattered by grief and suspense; but he made an effort this time to speak gently. "How can I say that, " he replied, "if the poor child's life depends on Miss Westerfield? I ask one favor— give me time to leave the house before she comes here. "

Mrs. Linley looked at him in amazement.

Her mother touched her arm; Randal tried by a sign to warn her to be careful. Their calmer minds had seen what the wife's agitation had prevented her from discovering. In Linley's position, the return of the governess was a trial to his self-control which he had every reason to dread: his look, his voice, his manner proclaimed it to persons capable of quietly observing him. He had struggled against his guilty passion—at what sacrifice of his own feelings no one knew but himself—and here was the temptation, at the very time when he was honorably resisting it, brought back to him by his wife! Her motive did unquestionably excuse, perhaps even sanction, what she had done; but this was an estimate of her conduct which commended itself to others. From his point of view—motive or no motive—he saw the old struggle against himself in danger of being renewed; he felt the ground that he had gained slipping from under him already.

In spite of the well-meant efforts made by her relatives to prevent it, Mrs. Linley committed the very error which it was the most important that she should avoid. She justified herself, instead of leaving it to events to justify her. "Miss Westerfield comes here, " she argued, "on an errand that is beyond reproach—an errand of mercy. Why should you leave the house? "

"In justice to you, " Linley answered.

Mrs. Presty could restrain herself no longer. "Drop it, Catherine! " she said in a whisper.

Catherine refused to drop it; Linley's short and sharp reply had irritated her. "After my experience, " she persisted, "have I no reason to trust you? "

"It is part of your experience, " he reminded her, "that I promised not to see Miss Westerfield again. "

"Own it at once! " she broke out, provoked beyond endurance; "though I may be willing to trust you—you are afraid to trust yourself. "

Unlucky Mrs. Presty interfered again. "Don't listen to her, Herbert. Keep out of harm's way, and you keep right. "

She patted him on the shoulder, as if she had been giving good advice to a boy. He expressed his sense of his mother-in-law's friendly offices in language which astonished her.

"Hold your tongue! "

"Do you hear that? " Mrs. Presty asked, appealing indignantly to her daughter.

Linley took his hat. "At what time do you expect Miss Westerfield to arrive? " he said to his wife.

She looked at the clock on the mantelpiece. "Before the half-hour strikes. Don't be alarmed, " she added, with an air of ironical sympathy; "you will have time to make your escape. "

He advanced to the door, and looked at her.

"One thing I beg you will remember, " he said. "Every half-hour while I am away (I am going to the farm) you are to send and let me know how Kitty is—and especially if Miss Westerfield justifies the experiment which the doctor has advised us to try. "

Having given those instructions he went out.

The sofa was near Mrs. Linley. She sank on it, overpowered by the utter destruction of the hopes that she had founded on the separation of Herbert and the governess. Sydney Westerfield was still in possession of her husband's heart!

Her mother was surely the right person to say a word of comfort to her. Randal made the suggestion—with the worst possible result. Mrs. Presty had not forgotten that she had been told—at her age, in her position as the widow of a Cabinet Minister—to hold her tongue. "Your brother has insulted me, " she said to Randal. He was weak enough to attempt to make an explanation. "I was speaking of my brother's wife, " he said. "Your brother's wife has allowed me to be insulted. " Having received that reply, Randal could only wonder. This woman went to church every Sunday, and kept a New Testament, bound in excellent taste, on her toilet-table! The occasion suggested reflection on the system which produces average Christians at the present time. Nothing more was said by Mrs. Presty; Mrs. Linley remained absorbed in her own bitter thoughts. In silence they waited for the return of the carriage, and the appearance of the governess.

Chapter XVIII.

The Nursemaid.

Pale, worn, haggard with anxiety, Sydney Westerfield entered the room, and looked once more on the faces which she had resigned herself never to see again. She appeared to be hardly conscious of the kind reception which did its best to set her at her ease.

"Am I in time? " were the first words that escaped her on entering the room. Reassured by the answer, she turned back to the door, eager to hurry upstairs to Kitty's bedside.

Mrs. Linley's gentle hand detained her.

The doctor had left certain instructions, warning the mother to guard against any accident that might remind Kitty of the day on which Sydney had left her. At the time of that bitter parting, the child had seen her governess in the same walking-dress which she wore now. Mrs. Linley removed the hat and cloak, and laid them on a chair.

"There is one other precaution which we must observe, " she said; "I must ask you to wait in my room until I find that you may show yourself safely. Now come with me. "

Mrs. Presty followed them, and begged earnestly for leave to wait the result of the momentous experiment, at the door of Kitty's bedroom. Her self-asserting manner had vanished; she was quiet, she was even humble. While the last chance for the child's life was fast becoming a matter of minutes only, the grandmother's better nature showed itself on the surface. Randal opened the door for them as the three went out together. He was in that state of maddening anxiety about his poor little niece in which men of his imaginative temperament become morbid, and say strangely inappropriate things. In the same breath with which he implored his sister-in-law to let him hear what had happened, without an instant of delay, he startled Mrs. Presty by one of his familiar remarks on the inconsistencies in her character. "You disagreeable old woman, " he whispered, as she passed him, "you have got a heart, after all. "

Left alone, he was never for one moment in repose, while the slow minutes followed each other in the silent house.

He walked about the room, he listened at the door, he arranged and disarranged the furniture. When the nursemaid descended from the upper regions with her mistress's message for him, he ran out to meet her; saw the good news in her smiling face; and, for the first and last time in his life kissed one of his brother's female servants. Susan—a well-bred young person, thoroughly capable in ordinary cases of saying "For shame, sir! " and looking as if she expected to feel an arm round her waist next—trembled with terror under that astounding salute. Her master's brother, a pattern of propriety up to that time, a man declared by her to be incapable of kissing a woman unless she had a right to insist on it in the licensed character of his wife, had evidently taken leave of his senses. Would he bite her next? No: he only looked confused, and said (how very extraordinary!) that he would never do it again. Susan gave her message gravely. Here was an unintelligible man; she felt the necessity of being careful in her choice of words.

"Miss Kitty stared at Miss Westerfield—only for a moment, sir—as if she didn't quite understand, and then knew her again directly. The doctor had just called. He drew up the blind to let the light in, and he looked, and he says: 'Only be careful'—" Tender-hearted Susan broke down, and began to cry. "I can't help it, sir; we are all so fond of Miss Kitty, and we are so happy. 'Only be careful' (those were the exact words, if you please), 'and I answer for her life. '—Oh, dear! what have I said to make him run away from me? "

Randal had left her abruptly, and had shut himself into the drawing-room. Susan's experience of men had not yet informed her that a true Englishman is ashamed to be seen (especially by his inferiors) with the tears in his eyes.

He had barely succeeded in composing himself, when another servant appeared—this time a man—with something to say to him.

"I don't know whether I have done right, sir, " Malcolm began. "There's a stranger downstairs among the tourists who are looking at the rooms and the pictures. He said he knew you. And he asked if you were not related to the gentleman who allowed travelers to see his interesting old house. "

"Well? "

"Well, sir, I said Yes. And then he wanted to know if you happened to be here at the present time. "

Randal cut the man's story short. "And you said Yes again, and he gave you his card. Let me look at it. "

Malcolm produced the card, and instantly received instructions to show the gentleman up. The name recalled the dinner at the London club—Captain Bennydeck.

Chapter XIX.

The Captain.

The fair complexion of the Captain's youthful days had been darkened by exposure to hard weather and extreme climates. His smooth face of twenty years since was scored by the telltale marks of care; his dark beard was beginning to present variety of color by means of streaks of gray; and his hair was in course of undisguised retreat from his strong broad forehead. Not rising above the middle height, the Captain's spare figure was well preserved. It revealed power and activity, severely tested perhaps at some former time, but capable even yet of endurance under trial. Although he looked older than his age, he was still, personally speaking, an attractive man. In repose, his eyes were by habit sad and a little weary in their expression. They only caught a brighter light when he smiled. At such times, helped by this change and by his simple, earnest manner, they recommended him to his fellow-creatures before he opened his lips. Men and women taking shelter with him, for instance, from the rain, found the temptation to talk with Captain Bennydeck irresistible; and, when the weather cleared, they mostly carried away with them the same favorable impression: "One would like to meet with that gentleman again. "

Randal's first words of welcome relieved the Captain of certain modest doubts of his reception, which appeared to trouble him when he entered the room. "I am glad to find you remember me as kindly as I remember you. " Those were his first words when he and Randal shook hands.

"You might have felt sure of that, " Randal said.

The Captain's modesty still doubted.

"You see, the circumstances were a little against me. We met at a dull dinner, among wearisome worldly men, full of boastful talk about themselves. It was all 'I did this, ' and 'I said that'—and the gentlemen who were present had always been right; and the gentlemen who were absent had always been wrong. And, oh, dear. when they came to politics, how they bragged about what they would have done if they had only been at the head of the Government; and how cruelly hard to please they were in the matter of wine! Do you remember recommending me to spend my next holiday in Scotland? "

"Perfectly. My advice was selfish—it really meant that I wanted to see you again. "

"And you have your wish, at your brother's house! The guide book did it. First, I saw your family name. Then, I read on and discovered that there were pictures at Mount Morven and that strangers were allowed to see them. I like pictures. And here I am. "

This allusion to the house naturally reminded Randal of the master. "I wish I could introduce you to my brother and his wife, " he said. "Unhappily their only child is ill—"

Captain Bennydeck started to his feet. "I am ashamed of having intruded on you, " he began. His new friend pressed him back into his chair without ceremony. "On the contrary, you have arrived at the best of all possible times—the time when our suspense is at an end. The doctor has just told us that his poor little patient is out of danger. You may imagine how happy we are. "

"And how grateful to God! " The Captain said those words in tones that trembled—speaking to himself.

Randal was conscious of feeling a momentary embarrassment. The character of his visitor had presented itself in a new light. Captain Bennydeck looked at him—understood him—and returned to the subject of his travels.

"Do you remember your holiday-time when you were a boy, and when you had to go back to school? " he asked with a smile. "My mind is in much the same state at leaving Scotland, and going back to my work in London. I hardly know which I admire most—your beautiful country or the people who inhabit it. I have had some pleasant talk with your poorer neighbors; the one improvement I could wish for among them is a keener sense of their religious duties. "

This was an objection new in Randal's experience of travelers in general.

"Our Highlanders have noble qualities, " he said. "If you knew them as well as I do, you would find a true sense of religion among them; not presenting itself, however, to strangers as strongly—I had almost said as aggressively—as the devotional feeling of the Lowland Scotch. Different races, different temperaments. "

"And all, " the Captain added, gravely and gently, "with souls to be saved. If I sent to these poor people some copies of the New Testament, translated into their own language, would my gift be accepted? "

Strongly interested by this time, in studying Captain Bennydeck's character on the side of it which was new to him, Randal owned that he observed with surprise the interest which his friend felt in perfect strangers. The Captain seemed to wonder why this impression should have been produced by what he had just said.

"I only try, " he answered, "to do what good I can, wherever I go. "

"Your life must be a happy one, " Randal said.

Captain Bennydeck's head drooped. The shadows that attend on the gloom of melancholy remembrance showed their darkening presence on his face. Briefly, almost sternly, he set Randal right.

"No, sir. "

"Forgive me, " the younger man pleaded, "if I have spoken thoughtlessly. "

"You have mistaken me, " the Captain explained; "and it is my fault. My life is an atonement for the sins of my youth. I have reached my fortieth year—and that one purpose is before me for the rest of my days. Sufferings and dangers which but few men undergo awakened my conscience. My last exercise of the duties of my profession associated me with an expedition to the Polar Seas. Our ship was crushed in the ice. Our march to the nearest regions inhabited by humanity was a hopeless struggle of starving men, rotten with scurvy, against the merciless forces of Nature. One by one my comrades dropped and died. Out of twenty men there were three left with a last flicker in them of the vital flame when the party of rescue found us. One of the three died on the homeward journey. One lived to reach his native place, and to sink to rest with his wife and children round his bed. The last man left, out of that band of martyrs to a hopeless cause, lives to be worthier of God's mercy—and tries to make God's creatures better and happier in this world, and worthier of the world that is to come. "

Randal's generous nature felt the appeal that had been made to it. "Will you let me take your hand, Captain? " he said.

They clasped hands in silence.

Captain Bennydeck was the first to speak again. That modest distrust of himself, which a man essentially noble and brave is generally the readiest of men to feel, seemed to be troubling him once more—just as it had troubled him when he first found himself in Randal's presence.

"I hope you won't think me vain, " he resumed; "I seldom say so much about myself as I have said to you. "

"I only wish you would say more, " Randal rejoined. "Can't you put off your return to London for a day or two? "

The thing was not to be done. Duties which it was impossible to trifle with called the Captain back. "It's quite likely, " he said, alluding pleasantly to the impression which he had produced in speaking of the Highlanders, "that I shall find more strangers to interest me in the great city. "

"Are they always strangers? " Randal asked. "Have you never met by accident with persons whom you may once have known? "

"Never—yet. But it may happen on my return. "

"In what way? "

"In this way. I have been in search of a poor girl who has lost both her parents: she has, I fear, been left helpless at the mercy of the world. Her father was an old friend of mine—once an officer in the Navy like myself. The agent whom I formerly employed (without success) to trace her, writes me word that he has reason to believe she has obtained a situation as pupil-teacher at a school in the suburbs of London; and I am going back (among other things) to try if I can follow the clew myself. Good-by, my friend. I am heartily sorry to go! "

"Life is made up of partings, " Randal answered.

"And of meetings, " the Captain wisely reminded him. "When you are in London, you will always hear of me at the club. "

Heartily reciprocating his good wishes, Randal attended Captain Bennydeck to the door. On the way back to the drawing-room, he found his mind dwelling, rather to his surprise, on the Captain's contemplated search for the lost girl.

Was the good man likely to find her? It seemed useless enough to inquire—and yet Randal asked himself the question. Her father had been described as an officer in the Navy. Well, and what did that matter? Inclined to laugh at his own idle curiosity, he was suddenly struck by a new idea. What had his brother told him of Miss Westerfield? *She* was the daughter of an officer in the Navy; *she* had been pupil-teacher at a school. Was it really possible that Sydney Westerfield could be the person whom Captain Bennydeck was attempting to trace? Randal threw up the window which overlooked the drive in front of the house. Too late! The carriage which had brought the Captain to Mount Morven was no longer in sight.

The one other course that he could take was to mention Captain Bennydeck's name to Sydney, and be guided by the result.

As he approached the bell, determining to send a message upstairs, he heard the door opened behind him. Mrs. Presty had entered the drawing-room, with a purpose (as it seemed) in which Randal was concerned.

Chapter XX.

The Mother-in-Law.

Strong as the impression was which Captain Bennydeck had produced on Randal, Mrs. Presty's first words dismissed it from his mind. She asked him if he had any message for his brother.

Randal instantly looked at the clock. "Has Catherine not sent to the farm, yet? " he asked in astonishment.

Mrs. Presty's mind seemed to be absorbed in her daughter. "Ah, poor Catherine! Worn out with anxiety and watching at Kitty's bedside. Night after night without any sleep; night after night tortured by suspense. As usual, she can depend on her old mother for sympathy. I have taken all her household duties on myself, till she is in better health. "

Randal tried again. "Mrs. Presty, am I to understand (after the plain direction Herbert gave) that no messenger has been sent to the farm? "

Mrs. Presty held her venerable head higher than ever, when Randal pronounced his brother's name. "I see no necessity for being in a hurry, " she answered stiffly, "after the brutal manner in which Herbert has behaved to me. Put yourself in my place—and imagine what you would feel if you were told to hold your tongue. "

Randal wasted no more time on ears that were deaf to remonstrance. Feeling the serious necessity of interfering to some good purpose, he asked where he might find his sister-in-law.

"I have taken Catherine into the garden, " Mrs. Presty announced. "The doctor himself suggested—no, I may say, ordered it. He is afraid that *she* may fall ill next, poor soul, if she doesn't get air and exercise. "

In Mrs. Linley's own interests, Randal resolved on advising her to write to her husband by the messenger; explaining that she was not to blame for the inexcusable delay which had already taken place. Without a word more to Mrs. Presty, he hastened out of the room. That inveterately distrustful woman called him back. She desired to know where he was going, and why he was in a hurry.

"I am going to the garden, " Randal answered.

"To speak to Catherine? "

"Yes. "

"Needless trouble, my dear Randal. She will be back in a quarter of an hour, and she will pass through this room on her way upstairs. "

Another quarter of an hour was a matter of no importance to Mrs. Presty! Randal took his own way—the way into the garden.

His silence and his determination to join his sister-in-law roused Mrs. Presty's ready suspicions; she concluded that he was bent on making mischief between her daughter and herself. The one thing to do in this case was to follow him instantly. The active old lady trotted out of the room, strongly inclined to think that the Evil Genius of the family might be Randal Linley after all!

They had both taken the shortest way to the garden; that is to say, the way through the library, which communicated at its furthest end with the corridor and the vaulted flight of stairs leading directly out of the house. Of the two doors in the drawing-room, one, on the left, led to the grand staircase and the hall; the other, on the right, opened on the backstairs, and on a side entrance to the house, used by the family when they were pressed for time, as well as by the servants.

The drawing-room had not been empty more than a few minutes when the door on the right was suddenly opened. Herbert Linley, entered with hurried, uncertain steps. He took the chair that was nearest to him, and dropped into it like a man overpowered by agitation or fatigue.

He had ridden from the farm at headlong speed, terrified by the unexplained delay in the arrival of the messenger from home. Unable any longer to suffer the torment of unrelieved suspense, he . had returned to make inquiry at the house. As he interpreted the otherwise inexplicable neglect of his instructions, the last chance of saving the child's life had failed, and his wife had been afraid to tell him the dreadful truth.

After an interval, he rose and went into the library.

It was empty, like the drawing-room. The bell was close by him. He lifted his hand to ring it—and drew back. As brave a man as ever lived, he knew what fear was now. The father's courage failed him before the prospect of summoning a servant, and hearing, for all he knew to the contrary, that his child was dead.

How long he stood there, alone and irresolute, he never remembered when he thought of it in after-days. All he knew was that there came a time when a sound in the drawing-room attracted his attention. It was nothing more important than the opening of a door.

The sound came from that side of the room which was nearest to the grand staircase—and therefore nearest also to the hall in one direction, and to the bed-chambers in the other.

Some person had entered the room. Whether it was one of the family or one of the servants, he would hear in either case what had happened in his absence. He parted the curtains over the library entrance, and looked through.

The person was a woman. She stood with her back turned toward the library, lifting a cloak off a chair. As she shook the cloak out before putting it on, she changed her position. He saw the face, never to be forgotten by him to the last day of his life. He saw Sydney Westerfield.

Chapter XXI.

The Governess.

Linley had one instant left, in which he might have drawn, back into the library in time to escape Sydney's notice. He was incapable of the effort of will. Grief and suspense had deprived him of that elastic readiness of mind which springs at once from thought to action. For a moment he hesitated. In that moment she looked up and saw him.

With a faint cry of alarm she let the cloak drop from her hands. As helpless as he was, as silent as he was, she stood rooted to the spot.

He tried to control himself. Hardly knowing what he said, he made commonplace excuses, as if he had been a stranger: "I am sorry to have startled you; I had no idea of finding you in this room. "

Sydney pointed to her cloak on the floor, and to her hat on a chair near it. Understanding the necessity which had brought her into the room, he did his best to reconcile her to the meeting that had followed.

"It's a relief to me to have seen you, " he said, "before you leave us. "

A relief to him to see her! Why? How? What did that strange word mean, addressed to *her?* She roused herself, and put the question to him.

"It's surely better for me, " he answered, "to hear the miserable news from you than from a servant. "

"What miserable news? " she asked, still as perplexed as ever.

He could preserve his self-control no longer; the misery in him forced its way outward at last. The convulsive struggles for breath which burst from a man in tears shook him from head to foot.

"My poor little darling! " he gasped. "My only child! "

All that was embarrassing in her position passed from Sydney's mind in an instant. She stepped close up to him; she laid her hand gently and fearlessly on his arm. "Oh, Mr. Linley, what dreadful mistake is this? "

His dim eyes rested on her with a piteous expression of doubt. He heard her—and he was afraid to believe her. She was too deeply distressed, too full of the truest pity for him, to wait and think before she spoke. "Yes! yes! " she cried, under the impulse of the moment. "The dear child knew me again, the moment I spoke to her. Kitty's recovery is only a matter of time. "

He staggered back—with a livid change in his face startling to see. The mischief done by Mrs. Presty's sense of injury had led already to serious results. If the thought in Linley, at that moment, had shaped itself into words, he would have said, "And Catherine never told me of it! " How bitterly he thought of the woman who had left him in suspense—how gratefully he felt toward the woman who had lightened his heart of the heaviest burden ever laid on it!

Innocent of all suspicion of the feeling that she had aroused, Sydney blamed her own want of discretion as the one cause of the change that she perceived in him. "How thoughtless, how cruel of me, " she said, "not to have been more careful in telling you the good news! Pray forgive me. "

"You thoughtless! you cruel! " At the bare idea of her speaking in that way of herself, his sense of what he owed to her defied all restraint. He seized her hands and covered them with grateful kisses. "Dear Sydney! dear, good Sydney! "

She drew back from him; not abruptly, not as if she felt offended. Her fine perception penetrated the meaning of those harmless kisses—the uncontrollable outburst of a sense of relief beyond the reach of expression in words. But she changed the subject. Mrs. Linley (she told him) had kindly ordered fresh horses to be put to the carriage, so that she might go back to her duties if the doctor sanctioned it.

She turned away to take up her cloak. Linley stopped her. "You can't leave Kitty, " he said, positively.

A faint smile brightened her face for a moment. "Kitty has fallen asleep—such a sweet, peaceful sleep! I don't think I should have left her but for that. The maid is watching at the bedside, and Mrs. Linley is only away for a little while. "

"Wait a few minutes, " he pleaded; "it's so long since we have seen each other. "

The tone in which he spoke warned her to persist in leaving him while her resolution remained firm. "I had arranged with Mrs. MacEdwin, " she began, "if all went well—"

"Speak of yourself, " he interposed. "Tell me if you are happy. "

She let this pass without a reply. "The doctor sees no harm, " she went on, "in my being away for a few hours. Mrs. MacEdwin has offered to send me here in the evening, so that I can sleep in Kitty's room. "

"You don't look well, Sydney. You are pale and worn—you are not happy. "

She began to tremble. For the second time, she turned away to take up her cloak. For the second time, he stopped her.

"Not just yet, " he said. "You don't know how it distresses me to see you so sadly changed. I remember the time when you were the happiest creature living. Do you remember it, too? "

"Don't ask me! " was all she could say.

He sighed as he looked at her. "It's dreadful to think of your young life, that ought to be so bright, wasting and withering among strangers. " He said those words with increasing agitation; his eyes rested on her eagerly with a wild look in them. She made a resolute effort to speak to him coldly—she called him "Mr. Linley"—she bade him good-by.

It was useless. He stood between her and the door; he disregarded what she had said as if he had not heard it. "Hardly a day passes, " he owned to her, "that I don't think of you. "

"You shouldn't tell me that! "

"How can I see you again—and not tell you? "

She burst out with a last entreaty. "For God's sake, let us say good-by! "

His manner became undisguisedly tender; his language changed in the one way of all others that was most perilous to her—he appealed to her pity: "Oh, Sydney, it's so hard to part with you! "

"Spare me! " she cried, passionately. "You don't know how I suffer. "

"My sweet angel, I do know it—by what I suffer myself! Do you ever feel for me as I feel for you? "

"Oh, Herbert! Herbert! "

"Have you ever thought of me since we parted? "

She had striven against herself, and against him, till her last effort at resistance was exhausted. In reckless despair she let the truth escape her at last.

"When do I ever think of anything else! I am a wretch unworthy of all the kindness that has been shown to me. I don't deserve your interest; I don't even deserve your pity. Send me away—be hard on me—be brutal to me. Have some mercy on a miserable creature whose life is one long hopeless effort to forget you! " Her voice, her look, maddened him. He drew her to his bosom; he held her in his arms; she struggled vainly to get away from him. "Oh, " she murmured, "how cruel you are! Remember, my dear one, remember how young I am, how weak I am. Oh, Herbert, I'm dying—dying—dying! " Her voice grew fainter and fainter; her head sank on his breast. He lifted her face to him with whispered words of love. He kissed her again and again.

The curtains over the library entrance moved noiselessly when they were parted. The footsteps of Catherine Linley were inaudible as she passed through, and entered the room.

She stood still for a moment in silent horror.

Not a sound warned them when she advanced. After hesitating for a moment, she raised her hand toward her husband, as if to tell him of her presence by a touch; drew it back, suddenly recoiling from her own first intention; and touched Sydney instead.

Then, and then only, they knew what had happened.

Face to face, those three persons—with every tie that had once united them snapped asunder in an instant—looked at each other. The man owed a duty to the lost creature whose weakness had appealed to his mercy in vain. The man broke the silence.

"Catherine—"

With immeasurable contempt looking brightly out of her steady eyes, his wife stopped him.

"Not a word! "

He refused to be silent. "It is I, " he said; "I only who am to blame. "

"Spare yourself the trouble of making excuses, " she answered; "they are needless. Herbert Linley, the woman who was once your wife despises you. "

Her eyes turned from him and rested on Sydney Westerfield.

"I have a last word to say to *you*. Look at me, if you can. "

Sydney lifted her head. She looked vacantly at the outraged woman before her, as if she saw a woman in a dream.

With the same terrible self-possession which she had preserved from the first—standing between her husband and her governess—Mrs. Linley spoke.

"Miss Westerfield, you have saved my child's life. " She paused—her eyes still resting on the girl's face. Deadly pale, she pointed to her husband, and said to Sydney: "Take him! "

She passed out of the room—and left them together.

THIRD BOOK.

Chapter XXII.

Retrospect.

The autumn holiday-time had come to an end; and the tourists had left Scotland to the Scots.

In the dull season, a solitary traveler from the North arrived at the nearest post-town to Mount Morven. A sketchbook and a color-box formed part of his luggage, and declared him to be an artist. Falling into talk over his dinner with the waiter at the hotel, he made inquiries about a picturesque house in the neighborhood, which showed that Mount Morven was well known to him by reputation. When he proposed paying a visit to the old border fortress the next day, the waiter said: "You can't see the house. " When the traveler asked Why, this man of few words merely added: "Shut up. "

The landlord made his appearance with a bottle of wine and proved to be a more communicative person in his relations with strangers. Presented in an abridged form, and in the English language, these (as he related them) were the circumstances under which Mount Morven had been closed to the public.

A complete dispersion of the family had taken place not long since. For miles round everybody was sorry for it. Rich and poor alike felt the same sympathy with the good lady of the house. She had been most shamefully treated by her husband, and by a good-for-nothing girl employed as governess. To put it plainly, the two had run away together; one report said they had gone abroad, and another declared that they were living in London. Mr. Linley's conduct was perfectly incomprehensible. He had always borne the highest character—a good landlord, a kind father, a devoted husband. And yet, after more than eight years of exemplary married life, he had disgraced himself. The minister of the parish, preaching on the subject, had attributed this extraordinary outbreak of vice on the part of an otherwise virtuous man, to a possession of the devil. Assuming "the devil, " in this case, to be only a discreet and clerical way of alluding from the pulpit to a woman, the landlord was inclined to agree with the minister. After what had happened, it was, of course, impossible that Mrs. Linley could remain in her husband's house.

She and her little girl, and her mother, were supposed to be living in retirement. They kept the place of their retreat a secret from everybody but Mrs. Linley's legal adviser, who was instructed to forward letters. But one other member of the family remained to be accounted for. This was Mr. Linley's younger brother, known at present to be traveling on the Continent. Two trustworthy old servants had been left in charge at Mount Morven—and there was the whole story; and that was why the house was shut up.

Chapter XXIII.

Separation.

In a cottage on the banks of one of the Cumberland Lakes, two ladies were seated at the breakfast-table. The windows of the room opened on a garden which extended to the water's edge, and on a boat-house and wooden pier beyond. On the pier a little girl was fishing, under the care of her maid. After a prevalence of rainy weather, the sun was warm this morning for the time of year; and the broad sheet of water alternately darkened and brightened as the moving masses of cloud now gathered and now parted over the blue beauty of the sky.

The ladies had finished their breakfast; the elder of the two—that is to say, Mrs. Presty—took up her knitting and eyed her silent daughter with an expression of impatient surprise.

"Another bad night, Catherine? "

The personal attractions that distinguished Mrs. Linley were not derived from the short-lived beauty which depends on youth and health. Pale as she was, her face preserved its fine outline; her features had not lost their grace and symmetry of form. Presenting the appearance of a woman who had suffered acutely, she would have been more than ever (in the eyes of some men) a woman to be admired and loved.

"I seldom sleep well now, " she answered, patiently.

"You don't give yourself a chance, " Mrs. Presty remonstrated. "Here's a fine morning—come out for a sail on the lake. To-morrow there's a concert in the town—let's take tickets. There's a want of what I call elastic power in your mind, Catherine—the very quality for which your father was so remarkable; the very quality which Mr. Presty used to say made him envy Mr. Norman. Look at your dress! Where's the common-sense, at your age, of wearing nothing but black? Nobody's dead who belongs to us, and yet you do your best to look as if you were in mourning. "

"I have no heart, mamma, to wear colors. "

Mrs. Presty considered this reply to be unworthy of notice. She went on with her knitting, and only laid it down when the servant brought in the letters which had arrived by the morning's post. They were but two in number—and both were for Mrs. Linley. In the absence of any correspondence of her own, Mrs. Presty took possession of her daughter's letters.

"One addressed in the lawyer's handwriting, " she announced; "and one from Randal. Which shall I open for you first? "

"Randal's letter, if you please. "

Mrs. Presty handed it across the table. "Any news is a relief from the dullness of this place, " she said. "If there are no secrets, Catherine, read it out. "

There were no secrets on the first page.

Randal announced his arrival in London from the Continent, and his intention of staying there for a while. He had met with a friend (formerly an officer holding high rank in the Navy) whom he was glad to see again—a rich man who used his wealth admirably in the interest of his poor and helpless fellow-creatures. A "Home, " established on a new plan, was just now engaging all his attention: he was devoting himself so unremittingly to the founding of this institution that his doctor predicted injury to his health at no distant date. If it was possible to persuade him to take a holiday, Randal might return to the Continent as the traveling-companion of his friend.

"This must be the man whom he first met at the club, " Mrs. Presty remarked. "Well, Catherine, I suppose there is some more of it. What's the matter? Bad news? "

"Something that I wish Randal had not written. Read it yourself—and don't talk of it afterward. "

Mrs. Presty read:

"I know nothing whatever of my unfortunate brother. If you think this is a too-indulgent way of alluding to a man who has so shamefully wronged you, let my conviction that he is already beginning to suffer the penalty of his crime plead my excuse.

Herbert's nature is, in some respects, better known to me than it is to you. I am persuaded that your hold on his respect and his devotion is shaken—not lost. He has been misled by one of those passing fancies, disastrous and even criminal in their results, to which men are liable when they are led by no better influence than the influence of their senses. It is not, and never will be, in the nature of women to understand this. I fear I may offend you in what I am now writing; but I must speak what I believe to be the truth, at any sacrifice. Bitter repentance (if he is not already feeling it) is in store for Herbert, when he finds himself tied to a person who cannot bear comparison with you. I say this, pitying the poor girl most sincerely, when I think of her youth and her wretched past life. How it will end I cannot presume to say. I can only acknowledge that I do not look to the future with the absolute despair which you naturally felt when I last saw you. "

Mrs. Presty laid the letter down, privately resolving to write to Randal, and tell him to keep his convictions for the future to himself. A glance at her daughter's face warned her, if she said anything, to choose a new subject.

The second letter still remained unnoticed. "Shall we see what the lawyer says? " she suggested—and opened the envelope. The lawyer had nothing to say. He simply inclosed a letter received at his office.

Mrs. Presty had long passed the age at which emotion expresses itself outwardly by a change of color. She turned pale, nevertheless, when she looked at the second letter.

The address was in Herbert Linley's handwriting.

Chapter XXIV.

Hostility.

When she was not eating her meals or asleep in her bed, absolute silence on Mrs. Presty's part was a circumstance without precedent in the experience of her daughter. Mrs. Presty was absolutely silent now. Mrs. Linley looked up.

She at once perceived the change in her mother's face and asked what it meant. "Mamma, you look as if something had frightened you. Is it anything in that letter? " She bent over the table, and looked a little closer at the letter. Mrs. Presty had turned it so that the address was underneath; and the closed envelope was visible still intact. "Why don't you open it? " Mrs. Linley asked.

Mrs. Presty made a strange reply. "I am thinking of throwing it into the fire. "

"My letter? "

"Yes; your letter. "

"Let me look at it first. "

"You had better not look at it, Catherine. "

Naturally enough, Mrs. Linley remonstrated. "Surely I ought to read a letter forwarded by my lawyer. Why are you hiding the address from me? Is it from some person whose handwriting we both know? " She looked again at her silent mother—reflected—and guessed the truth. "Give it to me directly, " she said; "my husband has written to me. "

Mrs. Presty's heavy eyebrows gathered into a frown. "Is it possible, " she asked sternly, "that you are still fond enough of that man to care about what he writes to you? " Mrs. Linley held out her hand for the letter. Her wise mother found it desirable to try persuasion next. "If you really won't give way, my dear, humor me for once. Will you let me read it to you? "

"Yes—if you promise to read every word of it. "

Mrs. Presty promised (with a mental reservation), and opened the letter.

At the two first words, she stopped and began to clean her spectacles. Had her own eyes deceived her? Or had Herbert Linley actually addressed her daughter—after having been guilty of the cruelest wrong that a husband can inflict on a wife—as "Dear Catherine"? Yes: there were the words, when she put her spectacles on again. Was he in his right senses? or had he written in a state of intoxication?

Mrs. Linley waited, with a preoccupied mind: she showed no signs of impatience or surprise. As it presently appeared, she was not thinking of the letter addressed to her by Herbert, but of the letter written by Randal. "I want to look at it again. " With that brief explanation she turned at once to the closing lines which had offended her when she first read them.

Mrs. Presty hazarded a guess at what was going on in her daughter's mind. "Now your husband has written to you, " she said, "are you beginning to think Randal's opinion may be worth considering again? " With her eyes still on Randal's letter, Mrs. Linley merely answered: "Why don't you begin? " Mrs. Presty began as follows, leaving out the familiarity of her son-in-law's address to his wife.

"I hope and trust you will forgive me for venturing to write to you, in consideration of the subject of my letter. I have something to say concerning our child. Although I have deserved the worst you can think of me, I believe you will not deny that even your love for our little Kitty (while we were living together) was not a truer love than mine. Bad as I am, my heart has that tender place left in it still. I cannot endure separation from my child. "

Mrs. Linley rose to her feet. The first vague anticipations of future atonement and reconciliation, suggested by her brother-in-law, no longer existed in her mind: she foresaw but too plainly what was to come. "Read faster, " she said, "or let me read it for myself. "

Mrs. Presty went on: "There is no wish, on my part, to pain you by any needless allusion to my claims as a father. My one desire is to enter into an arrangement which shall be as just toward you, as it is toward me. I propose that Kitty shall live with her father one half of the year, and shall return to her mother's care for the other half If there is any valid objection to this, I confess I fail to see it. "

Mrs. Linley could remain silent no longer.

"Does he see no difference, " she broke out, "between his position and mine? What consolation—in God's name, what consolation is left to me for the rest of my life but my child? And he threatens to separate us for six months in every year! And he takes credit to himself for an act of exalted justice on his part! Is there no such thing as shame in the hearts of men? "

Under ordinary circumstances, her mother would have tried to calm her. But Mrs. Presty had turned to the next page of the letter, at the moment when her daughter spoke.

What she found written, on that other side, produced a startling effect on her. She crumpled the letter up in her hand, and threw it into the fireplace. It fell under the grate instead of into the grate. With amazing activity for a woman of her age, she ran across the room to burn it. Younger and quicker, Mrs. Linley got to the fireplace first, and seized the letter. "There is something more! " she exclaimed. "And you are afraid of my knowing what it is. "

"Don't read it! " Mrs. Presty called out.

There was but one sentence left to read: "If your maternal anxiety suggests any misgiving, let me add that a woman's loving care will watch over our little girl while she is under my roof. You will remember how fond Miss Westerfield was of Kitty, and you will believe me when I tell you that she is as truly devoted to the child as ever. "

"I tried to prevent you from reading it, " said Mrs. Presty.

Mrs. Linley looked at her mother with a strange unnatural smile.

"I wouldn't have missed this for anything! " she said. "The cruelest of all separations is proposed to me—and I am expected to submit to it, because my husband's mistress is fond of my child! " She threw the letter from her with a frantic gesture of contempt and burst into a fit of hysterical laughter.

The old mother's instinct—not the old mother's reason—told her what to do. She drew her daughter to the open window, and called to Kitty to come in. The child (still amusing herself by fishing in the lake) laid down her rod. Mrs. Linley saw her running lightly along the little pier, on her way to the house. *That* influence effected what no other influence could have achieved. The outraged wife controlled herself, for the sake of her child. Mrs. Presty led her out to meet Kitty in the garden; waited until she saw them together; and returned to the breakfast-room.

Herbert Linley's letter lay on the floor; his discreet mother-in-law picked it up. It could do no more harm now, and there might be reasons for keeping the husband's proposal. "Unless I am very much mistaken, " Mrs. Presty concluded, "we shall hear more from the lawyer before long. " She locked up the letter, and wondered what her daughter would do next.

In half an hour Mrs. Linley returned—pale, silent, self-contained.

She seated herself at her desk; wrote literally one line; signed it without an instant's hesitation, and folded the paper. Before it was secured in the envelope, Mrs. Presty interfered with a characteristic request. "You are writing to Mr. Linley, of course, " she said. "May I see it? "

Mrs. Linley handed the letter to her. The one line of writing contained these words: "I refuse positively to part with my child. — Catherine Linley. "

"Have you considered what is likely to happen, when he gets this? " Mrs. Presty inquired.

"No, mamma. "

"Will you consult Randal? "

"I would rather not consult him. "

"Will you let me consult him for you? "

"Thank you—no. "

"Why not? "

"After what Randal has written to me, I don't attach any value to his opinion. " With that reply she sent her letter to the post, and went back again to Kitty.

After this, Mrs. Presty resolved to wait the arrival of Herbert Linley's answer, and to let events take their course. The view from the window (as she passed it, walking up and down the room) offered her little help in forecasting the future. Kitty had returned to her fishing; and Kitty's mother was walking slowly up and down the pier, deep in thought. Was she thinking of what might happen, and summoning the resolution which so seldom showed itself on ordinary occasions?

Chapter XXV.

Consultation.

No second letter arrived. But a telegram was received from the lawyer toward the end of the week.

"Expect me to-morrow on business which requires personal consultation. "

That was the message. In taking the long journey to Cumberland, Mrs. Linley's legal adviser sacrificed two days of his precious time in London. Something serious must assuredly have happened.

In the meantime, who was the lawyer?

He was Mr. Sarrazin, of Lincoln's Inn Fields.

Was he an Englishman or a Frenchman?

He was a curious mixture of both. His ancestors had been among the persecuted French people who found a refuge in England, when the priest-ridden tyrant, Louis the Fourteenth, revoked the Edict of Nantes. A British subject by birth, and a thoroughly competent and trustworthy man, Mr. Sarrazin labored under one inveterate delusion; he firmly believed that his original French nature had been completely eradicated, under the influence of our insular climate and our insular customs. No matter how often the strain of the lively French blood might assert itself, at inconvenient times and under regrettable circumstances, he never recognized this foreign side of his character. His excellent spirits, his quick sympathies, his bright mutability of mind—all those qualities, in short, which were most mischievously ready to raise distrust in the mind of English clients, before their sentiment changed for the better under the light of later experience—were attributed by Mr. Sarrazin to the exhilarating influence of his happy domestic circumstances and his successful professional career. His essentially English wife; his essentially English children; his whiskers, his politics, his umbrella, his pew at church, his plum pudding, his *Times* newspaper, all answered for him (he was accustomed to say) as an inbred member of the glorious nation that rejoices in hunting the fox, and believes in innumerable pills.

This excellent man arrived at the cottage, desperately fatigued after his long journey, but in perfect possession of his incomparable temper, nevertheless.

He afforded a proof of this happy state of mind, on sitting down to his supper. An epicure, if ever there was one yet, he found the solid part of the refreshments offered to him to consist of a chop. The old French blood curdled at the sight of it—but the true-born Englishman heroically devoted himself to the national meal. At the same time the French vivacity discovered a kindred soul in Kitty; Mr. Sarrazin became her intimate friend in five minutes. He listened to her and talked to her, as if the child had been his client, and fishing from the pier the business which had brought him from London. To Mrs. Presty's disgust, he turned up a corner of the table-cloth, when he had finished his chop, and began to conjure so deftly with the spoons and forks that poor little Kitty (often dull, now, under the changed domestic circumstances of her life) clapped her hands with pleasure, and became the joyous child of the happy old times once more. Mrs. Linley, flattered in her maternal love and her maternal pride, never thought of recalling this extraordinary lawyer to the business that was waiting to be discussed. But Mrs. Presty looked at the clock, and discovered that her grandchild ought to have been in bed half-an-hour ago.

"Time to say good-night, " the grandmother suggested.

The grandchild failed to see the subject of bed in the same light. "Oh, not yet, " she pleaded; "I want to speak to Mr. —" Having only heard the visitor's name once, and not finding her memory in good working order after the conjuring, Kitty hesitated. "Isn't your name something like Saracen? " she asked.

"Very like! " cried the genial lawyer. "Try my other name, my dear. I'm Samuel as well as Sarrazin. "

"Ah, that'll do, " said Kitty. "Grandmamma, before I go to bed, I've something to ask Samuel. "

Grandmamma persisted in deferring the question until the next morning. Samuel administered consolation before he said good-night. "I'll get up early, " he whispered, "and we'll go on the pier before breakfast and fish. "

Kitty expressed her gratitude in her own outspoken way. "Oh, dear, how nice it would be, Samuel, if you lived with us! " Mrs. Linley laughed for the first time, poor soul, since the catastrophe which had broken up her home. Mrs. Presty set a proper example. She moved her chair so that she faced the lawyer, and said: "Now, Mr. Sarrazin! "

He acknowledged that he understood what this meant, by a very unprofessional choice of words. "We are in a mess, " he began, "and the sooner we are out of it the better. "

"Only let me keep Kitty, " Mrs. Linley declared, "and I'll do whatever you think right. "

"Stick to that, dear madam, when you have heard what I have to tell you—and I shall not have taken my journey in vain. In the first place, may I look at the letter which I had the honor of forwarding some days since? "

Mrs. Presty gave him Herbert Linley's letter. He read it with the closest attention, and tapped the breast-pocket of his coat when he had done.

"If I didn't know what I have got here, " he remarked, "I should have said: Another person dictated this letter, and the name of the person is Miss Westerfield. "

"Just my idea! " Mrs. Presty exclaimed. "There can't be a doubt of it. "

"Oh, but there is a very great doubt of it, ma'am; and you will say so too when you know what your severe son-in-law threatens to do. " He turned to Mrs. Linley. "After having seen that pretty little friend of mine who has just gone to bed (how much nicer it would be for all of us if we could go to bed too!), I think I know how you answered your husband's letter. But I ought perhaps to see how you have expressed yourself. Have you got a copy? "

"It was too short, Mr. Sarrazin, to make a copy necessary. "

"Do you mean you can remember it? "

"I can repeat it word for word. This was my reply: I refuse, positively, to part with my child. "

"No more like that? "

"No more. "

Mr. Sarrazin looked at his client with undisguised admiration. "The only time in all my long experience, " he said, "in which I have found a lady's letter capable of expressing itself strongly in a few words. What a lawyer you will make, Mrs. Linley, when the rights of women invade my profession! "

He put his hand into his pocket and produced a letter addressed to himself.

Watching him anxiously, the ladies saw his bright face become overclouded with anxiety. "I am the wretched bearer of bad news, " he resumed, "and if I fidget in my chair, that is the reason for it. Let us get to the point—and let us get off it again as soon as possible. Here is a letter, written to me by Mr. Linley's lawyer. If you will take my advice you will let me say what the substance of it is, and then put it back in my pocket. I doubt if a woman has influenced these cruel instructions, Mrs. Presty; and, therefore, I doubt if a woman influenced the letter which led the way to them. Did I not say just now that I was coming to the point? and here I am wandering further and further away from it. A lawyer is human; there is the only excuse. Now, Mrs. Linley, in two words; your husband is determined to have little Miss Kitty; and the law, when he applies to it, is his obedient humble servant. "

"Do you mean that the law takes my child away from me? "

"I am ashamed, madam, to think that I live by the law; but that, I must own, is exactly what it is capable of doing in the present case. Compose yourself, I beg and pray. A time will come when women will remind men that the mother bears the child and feeds the child, and will insist that the mother's right is the best right of the two. In the meanwhile—"

"In the meanwhile, Mr. Sarrazin, I won't submit to the law. "

"Quite right, Catherine! " cried Mrs. Presty. "Exactly what I should do, in your place. "

Mr. Sarrazin listened patiently. "I am all attention, good ladies, " he said, with the gentlest resignation. "Let me hear how you mean to do it. "

The good ladies looked at each other. They discovered that it is one thing to set an abuse at defiance in words, and another thing to apply the remedy in deeds. The kind-hearted lawyer helped them with a suggestion. "Perhaps you think of making your escape with the child, and taking refuge abroad? "

Mrs. Linley eagerly accepted the hint. "The first train to-morrow morning starts at half-past seven, " she said. "We might catch some foreign steamer that sails from the east coast of Scotland. "

Mrs. Presty, keeping a wary eye on Mr. Sarrazin, was not quite so ready as her daughter in rushing at conclusions. "I am afraid, " she acknowledged, "our worthy friend sees some objection. What is it? "

"I don't presume to offer a positive opinion, ma'am; but I think Mr. Linley and his lawyer have their suspicions. Plainly speaking, I am afraid spies are set to watch us already. "

"Impossible! "

"You shall hear. I travel second-class; one saves money and one finds people to talk to—and at what sacrifice? Only a hard cushion to sit on! In the same carriage with me there was a very conversable person—a smart young man with flaming red hair. When we took the omnibus at your station here, all the passengers got out in the town except two. I was one exception, and the smart young man was the other. When I stopped at your gate, the omnibus went on a few yards, and set down my fellow-traveler at the village inn. My profession makes me sly. I waited a little before I rang your bell; and, when I could do it without being seen, I crossed the road, and had a look at the inn. There is a moon to-night; I was very careful. The young man didn't see me. But I saw a head of flaming hair, and a pair of amiable blue eyes, over the blind of a window; and it happened to be the one window of the inn which commands a full view of your gate. Mere suspicion, you will say! I can't deny it, and yet I have my reasons for suspecting. Before I left London, one of my clerks followed me in a great hurry to the terminus, and caught me as I was opening the carriage door. 'We have just made a discovery, ' he said; 'you and Mrs. Linley are to be reckoned up. ' Reckoned up is, if you please, detective English for being watched. My clerk might have repeated a false report, of course. And my fellow-traveler might have come all the way from London to look out of the window of an inn, in a Cumberland village. What do you think yourselves? "

It seemed to be easier to dispute the law than to dispute Mr. Sarrazin's conclusions.

"Suppose I choose to travel abroad, and to take my child with me, " Mrs. Linley persisted, "who has any right to prevent me? "

Mr. Sarrazin reluctantly reminded her that the father had a right. "No person—not even the mother—can take the child out of the father's custody, " he said, "except with the father's consent. His authority is the supreme authority—unless it happens that the law has deprived him of his privilege, and has expressly confided the child to the mother's care. Ha! " cried Mr. Sarrazin, twisting round in his chair and fixing his keen eyes on Mrs. Presty, "look at your good mother; *she* sees what I am coming to. "

"I see something more than you think, " Mrs. Presty answered. "If I know anything of my daughter's nature, you will find yourself, before long, on delicate ground. "

"What do you mean, mamma? "

Mrs. Presty had lived in the past age when persons occasionally used metaphor as an aid to the expression of their ideas. Being called upon to explain herself, she did it in metaphor, to her own entire satisfaction.

"Our learned friend here reminds me, my dear Catherine, of a traveler exploring a strange town. He takes a turning, in the confident expectation that it will reward him by leading him to some satisfactory result—and he finds himself in a blind alley, or, as the French put it (I speak French fluently), in a *cool de sack*. Do I make my meaning clear, Mr. Sarrazin? "

"Not the least in the world, ma'am. "

"How very extraordinary! Perhaps I have been misled by my own vivid imagination. Let me endeavor to express myself plainly—let me say that my fancy looks prophetically at what you are going to do, and sincerely wishes you well out of it. Pray go on. "

"And pray speak more plainly than my mother has spoken, " Mrs. Linley added. "As I understood what you said just now, there is a law, after all, that will protect me in the possession of my little girl. I don't care what it costs; I want that law. "

"May I ask first, " Mr. Sarrazin stipulated, "whether you are positively resolved not to give way to your husband in this matter of Kitty? "

"Positively. "

"One more question, if you please, on a matter of fact. I have heard that you were married in Scotland. Is that true? "

"Quite true. "

Mr. Sarrazin exhibited himself once more in a highly unprofessional aspect. He clapped his hands, and cried, "Bravo! " as if he had been in a theater.

Mrs. Linley caught the infection of the lawyer's excitement. "How dull I am! " she exclaimed. "There is a thing they call 'incompatibility of temper'—and married people sign a paper at the lawyer's and promise never to trouble each other again as long as they both live. And they're readier to do it in Scotland than they are in England. That's what you mean—isn't it? "

Mr. Sarrazin found it necessary to reassume his professional character.

"No, indeed, madam, " he said, "I should be unworthy of your confidence if I proposed nothing better than that. You can only secure the sole possession of little Kitty by getting the help of a judge—"

"Get it at once, " Mrs. Linley interposed.

"And you can only prevail on the judge to listen to you, " Mr. Sarrazin proceeded, "in one way. Summon your courage, madam. Apply for a divorce. "

There was a sudden silence. Mrs. Linley rose trembling, as if she saw—not good Mr. Sarrazin—but the devil himself tempting her. "Do you hear that? " she said to her mother.

Mrs. Presty only bowed.

"Think of the dreadful exposure! "

Mrs. Presty bowed again.

The lawyer had his opportunity now.

"Well, Mrs. Linley, " he asked, "what do you say? "

"No—never! " She made that positive reply; and disposed beforehand of everything that might have been urged, in the way of remonstrance and persuasion, by leaving the room. The two persons who remained, sitting opposite to each other, took opposite views.

"Mr. Sarrazin, she won't do it. "

"Mrs. Presty, she will. "

Chapter XXVI.

Decision.

Punctual to his fishing appointment with Kitty, Mr. Sarrazin was out in the early morning, waiting on the pier.

Not a breath of wind was stirring; the lazy mist lay asleep on the further shore of the lake. Here and there only the dim tops of the hills rose like shadows cast by the earth on the faint gray of the sky. Nearer at hand, the waters of the lake showed a gloomy surface; no birds flew over the colorless calm; no passing insects tempted the fish to rise. From time to time a last-left leaf on the wooded shore dropped noiselessly and died. No vehicles passed as yet on the lonely road; no voices were audible from the village; slow and straight wreaths of smoke stole their way out of the chimneys, and lost their vapor in the misty sky. The one sound that disturbed the sullen repose of the morning was the tramp of the lawyer's footsteps, as he paced up and down the pier. He thought of London and its ceaseless traffic, its roaring high tide of life in action—and he said to himself, with the strong conviction of a town-bred man: How miserable this is!

A voice from the garden cheered him, just as he reached the end of the pier for the fiftieth time, and looked with fifty-fold intensity of dislike at the dreary lake.

There stood Kitty behind the garden-gate, with a fishing-rod in each hand. A tin box was strapped on one side of her little body and a basket on the other. Burdened with these impediments, she required assistance. Susan had let her out of the house; and Samuel must now open the gate for her. She was pleased to observe that the raw morning had reddened her friend's nose; and she presented her own nose to notice as exhibiting perfect sympathy in this respect. Feeling a misplaced confidence in Mr. Sarrazin's knowledge and experience as an angler, she handed the fishing-rods to him. "My fingers are cold, " she said; "you bait the hooks. " He looked at his young friend in silent perplexity; she pointed to the tin box. "Plenty of bait there, Samuel; we find maggots do best. " Mr. Sarrazin eyed the box with undisguised disgust; and Kitty made an unexpected discovery. "You seem to know nothing about it, " she said. And Samuel answered, cordially, "Nothing! " In five minutes more he found himself by the side of his young friend — with his hook baited, his line in the water, and strict injunctions to keep an eye on the float.

They began to fish.

Kitty looked at her companion, and looked away again in silence. By way of encouraging her to talk, the good-natured lawyer alluded to what she had said when they parted overnight. "You wanted to ask me something, " he reminded her. "What is it? "

Without one preliminary word of warning to prepare him for the shock, Kitty answered: "I want you to tell me what has become of papa, and why Syd has gone away and left me. You know who Syd is, don't you? "

The only alternative left to Mr. Sarrazin was to plead ignorance. While Kitty was instructing him on the subject of her governess, he had time to consider what he should say to her next. The result added one more to the lost opportunities of Mr. Sarrazin's life.

"You see, " the child gravely continued, "you are a clever man; and you have come here to help mamma. I have got that much out of grandmamma, if I have got nothing else. Don't look at me; look at your float. My papa has gone away and Syd has left me without even saying good-by, and we have given up our nice old house in Scotland and come to live here. I tell you I don't understand it. If you see your float begin to tremble, and then give a little dip down as if it was going to sink, pull your line out of the water; you will most likely find a fish at the end of it. When I ask mamma what all this means, she says there is a reason, and I am not old enough to understand it, and she looks unhappy, and she gives me a kiss, and it ends in that way. You've got a bite; no you haven't; it's only a nibble; fish are so sly. And grandmamma is worse still. Sometimes she tells me I'm a spoiled child; and sometimes she says well-behaved little girls don't ask questions. That's nonsense — and I think it's hard on me. You look uncomfortable. Is it my fault? I don't want to bother you; I only want to know why Syd has gone away. When I was younger I might have thought the fairies had taken her. Oh, no! that won't do any longer; I'm too old. Now tell me. "

Mr. Sarrazin weakly attempted to gain time: he looked at his watch. Kitty looked over his shoulder: "Oh, we needn't be in a hurry;

breakfast won't be ready for half an hour yet. Plenty of time to talk of Syd; go on. "

Most unwisely (seeing that he had to deal with a clever child, and that child a girl), Mr. Sarrazin tried flat denial as a way out of the difficulty. He said: "I don't know why she has gone away. " The next question followed instantly: "Well, then, what do you *think* about it? " In sheer despair, the persecuted friend said the first thing that came into his head.

"I think she has gone to be married. "

Kitty was indignant.

"Gone to be married, and not tell me! " she exclaimed. "What do you mean by that? "

Mr. Sarrazin's professional experience of women and marriages failed to supply him with an answer. In this difficulty he exerted his imagination, and invented something that no woman ever did yet. "She's waiting, " he said, "to see how her marriage succeeds, before she tells anybody about it. "

This sounded probable to the mind of a child.

"I hope she hasn't married a beast, " Kitty said, with a serious face and an ominous shake of the head. "When shall I hear from Syd? "

Mr. Sarrazin tried another prevarication—with better results this time. "You will be the first person she writes to, of course. " As that excusable lie passed his lips, his float began to tremble. Here was a chance of changing the subject—"I've got a fish! " he cried.

Kitty was immediately interested. She threw down her own rod, and assisted her ignorant companion. A wretched little fish appeared in the air, wriggling. "It's a roach, " Kitty pronounced. "It's in pain, " the merciful lawyer added; "give it to me. " Kitty took it off the hook, and obeyed. Mr. Sarrazin with humane gentleness of handling put it back into the water. "Go, and God bless you, " said this excellent man, as the roach disappeared joyously with a flick of its tail. Kitty was scandalized. "That's not sport! " she said. "Oh, yes, it is, " he answered—"sport to the fish. "

They went on with their angling. What embarrassing question would Kitty ask next? Would she want to be told why her father had left her? No: the last image in the child's mind had been the image of Sydney Westerfield. She was still thinking of it when she spoke again.

"I wonder whether you're right about Syd? " she began. "You might be mistaken, mightn't you? I sometimes fancy mamma and Sydney may have had a quarrel. Would you mind asking mamma if that's true? " the affectionate little creature said, anxiously. "You see, I can't help talking of Syd, I'm so fond of her; and I do miss her so dreadfully every now and then; and I'm afraid—oh, dear, dear, I'm afraid I shall never see her again! " She let her rod drop on the pier, and put her little hands over her face and burst out crying.

Shocked and distressed, good Mr. Sarrazin kissed her, and consoled her, and told another excusable lie.

"Try to be comforted, Kitty; I'm sure you will see her again. "

His conscience reproached him as he held out that false hope. It could never be! The one unpardonable sin, in the judgment of fallible human creatures like herself, was the sin that Sydney Westerfield had committed. Is there something wrong in human nature? or something wrong in human laws? All that is best and noblest in us feels the influence of love—and the rules of society declare that an accident of position shall decide whether love is a virtue or a crime.

These thoughts were in the lawyer's mind. They troubled him and disheartened him: it was a relief rather than an interruption when he felt Kitty's hand on his arm. She had dried her tears, with a child's happy facility in passing from one emotion to another, and was now astonished and interested by a marked change in the weather.

"Look for the lake! " she cried. "You can't see it. "

A dense white fog was closing round them. Its stealthy advance over the water had already begun to hide the boathouse at the end of the pier from view. The raw cold of the atmosphere made the child shiver. As Mr. Sarrazin took her hand to lead her indoors, he turned and looked back at the faint outline of the boathouse, disappearing in the fog. Kitty wondered. "Do you see anything? " she asked.

He answered that there was nothing to see, in the absent tone of a man busy with his own thoughts. They took the garden path which led to the cottage. As they reached the door he roused himself, and looked round again in the direction of the invisible lake.

"Was the boat-house of any use now, " he inquired—"was there a boat in it, for instance? " "There was a capital boat, fit to go anywhere. " "And a man to manage it? " "To be sure! the gardener was the man; he had been a sailor once; and he knew the lake as well as—" Kitty stopped, at a loss for a comparison. "As well as you know your multiplication table? " said Mr. Sarrazin, dropping his serious questions on a sudden. Kitty shook her head. "Much better, " she honestly acknowledged.

Opening the breakfast-room door they saw Mrs. Presty making coffee. Kitty at once retired. When she had been fishing, her grandmamma inculcated habits of order by directing her to take the rods to pieces, and to put them away in their cases in the lumber-room. While she was absent, Mr. Sarrazin profited by the opportunity, and asked if Mrs. Linley had thought it over in the night, and had decided on applying for a Divorce.

"I know nothing about my daughter, " Mrs. Presty answered, "except that she had a bad night. Thinking, no doubt, over your advice, " the old lady added with a mischievous smile.

"Will you kindly inquire if Mrs. Linley has made up her mind yet? " the lawyer ventured to say.

"Isn't that your business? " Mrs. Presty asked slyly. "Suppose you write a little note, and I will send it up to her room. " The worldly-wisdom which prompted this suggestion contemplated a possible necessity for calling a domestic council, assembled to consider the course of action which Mrs. Linley would do well to adopt. If the influence of her mother was among the forms of persuasion which might be tried, that wary relative maneuvered to make the lawyer speak first, and so to reserve to herself the advantage of having the last word.

Patient Mr. Sarrazin wrote the note.

He modestly asked for instructions; and he was content to receive them in one word—Yes or No. In the event of the answer being Yes, he would ask for a few minutes' conversation with Mrs. Linley, at her earliest convenience. Tha t was all.

The reply was returned in a form which left Yes to be inferred: "I will receive you as soon as you have finished your breakfast. "

Chapter XXVII.

Resolution.

Having read Mrs. Linley's answer, Mr. Sarrazin looked out of the breakfast-room window, and saw that the fog had reached the cottage. Before Mrs. Presty could make any remark on the change in the weather, he surprised her by an extraordinary question.

"Is there an upper room here, ma'am, which has a view of the road before your front gate? "

"Certainly! "

"And can I go into it without disturbing anybody? "

Mrs. Presty said, "Of course! " with an uplifting of her eye brows which expressed astonishment not unmixed with suspicion. "Do you want to go up now? " she added, "or will you wait till you have had your breakfast? "

"I want to go up, if you please, before the fog thickens. Oh, Mrs. Presty, I am ashamed to trouble you! Let the servant show me the room. "

No. For the first time in her life Mrs. Presty insisted on doing servant's duty. If she had been crippled in both legs her curiosity would have helped her to get up the stairs on her hands. "There! " she said, opening the door of the upper room, and placing herself exactly in the middle of it, so that she could see all round her: "Will that do for you? "

Mr. Sarrazin went to the window; hid himself behind the curtain; and cautiously peeped out. In half a minute he turned his back on the misty view of the road, and said to himself: "Just what I expected. "

Other women might have asked what this mysterious proceeding meant. Mrs. Presty's sense of her own dignity adopted a system of independent discovery. To Mr. Sarrazin's amusement, she imitated him to his face. Advancing to the window, she, too, hid herself behind the curtain, and she, too, peeped out. Still following her model, she next turned her back on the view—and then she became herself again. "Now we have both looked out of window, " she said to the lawyer, in her own inimitably impudent way, "suppose we compare our impressions. "

This was easily done. They had both seen the same two men walking backward and forward, opposite the front gate of the cottage. Before the advancing fog made it impossible to identify him, Mr. Sarrazin had recognized in one of the men his agreeable fellow-traveler on the journey from London. The other man—a stranger—was in all probability an assistant spy obtained in the neighborhood. This discovery suggested serious embarrassment in the future. Mrs. Presty asked what was to be done next. Mr. Sarrazin answered: "Let us have our breakfast. "

In another quarter of an hour they were both in Mrs. Linley's room.

Her agitated manner, her reddened eyes, showed that she was still suffering under the emotions of the past night. The moment the lawyer approached her, she crossed the room with hurried steps, and took both his hands in her trembling grasp. "You are a good man, you are a kind man, " she said to him wildly; "you have my truest respect and regard. Tell me, are you—really—really—really sure that the one way in which I can keep my child with me is the way you mentioned last night? "

Mr. Sarrazin led her gently back to her chair.

The sad change in her startled and distressed him. Sincerely, solemnly even, he declared that the one alternative before her was the alternative that he had mentioned. He entreated her to control herself. It was useless, she still held him as if she was holding to her last hope.

"Listen to me! " she cried. "There's something more; there's another chance for me. I must, and will, know what you think of it. "

"Wait a little. Pray wait a little! "

"No! not a moment. Is there any hope in appealing to the lawyer whom Mr. Linley has employed? Let me go back with you to London. I will persuade him to exert his influence—I will go down on my knees to him—I will never leave him till I have won him over to my side—I will take Kitty with me; he shall see us both, and pity us, and help us! "

"Hopeless. Quite hopeless, Mrs. Linley. "

"Oh, don't say that! "

"My dear lady, my poor dear lady, I must say it. The man you are talking of is the last man in the world to be influenced as you suppose. He is notoriously a lawyer, and nothing but a lawyer. If you tried to move him to pity you, he would say, 'Madam, I am doing my duty to my client'; and he would ring his bell and have you shown out. Yes! even if he saw you crushed and crying at his feet. "

Mrs. Presty interfered for the first time.

"In your place, Catherine, " she said, "I would put my foot down on that man and crush *him*. Consent to the Divorce, and you may do it. "

Mrs. Linley lay prostrate in her chair. The excitement which had sustained her thus far seemed to have sunk with the sinking of her last hope. Pale, exhausted, yielding to hard necessity, she looked up when her mother said, "Consent to the Divorce, " and answered, "I have consented. "

"And trust me, " Mr. Sarrazin said fervently, "to see that Justice is done, and to protect you in the meanwhile. "

Mrs. Presty added her tribute of consolation.

"After all, " she asked, "what is there to terrify you in the prospect of a Divorce? You won't hear what people say about it—for we see no society now. And, as for the newspapers, keep them out of the house. "

Mrs. Linley answered with a momentary revival of energy

"It is not the fear of exposure that has tortured me, " she said. "When I was left in the solitude of the night, my heart turned to Kitty; I felt that any sacrifice of myself might be endured for her sake. It's the remembrance of my marriage, Mr. Sarrazin, that is the terrible trial to me. Those whom God has joined together, let no man put asunder. Is there nothing to terrify me in setting that solemn command at defiance? I do it—oh, I do it—in consenting to the Divorce! I renounce the vows which I bound myself to respect in the presence of God; I profane the remembrance of eight happy years, hallowed by true love. Ah, you needn't remind me of what my husband has done. I don't forget how cruelly he has wronged me; I don't forget that his own act has cast me from him. But whose act destroys our marriage? Mine, mine! Forgive me, mamma; forgive me, my kind friend—the horror that I have of myself forces its way to my lips. No more of it! My child is my one treasure left. What must I do next? What must I sign? What must I sacrifice? Tell me—and it shall be done. I submit! I submit! "

Delicately and mercifully Mr. Sarrazin answered that sad appeal.

All that his knowledge, experience and resolution could suggest he addressed to Mrs. Presty. Mrs. Linley could listen or not listen, as her own wishes inclined. In the one case or in the other, her interests would be equally well served. The good lawyer kissed her hand. "Rest, and recover, " he whispered. And then he turned to her mother—and became a man of business once more.

"The first thing I shall do, ma'am, is to telegraph to my agent in Edinburgh. He will arrange for the speediest possible hearing of our case in the Court of Session. Make your mind easy so far. "

Mrs. Presty's mind was by this time equally inaccessible to information and advice. "I want to know what is to be done with those two men who are watching the gate, " was all she said in the way of reply.

Mrs. Linley raised her head in alarm.

"Two! " she exclaimed—and looked at Mr. Sarrazin. "You only spoke of one last night. "

"And I add another this morning. Rest your poor head, Mrs. Linley, I know how it aches; I know how it burns. " He still persisted in speaking to Mrs. Presty. "One of those two men will follow me to the station, and see me off on my way to London. The other will look after you, or your daughter, or the maid, or any other person who may try to get away into hiding with Kitty. And they are both keeping close to the gate, in the fear of losing sight of us in the fog. "

The Evil Genius

"I wish we lived in the Middle Ages! " said Mrs. Presty.

"What would be the use of that, ma'am? "

"Good heavens, Mr. Sarrazin, don't you see? In those grand old days you would have taken a dagger, and the gardener would have taken a dagger, and you would have stolen out, and stabbed those two villains as a matter of course. And this is the age of progress! The vilest rogue in existence is a sacred person whose life we are bound to respect. Ah, what good that national hero would have done who put his barrels of gunpowder in the right place on the Fifth of November! I have always said it, and I stick to it, Guy Fawkes was a great statesman. "

In the meanwhile Mrs. Linley was not resting, and not listening to the expression of her mother's political sentiments. She was intently watching Mr. Sarrazin's face.

"There is danger threatening us, " she said. "Do you see a way out of it? "

To persist in trying to spare her was plainly useless; Mr. Sarrazin answered her directly.

"The danger of legal proceedings to obtain possession of the child, " he said, "is more near and more serious than I thought it right to acknowledge, while you were in doubt which way to decide. I was careful—too careful, perhaps—not to unduly influence you in a matter of the utmost importance to your future life. But you have made up your mind. I don't scruple now to remind you that an interval of time must pass before the decree for your Divorce can be pronounced, and the care of the child be legally secured to the mother. The only doubt and the only danger are there. If you are not frightened by the prospect of a desperate venture which some women would shrink from, I believe I see a way of baffling the spies. "

Mrs. Linley started to her feet. "Say what I am to do, " she cried, "and judge for yourself if I am as easily frightened as some women. "

The lawyer pointed with a persuasive smile to her empty chair. "If you allow yourself to be excited, " he said, "you will frighten me. Please—oh, please sit down again! "

Mrs. Linley felt the strong will, asserting itself in terms of courteous entreaty. She obeyed. Mrs. Presty had never admired the lawyer as she admired him now. "Is that how you manage your wife? " she asked.

Mr. Sarrazin was equal to the occasion, whatever it might be. "In your time, ma'am, " he said, "did you reveal the mysteries of conjugal life? " He turned to Mrs. Linley. "I have something to ask first, " he resumed, "and then you shall hear what I propose. How many people serve you in this cottage? "

"Three. Our landlady, who is housekeeper and cook. Our own maid. And the landlady's daughter, who does the housework. "

"Any out-of-door servants? "

"Only the gardener. "

"Can you trust these people? "

"In what way, Mr. Sarrazin? "

"Can you trust them with a secret which only concerns yourself? "

"Certainly! The maid has been with us for years; no truer woman ever lived. The good old landlady often drinks tea with us. Her daughter is going to be married; and I have given the wedding-dress. As for the gardener, let Kitty settle the matter with him, and I answer for the rest. Why are you pointing to the window? "

"Look out, and tell me what you see. "

"I see the fog. "

"And I, Mrs. Linley, have seen the boathouse. While the spies are watching your gate, what do you say to crossing the lake, under cover of the fog? "

FOURTH BOOK.

Chapter XXVIII.

Mr. Randal Linley.

Winter had come and gone; spring was nearing its end, and London still suffered under the rigid regularity of easterly winds. Although in less than a week summer would begin with the first of June, Mr. Sarrazin was glad to find his office warmed by a fire, when he arrived to open the letters of the day.

The correspondence in general related exclusively to proceedings connected with the law. Two letters only presented an exception to the general rule. The first was addressed in Mrs. Linley's handwriting, and bore the postmark of Hanover. Kitty's mother had not only succeeded in getting to the safe side of the lake—she and her child had crossed the German Ocean as well. In one respect her letter was a remarkable composition. Although it was written by a lady, it was short enough to be read in less than a minute:

"MY DEAR MR. SARRAZIN—I have just time to write by this evening's post. Our excellent courier has satisfied himself that the danger of discovery has passed away. The wretches have been so completely deceived that they are already on their way back to England, to lie in wait for us at Folkestone and Dover. To-morrow morning we leave this charming place—oh, how unwillingly! —for Bremen, to catch the steamer to Hull. You shall hear from me again on our arrival. Gratefully yours,

CATHERINE LINLEY. "

Mr. Sarrazin put this letter into a private drawer and smiled as he turned the key. "Has she made up her mind at last? " he asked himself. "But for the courier, I shouldn't feel sure of her even now. "

The second letter agreeably surprised him. It was announced that the writer had just returned from the United States; it invited him to dinner that evening; and it was signed "Randal Linley. " In Mr. Sarrazin's estimation, Randal had always occupied a higher place than his brother. The lawyer had known Mrs. Linley before her marriage, and had been inclined to think that she would have done wisely if she had given her hand to the younger brother instead of the elder. His acquaintance with Randal ripened rapidly into friendship. But his relations with Herbert made no advance toward intimacy: there was a gentlemanlike cordiality between them, and nothing more.

At seven o'clock the two friends sat at a snug little table, in the private room of a hotel, with an infinite number of questions to ask of each other, and with nothing to interrupt them but a dinner of such extraordinary merit that it insisted on being noticed, from the first course to the last.

Randal began. "Before we talk of anything else, " he said, "tell me about Catherine and the child. Where are they? "

"On their way to England, after a residence in Germany. "

"And the old lady? "

"Mrs. Presty has been staying with friends in London. "

"What! have they parted company? Has there been a quarrel? "

"Nothing of the sort; a friendly separation, in the strictest sense of the word. Oh, Randal, what are you about? Don't put pepper into this perfect soup. It's as good as the *gras double* at the Cafe Anglais in Paris. "

"So it is; I wasn't paying proper attention to it. But I am anxious about Catherine. Why did she go abroad? "

"Haven't you heard from her? "

"Not for six months or more. I innocently vexed her by writing a little too hopefully about Herbert. Mrs. Presty answered my letter, and recommended me not to write again. It isn't like Catherine to bear malice. "

"Don't even think such a thing possible! " the lawyer answered, earnestly. "Attribute her silence to the right cause. Terrible anxieties have been weighing on her mind since you went to America. "

"Anxieties caused by my brother? Oh, I hope not! "

"Caused entirely by your brother—if I must tell the truth. Can't you guess how? "

"Is it the child? You don't mean to tell me that Herbert has taken Kitty away from her mother! "

"While I am her mother's lawyer, my friend, your brother won't do that. Welcome back to England in the first glass of sherry; good wine, but a little too dry for my taste. No, we won't talk of domestic troubles just yet. You shall hear all about it after dinner. What made you go to America? You haven't been delivering lectures, have you? "

"I have been enjoying myself among the most hospitable people in the world. "

Mr. Sarrazin shook his head; he had a case of copyright in hand just then. "A people to be pitied, " he said.

"Why? "

"Because their Government forgets what is due to the honor of the nation. "

"How? "

"In this way. The honor of a nation which confers right of property in works of art, produced by its own citizens, is surely concerned in protecting from theft works of art produced by other citizens. "

"That's not the fault of the people. "

"Certainly not. I have already said it's the fault of the Government. Let's attend to the fish now. "

Randal took his friend's advice. "Good sauce, isn't it? " he said.

The epicure entered a protest. "Good? " he repeated. "My dear fellow, it's absolute perfection. I don't like to cast a slur on English cookery. But think of melted butter, and tell me if anybody but a foreigner (I don't like foreigners, but I give them their due) could have produced this white wine sauce? So you really had no particular motive in going to America? "

"On the contrary, I had a very particular motive. Just remember what my life used to be when I was in Scotland—and look at my life now! No Mount Morven; no model farm to look after; no pleasant Highland neighbors; I can't go to my brother while he is leading his present life; I have hurt Catherine's feelings; I have lost dear little Kitty; I am not obliged to earn my living (more's the pity); I don't care about politics; I have a pleasure in eating harmless creatures, but no pleasure in shooting them. What is there left for me to do, but to try change of scene, and go roaming around the world, a restless creature without an object in life? Have I done something wrong again? It isn't the pepper this time—and yet you're looking at me as if I was trying your temper. "

The French side of Mr. Sarrazin's nature had got the better of him once more. He pointed indignantly to a supreme preparation of fowl on his friend's plate. "Do I actually see you picking out your truffles, and putting them on one side? " he asked.

"Well, " Randal acknowledged, "I don't care about truffles. "

Mr. Sarrazin rose, with his plate in his hand and his fork ready for action. He walked round the table to his friend's side, and reverently transferred the neglected truffles to his own plate. "Randal, you will live to repent this, " he said solemnly. "In the meantime, I am the gainer. " Until he had finished the truffles, no word fell from his lips. "I think I should have enjoyed them more, " he remarked, "if I had concentrated my attention by closing my eyes; but you would have thought I was going to sleep. " He recovered his English nationality, after this, until the dessert had been placed on the table, and the waiter was ready to leave the room. At that auspicious moment, he underwent another relapse. He insisted on sending his compliments and thanks to the cook.

"At last, " said Randal, "we are by ourselves—and now I want to know why Catherine went to Germany. "

Chapter XXIX.

Mr. Sarrazin.

As a lawyer, Randal's guest understood that a narrative of events can only produce the right effect, on one condition: it must begin at the beginning. Having related all that had been said and done during his visit to the cottage, including his first efforts in the character of an angler under Kitty's supervision, he stopped to fill his glass again—and then astonished Randal by describing the plan that he had devised for escaping from the spies by crossing the lake in the fog.

"What did the ladies say to it? " Randal inquired. "Who spoke first? "

"Mrs. Presty, of course! She objected to risk her life on the water, in a fog. Mrs. Linley showed a resolution for which I was not prepared. She thought of Kitty, saw the value of my suggestion, and went away at once to consult with the landlady. In the meantime I sent for the gardener, and told him what I was thinking of. He was one of those stolid Englishmen, who possess resources which don't express themselves outwardly. Judging by his face, you would have said he was subsiding into a slumber under the infliction of a sermon, instead of listening to a lawyer proposing a stratagem. When I had done, the man showed the metal he was made of. In plain English, he put three questions which gave me the highest opinion of his intelligence. 'How much luggage, sir? ' 'As little as they can conveniently take with them, ' I said. 'How many persons? ' 'The two ladies, the child, and myself. ' 'Can you row, sir? ' 'In any water you like, Mr. Gardener, fresh or salt'. Think of asking Me, an athletic Englishman, if I could row! In an hour more we were ready to embark, and the blessed fog was thicker than ever. Mrs. Presty yielded under protest; Kitty was wild with delight; her mother was quiet and resigned. But one circumstance occurred that I didn't quite understand—the presence of a stranger on the pier with a gun in his hand. "

"You don't mean one of the spies? "

"Nothing of the sort; I mean an idea of the gardener's. He had been a sailor in his time—and that's a trade which teaches a man (if he's good for anything) to think, and act on his thought, at one and the same moment. He had taken a peep at the blackguards in front of the house, and had recognized the shortest of the two as a native of the place, perfectly well aware that one of the features attached to the cottage was a boathouse. 'That chap is not such a fool as he looks, ' says the gardener. 'If he mentions the boat-house, the other fellow from London may have his suspicions. I thought I would post my son on the pier—that quiet young man there with the gun—to keep a lookout. If he sees another boat (there are half a dozen on this side of the lake) putting off after us, he has orders to fire, on the chance of our hearing him. A little notion of mine, sir, to prevent our being surprised in the fog. Do you see any objection to it? ' Objection! In the days when diplomacy was something more than a solemn pretense, what a member of Congress that gardener would have made! Well, we shipped our oars, and away we went. Not quite haphazard—for we had a compass with us. Our course was as straight as we could go, to a village on the opposite side of the lake, called Brightfold. Nothing happened for the first quarter of an hour—and then, by the living Jingo (excuse my vulgarity), we heard the gun! "

"What did you do? "

"Went on rowing, and held a council. This time I came out as the clever one of the party. The men were following us in the dark; they would have to guess at the direction we had taken, and they would most likely assume (in such weather as we had) that we should choose the shortest way across the lake. At my suggestion we changed our course, and made for a large town, higher up on the shore, called Tawley. We landed, and waited for events, and made no discovery of another boat behind us. The fools had justified my confidence in them—they had gone to Brightfold. There was half-an-hour to spare before the next train came to Tawley; and the fog was beginning to lift on that side of the lake. We looked at the shops; and I made a purchase in the town. "

"Stop a minute, " said Randal. "Is Brightfold on the railway? "

"No. "

"Is there an electric telegraph at the place? "

"Yes. "

"That was awkward, wasn't it? The first thing those men would do would be to telegraph to Tawley. "

"Not a doubt of it. How would they describe us, do you think? "

Randal answered. "A middle-aged gentleman—two ladies, one of them elderly—and a little girl. Quite enough to identify you at Tawley, if the station-master understood the message. "

"Shall I tell you what the station-master discovered, with the message in his hand? No elderly lady, no middle-aged gentleman; nothing more remarkable than *one* lady—and a little boy. "

Randal's face brightened. "You parted company, of course, " he said; "and you disguised Kitty! How did you manage it? "

"Didn't I say just now that we looked at the shops, and that I made a purchase in the town? A boy's ready-made suit—not at all a bad fit for Kitty! Mrs. Linley put on the suit, and tucked up the child's hair under a straw hat, in an empty yard—no idlers about in that bad weather. We said good-by, and parted, with grievous misgivings on my side, which proved (thank God!) to have been quite needless. Kitty and her mother went to the station, and Mrs. Presty and I hired a carriage, and drove away to the head of the lake, to catch the train to London. Do you know, Randal, I have altered my opinion of Mrs. Presty? "

Randal smiled. "You too have found something in that old woman, " he said, "which doesn't appear on the surface. "

"The occasion seems to bring that something out, " the lawyer remarked. "When I proposed the separation, and mentioned my reasons, I expected to find some difficulty in persuading Mrs. Presty to give up the adventurous journey with her daughter and her grandchild. I reminded her that she had friends in London who would receive her, and got snubbed for taking the liberty. 'I know that as well as you do. Come along—I'm ready to go with you. ' It isn't agreeable to my self-esteem to own it, but I expected to hear her say that she would consent to any sacrifice for the sake of her dear daughter. No such clap-trap as that passed her lips. She owned the true motive with a superiority to cant which won my sincerest respect. 'I'll do anything, ' she said, 'to baffle Herbert Linley and the spies he has set to watch us. ' I can't tell you how glad I was that she

179

had her reward on the same day. We were too late at the station, and we had to wait for the next train. And what do you think happened? The two scoundrels followed us instead of following Mrs. Linley! They had inquired no doubt at the livery stables where we hired the carriage—had recognized the description of us—and had taken the long journey to London for nothing. Mrs. Presty and I shook hands at the terminus the best friends that ever traveled together with the best of motives. After that, I think I deserve another glass of wine. "

"Go on with your story, and you shall have another bottle! " cried Randal. "What did Catherine and the child do after they left you? "

"They did the safest thing—they left England. Mrs. Linley distinguished herself on this occasion. It was her excellent idea to avoid popular ports of departure, like Folkestone and Dover, which were sure to be watched, and to get away (if the thing could be done) from some place on the east coast. We consulted our guide and found that a line of steamers sailed from Hull to Bremen once a week. A tedious journey from our part of Cumberland, with some troublesome changing of trains, but they got there in time to embark. My first news of them reached me in a telegram from Bremen. There they waited for further instructions. I sent the instructions by a thoroughly capable and trustworthy man—an Italian courier, known to me by an experience of twenty years. Shall I confess it? I thought I had done rather a clever thing in providing Mrs. Linley with a friend in need while I was away from her. "

"I think so, too, " said Randal.

"Wrong, completely wrong. I had made a mistake—I had been too clever, and I got my reward accordingly. You know how I advised Mrs. Linley? "

"Yes. You persuaded her, with the greatest difficulty, to apply for a Divorce. "

"Very well. I had made all the necessary arrangements for the trial, when I received a letter from Germany. My charming client had changed her mind, and declined to apply for the Divorce. There was my reward for having been too clever! "

"I don't understand you. "

"My dear fellow, you are dull to-night. I had been so successful in protecting Mrs. Linley and the child, and my excellent courier had found such a charming place of retreat for them in one of the suburbs of Hanover, that 'she saw no reason now for taking the shocking course that I had recommended to her—so repugnant to all her most cherished convictions; so sinful and so shameful in its doing of evil that good might come. Experience had convinced her that (thanks to me) there was no fear of Kitty being discovered and taken from her. She therefore begged me to write to my agent in Edinburgh, and tell him that her application to the court was withdrawn. ' Ah, you understand my position at last. The headstrong woman was running a risk which renewed all my anxieties. By every day's post I expected to hear that she had paid the penalty of her folly, and that your brother had succeeded in getting possession of the child. Wait a little before you laugh at me. But for the courier, the thing would have really happened a week since. "

Randal looked astonished. "Months must have passed, " he objected. "Surely, after that lapse of time, Mrs. Linley must have been safe from discovery. "

"Take your own positive view of it! I only know that the thing happened. And why not? The luck had begun by being on one side—why shouldn't the other side have had its turn next? "

"Do you really believe in luck? "

"Devoutly. A lawyer must believe in something. He knows the law too well to put any faith in that: and his clients present to him (if he is a man of any feeling) a hideous view of human nature. The poor devil believes in luck—rather than believe in nothing. I think it quite likely that accident helped the person employed by the husband to discover the wife and child. Anyhow, Mrs. Linley and Kitty were seen in the streets of Hanover; seen, recognized, and followed. The courier happened to be with them—luck again! For thirty years and more, he had been traveling in every part of Europe; there was not a landlord of the smallest pretensions anywhere who didn't know him and like him. 'I pretended not to see that anybody was following us, ' he said (writing from Hanover to relieve my anxiety); 'and I took the ladies to a hotel. The hotel possessed two merits from our point of view—it had a way out at the back, through the stables, and it was kept by a landlord who was an excellent good friend of mine. I arranged with him what he was to say when inquiries were made; and I kept my poor ladies prisoners in their lodgings for three days. The end of it is that Mr. Linley's policeman has gone away to watch the Channel steam-service, while we return quietly by way of Bremen and Hull. ' There is the courier's account of it. I have only to add that poor Mrs. Linley has been fairly frightened into submission. She changes her mind again, and pledges herself once more to apply for the Divorce. If we are only lucky enough to get our case heard without any very serious delay, I am not afraid of my client slipping through my fingers for the second time. When will the courts of session be open to us? You have lived in Scotland, Randal—"

"But I haven't lived in the courts of law. I wish I could give you the information you want. "

Mr. Sarrazin looked at his watch. "For all I know to the contrary, " he said, "we may be wasting precious time while we are talking here. Will you excuse me if I go away to my club? "

"Are you going in search of information? "

"Yes. We have some inveterate old whist-players who are always to be found in the card-room. One of them formerly practiced, I believe, in the Scotch courts. It has just occurred to me that the chance is worth trying. "

"Will you let me know if you succeed? " Randal asked.

The lawyer took his hand at parting. "You seem to be almost as anxious about it as I am, " he said.

"To tell you the truth, I am a little alarmed when I think of Catherine. If there is another long delay, how do we know what may happen before the law has confirmed the mother's claim to the child? Let me send one of the servants here to wait at your club. Will you give him a line telling me when the trial is likely to take place? "

"With the greatest pleasure. Good-night. "

Left alone, Randal sat by the fireside for a while, thinking of the future. The prospect, as he saw it, disheartened him. As a means of employing his mind on a more agreeable subject for reflection, he opened his traveling desk and took out two or three letters. They had been addressed to him, while he was in America, by Captain Bennydeck.

The captain had committed an error of which most of us have been guilty in our time. He had been too exclusively devoted to work that interested him to remember what was due to the care of his health. The doctor's warnings had been neglected; his over-strained nerves had given way; and the man whose strong constitution had resisted cold and starvation in the Arctic wastes, had broken down under stress of brain-work in London.

This was the news which the first of the letters contained.

The second, written under dictation, alluded briefly to the remedies suggested. In the captain's case, the fresh air recommended was the air of the sea. At the same time he was forbidden to receive either letters or telegrams, during his absence from town, until the doctor had seen him again. These instructions pointed, in Captain Bennydeck's estimation, to sailing for pleasure's sake, and therefore to hiring a yacht.

The third and last letter announced that the yacht had been found, and described the captain's plans when the vessel was ready for sea.

He proposed to sail here and there about the Channel, wherever it might please the wind to take him. Friends would accompany him, but not in any number. The yacht was not large enough to accommodate comfortably more than one or two guests at a time. Every now and then, the vessel would come to an anchor in the bay of the little coast town of Sandyseal, to accommodate friends going and coming and (in spite of medical advice) to receive letters. "You may have heard of Sandyseal, " the Captain wrote, "as one of the places which have lately been found out by the doctors. They are recommending the air to patients suffering from nervous disorders all over England. The one hotel in the place, and the few cottages which let lodgings, are crammed, as I hear, and the speculative builder is beginning his operations at such a rate that Sandyseal will be no longer recognizable in a few months more. Before the crescents and terraces and grand hotels turn the town into a fashionable watering-place, I want to take a last look at scenes familiar to me under their old aspect. If you are inclined to wonder at my feeling such a wish as this, I can easily explain myself. Two miles inland from Sandyseal, there is a lonely old moated house. In that house I was born. When you return from America, write to me at the post-office, or at the hotel (I am equally well known in both places), and let us arrange for a speedy meeting. I wish I could ask you to come and see me in my birth-place. It was sold, years since, under instructions in my father's will, and was purchased for the use of a community of nuns. We may look at the outside, and we can do no more. In the meantime, don't despair of my recovery; the sea is my old friend, and my trust is in God's mercy. "

These last lines were added in a postscript:

"Have you heard any more of that poor girl, the daughter of my old friend Roderick Westerfield — whose sad story would never have been known to me but for you? I feel sure that you have good reasons for not telling me the name of the man who has misled her, or the address at which she may be found. But you may one day be at liberty to break your silence. In that case, don't hesitate to do so because there may happen to be obstacles in my way. No difficulties discourage me, when my end in view is the saving of a soul in peril. "

Randal returned to his desk to write to the Captain. He had only got as far as the first sentences, when the servant returned with the lawyer's promised message. Mr. Sarrazin's news was communicated in these cheering terms:

"I am a firmer believer in luck than ever. If we only make haste — and won't I make haste! — we may get the Divorce, as I calculate, in three weeks' time. "

Chapter XXX.

The Lord President.

Mrs. Linley's application for a Divorce was heard in the first division of the Court of Session at Edinburgh, the Lord President being the judge.

To the disappointment of the large audience assembled, no defense was attempted on the part of the husband—a wise decision, seeing that the evidence of the wife and her witnesses was beyond dispute. But one exciting incident occurred toward the close of the proceedings. Sudden illness made Mrs. Linley's removal necessary, at the moment of all others most interesting to herself—the moment before the judge's decision was announced.

But, as the event proved, the poor lady's withdrawal was the most fortunate circumstance that could have occurred, in her own interests. After condemning the husband's conduct with unsparing severity, the Lord President surprised most of the persons present by speaking of the wife in these terms:

"Grievously as Mrs. Linley has been injured, the evidence shows that she was herself by no means free from blame. She has been guilty, to say the least of it, of acts of indiscretion. When the criminal attachment which had grown up between Mr. Herbert Linley and Miss Westerfield had been confessed to her, she appears to have most unreasonably overrated whatever merit there might have been in their resistance to the final temptation. She was indeed so impulsively ready to forgive (without waiting to see if the event justified the exercise of mercy) that she owns to having given her hand to Miss Westerfield, at parting, not half an hour after that young person's shameless forgetfulness of the claims of modesty, duty and gratitude had been first communicated to her. To say that this was the act of an inconsiderate woman, culpably indiscreet and, I had almost added, culpably indelicate, is only to say what she has deserved. On the next occasion to which I feel bound to advert, her conduct was even more deserving of censure. She herself appears to have placed the temptation under which he fell in her husband's way, and so (in some degree at least) to have provoked the catastrophe which has brought her before this court. I allude, it is needless to say, to her having invited the governess—then out of harm's way; then employed elsewhere—to return to her house, and to risk (what actually occurred) a meeting with Mr. Herbert Linley when no third person happened to be present. I know that the maternal motive which animated Mrs. Linley is considered, by many persons, to excuse and even to justify that most regrettable act; and I have myself allowed (I fear weakly allowed) more than due weight to this consideration in pronouncing for the Divorce. Let me express the earnest hope that Mrs. Linley will take warning by what has happened; and, if she finds herself hereafter placed in other circumstances of difficulty, let me advise her to exercise more control over impulses which one might expect perhaps to find in a young girl, but which are neither natural nor excusable in a woman of her age. "

His lordship then decreed the Divorce in the customary form, giving the custody of the child to the mother.

* * * * *

As fast as a hired carriage could take him, Mr. Sarrazin drove from the court to Mrs. Linley's lodgings, to tell her that the one great object of securing her right to her child had been achieved.

At the door he was met by Mrs. Presty. She was accompanied by a stranger, whose medical services had been required. Interested professionally in hearing the result of the trial, this gentleman volunteered to communicate the good news to his patient. He had been waiting to administer a composing draught, until the suspense from which Mrs. Linley was suffering might be relieved, and a reasonable hope be entertained that the medicine would produce the right effect. With that explanation he left the room.

While the doctor was speaking, Mrs. Presty was drawing her own conclusions from a close scrutiny of Mr. Sarrazin's face.

"I am going to make a disagreeable remark, " she announced. "You look ten years older, sir, than you did when you left us this morning to go to the Court. Do me a favor—come to the sideboard. " The lawyer having obeyed, she poured out a glass of wine. "There is the remedy, " she resumed, "when something has happened to worry you. "

"'Worry' isn't the right word, " Mr. Sarrazin declared. "I'm furious! It's a most improper thing for a person in my position to say of a person in the Lord President's position; but I do say it—he ought to be ashamed of himself. "

"After giving us our Divorce! " Mrs. Presty exclaimed. "What has he done? "

Mr. Sarrazin repeated what the judge had said of Mrs. Linley. "In my opinion, " he added, "such language as that is an insult to your daughter. "

"And yet, " Mrs. Presty repeated, "he has given us our Divorce. " She returned to the sideboard, poured out a second dose of the remedy against worry, and took it herself. "What sort of character does the Lord President bear? " she asked when she had emptied her glass.

This seemed to be an extraordinary question to put, under the circumstances. Mr. Sarrazin answered it, however, to the best of his ability. "An excellent character, " he said—"that's the unaccountable part of it. I hear that he is one of the most careful and considerate men who ever sat on the bench. Excuse me, Mrs. Presty, I didn't intend to produce that impression on you. "

"What impression, Mr. Sarrazin? "

"You look as if you thought there was some excuse for the judge. "

"That's exactly what I do think. "

"You find an excuse for him? "

"I do. "

"What is it, ma'am? "

"Constitutional infirmity, sir. "

"May I ask of what nature? "

"You may. Gout. "

Mr. Sarrazin thought he understood her at last. "You know the Lord President, " he said.

Mrs. Presty denied it positively. "No, Mr. Sarrazin, I don't get at it in that way. I merely consult my experience of another official person of high rank, and apply it to the Lord President. You know that my first husband was a Cabinet Minister? "

"I have heard you say so, Mrs. Presty, on more than one occasion. "

"Very well. You may also have heard that the late Mr. Norman was a remarkably well-bred man. In and out of the House of Commons, courteous almost to a fault. One day I happened to interrupt him when he was absorbed over an Act of Parliament. Before I could apologize—I tell you this in the strictest confidence—he threw the Act of Parliament at my head. Ninety-nine women out of a hundred would have thrown it back again. Knowing his constitution, I decided on waiting a day or two. On the second day, my anticipations were realized. Mr. Norman's great toe was as big as my fist and as red as a lobster; he apologized for the Act of Parliament with tears in his eyes. Suppressed gout in Mr. Norman's temper; suppressed gout in the Lord President's temper. *He* will have a toe; and, if I can prevail upon my daughter to call upon him, I have not the least doubt he will apologize to her with tears in *his* eyes. "

This interesting experiment was never destined to be tried. Right or wrong, Mrs. Presty's theory remained the only explanation of the judge's severity. Mr. Sarrazin attempted to change the subject. Mrs. Presty had not quite done with it yet. "There is one more thing I want to say, " she proceeded. "Will his lordship's remarks appear in the newspapers? "

"Not a doubt of it. "

"In that case I will take care (for my daughter's sake) that no newspapers enter the house to-morrow. As for visitors, we needn't be afraid of them. Catherine is not likely to be able to leave her room; the worry of this miserable business has quite broken her down. "

The doctor returned at that moment.

Without taking the old lady's gloomy view of his patient, he admitted that she was in a low nervous condition, and he had reason to suppose, judging by her reply to a question which he had ventured to put, that she had associations with Scotland which made a visit to that country far from agreeable to her. His advice was that she should leave Edinburgh as soon as possible, and go South. If the change of climate led to no improvement, she would at least be in a position to consult the best physicians in London. In a day or two more it would be safe to remove her—provided she was not permitted to exhaust her strength by taking long railway journeys.

Having given his advice, the doctor took leave. Soon after he had gone, Kitty made her appearance, charged with a message from Mrs. Linley's room.

"Hasn't the physic sent your mother to sleep yet? " Mrs. Presty inquired.

Kitty shook her head. "Mamma wants to go away tomorrow, and no physic will make her sleep till she has seen you, and settled about it. That's what she told me to say. If *I* behaved in that way about my physic, I should catch it. "

Mrs. Presty left the room; watched by her granddaughter with an appearance of anxiety which it was not easy to understand.

"What's the matter? " Mr. Sarrazin asked. "You look very serious to-day. "

Kitty held up a warning hand. "Grandmamma sometimes listens at doors, " she whispered; "I don't want her to hear me. " She waited a little longer, and then approached Mr. Sarrazin, frowning mysteriously. "Take me up on your knee, " she said. "There's something wrong going on in this house. "

Mr. Sarrazin took her on his knee, and rashly asked what had gone wrong. Kitty's reply puzzled him.

"I go to mamma's room every morning when I wake, " the child began. "I get into her bed, and I give her a kiss, and I say 'Good-morning'—and sometimes, if she isn't in a hurry to get up, I stop in her bed, and go to sleep again. Mamma thought I was asleep this morning. I wasn't asleep—I was only quiet. I don't know why I was quiet. "

Mr. Sarrazin's kindness still encouraged her. "Well, " he said, "and what happened after that? "

"Grandmamma came in. She told mamma to keep up her spirits. She says, 'It will all be over in a few hours more. ' She says, 'What a burden it will be off your mind! ' She says, 'Is that child asleep? ' And mamma says, 'Yes. ' And grandmamma took one of mamma's towels. And I thought she was going to wash herself. What would *you* have thought? "

Mr. Sarrazin began to doubt whether he would do well to discuss Mrs. Presty's object in taking the towel. He only said, "Go on. "

"Grandmamma dipped it into the water-jug, " Kitty continued, with a grave face; "but she didn't wash herself. She went to one of mamma's boxes. Though she's so old, she's awfully strong, I can tell you. She rubbed off the luggage-label in no time. Mamma says, 'What are you doing that for? ' And grandmamma says—this is the dreadful thing that I want you to explain; oh, I can remember it all; it's like learning lessons, only much nicer—grandmamma says, 'Before the day's over, the name on your boxes will be your name no longer. '"

Mr. Sarrazin now became aware of the labyrinth into which his young friend had innocently led him. The Divorce, and the wife's inevitable return (when the husband was no longer the husband) to her maiden name—these were the subjects on which Kitty's desire for enlightenment applied to the wisest person within her reach, her mother's legal adviser.

Mr. Sarrazin tried to put her off his knee. She held him round the neck. He thought of the railway as a promising excuse, and told her he must go back to London. She held him a little tighter. "I really can't wait, my dear; " he got up as he said it. Kitty hung on to him with her legs as well as her arms, and finding the position uncomfortable, lost her temper. "Mamma's going to have a new name, " she shouted, as if the lawyer had suddenly become deaf. "Grandmamma says she must be Mrs. Norman. And I must be Miss Norman. I won't! Where's papa? I want to write to him; I know he won't allow it. Do you hear? Where's papa? "

She fastened her little hands on Mr. Sarrazin's coat collar and tried to shake him, in a fury of resolution to know what it all meant. At that critical moment Mrs. Presty opened the door, and stood petrified on the threshold.

"Hanging on to Mr. Sarrazin with her arms *and* her legs! " exclaimed the old lady. "You little wretch, which are you, a monkey or a child? "

The lawyer gently deposited Kitty on the floor.

"Mind this, Samuel, " she whispered, as he set her down on her feet, "I won't be Miss Norman. "

Mrs. Presty pointed sternly at the open door. "You were screaming just now, when quiet in the house is of the utmost importance to your mother. If I hear you again, bread and water and no doll for the rest of the week. "

Kitty retired in disgrace, and Mrs. Presty sharpened her tongue on Mr. Sarrazin next. "I'm astonished, sir, at your allowing that impudent grandchild of mine to take such liberties with you. Who would suppose that you were a married man, with children of your own? "

"That's just the reason, my dear madam, " Mr. Sarrazin smartly replied. "I romp with my own children—why not with Kitty? Can I do anything for you in London? " he went on, getting a little nearer to the door; "I leave Edinburgh by the next train. And I promise you, " he added, with the spirit of mischief twinkling in his eyes, "this shall be my last confidential interview with your grandchild. When she wants to ask any more questions, I transfer her to you. "

Mrs. Presty looked after the retreating lawyer thoroughly mystified. What "confidential interview"? What "questions"? After some consideration, her experience of her granddaughter suggested that a little exercise of mercy might be attended with the right result. She looked at a cake on the sideboard. "I have only to forgive Kitty, " she decided, "and the child will talk about it of her own accord. "

Chapter XXXI.

Mr. Herbert Linley.

Of the friends and neighbors who had associated with Herbert Linley, in bygone days, not more than two or three kept up their intimacy with him at the later time of his disgrace. Those few, it is needless to say, were men.

One of the faithful companions, who had not shrunk from him yet, had just left the London hotel at which Linley had taken rooms for Sydney Westerfield and himself—in the name of Mr. and Mrs. Herbert. This old friend had been shocked by the change for the worse which he had perceived in the fugitive master of Mount Morven. Linley's stout figure of former times had fallen away, as if he had suffered under long illness; his healthy color had faded; he made an effort to assume the hearty manner that had once been natural to him which was simply pitiable to see. "After sacrificing all that makes life truly decent and truly enjoyable for a woman, he has got nothing, not even false happiness, in return! " With that dreary conclusion the retiring visitor descended the hotel steps, and went his way along the street.

Linley returned to the newspaper which he had been reading when his friend was shown into the room.

Line by line he followed the progress of the law report, which informed its thousands of readers that his wife had divorced him, and had taken lawful possession of his child. Word by word, he dwelt with morbid attention on the terms of crushing severity in which the Lord President had spoken of Sydney Westerfield and of himself. Sentence by sentence he read the reproof inflicted on the unhappy woman whom he had vowed to love and cherish. And then—even then—urged by his own self-tormenting suspicion, he looked for more. On the opposite page there was a leading article, presenting comments on the trial, written in the tone of lofty and virtuous regret; taking the wife's side against the judge, but declaring, at the same time, that no condemnation of the conduct of the husband and the governess could be too merciless, and no misery that might overtake them in the future more than they had deserved.

He threw the newspaper on the table at his side, and thought over what he had read.

If he had done nothing else, he had drained the bitter cup to the dregs. When he looked back, he saw nothing but the life that he had wasted. When his thoughts turned to the future, they confronted a prospect empty of all promise to a man still in the prime of life. Wife and child were as completely lost to him as if they had been dead— and it was the wife's doing. Had he any right to complain? Not the shadow of a right. As the newspapers said, he had deserved it.

The clock roused him, striking the hour.

He rose hurriedly, and advanced toward the window. As he crossed the room, he passed by a mirror. His own sullen despair looked at him in the reflection of his face. "She will be back directly, " he remembered; "she mustn't see me like this! " He went on to the window to divert his mind (and so to clear his face) by watching the stream of life flowing by in the busy street. Artificial cheerfulness, assumed love in Sydney's presence—that was what his life had come to already.

If he had known that she had gone out, seeking a temporary separation, with *his* fear of self-betrayal—if he had suspected that she, too, had thoughts which must be concealed: sad forebodings of losing her hold on his heart, terrifying suspicions that he was already comparing her, to her own disadvantage, with the wife whom he had deserted—if he had made these discoveries, what would the end have been? But she had, thus far, escaped the danger of exciting his distrust. That she loved him, he knew. That she had begun to doubt his attachment to her he would not have believed, if his oldest friend had declared it on the best evidence. She had said to him, that morning, at breakfast: "There was a good woman who used to let lodgings here in London, and who was very kind to me when I was a child; " and she had asked leave to go to the house, and inquire if that friendly landlady was still living—with nothing visibly constrained in her smile, and with no faltering tone in her voice. It was not until she was out in the street that the tell-tale tears came into her eyes, and the bitter sigh broke from her, and mingled its little unheard misery with the grand rise and fall of the tumult of London life. While he was still at the window, he saw her crossing the street on her way back to him. She came into the room with her complexion heightened by exercise; she kissed him, and said with her pretty smile: "Have you been lonely without me? " Who would have supposed that the torment of distrust, and the dread of desertion, were busy at this woman's heart?

He placed a chair for her, and seating himself by her side asked if she felt tired. Every attention that she could wish for from the man whom she loved, offered with every appearance of sincerity on the surface! She met him halfway, and answered as if her mind was quite at ease.

"No, dear, I'm not tired—but I'm glad to get back. "

"Did you find your old landlady still alive? "

"Yes. But oh, so altered, poor thing! The struggle for life must have been a hard one, since I last saw her. "

"She didn't recognize you, of course? "

"Oh! no. She looked at me and my dress in great surprise and said her lodgings were hardly fit for a young lady like me. It was too sad. I said I had known her lodgings well, many years ago—and, with that to prepare her, I told her who I was. Ah, it was a melancholy meeting for both of us. She burst out crying when I kissed her; and I had to tell her that my mother was dead, and my brother lost to me in spite of every effort to find him. I asked to go into the kitchen, thinking the change would be a relief to both of us. The kitchen used to be a paradise to me in those old days; it was so warm to a half-starved child—and I always got something to eat when I was there. You have no idea, Herbert, how poor and how empty the place looked to me now. I was glad to get out of it, and go upstairs. There was a lumber-room at the top of the house; I used to play in it, all by myself. More changes met me the moment I opened the door. "

"Changes for the better? "

"My dear, it couldn't have changed for the worse! My dirty old play-room was cleaned and repaired; the lumber taken away, and a nice little bed in one corner. Some clerk in the City had taken the room—I shouldn't have known it again. But there was another surprise waiting for me; a happy surprise this time. In cleaning out the garret, what do you think the landlady found? Try to guess. "

Anything to please her! Anything to make her think that he was as fond of her as ever! "Was it something you had left behind you, " he said, "at the time when you lodged there. "

"Yes! you are right at the first guess—a little memorial of my father. Only some torn crumpled leaves from a book of children's songs that he used to teach me to sing; and a small packet of his letters, which my mother may have thrown aside and forgotten. See! I have brought them back with me; I mean to look over the letters at once— but this doesn't interest you? "

"Indeed it does. "

He made that considerate reply mechanically, as if thinking of something else. She was afraid to tell him plainly that she saw this; but she could venture to say that he was not looking well. "I have noticed it for some time past, " she confessed. "You have been accustomed to live in the country; I am afraid London doesn't agree with you. "

He admitted that she might be right; still speaking absently, still thinking of the Divorce. She laid the packet of letters and the poor relics of the old song-book on the table, and bent over him. Tenderly, and a little timidly, she put her arm around his neck. "Let us try some purer air, " she suggested; "the seaside might do you good. Don't you think so? "

"I daresay, my dear. Where shall we go? "

"Oh, I leave that to you. "

"No, Sydney. It was I who proposed coming to London. You shall decide this time. "

She submitted, and promised to think of it. Leaving him, with the first expression of trouble that had shown itself in her face, she took up the songs and put them into the pocket of her dress. On the point of removing the letters next, she noticed the newspaper on the table. "Anything interesting to-day? " she asked—and drew the newspaper toward her to look at it. He took it from her suddenly, almost roughly. The next moment he apologized for his rudeness. "There is nothing worth reading in the paper, " he said, after begging her pardon. "You don't care about politics, do you? "

Instead of answering, she looked at him attentively.

The heightened color which told of recent exercise, healthily enjoyed, faded from her face. She was silent; she was pale. A little confused, he smiled uneasily. "Surely, " he resumed, trying to speak gayly, "I haven't offended you? "

"There is something in the newspaper, " she said, "which you don't want me to read. "

He denied it—but he still kept the newspaper in his own possession. Her voice sank low; her face turned paler still.

"Is it all over? " she asked. "And is it put in the newspaper? "

"What do you mean? "

"I mean the Divorce. "

He went back again to the window and looked out. It was the easiest excuse that he could devise for keeping his face turned away from her. She followed him.

"I don't want to read it, Herbert. I only ask you to tell me if you are a free man again. "

Quiet as it was, her tone left him no alternative but to treat her brutally or to reply. Still looking out at the street, he said "Yes. "

"Free to marry, if you like? " she persisted.

He said "Yes" once more—and kept his face steadily turned away from her. She waited a while. He neither moved nor spoke.

Surviving the slow death little by little of all her other illusions, one last hope had lingered in her heart. It was killed by that cruel look, fixed on the view of the street.

"I'll try to think of a place that we can go to at the seaside. " Having said those words she slowly moved away to the door, and turned back, remembering the packet of letters. She took it up, paused, and looked toward the window. The streets still interested him. She left the room.

Chapter XXXII.

Miss Westerfield.

She locked the door of her bedchamber, and threw off her walking-dress; light as it was, she felt as if it would stifle her. Even the ribbon round her neck was more than she could endure and breathe freely. Her overburdened heart found no relief in tears. In the solitude of her room she thought of the future. The dreary foreboding of what it might be, filled her with a superstitious dread from which she recoiled. One of the windows was open already; she threw up the other to get more air. In the cooler atmosphere her memory recovered itself; she recollected the newspaper, that Herbert had taken from her. Instantly she rang for the maid. "Ask the first waiter you see downstairs for today's newspaper; any one will do, so long as I don't wait for it. " The report of the Divorce—she was in a frenzy of impatience to read what *he* had read—the report of the Divorce.

When her wish had been gratified, when she had read it from beginning to end, one vivid impression only was left on her mind. She could think of nothing but what the judge had said, in speaking of Mrs. Linley.

A cruel reproof, and worse than cruel, a public reproof, administered to the generous friend, the true wife, the devoted mother—and for what? For having been too ready to forgive the wretch who had taken her husband from her, and had repaid a hundred acts of kindness by unpardonable ingratitude.

She fell on her knees; she tried wildly to pray for inspiration that should tell her what to do. "Oh, God, how can I give that woman back the happiness of which I have robbed her! "

The composing influence of prayer on a troubled mind was something that she had heard of. It was not something that she experienced now. An overpowering impatience to make the speediest and completest atonement possessed her. Must she wait till Herbert Linley no longer concealed that he was weary of her, and cast her off? No! It should be her own act that parted them, and that did it at once. She threw open the door, and hurried half-way down the stairs before she remembered the one terrible obstacle in her way—the Divorce.

Slowly and sadly she submitted, and went back to her room.

There was no disguising it; the two who had once been husband and wife were parted irrevocably—by the wife's own act. Let him repent ever so sincerely, let him be ever so ready to return, would the woman whose faith Herbert Linley had betrayed take him back? The Divorce, the merciless Divorce, answered: —No!

She paused, thinking of the marriage that was now a marriage no more. The toilet-table was close to her; she looked absently at her haggard face in the glass. What a lost wretch she saw! The generous impulses which other women were free to feel were forbidden luxuries to her. She was ashamed of her wickedness; she was eager to sacrifice herself, for the good of the once-dear friend whom she had wronged. Useless longings! Too late! too late!

She regretted it bitterly. Why?

Comparing Mrs. Linley's prospects with hers, was there anything to justify regret for the divorced wife? She had her sweet little child to make her happy; she had a fortune of her own to lift her above sordid cares; she was still handsome, still a woman to be admired. While she held her place in the world as high as ever, what was the prospect before Sydney Westerfield? The miserable sinner would end as she had deserved to end. Absolutely dependent on a man who was at that moment perhaps lamenting the wife whom he had deserted and lost, how long would it be before she found herself an outcast, without a friend to help her—with a reputation hopelessly lost—face to face with the temptation to drown herself or poison herself, as other women had drowned themselves or poisoned themselves, when the brightest future before them was rest in death?

If she had been a few years older, Herbert Linley might never again have seen her a living creature. But she was too young to follow any train of repellent thought persistently to its end. The man she had guiltily (and yet how naturally) loved was lord and master in her heart, doubt him as she might. Even in his absence he pleaded with her to have some faith in him still.

She reviewed his language and his conduct toward her, when she had returned that morning from her walk. He had been kind and considerate; he had listened to her little story of the relics of her father, found in the garret, as if her interests were his interests. There had been nothing to disappoint her, nothing to complain of, until she had rashly attempted to discover whether he was free to make her his wife. She had only herself to blame if he was cold and distant when she had alluded to that delicate subject, on the day when he first knew that the Divorce had been granted and his child had been taken from him. And yet, he might have found a kinder way of reproving a sensitive woman than looking into the street—as if he had forgotten her in the interest of watching the strangers passing by! Perhaps he was not thinking of the strangers; perhaps his mind was dwelling fondly and regretfully on his wife?

Instinctively, she felt that her thoughts were leading her back again to a state of doubt from which her youthful hopefulness recoiled. Was there nothing she could find to do which would offer some other subject to occupy her mind than herself and her future?

Looking absently round the room, she noticed the packet of her father's letters placed on the table by her bedside.

The first three letters that she examined, after untying the packet, were briefly written, and were signed by names unknown to her. They all related to race-horses, and to cunningly devised bets which were certain to make the fortunes of the clever gamblers on the turf who laid them. Absolute indifference on the part of the winners to the ruin of the losers, who were not in the secret, was the one feeling in common, which her father's correspondents presented. In mercy to his memory she threw the letters into the empty fireplace, and destroyed them by burning.

The next letter which she picked out from the little heap was of some length, and was written in a clear and steady hand. By comparison with the blotted scrawls which she had just burned, it looked like the letter of a gentleman. She turned to the signature. The strange surname struck her; it was "Bennydeck. "

Not a common name, and not a name which seemed to be altogether unknown to her. Had she heard her father mention it at home in the time of her early childhood? There were no associations with it that she could now call to mind.

She read the letter. It addressed her father familiarly as "My dear Roderick, " and it proceeded in these words: —

"The delay in the sailing of your ship offers me an opportunity of writing to you again. My last letter told you of my father's death. I was then quite unprepared for an event which has happened, since that affliction befell me. Prepare yourself to be surprised. Our old moated house at Sandyseal, in which we have spent so many happy holidays when we were schoolfellows, is sold.

"You will be almost as sorry as I was to hear this; and you will be quite as surprised as I was, when I tell you that Sandyseal Place has become a Priory of English Nuns, of the order of St. Benedict.

"I think I see you look up from my letter, with your big black eyes staring straight before you, and say and swear that this must be one of my mystifications. Unfortunately (for I am fond of the old house in which I was born) it is only too true. The instructions in my father's will, under which Sandyseal has been sold, are peremptory. They are the result of a promise made, many years since, to his wife.

"You and I were both very young when my poor mother died; but I think you must remember that she, like the rest of her family, was a Roman Catholic.

"Having reminded you of this, I may next tell you that Sandyseal Place was my mother's property. It formed part of her marriage portion, and it was settled on my father if she died before him, and if she left no female child to survive her. I am her only child. My father was therefore dealing with his own property when he ordered the house to be sold. His will leaves the purchase money to me. I would rather have kept the house.

"But why did my mother make him promise to sell the place at his death?

"A letter, attached to my father's will, answers this question, and tells a very sad story. In deference to my mother's wishes it was kept strictly a secret from me while my father lived.

"There was a younger sister of my mother's who was the beauty of the family; loved and admired by everybody who was acquainted with her. It is needless to make this long letter longer by dwelling on the girl's miserable story. You have heard it of other girls, over and over again. She loved and trusted; she was deceived and deserted. Alone and friendless in a foreign country; her fair fame blemished;

her hope in the future utterly destroyed, she attempted to drown herself. This took place in France. The best of good women—a Sister of Charity—happened to be near enough to the river to rescue her. She was sheltered; she was pitied; she was encouraged to return to her family. The poor deserted creature absolutely refused; she could never forget that she had disgraced them. The good Sister of Charity won her confidence. A retreat which would hide her from the world, and devote her to religion for the rest of her days, was the one end to her wasted life that she longed for. That end was attained in a Priory of Benedictine Nuns, established in France. There she found protection and peace—there she passed the remaining years of her life among devoted Sister-friends—and there she died a quiet and even a happy death.

"You will now understand how my mother's grateful remembrance associated her with the interests of more than one community of Nuns; and you will not need to be told what she had in mind when she obtained my father's promise at the time of her last illness.

"He at once proposed to bequeath the house as a free gift to the Benedictines. My mother thanked him and refused. She was thinking of me. 'If our son fails to inherit the house from his father, ' she said, 'it is only right that he should have the value of the house in money. Let it be sold. '

"So here I am—rich already—with this additional sum of money in my banker's care.

"My idea is to invest it in the Funds, and to let it thrive at interest, until I grow older, and retire perhaps from service in the Navy. The later years of my life may well be devoted to the founding of a charitable institution, which I myself can establish and direct. If I die first—oh, there is a chance of it! We may have a naval war, perhaps, or I may turn out one of those incorrigible madmen who risk their lives in Arctic exploration. In case of the worst, therefore, I shall leave the interests of my contemplated Home in your honest and capable hands. For the present good-by, and a prosperous voyage outward bound. "

So the letter ended.

Sydney dwelt with reluctant attention on the latter half of it. The story of the unhappy favorite of the family had its own melancholy and sinister interest for her. She felt the foreboding that it might, in some of its circumstances, be her story too—without the peaceful end. Into what community of merciful women could *she* be received, in her sorest need? What religious consolations would encourage her penitence? What prayers, what hopes, would reconcile her, on her death-bed, to the common doom?

She sighed as she folded up Captain Bennydeck's letter and put it in her bosom, to be read again. "If my lot had fallen among good people, " she thought, "perhaps I might have belonged to the Church which took care of that poor girl. "

Her mind was still pursuing its own sad course of inquiry; she was wondering in what part of England Sandyseal might be; she was asking herself if the Nuns at the old moated house ever opened their doors to women, whose one claim on their common Christianity was the claim to be pitied—when she heard Linley's footsteps approaching the door.

His tone was kind; his manner was gentle; his tender interest in her seemed to have revived. Her long absence had alarmed him; he feared she might be ill. "I was only thinking, " she said. He smiled, and sat down by her, and asked if she had been thinking of the place that they should go to when they left London.

Chapter XXXIII.

Mrs. Romsey.

The one hotel in Sandyseal was full, from the topmost story to the ground floor; and by far the larger half of the landlord's guests were invalids sent to him by the doctors.

To persons of excitable temperament, in search of amusement, the place offered no attractions. Situated at the innermost end of a dull little bay, Sandyseal—so far as any view of the shipping in the Channel was concerned—might have been built on a remote island in the Pacific Ocean. Vessels of any importance kept well out of the way of treacherous shoals and currents lurking at the entrance of the bay. The anchorage ground was good; but the depth of water was suited to small vessels only—to shabby old fishing-smacks which seldom paid their expenses, and to dirty little coasters carrying coals and potatoes. At the back of the hotel, two slovenly rows of cottages took their crooked course inland. Sailing masters of yachts, off duty, sat and yawned at the windows; lazy fishermen looked wearily at the weather over their garden gates; and superfluous coastguards gathered together in a wooden observatory, and leveled useless telescopes at an empty sea. The flat open country, with its few dwarf trees and its mangy hedges, lay prostrate under the sky in all the desolation of solitary space, and left the famous restorative air free to build up dilapidated nerves, without an object to hinder its passage at any point of the compass. The lonely drab-colored road that led to the nearest town offered to visitors, taking airings, a view of a low brown object in the distance, said to be the convent in which the Nuns lived, secluded from mortal eyes. At one side of the hotel, the windows looked on a little wooden pier, sadly in want of repair. On the other side, a walled inclosure accommodated yachts of light tonnage, stripped of their rigging, and sitting solitary on a bank of mud until their owners wanted them. In this neighborhood there was a small outlying colony of shops: one that sold fruit and fish; one that dealt in groceries and tobacco; one shut up, with a bill in the window inviting a tenant; and one, behind the Methodist Chapel, answering the double purpose of a post-office and a storehouse for ropes and coals. Beyond these objects there was nothing (and this was the great charm of the place) to distract the attention of invalids, following the doctor's directions, and from morning to night taking care of their health.

The time was evening; the scene was one of the private sitting-rooms in the hotel; and the purpose in view was a little tea-party.

Rich Mrs. Romsey, connected with commerce as wife of the chief partner in the firm of Romsey & Renshaw, was staying at the hotel in the interests of her three children. They were of delicate constitution; their complete recovery, after severe illness which had passed from one to the other, was less speedy than had been anticipated; and the doctor had declared that the nervous system was, in each case, more or less in need of repair. To arrive at this conclusion, and to recommend a visit to Sandyseal, were events which followed each other (medically speaking) as a matter of course.

The health of the children had greatly improved; the famous air had agreed with them, and the discovery of new playfellows had agreed with them. They had made acquaintance with Lady Myrie's well-bred boys, and with Mrs. Norman's charming little Kitty. The most cordial good-feeling had established itself among the mothers. Owing a return for hospitalities received from Lady Myrie and Mrs. Norman, Mrs. Romsey had invited the two ladies to drink tea with her in honor of an interesting domestic event. Her husband, absent on the Continent for some time past, on business connected with his firm, had returned to England, and had that evening joined his wife and children at Sandyseal.

Lady Myrie had arrived, and Mr. Romsey had been presented to her. Mrs. Norman, expected to follow, was represented by a courteous note of apology. She was not well that evening, and she begged to be excused.

"This is a great disappointment, " Mrs. Romsey said to her husband. "You would have been charmed with Mrs. Norman—highly-bred, accomplished, a perfect lady. And she leaves us to-morrow. The departure will not be an early one; and I shall find an opportunity, my dear, of introducing you to my friend and her sweet little Kitty. "

Mr. Romsey looked interested for a moment, when he first heard Mrs. Norman's name. After that, he slowly stirred his tea, and seemed to be thinking, instead of listening to his wife.

"Have you made the lady's acquaintance here? " he inquired.

"Yes—and I hope I have made a friend for life, " Mrs. Romsey said with enthusiasm.

"And so do I, " Lady Myrie added.

Mr. Romsey went on with his inquiries.

"Is she a handsome woman? "

Both the ladies answered the question together. Lady Myrie described Mrs. Norman, in one dreadful word, as "Classical. " By comparison with this, Mrs. Romsey's reply was intelligible. "Not even illness can spoil her beauty! "

"Including the headache she has got to-night? " Mr. Romsey suggested.

"Don't be ill-natured, dear! Mrs. Norman is here by the advice of one of the first physicians in London; she has suffered under serious troubles, poor thing. "

Mr. Romsey persisted in being ill-natured. "Connected with her husband? " he asked.

Lady Myrie entered a protest. She was a widow; and it was notorious among her friends that the death of her husband had been the happiest event in her married life. But she understood her duty to herself as a respectable woman.

"I think, Mr. Romsey, you might have spared that cruel allusion, " she said with dignity.

Mr. Romsey apologized. He had his reasons for wishing to know something more about Mrs. Norman; he proposed to withdraw his last remark, and to put his inquiries under another form. Might he ask his wife if anybody had seen *Mr.* Norman?

"No. "

"Or heard of him? "

Mrs. Romsey answered in the negative once more, and added a question on her own account. What did all this mean?

"It means, " Lady Myrie interposed, "what we poor women are all exposed to—scandal. " She had not yet forgiven Mr. Romsey's allusion, and she looked at him pointedly as she spoke. There are some impenetrable men on whom looks produce no impression. Mr. Romsey was one of them. He turned to his wife, and said, quietly: "What I mean is, that I know more of Mrs. Norman than you do. I have heard of her—never mind how or where. She is a lady who has been celebrated in the newspapers. Don't be alarmed. She is no less a person than the divorced Mrs. Linley. "

The two ladies looked at each other in blank dismay. Restrained by a sense of conjugal duty, Mrs. Romsey only indulged in an exclamation. Lady Myrie, independent of restraint, expressed her opinion, and said: "Quite impossible! "

"The Mrs. Norman whom I mean, " Mr. Romsey went on, "has, as I have been told, a mother living. The old lady has been twice married. Her name is Mrs. Presty. "

This settled the question. Mrs. Presty was established, in her own proper person, with her daughter and grandchild at the hotel. Lady Myrie yielded to the force of evidence; she lifted her hands in horror: "This is too dreadful! "

Mrs. Romsey took a more compassionate view of the disclosure. "Surely the poor lady is to be pitied? " she gently suggested.

Lady Myrie looked at her friend in astonishment. "My dear, you must have forgotten what the judge said about her. Surely you read the report of the case in the newspapers? "

"No; I heard of the trial, and that's all. What did the judge say? "

"Say? " Lady Myrie repeated. "What did he not say! His lordship declared that he had a great mind not to grant the Divorce at all. He spoke of this dreadful woman who has deceived us in the severest terms; he said she had behaved in a most improper manner. She had encouraged the abominable governess; and if her husband had yielded to temptation, it was her fault. And more besides, that I don't remember. "

Mr. Romsey's wife appealed to him in despair. "What am I to do? " she asked, helplessly.

"Do nothing, " was the wise reply. "Didn't you say she was going away to-morrow? "

"That's the worst of it! " Mrs. Romsey declared. "Her little girl Kitty gives a farewell dinner to-morrow to our children; and I've promised to take them to say good-by. "

Lady Myrie pronounced sentence without hesitation. "Of course your girls mustn't go. Daughters! Think of their reputations when they grow up! "

"Are you in the same scrape with my wife? " Mr. Romsey asked.

Lady Myrie corrected his language. "I have been deceived in the same way, " she said. "Though my children are boys (which perhaps makes a difference) I feel it is my duty as a mother not to let them get into bad company. I do nothing myself in an underhand way. No excuses! I shall send a note and tell Mrs. Norman why she doesn't see my boys to-morrow. "

"Isn't that a little hard on her? " said merciful Mrs. Romsey.

Mr. Romsey agreed with his wife, on grounds of expediency. "Never make a row if you can help it, " was the peaceable principle to which this gentleman committed himself. "Send word that the children have caught colds, and get over it in that way. "

Mrs. Romsey looked gratefully at her admirable husband. "Just the thing! " she said, with an air of relief.

Lady Myrie's sense of duty expressed itself, with the strictest adherence to the laws of courtesy. She rose, smiled resignedly, and said, "Good-night. "

Almost at the same moment, innocent little Kitty astonished her mother and her grandmother by appearing before them in her night-gown, after she had been put to bed nearly two hours since.

"What will this child do next? " Mrs. Presty exclaimed.

Kitty told the truth. "I can't go to sleep, grandmamma. "

"Why not, my darling? " her mother asked.

"I'm so excited, mamma. "

"About what, Kitty? "

"About my dinner-party to-morrow. Oh, " said the child, clasping her hands earnestly as she thought of her playfellows, "I do so hope it will go off well! "

The Evil Genius

Chapter XXXIV.

Mrs. Presty.

Belonging to the generation which has lived to see the Age of Hurry, and has no sympathy with it, Mrs. Presty entered the sitting-room at the hotel, two hours before the time that had been fixed for leaving Sandyseal, with her mind at ease on the subject of her luggage. "My boxes are locked, strapped and labeled; I hate being hurried. What's that you're reading? " she asked, discovering a book on her daughter's lap, and a hasty action on her daughter's part, which looked like trying to hide it.

Mrs. Norman made the most common, and—where the object is to baffle curiosity—the most useless of prevaricating replies. When her mother asked her what she was reading she answered: "Nothing. "

"Nothing! " Mrs. Presty repeated with an ironical assumption of interest. "The work of all others, Catherine, that I most want to read. " She snatched up the book; opened it at the first page, and discovered an inscription in faded ink which roused her indignation. "To dear Catherine, from Herbert, on the anniversary of our marriage. " What unintended mockery in those words, read by the later light of the Divorce! "Well, this is mean, " said Mrs. Presty. "Keeping that wretch's present, after the public exposure which he has forced on you. Oh, Catherine! "

Catherine was not quite so patient with her mother as usual. "Keeping my best remembrance of the happy time of my life, " she answered.

"Misplaced sentiment, " Mrs. Presty declared; "I shall put the book out of the way. Your brain is softening, my dear, under the influence of this stupefying place. "

Catherine asserted her own opinion against her mother's opinion, for the second time. "I have recovered my health at Sandyseal, " she said. "I like the place, and I am sorry to leave it. "

"Give me the shop windows, the streets, the life, the racket, and the smoke of London, " cried Mrs. Presty. "Thank Heaven, these rooms are let over our heads, and out we must go, whether we like it or not. "

This expression of gratitude was followed by a knock at the door, and by a voice outside asking leave to come in, which was, beyond all doubt, the voice of Randal Linley. With Catherine's book still in her possession, Mrs. Presty opened the table-drawer, threw it in, and closed the drawer with a bang. Discovering the two ladies, Randal stopped in the doorway, and stared at them in astonishment.

"Didn't you expect to see us? " Mrs. Presty inquired.

"I heard you were here, from our friend Sarrazin, " Randal said; "but I expected to see Captain Bennydeck. Have I mistaken the number? Surely these are his rooms? "

Catherine attempted to explain. "They *were* Captain Bennydeck's rooms, " she began; "but he was so kind, although we are perfect strangers to him—"

Mrs. Presty interposed. "My dear Catherine, you have not had my advantages; you have not been taught to make a complicated statement in few words. Permit me to seize the points (in the late Mr. Presty's style) and to put them in the strongest light. This place, Randal, is always full; and we didn't write long enough beforehand to secure rooms. Captain Bennydeck happened to be downstairs when he heard that we were obliged to go away, and that one of us was a lady in delicate health. This sweetest of men sent us word that we were welcome to take his rooms, and that he would sleep on board his yacht. Conduct worthy of Sir Charles Grandison himself. When I went downstairs to thank him, he was gone—and here we have been for nearly three weeks; sometimes seeing the Captain's yacht, but, to our great surprise, never seeing the Captain himself. "

"There's nothing to be surprised at, Mrs. Presty. Captain Bennydeck likes doing kind things, and hates being thanked for it. I expected him to meet me here to-day. "

Catherine went to the window. "He is coming to meet you, " she said. "There is his yacht in the bay. "

"And in a dead calm, " Randal added, joining her. "The vessel will not get here, before I am obliged to go away again. "

Catherine looked at him timidly. "Do I drive you away? " she asked, in tones that faltered a little.

Randal wondered what she could possibly be thinking of and acknowledged it in so many words.

"She is thinking of the Divorce, " Mrs. Presty explained. "You have heard of it, of course; and perhaps you take your brother's part? "

"I do nothing of the sort, ma'am. My brother has been in the wrong from first to last. " He turned to Catherine. "I will stay with you as long as I can, with the greatest pleasure, " he said earnestly and kindly. "The truth is, I am on my way to visit some friends; and if Captain Bennydeck had got here in time to see me, I must have gone away to the junction to catch the next train westward, just as I am going now. I had only two words to say to the Captain about a person in whom he is interested—and I can say them in this way. " He wrote in pencil on one of his visiting cards, and laid it on the table. "I shall be back in London, in a week, " he resumed, "and you will tell me at what address I can find you. In the meanwhile, I miss Kitty. Where is she? "

Kitty was sent for. She entered the room looking unusually quiet and subdued—but, discovering Randal, became herself again in a moment, and jumped on his knee.

"Oh, Uncle Randal, I'm so glad to see you! " She checked herself, and looked at her mother. "May I call him Uncle Randal? " she asked. "Or has *he* changed his name, too? "

Mrs. Presty shook a warning forefinger at her granddaughter, and reminded Kitty that she had been told not to talk about names. Randal saw the child's look of bewilderment, and felt for her. "She may talk as she pleases to me, " he said "but not to strangers. She understands that, I am sure. "

Kitty laid her cheek fondly against her uncle's cheek. "Everything is changed, " she whispered. "We travel about; papa has left us, and Syd has left us, and we have got a new name. We are Norman now. I wish I was grown up, and old enough to understand it. "

Randal tried to reconcile her to her own happy ignorance. "You have got your dear good mother, " he said, "and you have got me, and you have got your toys—"

"And some nice boys and girls to play with, " cried Kitty, eagerly following the new suggestion. "They are all coming here directly to dine with me. You will stay and have dinner too, won't you? "

Randal promised to dine with Kitty when they met in London. Before he left the room he pointed to his card on the table. "Let my friend see that message, " he said, as he went out.

The moment the door had closed on him, Mrs. Presty startled her daughter by taking up the card and looking at what Randal had written on it. "It isn't a letter, Catherine; and you know how superior I am to common prejudices. " With that defense of her proceeding, she coolly read the message:

"I am sorry to say that I can tell you nothing more of your old friend's daughter as yet. I can only repeat that she neither needs nor deserves the help that you kindly offer to her. "

Mrs. Presty laid the card down again and owned that she wished Randal had been a little more explicit. "Who can it be? " she wondered. "Another young hussy gone wrong? "

Kitty turned to her mother with a look of alarm. "What's a hussy? " she asked. "Does grandmamma mean me? " The great hotel clock in the hall struck two, and the child's anxieties took a new direction. "Isn't it time my little friends came to see me? " she said.

It was half an hour past the time. Catherine proposed to send to Lady Myrie and Mrs. Romsey, and inquire if anything had happened to cause the delay. As she told Kitty to ring the bell, the waiter came in with two letters, addressed to Mrs. Norman.

Mrs. Presty had her own ideas, and drew her own conclusions. She watched Catherine attentively. Even Kitty observed that her mother's face grew paler and paler as she read the letters. "You look as if you were frightened, mamma. " There was no reply. Kitty began to feel so uneasy on the subject of her dinner and her guests, that she actually ventured on putting a question to her grandmother.

"Will they be long, do you think, before they come? " she asked.

The old lady's worldly wisdom had passed, by this time from a state of suspicion to a state of certainty. "My child, " she answered, "they won't come at all. "

Kitty ran to her mother, eager to inquire if what Mrs. Presty had told her could possibly be true. Before a word had passed her lips, she shrank back, too frightened to speak.

Never, in her little experience, had she been startled by such a look in her mother's face as the look that confronted her now. For the first time Catherine saw her child trembling at the sight of her. Before that discovery, the emotions that shook her under the insult which she had received lost their hold. She caught Kitty up in her arms. "My darling, my angel, it isn't you I am thinking of. I love you! —I love you! In the whole world there isn't such a good child, such a sweet, lovable, pretty child as you are. Oh, how disappointed she looks—she's crying. Don't break my heart! —don't cry! " Kitty held up her head, and cleared her eyes with a dash of her hand. "I won't cry, mamma. " And child as she was, she was as good as her word. Her mother looked at her and burst into tears.

Perversely reluctant, the better nature that was in Mrs. Presty rose to the surface, forced to show itself. "Cry, Catherine, " she said kindly; "it will do you good. Leave the child to me. "

With a gentleness that astonished Kitty, she led her little granddaughter to the window, and pointed to the public walk in front of the house. "I know what will comfort you, " the wise old woman began; "look out of the window. " Kitty obeyed.

"I don't see my little friends coming, " she said. Mrs. Presty still pointed to some object on the public walk. "That's better than nothing, isn't it? " she persisted. "Come with me to the maid; she shall go with you, and take care of you. " Kitty whispered, "May I give mamma a kiss first? " Sensible Mrs. Presty delayed the kiss for a while. "Wait till you come back, and then you can tell your mamma what a treat you have had. " Arrived at the door on their way out, Kitty whispered again: "I want to say something"—"Well, what is it? "—"Will you tell the donkey-boy to make him gallop? "—"I'll tell the boy he shall have sixpence if you are satisfied; and you will see what he does then. " Kitty looked up earnestly in her grandmother's face. "What a pity it is you are not always like what you are now! " she said. Mrs. Presty actually blushed.

Chapter XXXV.

Captain Bennydeck.

For some time, Catherine and her mother had been left together undisturbed.

Mrs. Presty had read (and destroyed) the letters of Lady Myrie and Mrs. Romsey, with the most unfeigned contempt for the writers— had repeated what the judge had really said, as distinguished from Lady Myrie's malicious version of it—and had expressed her intention of giving Catherine a word of advice, when she was sufficiently composed to profit by it. "You have recovered your good looks, after that fit of crying, " Mrs. Presty admitted, "but not your good spirits. What is worrying you now? "

"I can't help thinking of poor Kitty. "

"My dear, the child wants nobody's pity. She's blowing away all her troubles by a ride in the fresh air, on the favorite donkey that she feeds every morning. Yes, yes, you needn't tell me you are in a false position; and nobody can deny that it's shameful to make the child feel it. Now listen to me. Properly understood, those two spiteful women have done you a kindness. They have as good as told you how to protect yourself in the time to come. Deceive the vile world, Catherine, as it deserves to be deceived. Shelter yourself behind a respectable character that will spare you these insults in the future. " In the energy of her conviction, Mrs. Presty struck her fist on the table, and finished in three audacious words: "Be a Widow! "

It was plainly said—and yet Catherine seemed to be at a loss to understand what her mother meant.

"Don't doubt about it, " Mrs. Presty went on; "do it. Think of Kitty if you won't think of yourself. In a few years more she will be a young lady. She may have an offer of marriage which may be everything we desire. Suppose her sweetheart's family is a religious family; and suppose your Divorce, and the judge's remarks on it, are discovered. What will happen then? "

"Is it possible that you are in earnest? " Catherine asked. "Have you seriously thought of the advice that you are giving me? Setting aside the deceit, you know as well as I do that Kitty would ask questions. Do you think I can tell my child that her father is dead? A lie—and such a dreadful lie as that? "

"Nonsense! " said Mrs. Presty..

"Nonsense? " Catherine repeated indignantly.

"Rank nonsense, " her mother persisted. "Hasn't your situation forced you to lie already? When the child asks why her father and her governess have left us, haven't you been obliged to invent excuses which are lies? If the man who was once your husband isn't as good as dead to *you*, I should like to know what your Divorce means! My poor dear, do you think you can go on as you are going on now? How many thousands of people have read the newspaper account of the trial? How many hundreds of people—interested in a handsome woman like you—will wonder why they never see Mr. Norman? What? You will go abroad again? Go where you may, you will attract attention; you will make an enemy of every ugly woman who looks at you. Strain at a gnat, Catherine, and swallow a camel. It's only a question of time. Sooner or later you will be a Widow. Here's the waiter again. What does the man want now? "

The waiter answered by announcing:

"Captain Bennydeck. "

Catherine's mother was nearer to the door than Catherine; she attracted the Captain's attention first. He addressed his apologies to her. "Pray excuse me for disturbing you—"

Mrs. Presty had an eye for a handsome man, irrespective of what his age might be. In the language of the conjurors a "magic change" appeared in her; she became brightly agreeable in a moment.

"Oh, Captain Bennydeck, you mustn't make excuses for coming into your own room! "

Captain Bennydeck went on with his excuses, nevertheless. "The landlady tells me that I have unluckily missed seeing Mr. Randal Linley, and that he has left a message for me. I shouldn't otherwise have ventured—"

Mrs. Presty stopped him once more. The Captain's claim to the Captain's rooms was the principle on which she took her stand. She revived the irresistible smiles which had conquered Mr. Norman and Mr. Presty. "No ceremony, I beg and pray! You are at home here— take the easy-chair! "

Catherine advanced a few steps; it was time to stop her mother, if the thing could be done. She felt just embarrassment enough to heighten her color, and to show her beauty to the greatest advantage. It literally staggered the Captain, the moment he looked at her. His customary composure, as a well-bred man, deserted him; he bowed confusedly; he had not a word to say. Mrs. Presty seized her opportunity, and introduced them to each other. "My daughter Mrs. Norman—Captain Bennydeck. " Compassionating him under the impression that he was a shy man, Catherine tried to set him at his ease. "I am indeed glad to have an opportunity of thanking you, " she said, inviting him by a gesture to be seated. "In this delightful air, I have recovered my health, and I owe it to your kindness. "

The Captain regained his self-possession. Expressions of gratitude had been addressed to him which, in his modest estimate of himself, he could not feel that he had deserved.

"You little know, " he replied, "under what interested motives I have acted. When I established myself in this hotel, I was fairly driven out of my yacht by a guest who went sailing with me. "

Mrs. Presty became deeply interested. "Dear me, what did he do? "

Captain Bennydeck answered gravely: "He snored. "

Catherine was amused; Mrs. Presty burst out laughing; the Captain's dry humor asserted itself as quaintly as ever. "This is no laughing matter, " he resumed, looking at Catherine. "My vessel is a small one. For two nights the awful music of my friend's nose kept me sleepless. When I woke him, and said, 'Don't snore, ' he apologized in the sweetest manner, and began again. On the third day I anchored in the bay here, determined to get a night's rest on shore. A dispute about the price of these rooms offered them to me. I sent a note of apology on board—and slept peacefully. The next morning, my sailing master informed me that there had been what he called 'a little swell in the night. ' He reported the sounds made by my friend on this occasion to have been the awful sounds of seasickness. 'The gentleman left the yacht, sir, the first thing this morning, ' he said; 'and he's gone home by railway. ' On the day when you happened to arrive, my cabin was my own again; and I can honestly thank you for relieving me of my rooms. Do you make a long stay, Mrs. Norman? "

Catherine answered that they were going to London by the next train. Seeing Randal's card still unnoticed on the table, she handed it to the Captain.

"Is Mr. Linley an old friend of yours? " he asked, as he took the card.

Mrs. Presty hastened to answer in the affirmative for her daughter. It was plain that Randal had discreetly abstained from mentioning his true connection with them. Would he preserve the same silence if the Captain spoke of his visit to Mrs. Norman, when he and his friend met next? Mrs. Presty's mind might have been at ease on that subject, if she had known how to appreciate Randal's character and Randal's motives. The same keen sense of the family disgrace, which had led him to conceal from Captain Bennydeck his brother's illicit relations with Sydney Westerfield, had compelled him to keep secret his former association, as brother-in-law, with the divorced wife. Her change of name had hitherto protected her from discovery by the Captain, and would in all probability continue to protect her in the future. The good Bennydeck had been enjoying himself at sea when the Divorce was granted, and when the newspapers reported the proceedings. He rarely went to his club, and he never associated with persons of either sex to whom gossip and scandal are as the breath of their lives. Ignorant of these circumstances, and remembering what had happened on that day, Mrs. Presty looked at him with some anxiety on her daughter's account, while he was reading the message on Randal's card. There was little to see. His fine face expressed a quiet sorrow, and he sighed as he put the card back in his pocket.

An interval of silence followed. Captain Bennydeck was thinking over the message which he had just read. Catherine and her mother were looking at him with the same interest, inspired by very different motives. The interview so pleasantly begun was in some danger of lapsing into formality and embarrassment, when a new personage appeared on the scene.

Kitty had returned in triumph from her ride. "Mamma! the donkey did more than gallop—he kicked, and I fell off. Oh, I'm not hurt! " cried the child, seeing the alarm in her mother's face. "Tumbling off is such a funny sensation. It isn't as if you fell on the ground; it's as if the ground came up to *you* and said—Bump! " She had got as far as that, when the progress of her narrative was suspended by the discovery of a strange gentleman in the room.

The smile that brightened the captain's face, when Kitty opened the door, answered for him as a man who loved children. "Your little girl, Mrs. Norman? " he said.

"Yes. "

(A common question and a common reply. Nothing worth noticing, in either the one or the other, at the time—and yet they proved to be important enough to turn Catherine's life into a new course.)

In the meanwhile, Kitty had been whispering to her mother. She wanted to know the strange gentleman's name. The Captain heard her. "My name is Bennydeck, " he said; "will you come to me? "

Kitty had heard the name mentioned in connection with a yacht. Like all children, she knew a friend the moment she looked at him. "I've seen your pretty boat, sir, " she said, crossing the room to Captain Bennydeck. "Is it very nice when you go sailing? "

"If you were not going back to London, my dear, I should ask your mamma to let me take you sailing with me. Perhaps we shall have another opportunity. "

The Captain's answer delighted Kitty. "Oh, yes, tomorrow or next day! " she suggested. "Do you know where to find me in London? Mamma, where do I live, when I am in London? " Before her mother could answer, she hit on a new idea. "Don't tell me; I'll find it for myself. It's on grandmamma's boxes, and they're in the passage. "

Captain Bennydeck's eyes followed her, as she left the room, with an expression of interest which more than confirmed the favorable impression that he had already produced on Catherine. She was on the point of asking if he was married, and had children of his own, when Kitty came back, and declared the right address to be Buck's

Hotel, Sydenham. "Mamma puts things down for fear of forgetting them, " she added. "Will you put down Buck? "

The Captain took out his pocketbook, and appealed pleasantly to Mrs. Norman. "May I follow your example? " he asked. Catherine not only humored the little joke, but, gratefully remembering his kindness, said: "Don't forget, when you are in London, that Kitty's invitation is my invitation, too. " At the same moment, punctual Mrs. Presty looked at her watch, and reminded her daughter that railways were not in the habit of allowing passengers to keep them waiting. Catherine rose, and gave her hand to the Captain at parting. Kitty improved on her mother's form of farewell; she gave him a kiss and whispered a little reminder of her own: "There's a river in London— don't forget your boat. "

Captain Bennydeck opened the door for them, secretly wishing that he could follow Mrs. Norman to the station and travel by the same train.

Mrs. Presty made no attempt to remind him that she was still in the room. Where her family interests were concerned, the old lady was capable (on very slight encouragement) of looking a long way into the future. She was looking into the future now. The Captain's social position was all that could be desired; he was evidently in easy pecuniary circumstances; he admired Catherine and Catherine's child. If he only proved to be a single man, Mrs. Presty's prophetic soul, without waiting an instant to reflect, perceived a dazzling future. Captain Bennydeck approached to take leave. "Not just yet, " pleaded the most agreeable of women; "my luggage was ready two hours ago. Sit down again for a few minutes. You seem to like my little granddaughter. "

"If I had such a child as that, " the Captain answered, "I believe I should be the happiest man living. "

"Ah, my dear sir, all isn't gold that glitters, " Mrs. Presty remarked. "That proverb must have been originally intended to apply to children. May I presume to make you the subject of a guess? I fancy you are not a married man. "

The Captain looked a little surprised. "You are quite right, " he said; "I have never been married. "

At a later period, Mrs. Presty owned that she felt an inclination to reward him for confessing himself to be a bachelor, by a kiss. He innocently checked that impulse by putting a question. "Had you any particular reason, " he asked, "for guessing that I was a single man? "

Mrs. Presty modestly acknowledged that she had only her own experience to help her. "You wouldn't be quite so fond of other people's children, " she said, "if you were a married man. Ah, your time will come yet—I mean your wife will come. "

He answered this sadly. "My time has gone by. I have never had the opportunities that have been granted to some favored men. " He thought of the favored man who had married Mrs. Norman. Was her husband worthy of his happiness? "Is Mr. Norman with you at this place? " the Captain asked.

Serious issues depended on the manner in which this question was answered. For one moment, and for one moment only, Mrs. Presty hesitated. Then (in her daughter's interest, of course) she put Catherine in the position of a widow, in the least blamable of all possible ways, by honestly owning the truth.

"There is no Mr. Norman, " she said.

"Your daughter is a widow! " cried the Captain, perfectly unable to control his delight at that discovery.

"What else should she be? " Mrs. Presty replied, facetiously.

What else, indeed! If "no Mr. Norman" meant (as it must surely mean) that Mr. Norman was dead, and if the beautiful mother of Kitty was an honest woman, her social position was beyond a doubt. Captain Bennydeck felt a little ashamed of his own impetuosity. Before he had made up his mind what to say next, the unlucky waiter (doomed to be a cause of disturbance on that day) appeared again.

"I beg your pardon, ma'am, " he said; "the lady and gentleman who have taken these rooms have just arrived. "

Mrs. Presty got up in a hurry, and cordially shook hands with the Captain. Looking round, she took up the railway guide and her knitting left on the table. Was there anything else left about? There was nothing to be seen. Mrs. Presty crossed the passage to her daughter's bedroom, to hurry the packing. Captain Bennydeck went downstairs, on his way back to the yacht.

In the hall of the hotel he passed the lady and gentleman—and, of course, noticed the lady. She was little and dark and would have been pretty, if she had not looked ill and out of spirits. What would he have said, what would he have done, if he had known that those two strangers were Randal Linley's brother and Roderick Westerfield's daughter?

Chapter XXXVI

Mr. and Mrs. Herbert.

The stealthy influence of distrust fastens its hold on the mind by slow degrees. Little by little it reaches its fatal end, and disguises delusion successfully under the garb of truth.

Day after day, the false conviction grew on Sydney's mind that Herbert Linley was comparing the life he led now with the happier life which he remembered at Mount Morven. Day after day, her unreasoning fear contemplated the time when Herbert Linley would leave her friendless, in the world that had no place in it for women like herself. Delusion—fatal delusion that looked like truth! Morally weak as he might be, the man whom she feared to trust had not yet entirely lost the sense which birth and breeding had firmly fastened in him—the sense of honor. Acting under that influence, he was (if the expression may be permitted) consistent even in inconsistency. With equal sincerity of feeling, he reproached himself for his infidelity toward the woman whom he had deserted, and devoted himself to his duty toward the woman whom he had misled. In Sydney's presence—suffer as he might under the struggle to maintain his resolution when he was alone—he kept his intercourse with her studiously gentle in manner, and considerate in language; his conduct offered assurances for the future which she could only see through the falsifying medium of her own distrust.

In the delusion that now possessed her she read, over and over again, the letter which Captain Bennydeck had addressed to her father; she saw, more and more clearly, the circumstances which associated her situation with the situation of the poor girl who had closed her wasted life among the nuns in a French convent.

Two results followed on this state of things.

When Herbert asked to what part of England they should go, on leaving London, she mentioned Sandyseal as a place that she had heard of, and felt some curiosity to see. The same day—bent on pleasing her, careless where he lived now, at home or abroad—he wrote to engage rooms at the hotel.

A time followed, during which they were obliged to wait until rooms were free. In this interval, brooding over the melancholy absence of a friend or relative in whom she could confide, her morbid dread of the future decided her on completing the parallel between herself and that other lost creature of whom she had read. Sydney opened communication anonymously with the Benedictine community at Sandyseal.

She addressed the Mother Superior; telling the truth about herself with but one concealment, the concealment of names. She revealed her isolated position among her fellow-creatures; she declared her fervent desire to repent of her wickedness, and to lead a religious life; she acknowledged her misfortune in having been brought up by persons careless of religion, and she confessed to having attended a Protestant place of worship, as a mere matter of form connected with the duties of a teacher at a school. "The religion of any Christian woman who will help me to be more like herself, " she wrote, "is the religion to which I am willing and eager to belong. If I come to you in my distress, will you receive me? " To that simple appeal, she added a request that an answer might be addressed to "S. W., Post-office, Sandyseal. "

When Captain Bennydeck and Sydney Westerfield passed each other as strangers, in the hall of the hotel, that letter had been posted in London a week since.

The servant showed "Mr. and Mrs. Herbert" into their sitting-room, and begged that they would be so good as to wait for a few minutes, while the other rooms were being prepared for them.

Sydney seated herself in silence. She was thinking of her letter, and wondering whether a reply was waiting for her at the post-office.

Moving toward the window to look at the view, Herbert paused to examine some prints hanging on the walls, which were superior as works of art to the customary decorations of a room at a hotel. If he had gone straight to the window he might have seen his divorced wife, his child, and his wife's mother, getting into the carriage which took them to the railway station.

"Come, Sydney, " he said, "and look at the sea. "

She joined him wearily, with a faint smile. It was a calm, sunny day. Bathing machines were on the beach; children were playing here and there; and white sails of pleasure boats were visible in the offing. The dullness of Sandyseal wore a quiet homely aspect which was pleasant to the eyes of strangers. Sydney said, absently, "I think I shall like the place. " And Herbert added: "Let us hope that the air will make you feel stronger. " He meant it and said it kindly—but, instead of looking at her while he spoke, he continued to look at the view. A woman sure of her position would not have allowed this trifling circumstance, even if she had observed it, to disturb her. Sydney thought of the day in London when he had persisted in looking out at the street, and returned in silence to her chair.

Had he been so unfortunate as to offend her? And in what way? As that doubt occurred to Herbert his mind turned to Catherine. *She* never took offense at trifles; a word of kindness from him, no matter how unimportant it might be, always claimed affectionate acknowledgment in the days when he was living with his wife. In another moment he had dismissed that remembrance, and could trust himself to return to Sydney.

"If you find that Sandyseal confirms your first impression, " he said, "let me know it in time, so that I may make arrangements for a longer stay. I have only taken the rooms here for a fortnight. "

"Thank you, Herbert; I think a fortnight will be long enough. "

"Long enough for you? " he asked.

Her morbid sensitiveness mistook him again; she fancied there was an undernote of irony in his tone.

"Long enough for both of us, " she replied.

He drew a chair to her side. "Do you take it for granted, " he said, smiling, "that I shall get tired of the place first? "

She shrank, poor creature, even from his smile. There was, as she thought, something contemptuous in the good-humor of it.

"We have been to many places, " she reminded him, "and we have got tired of them together. "

"Is that my fault? "

"I didn't say it was. "

He got up and approached the bell. "I think the journey has a little over-tired you, " he resumed. "Would you like to go to your room? "

"I will go to my room, if you wish it. "

He waited a little, and answered her as quietly as ever. "What I really wish, " he said, "is that we had consulted a doctor while we were in London. You seem to be very easily irritated of late. I observe a change in you, which I willingly attribute to the state of your health—"

She interrupted him. "What change do you mean? "

"It's quite possible I may be mistaken, Sydney. But I have more than once, as I think, seen something in your manner which suggests that you distrust me. "

"I distrust the evil life we are leading, " she burst out, "and I see the end of it coming. Oh, I don't blame you! You are kind and considerate, you do your best to hide it; but you have lived long enough with me to regret the woman whom you have lost. You begin to feel the sacrifice you have made—and no wonder. Say the word, Herbert, and I release you. "

"I will never say the word! "

She hesitated—first inclined, then afraid, to believe him. "I have grace enough left in me, " she went on, "to feel the bitterest repentance for the wrong that I have done to Mrs. Linley. When it ends, as it must end, in our parting, will you ask your wife—? "

Even his patience began to fail him; he refused—firmly, not angrily—to hear more. "She is no longer my wife, " he said.

Sydney's bitterness and Sydney's penitence were mingled, as opposite emotions only *can* be mingled in a woman's breast. "Will you ask your wife to forgive you? " she persisted.

"After we have been divorced at her petition? " He pointed to the window as he said it. "Look at the sea. If I was drowning out yonder, I might as well ask the sea to forgive me. "

He produced no effect on her. She ignored the Divorce; her passionate remorse asserted itself as obstinately as ever. "Mrs. Linley is a good woman, " she insisted; "Mrs. Linley is a Christian woman. "

"I have lost all claim on her—even the claim to remember her virtues, " he answered, sternly. "No more of it, Sydney! I am sorry I have disappointed you; I am sorry if you are weary of me. "

At those last words her manner changed. "Wound me as cruelly as you please, " she said, humbly. "I will try to bear it. "

"I wouldn't wound you for the world! Why do you persist in distressing me? Why do you feel suspicion of me which I have not deserved? " He stopped, and held out his hand. "Don't let us quarrel, Sydney. Which will you do? Keep your bad opinion of me, or give me a fair trial? "

She loved him dearly; she was so young—and the young are so ready to hope! Still, she struggled against herself. "Herbert! is it your pity for me that is speaking now? "

He left her in despair. "It's useless! " he said, sadly. "Nothing will conquer your inveterate distrust. "

She followed him. With a faint cry of entreaty she made him turn to her, and held him in a trembling embrace, and rested her head on his bosom. "Forgive me—be patient with me—love me. " That was all she could say.

He attempted to calm her agitation by speaking lightly. "At last, Sydney, we are friends again! " he said.

Friends? All the woman in her recoiled from that insufficient word. "Are we Lovers? " she whispered.

"Yes! "

With that assurance her anxious heart was content. She smiled; she looked out at the sea with a new appreciation of the view. "The air of this place will do me good now, " she said. "Are my eyes red, Herbert? Let me go and bathe them, and make myself fit to be seen. "

She rang the bell. The chambermaid answered it, ready to show the other rooms. She turned round at the door.

"Let's try to make our sitting-room look like home, " she suggested. "How dismal, how dreadfully like a thing that doesn't belong to us, that empty table looks! Put some of your books and my keepsakes on it, while I am away. I'll bring my work with me when I come back. "

He had left his travelers' bag on a chair, when he first came in. Now that he was alone, and under no restraint, he sighed as he unlocked the bag. "Home? " he repeated; "we have no home. Poor girl! poor unhappy girl! Let me help her to deceive herself. "

He opened the bag. The little fragile presents, which she called her "keepsakes, " had been placed by her own hands in the upper part of the bag, so that the books should not weigh on them, and had been carefully protected by wrappings of cotton wool. Taking them out, one by one, Herbert found a delicate china candlestick (intended to hold a wax taper) broken into two pieces, in spite of the care that had been taken to preserve it. Of no great value in itself, old associations made the candlestick precious to Sydney. It had been broken at the stem and could be easily mended so as to keep the accident concealed. Consulting the waiter, Herbert discovered that the fracture could be repaired at the nearest town, and that the place would be within reach when he went out for a walk. In fear of another disaster, if he put it back in the bag, he opened a drawer in the table, and laid the two fragments carefully inside, at the further end. In doing this, his hand touched something that had been already placed in the drawer. He drew it out, and found that it was a book—the same book that Mrs. Presty (surely the evil genius of the family again!) had hidden from Randal's notice, and had forgotten when she left the hotel.

Herbert instantly recognized the gilding on the cover, imitated from a design invented by himself. He remembered the inscription, and yet he read it again:

"To dear Catherine, from Herbert, on the anniversary of our marriage. "

The book dropped from his hand on the table, as if it had been a new discovery, torturing him with a new pain.

His wife (he persisted in thinking of her as his wife) must have occupied the room—might perhaps have been the person whom he had succeeded, as a guest at the hotel. Did she still value his present to her, in remembrance of old times? No! She valued it so little that she had evidently forgotten it. Perhaps her maid might have included it among the small articles of luggage when they left home, or dear little Kitty might have put it into one of her mother's trunks. In any case, there it was now, abandoned in the drawer of a table at a hotel.

"Oh, " he thought bitterly, "if I could only feel as coldly toward Catherine as she feels toward me! " His resolution had resisted much; but this final trial of his self-control was more than he could sustain. He dropped into a chair—his pride of manhood recoiled from the contemptible weakness of crying—he tried to remember that she had divorced him, and taken his child from him. In vain! in vain! He burst into tears.

Chapter XXXVII.

Mrs. Norman.

With a heart lightened by reconciliation (not the first reconciliation unhappily), with hopes revived, and sweet content restored, Sydney's serenity of mind was not quite unruffled. Her thoughts were not dwelling on the evil life which she had honestly deplored, or on the wronged wife to whom she had been eager to make atonement. Where is the woman whose sorrows are not thrown into the shade by the bright renewal of love? The one anxiety that troubled Sydney was caused by remembrance of the letter which she had sent to the convent at Sandyseal.

As her better mind now viewed it, she had doubly injured Herbert—first in distrusting him; then by appealing from him to the compassion of strangers.

If the reply for which she had rashly asked was waiting for her at that moment—if the mercy of the Mother Superior was ready to comfort and guide her—what return could she make? how could she excuse herself from accepting what was offered in kindly reply to her own petition? She had placed herself, for all she knew to the contrary, between two alternatives of ingratitude equally unendurable, equally degrading. To feel this was to feel the suspense which, to persons of excitable temperament, is of all trials the hardest to bear. The chambermaid was still in her room—Sydney asked if the post-office was near to the hotel.

The woman smiled. "Everything is near us, ma'am, in this little place. Can we send to the post-office for you? "

Sydney wrote her initials. "Ask, if you please, for a letter addressed in that way. " She handed the memorandum to the chambermaid. "Corresponding with her lover under her husband's nose! " That was how the chambermaid explained it below stairs, when the porter remarked that initials looked mysterious.

The Mother Superior had replied. Sydney trembled as she opened the letter. It began kindly.

"I believe you, my child, and I am anxious to help you. But I cannot correspond with an unknown person. If you decide to reveal yourself, it is only right to add that I have shown your letter to the Reverend Father who, in temporal as in spiritual things, is our counselor and guide. To him I must refer you, in the first instance. His wisdom will decide the serious question of receiving you into our Holy Church, and will discover, in due time, if you have a true vocation to a religious life. With the Father's sanction, you may be sure of my affectionate desire to serve you. "

Sydney put the letter back in the envelope, feeling gratefully toward the Mother Superior, but determined by the conditions imposed on her to make no further advance toward the Benedictine community.

Even if her motive in writing to the convent had remained unchallenged, the allusions to the priest would still have decided her on taking this step. The bare idea of opening her inmost heart, and telling her saddest secrets, to a man, and that man a stranger, was too repellent to be entertained for a moment. In a few lines of reply, gratefully and respectfully written, she thanked the Mother Superior, and withdrew from the correspondence.

The letter having been closed, and posted in the hotel box, she returned to the sitting-room free from the one doubt that had troubled her; eager to show Herbert how truly she believed in him, how hopefully she looked to the future.

With a happy smile on her lips she opened the door. She was on the point of asking him playfully if he had felt surprised at her long absence—when the sight that met her eyes turned her cold with terror in an instant.

His arms were stretched out on the table; his head was laid on them, despair confessed itself in his attitude; grief spoke in the deep sobbing breaths that shook him. Love and compassion restored Sydney's courage; she advanced to raise him in her arms—and stopped once more. The book on the table caught her eye. He was still unconscious of her presence; she ventured to open it. She read the inscription—looked at him—looked back at the writing—and knew the truth at last.

The rigor of the torture that she suffered paralyzed all outward expression of pain. Quietly she put the book back on the table. Quietly she touched him, and called him by his name.

He started and looked up; he made an attempt to speak to her in his customary tone. "I didn't hear you come in, " he said.

She pointed to the book, without the slightest change in her face or her manner.

"I have read the inscription to your wife, " she answered; "I have seen you while you thought you were alone; the mercy which has so long kept the truth from me is mercy wasted now. Your bonds are broken, Herbert. You are a free man. "

He affected not to have understood her. She let him try to persuade her of it, and made no reply. He declared, honestly declared, that what she had said distressed him. She listened in submissive silence. He took her hand, and kissed it. She let him kiss it, and let him drop it at her side. She frightened him; he began to fear for her reason. There was silence—long, horrid, hopeless silence.

She had left the door of the room open. One of the servants of the hotel appeared outside in the passage. He spoke to some person behind him. "Perhaps the book has been left in here, " he suggested. A gentle voice answered: "I hope the lady and gentleman will excuse me, if I ask leave to look for my book. " She stepped into the room to make her apologies.

Herbert Linley and Sydney Westerfield looked at the woman whom they had outraged. The woman whom they had outraged paused, and looked back at them.

The hotel servant was surprised at their not speaking to each other. He was a stupid man; he thought the gentlefolks were strangely unlike gentlefolks in general; they seemed not to know what to say. Herbert happened to be standing nearest to him; he felt that it would be civil to the gentleman to offer a word of explanation.

"The lady had these rooms, sir. She has come back from the station to look for a book that has been left behind. "

Herbert signed to him to go. As the man turned to obey, he drew back. Sydney had moved to the door before him, to leave the room. Herbert refused to permit it. "Stay here, " he said to her gently; "this room is yours. "

Sydney hesitated. Herbert addressed her again. He pointed to his divorced wife. "You see how that lady is looking at you, " he said; "I beg that you will not submit to insult from anybody. "

Sydney obeyed him: she returned to the room.

Catherine's voice was heard for the first time. She addressed herself to Sydney with a quiet dignity—far removed from anger, further removed still from contempt.

"You were about to leave the room, " she said. "I notice—as an act of justice to *you*—that my presence arouses some sense of shame. "

Herbert turned to Sydney; trying to recover herself, she stood near the table. "Give me the book, " he said; "the sooner this comes to an end the better for her, the better for us. " Sydney gave him the book. With a visible effort, he matched Catherine's self-control; after all, she had remembered his gift! He offered the book to her.

She still kept her eyes fixed on Sydney—still spoke to Sydney.

"Tell him, " she said, "that I refuse to receive the book. "

Sydney attempted to obey. At the first words she uttered, Herbert checked her once more.

"I have begged you already not to submit to insult. " He turned to Catherine. "The book is yours, madam. Why do you refuse to take it? "

She looked at him for the first time. A proud sense of wrong flashed at him its keenly felt indignation in her first glance. "Your hands and her hands have touched it, " she answered. "I leave it to *you* and to *her*. "

Those words stung him. "Contempt, " he said, "is bitter indeed on your lips. "

"Do you presume to resent my contempt? "

"I forbid you to insult Miss Westerfield. " With that reply, he turned to Sydney. "You shall not suffer while I can prevent it, " he said tenderly, and approached to put his arm round her. She looked at Catherine, and drew back from his embrace, gently repelling him by a gesture.

Catherine felt and respected the true delicacy, the true penitence, expressed in that action. She advanced to Sydney. "Miss Westerfield, " she said, "I will take the book—from you. "

Sydney gave back the book without a word; in her position silence was the truest gratitude. Quietly and firmly Catherine removed the blank leaf on which Herbert had written, and laid it before him on the table. "I return your inscription. It means nothing now. " Those words were steadily pronounced; not the slightest appearance of temper accompanied them. She moved slowly to the door and looked back at Sydney. "Make some allowance for what I have suffered, " she said gently. "If I have wounded you, I regret it. " The faint sound of her dress on the carpet was heard in the perfect stillness, and lost again. They saw her no more.

Herbert approached Sydney. It was a moment when he was bound to assure her of his sympathy. He felt for her. In his inmost heart he felt for her. As he drew nearer, he saw tears in her eyes; but they seemed to have risen without her knowledge. Hardly conscious of his presence, she stood before him—lost in thought.

He endeavored to rouse her. "Did I protect you from insult? " he asked.

She said absently: "Yes! "

"Will you do as I do, dear? Will you try to forget? "

She said: "I will try to atone, " and moved toward the door of her room. The reply surprised him; but it was no time then to ask for an explanation.

"Would you like to lie down, Sydney, and rest? "

"Yes. "

She took his arm. He led her to the door of her room. "Is there anything else I can do for you? " he asked.

"Nothing, thank you. "

She closed the door—and abruptly opened it again. "One thing more, " she said. "Kiss me. "

He kissed her tenderly. Returning to the sitting-room, he looked back across the passage. Her door was shut.

His head was heavy; his mind felt confused. He threw himself on the sofa—utterly exhausted by the ordeal through which he had passed. In grief, in fear, in pain, the time still comes when Nature claims her rights. The wretched worn-out man fell into a restless sleep. He was awakened by the waiter, laying the cloth for dinner. "It's just ready, sir, " the servant announced; "shall I knock at the lady's door? "

Herbert got up and went to her room.

He entered softly, fearing to disturb her if she too had slept. No sign of her was to be seen. She had evidently not rested on her bed. A morsel of paper lay on the smooth coverlet. There was only a line written on it: "You may yet be happy—and it may perhaps be my doing. "

He stood, looking at that last line of her writing, in the empty room. His despair and his submission spoke in the only words that escaped him:

"I have deserved it! "

FIFTH BOOK.

Chapter XXXVIII.

Hear the Lawyer.

"Mr. Herbert Linley, I ask permission to reply to your inquiries in writing, because it is quite likely that some of the opinions you will find here might offend you if I expressed them personally. I can relieve your anxiety on the subject of Miss Sydney Westerfield. But I must be allowed to do so in my own way—without any other restraints than those which I think it becoming to an honorable man to impose on himself.

"You are quite right in supposing that Miss Westerfield had heard me spoken of at Mount Morven, as the agent and legal adviser of the lady who was formerly your wife. What purpose led her to apply to me, under these circumstances, you will presently discover. As to the means by which she found her way to my office, I may remind you that any directory would give her the necessary information.

"Miss Westerfield's object was to tell me, in the first place, that her guilty life with you was at an end. She has left your protection—not to return to it. I was sorry to see (though she tried to hide it from me) how keenly she felt the parting. You have been dearly loved by two sweet women, and they have thrown their hearts away on you—as women will.

"Having explained the circumstances so far, Miss Westerfield next mentioned the motive which had brought her to my office. She asked if I would inform her of Mrs. Norman's address.

"This request, I confess, astonished me.

"To my mind she was, of all persons, the last who ought to contemplate communicating in any way with Mrs. Norman. I say this to you; but I refrained from saying it to her. What I did venture to do was to ask for her reasons. She answered that they were reasons which would embarrass her if she communicated them to a stranger.

"After this reply, I declined to give her the information she wanted.

"Not unprepared, as it appeared to me, for my refusal, she asked next if I was willing to tell her where she might find your brother, Mr. Randal Linley. In this case I was glad to comply with her request. She could address herself to no person worthier to advise her than your brother. In giving her his address in London, I told her that he was absent on a visit to some friends, and that he was expected to return in a week's time.

"She thanked me, and rose to go.

"I confess I was interested in her. Perhaps I thought of the time when she might have been as dear to her father as my own daughters are to me. I asked if her parents were living: they were dead. My next question was: 'Have you any friends in London? ' She answered: 'I have no friends. ' It was said with a resignation so very sad in so young a creature that I was really distressed. I ran the risk of offending her—and asked if she felt any embarrassment in respect of money. She said: 'I have some small savings from my salary when I was a governess. ' The change in her tone told me that she was alluding to the time of her residence at Mount Morven. It was impossible to look at this friendless girl, and not feel some anxiety about the lodging which she might have chosen in such a place as London. She had fortunately come to me from the railway, and had not thought yet of where she was to live. At last I was able to be of some use to her. My senior clerk took care of Miss Westerfield, and left her among respectable people, in whose house she could live cheaply and safely. Where that house is, I refuse (for her sake) to tell you. She shall not be disturbed.

"After a week had passed I received a visit from my good friend, Randal Linley.

"He had on that day seen Miss Westerfield. She had said to him what she had said to me, and had repeated the request which I thought it unwise to grant; owning to your brother, however, the motives which she had refused to confide to me. He was so strongly impressed by the sacrifice of herself which this penitent woman had made, that he was at first disposed to trust her with Mrs. Norman's address.

"Reflection, however, convinced him that her motives, pure and disinterested as they undoubtedly were, did not justify him in letting her expose herself to the consequences which might follow the proposed interview. All that he engaged to do was to repeat to Mrs. Norman what Miss Westerfield had said, and to inform the young lady of the result.

"In the intervals of business, I had felt some uneasiness when I thought of Miss Westerfield's prospects. Your good brother at once set all anxiety on this subject at rest.

"He proposed to place Miss Westerfield under the care of an old and dear friend of her late father—Captain Bennydeck. Her voluntary separation from you offered to your brother, and to the Captain, the opportunity for which they had both been waiting. Captain Bennydeck was then cruising at sea in his yacht. Immediately on his return, Miss Westerfield's inclination would be consulted, and she would no doubt eagerly embrace the opportunity of being introduced to her father's friend.

"I have now communicated all that I know, in reply to the questions which you have addressed to me. Let me earnestly advise you to make the one reparation to this poor girl which is in your power. Resign yourself to a separation which is not only for her good, but for yours. —SAMUEL SARRAZIN. "

Chapter XXXIX.

Listen to Reason.

Not having heard from Captain Bennydeck for some little time, Randal thought it desirable in Sydney's interests to make inquiries at his club. Nothing was known of the Captain's movements there. On the chance of getting the information that he wanted, Randal wrote to the hotel at Sandyseal.

The landlord's reply a little surprised him.

Some days since, the yacht had again appeared in the bay. Captain Bennydeck had landed, to all appearance in fairly good health; and had left by an early train for London. The sailing-master announced that he had orders to take the vessel back to her port—with no other explanation than that the cruise was over. This alternative in the Captain's plans (terminating the voyage a month earlier than his arrangements had contemplated) puzzled Randal. He called at his friend's private residence, only to hear from the servants that they had seen nothing of their master. Randal waited a while in London, on the chance that Bennydeck might pay him a visit.

During this interval his patience was rewarded in an unexpected manner. He discovered the Captain's address by means of a letter from Catherine, dated "Buck's Hotel, Sydenham. " Having gently reproached him for not writing to her or calling on her, she invited him to dinner at the hotel. Her letter concluded in these words: "You will only meet one person besides ourselves—your friend, and (since we last met) our friend too. Captain Bennydeck has got tired of the sea. He is staying at this hotel, to try the air of Sydenham, and he finds that it agrees with him. "

These lines set Randal thinking seriously.

To represent Bennydeck as being "tired of the sea, " and as being willing to try, in place of the breezy Channel, the air of a suburb of London, was to make excuses too perfectly futile and absurd to deceive any one who knew the Captain. In spite of the appearance of innocence which pervaded Catherine's letter, the true motive for breaking off his cruise might be found, as Randal concluded, in Catherine herself. Her residence at the sea-side, helped by the lapse of time, had restored to her personal attractions almost all they had lost under the deteriorating influences of care and grief; and her change of name must have protected her from a discovery of the Divorce which would have shocked a man so sincerely religious as Bennydeck. Had her beauty fascinated him? Was she aware of the interest that he felt in her? and was it secretly understood and returned? Randal wrote to accept the invitation; determining to present himself before the appointed hour, and to question Catherine privately, without giving her the advantage over him of preparing herself for the interview.

In the short time that passed before the day of the dinner, distressing circumstances strengthened his resolution. After months of separation, he received a visit from Herbert.

Was this man—haggard, pallid, shabby, looking at him piteously with bloodshot eyes—the handsome, pleasant, prosperous brother whom he remembered? Randal was so grieved, that he was for a moment unable to utter a word. He could only point to a seat. Herbert dropped into the chair as if he was reduced to the last extremity of fatigue. And yet he spoke roughly; he looked like an angry man brought to bay.

"I seem to frighten you, " he said.

"You distress me, Herbert, more than words can say. "

"Give me a glass of wine. I've been walking—I don't know where. A long distance; I'm dead beat. "

He drank the wine greedily. Whatever reviving effect it might otherwise have produced on him, it made no change in the threatening gloom of his manner. In a man morally weak, calamity (suffered without resisting power) breaks its way through the surface which exhibits a gentleman, and shows the naked nature which claims kindred with our ancestor the savage.

"Do you feel better, Herbert? "

He put down the empty glass, taking no notice of his brother's question. "Randal, " he said, "you know where Sydney is. "

Randal admitted it.

"Give me her address. My mind's in such a state I can't remember it; write it down. "

"No, Herbert. "

"You won't write it? and you won't give it? "

"I will do neither the one nor the other. Go back to your chair; fierce looks and clinched fists don't frighten me. Miss Westerfield is quite right in separating herself from you. And you are quite wrong in wishing to go back to her. There are my reasons. Try to understand them. And, once again, sit down. "

He spoke sternly—with his heart aching for his brother all the time. He was right. The one way is the positive way, when a man who suffers trouble is degraded by it.

The poor wretch sank under Randal's firm voice and steady eye.

"Don't be hard on me, " he said. "I think a man in my situation is to be pitied—especially by his brother. I'm not like you; I'm not accustomed to live alone. I've been accustomed to having a kind woman to talk to me, and take care of me. You don't know what it is to be used to seeing a pretty creature, always nicely dressed, always about the room—thinking so much of you, and so little of herself— and then to be left alone as I am left, out in the dark. I haven't got my wife; she has thrown me over, and taken my child away from me. And, now, Sydney's taken away from me next. I'm alone. Do you hear that? Alone! Take the poker there out of the fireplace. Give me back Sydney, or knock out my brains. I haven't courage enough to do it for myself. Oh, why did I engage that governess! I was so happy, Randal, with Catherine and little Kitty. "

He laid his head wearily on the back of his chair. Randal offered him more wine; he refused it.

"I'm afraid, " he said. "Wine maddens me if I take too much of it. You have heard of men forgetting their sorrows in drink. I tried it yesterday; it set my brains on fire; I'm feeling that glass I took just now. No! I'm not faint. It eases my head when I rest like this. Shake hands, Randal; we have never had any unfriendly words; we mustn't begin now. There's something perverse about me. I didn't know how fond I was of Sydney till I lost her; I didn't know how fond I was of my wife till I left her. " He paused, and put his hand to his fevered head. Was his mind wandering into some other train of thought? He astonished his brother by a new entreaty—the last imaginable entreaty that Randal expected to hear. "Dear old fellow, I want you to do me a favor. Tell me where my wife is living now? "

"Surely, " Randal answered, "you know that she is no longer your wife? "

"Never mind that! I have something to say to her. "

"You can't do it. "

"Can *you* do it? Will you give her a message? "

"Let me hear what it is first. "

Herbert lifted his head, and laid his hand earnestly on his brother's arm. When he said his next words he was almost like his old self again.

"Say that I'm lonely, say that I'm dying for want of a little comfort—ask her to let me see Kitty. "

His tone touched Randal to the quick. "I feel for you, Herbert, " he said, warmly. "She shall have your message; all that I can do to persuade her shall be done. "

"As soon as possible? "

"Yes—as soon as possible. "

"And you won't forget? No, no; of course you won't forget. " He tried to rise, and fell back again into his chair. "Let me rest a little, " he pleaded, "if I'm not in the way. I'm not fit company for you, I know; I'll go when you tell me. "

Randal refused to let him go at all. "You will stay here with me; and if I happen to be away, there will be somebody in the house, who is almost as fond of you as I am. " He mentioned the name of one of the old servants at Mount Morven, who had attached himself to Randal after the breakup of the family. "And now rest, " he said, "and let me put this cushion under your head. "

Herbert answered: "It's like being at home again"—and composed himself to rest.

Chapter XL.

Keep Your Temper.

On the next day but one, Randal arranged his departure for Sydenham, so as to arrive at the hotel an hour before the time appointed for the dinner. His prospects of success, in pleading for a favorable reception of his brother's message, were so uncertain that he refrained—in fear of raising hopes which he might not be able to justify—from taking Herbert into his confidence. No one knew on what errand he was bent, when he left the house. As he took his place in the carriage, the newspaper boy appeared at the window as usual. The new number of a popular weekly journal had that day been published. Randal bought it.

After reading one or two of the political articles, he arrived at the columns specially devoted to "Fashionable Intelligence. " Caring nothing for that sort of news, he was turning over the pages in search of the literary and dramatic articles, when a name not unfamiliar to him caught his eye. He read the paragraph in which it appeared.

"The charming widow, Mrs. Norman, is, we hear, among the distinguished guests staying at Buck's Hotel. It is whispered that the lady is to be shortly united to a retired naval officer of Arctic fame; now better known, perhaps, as one of our leading philanthropists. "

The allusion to Bennydeck was too plain to be mistaken. Randal looked again at the first words in the paragraph. "The charming widow! " Was it possible that this last word referred to Catherine? To suppose her capable of assuming to be a widow, and—if the child asked questions—of telling Kitty that her father was dead, was, in Randal's estimation, to wrong her cruelly. With his own suspicions steadily contradicting him, he arrived at the hotel, obstinately believing that "the charming widow" would prove to be a stranger.

A first disappointment was in store for him when he entered the house. Mrs. Norman and her little daughter were out driving with a friend, and were expected to return in good time for dinner. Mrs. Presty was at home; she was reported to be in the garden of the hotel.

Randal found her comfortably established in a summerhouse, with her knitting in her hands, and a newspaper on her lap. She advanced to meet him, all smiles and amiability. "How nice of you to come so soon! " she began. Her keen penetration discovered something in his face which checked the gayety of her welcome. "You don't mean to say that you are going to spoil our pleasant little dinner by bringing bad news! " she added, looking at him suspiciously.

"It depends on you to decide that, " Randal replied.

"How very complimentary to a poor useless old woman! Don't be mysterious, my dear. I don't belong to the generation which raises storms in tea-cups, and calls skirmishes with savages battles. Out with it! "

Randal handed his paper to her, open at the right place. "There is my news, " he said.

Mrs. Presty looked at the paragraph, and handed *her* newspaper to Randal.

"I am indeed sorry to spoil your dramatic effect, " she said. "But you ought to have known that we are only half an hour behind you, at Sydenham, in the matter of news. The report is premature, my good friend. But if these newspaper people waited to find out whether a report is true or false, how much gossip would society get in its favorite newspapers? Besides, if it isn't true now, it will be true next week. The author only says, 'It's whispered. ' How delicate of him! What a perfect gentleman! "

"Am I really to understand, Mrs. Presty, that Catherine—"

"You are to understand that Catherine is a widow. I say it with pride, a widow of my making! "

"If this is one of your jokes, ma'am—"

"Nothing of the sort, sir. "

"Are you aware, Mrs. Presty, that my brother—"

"Oh, don't talk of your brother! He's an obstacle in our way, and we have been compelled to get rid of him. "

Randal drew back a step. Mrs. Presty's audacity was something more than he could understand. "Is this woman mad? " he said to himself.

"Sit down, " said Mrs. Presty. "If you are determined to make a serious business of it—if you insist on my justifying myself—you are to be pitied for not possessing a sense of humor, but you shall have your own way. I am put on my defense. Very well. You shall hear how my divorced daughter and my poor little grandchild were treated at Sandyseal, after you left us. "

Having related the circumstances, she suggested that Randal should put himself in Catherine's place, before he ventured on expressing an opinion. "Would you have exposed yourself to be humiliated again in the same way? " she asked. "And would you have seen your child made to suffer as well as yourself? "

"I should have kept in retirement for the future, " he answered, "and not have trusted my child and myself among strangers in hotels. "

"Ah, indeed? And you would have condemned your poor little daughter to solitude? You would have seen her pining for the company of other children, and would have had no mercy on her? I wonder what you would have done when Captain Bennydeck paid us a visit at the seaside? He was introduced to Mrs. Norman, and to Mrs. Norman's little girl, and we were all charmed with him. When he and I happened to be left together he naturally wondered, after having seen the beautiful wife, where the lucky husband might be. If he had asked you about Mr. Norman, how would you have answered him? "

"I should have told the truth. "

"You would have said there was no Mr. Norman? "

"Yes. "

"Exactly what I did! And the Captain of course concluded (after having been introduced to Kitty) that Mrs. Norman was a widow. If I had set him right, what would have become of my daughter's reputation? If I had told the truth at this hotel, when everybody wanted to know what Mrs. Norman, that handsome lady, was— what would the consequences have been to Catherine and her little girl? No! no! I have made the best of a miserable situation; I have consulted the tranquillity of a cruelly injured woman and an innocent child—with this inevitable result; I have been obliged to treat your brother like a character in a novel. I have ship-wrecked Herbert as the shortest way of answering inconvenient questions. Vessel found bottom upward in the middle of the Atlantic, and everybody on board drowned, of course. Worse stories have been printed; I do assure you, worse stories have been printed. "

Randal decided on leaving her. "Have you done all this with Catherine's consent? " he asked as he got up from his chair.

"Catherine submits to circumstances, like a sensible woman. "

"Does she submit to your telling Kitty that her father is dead? "

For the first time Mrs. Presty became serious.

"Wait a minute, " she answered. "Before I consented to answer the child's inquiries, I came to an understanding with her mother. I said, 'Will you let Kitty see her father again? '"

The very question which Randal had promised to ask in his brother's interests! "And how did Catherine answer you? " he inquired.

"Honestly. She said: 'I daren't! ' After that, I had her mother's authority for telling Kitty that she would never see her father again. She asked directly if her father was dead—"

"That will do, Mrs. Presty. Your defense is thoroughly worthy of your conduct in all other respects. "

"Say thoroughly worthy of the course forced upon me and my daughter by your brother's infamous conduct—and you will be nearer the mark! "

Randal passed this over without notice. "Be so good, " he said, "as to tell Catherine that I try to make every possible allowance for her, but that I cannot consent to sit at her dinner-table, and that I dare not face my poor little niece, after what I have heard. "

Mrs. Presty recovered all her audacity. "A very wise decision, " she remarked. "Your sour face would spoil the best dinner that ever was put on the table. Have you any message for Captain Bennydeck? "

Randal asked if his friend was then at the hotel.

Mrs. Presty smiled significantly. "Not at the hotel, just now. "

"Where is he? "

"Where he is every day, about this time—out driving with Catherine and Kitty. "

It was a relief to Randal—in the present state of Catherine's relations toward Bennydeck—to return to London without having seen his friend.

He took leave of Mrs. Presty with the formality due to a stranger—he merely bowed. That incorrigible old woman treated him with affectionate familiarity in return.

"Good-by, dear Randal. One moment before you go! Will it be of any use if we invite you to the marriage? "

Arrived at the station, Randal found that he must wait for the train. While he was walking up and down the platform with a mind doubly distressed by anxiety about his brother and anxiety about Sydney, the train from London came in. He stood, looking absently at the passengers leaving the carriage on the opposite side of the platform. Suddenly, a voice that he knew was audible, asking the way to Buck's Hotel. He crossed the line in an instant, and found himself face to face with Herbert.

Chapter XLI.

Make the Best of It.

For a moment the two men looked at each other without speaking. Herbert's wondering eyes accurately reflected his brother's astonishment.

"What are you doing here? " he asked. Suspicion overclouded his face as he put the question. "You have been to the hotel? " he burst out; "you have seen Catherine? "

Randal could deny that he had seen Catherine, with perfect truth—and did deny it in the plainest terms. Herbert was satisfied. "In all my remembrance of you, " he said, "you have never told me a lie. We have both seen the same newspaper, of course—and you have been the first to clear the thing up. That's it, isn't it? "

"I wonder who this other Mrs. Norman is; did you find out? "

"No. "

"She's not Catherine, at any rate; I, for one, shall go home with a lighter heart. " He took his brother's arm, to return to the other platform. "Do you know, Randal, I was almost afraid that Catherine was the woman. The devil take the thing, and the people who write in it! "

He snatched a newspaper out of his pocket as he spoke—tore it in half—and threw it away. "Malcolm meant well, poor fellow, " he said, referring to the old servant, "but he made a miserable man of me for all that. "

Not satisfied with gossip in private, the greedy public appetite devours gossip in print, and wants more of it than any one editor can supply. Randal picked up the torn newspaper. It was not the newspaper which he had bought at the station. Herbert had been reading a rival journal, devoted to the interests of Society—in which the report of Mrs. Norman's marriage was repeated, with this difference, that it boldly alluded to Captain Bennydeck by name. "Did Malcolm give you this? " Randal asked.

"Yes; he and the servant next door subscribe to take it in; and Malcolm thought it might amuse me. It drove me out of the house and into the railway. If it had driven me out of mind, I shouldn't have been surprised. "

"Gently, Herbert! Supposing the report had been true—? "

"After what you have told me, why should I suppose anything of the sort? "

"Don't be angry; and do pray remember that the Divorce allows you and Catherine to marry again, if you like. "

Herbert became more unreasonable than ever. "If Catherine does think of marrying again, " he said, "the man will have to reckon first with me. But that is not the point. You seem to have forgotten that the woman at Buck's Hotel is described as a Widow. The bare doubt that my divorced wife might be the woman was bad enough—but what I wanted to find out was how she had passed off her false pretense on our child. *That* was what maddened me! No more of it now. Have you seen Catherine lately? "

"Not lately. "

"I suppose she is as handsome as ever. When will you ask her to let me see Kitty? "

"Leave that to me, " was the one reply which Randal could venture to make at the moment.

The serious embarrassments that surrounded him were thickening fast. His natural frank nature urged him to undeceive Herbert. If he followed his inclinations, in the near neighborhood of the hotel, who could say what disasters might not ensue, in his brother's present frame of mind? If he made the disclosure on their return to the house, he would be only running the same risk of consequences, after an interval of delay; and, if he remained silent, the march of events might, at any moment, lead to the discovery of what he had concealed. Add to this, that his confidence in Catherine had been rudely shaken. Having allowed herself to be entrapped into the deception proposed by her mother, and having thus far persevered in that deception, were the chances in favor of her revealing her true position—especially if she was disposed to encourage Bennydeck's suit? Randal's loyalty to Catherine hesitated to decide that serious question against the woman whom he had known, trusted, and admired for so many years. In any event, her second marriage would lead to one disastrous result. It would sooner or later come to Herbert's ears. In the meantime, after what Mrs. Presty had confessed, the cruel falsehood which had checked poor Kitty's natural inquiries raised an insuperable obstacle to a meeting between father and child.

If Randal shrank from the prospect which thus presented itself to him, in his relations with his brother, and if his thoughts reverted to Sydney Westerfield, other reasons for apprehension found their way into his mind.

He had promised to do his best toward persuading Catherine to grant Sydney an interview. To perform that promise appeared to be now simply impossible. Under the exasperating influence of a disappointment for which she was not prepared, it was hard to say what act of imprudence Sydney might not commit. Even the chance of successfully confiding her to Bennydeck's protection had lost something of its fair promise, since Randal's visit to Sydenham. That the Captain would welcome his friend's daughter as affectionately as if she had been his own child, was not to be doubted for a moment. But that she would receive the same unremitting attention, while he was courting Catherine, which would have been offered to her under other circumstances, was not to be hoped. Be the results, however, what they might, Randal could see but one plain course before him now. He decided on hastening Sydney's introduction to Bennydeck, and on writing at once to prepare the Captain for that event.

Even this apparently simple proceeding required examination in its different bearings, before he could begin his letter.

Would he be justified in alluding to the report which associated Bennydeck with Catherine? Considerations of delicacy seemed to forbid taking this liberty, even with an intimate friend. It was for the Captain to confirm what Mrs. Presty had said of him, if he thought it desirable to touch on the subject in his reply. Besides, looking to Catherine's interest—and not forgetting how she had suffered—had Randal any right to regard with other than friendly feelings a second marriage, which united her to a man morally and intellectually the superior of her first husband? What happier future could await her—especially if she justified Randal's past experience of all that was candid and truthful in her character—than to become his friend's wife?

Written under the modifying influence of these conclusions, his letter contained the few words that follow:

"I have news for you which I am sure you will be glad to hear. Your old friend's daughter has abandoned her sinful way of life, and has made sacrifices which prove the sincerity of her repentance. Without entering into particulars which may be mercifully dismissed from notice, let me only assure you that I answer for Sydney Westerfield as being worthy of the fatherly interest which you feel in her. Shall I say that she may expect an early visit from you, when I see her to-morrow? I don't doubt that I am free already to do this; but it will encourage the poor girl, if I can speak with your authority. "

He added Sydney's address in a postscript, and dispatched his letter that evening.

On the afternoon of the next day two letters were delivered to Randal, bearing the Sydenham postmark.

The first which he happened to take up was addressed to him in Mrs. Presty's handwriting. His opinion of this correspondent was expressed in prompt action—he threw the letter, unopened, into the waste-paper basket.

The next letter was from Bennydeck, written in the kindest terms, but containing no allusion to any contemplated change in his life. He would not be able (he wrote) to leave Sydenham for a day or two. No explanation of the cause of this delay followed. But it might, perhaps, be excusable to infer that the marriage had not yet been decided on, and that the Captain's proposals were still waiting for Catherine's reply.

Randal put the letter in his pocket and went at once to Sydney's lodgings.

Chapter XLII.

Try to Excuse Her.

The weather had been unusually warm. Of all oppressive summers a hot summer in London is the hardest to endure. The little exercise that Sydney could take was, as Randal knew, deferred until the evening. On asking for her, he was surprised to hear that she had gone out.

"Is she walking? " he asked, "on a day such as this? "

No: she was too much overcome by the heat to be able to walk. The landlady's boy had been sent to fetch a cab, and he had heard Miss Westerfield tell the driver to go to Lincoln's Inn Fields.

The address at once reminded Randal of Mr. Sarrazin. On the chance of making a discovery, he went to the lawyer's office. It had struck him as being just possible that Sydney might have called there for the second time; and, on making inquiry, he found that his surmise was correct. Miss Westerfield had called, and had gone away again more than an hour since.

Having mentioned this circumstance, good Mr. Sarrazin rather abruptly changed the subject.

He began to talk of the weather, and, like everybody else, he complained of the heat. Receiving no encouragement so far, he selected politics as his next topic. Randal was unapproachably indifferent to the state of parties, and the urgent necessity for reform. Still bent, as it seemed, on preventing his visitor from taking a leading part in the conversation, Mr. Sarrazin tried the exercise of hospitality next. He opened his cigar-case, and entered eagerly into the merits of his cigars; he proposed a cool drink, and described the right method of making it as distinguished from the wrong. Randal was not thirsty, and was not inclined to smoke. Would the pertinacious lawyer give way at last? In appearance, at least, he submitted to defeat. "You want something of me, my friend, " he said, with a patient smile. "What is it? "

"I want to know why Miss Westerfield called on you? "

Randal flattered himself that he had made a prevaricating reply simply impossible. Nothing of the sort! Mr. Sarrazin slipped through his fingers once more. The unwritten laws of gallantry afforded him a refuge now.

"The most inviolate respect, " he solemnly declared, "is due to a lady's confidence—and, what is more, to a young lady's confidence—and, what is more yet, to a pretty young lady's confidence. The sex, my dear fellow! Must I recall your attention to what is due to the sex? "

This little outbreak of the foreign side of his friend's character was no novelty to Randal. He remained as indifferent to the inviolate claims of the sex as if he had been an old man of ninety.

"Did Miss Westerfield say anything about me? " was his next question.

Slippery Mr. Sarrazin slid into another refuge: he entered a protest.

"Here is a change of persons and places! " he exclaimed. "Am I a witness of the court of justice—and are you the lawyer who examines me? My memory is defective, my learned friend. *Non mi ricordo.* I know nothing about it. "

Randal changed his tone. "We have amused ourselves long enough, " he said. "I have serious reasons, Sarrazin, for wishing to know what passed between Miss Westerfield and you—and I trust my old friend to relieve my anxiety. "

The lawyer was accustomed to say of himself that he never did things by halves. His answer to Randal offered a proof of his accurate estimate of his own character.

"Your old friend will deserve your confidence in him, " he answered. "You want to know why Miss Westerfield called here. Her object in view was to twist me round her finger—and I beg to inform you that she has completely succeeded. My dear Randal, this pretty creature's cunning is remarkable even for a woman. I am an old lawyer, skilled in the ways of the world—and a young girl has completely overreached me. She asked—oh, heavens, how innocently! —if Mrs. Norman was likely to make a long stay at her present place of residence. "

Randal interrupted him. "You don't mean to tell me you have given her Catherine's address? "

"Buck's Hotel, Sydenham, " Mr. Sarrazin answered. "She has got the address down in her nice little pocketbook. "

"What amazing weakness! " Randal exclaimed.

Mr. Sarrazin cordially agreed with him. "Amazing weakness, as you say. Pretty Miss Sydney has extracted more things, besides the address. She knows that Mrs. Norman is here on business relating to new investments of her money. She knows besides that one of the trustees is keeping us waiting. She also made sensible remarks. She mentioned having heard Mrs. Norman say that the air of London never agreed with her; and she hoped that a comparatively healthy neighborhood had been chosen for Mrs. Norman's place of residence. This, you see, was leading up to the discovery of the address. The spirit of mischief possessed me; I allowed Miss Westerfield to take a little peep at the truth. 'Mrs. Norman is not actually in London, ' I said; 'she is only in the neighborhood. ' For what followed on this, my experience of ladies ought to have prepared me. I am ashamed to say *this* lady took me completely by surprise. "

"What did she do? "

"Fell on her knees, poor dear—and said: 'Oh, Mr. Sarrazin, be kinder to me than you have ever been yet; tell me where Mrs. Norman is! '—I put her back in her chair, and I took her handkerchief out of her pocket and I wiped her eyes. "

"And then you told her the address? "

"I was near it, but I didn't do it yet. I asked what you had done in the matter. Alas, your kind heart has led you to promise more than you could perform. She had waited to hear from you if Mrs. Norman consented to see her, and had waited in vain. Hard on her, wasn't it? I was sorry, but I was still obdurate. I only felt the symptoms which warned me that I was going to make a fool of myself, when she let me into her secret for the first time, and said plainly what she wanted with Mrs. Norman. Her tears and her entreaties I had resisted. The confession of her motives overpowered me. It is right, " cried Mr. Sarrazin, suddenly warming into enthusiasm, "that these two women should meet. Remember how that poor girl has proved that her repentance is no sham. I say, she has a right to tell, and the lady whom she has injured has a right to hear, what she has done to atone for the past, what confession she is willing to make to the one woman in the world (though she *is* a divorced woman) who is most interested in hearing what Miss Westerfield's life has been with that wretched brother of yours. Ah, yes, I know what the English cant might say. Away with the English cant! it is the worst obstacle to the progress of the English nation! "

Randal listened absently: he was thinking.

There could be little doubt to what destination Sydney Westerfield had betaken herself, when she left the lawyer's office. At that moment, perhaps, she and Catherine were together—and together alone.

Mr. Sarrazin had noticed his friend's silence. "Is it possible you don't agree with me? " he asked.

"I don't feel as hopefully as you do, if these two ladies meet. "

"Ah, my friend, you are not a sanguine man by nature. If Mrs. Norman treats our poor Sydney just as a commonplace ill-tempered woman would treat her, I shall be surprised indeed. Say, if you like, that she will be insulted—of this I am sure, she will not return it; there is no expiation that is too bitter to be endured by that resolute little creature. Her fine nature has been tempered by adversity. A hard life has been Sydney's, depend upon it, in the years before you and I met with her. Good heavens! What would my wife say if she heard me? The women are nice, but they have their drawbacks. Let us wait till tomorrow, my dear boy; and let us believe in Sydney without allowing our wives—I beg your pardon, I mean *my* wife—to suspect in what forbidden directions our sympathies are leading us. Oh, for shame! "

Who could persist in feeling depressed in the company of such a man as this? Randal went home with the influence of Mr. Sarrazin's sanguine nature in undisturbed possession of him, until his old servant's gloomy face confronted him at the door.

"Anything gone wrong, Malcolm? "

"I'm sorry to say, sir, Mr. Herbert has left us. "

"Left us! Why? "

"I don't know, sir. "

"Where has he gone? "

"He didn't tell me. "

"Is there no letter? No message? "

"There's a message, sir. Mr. Herbert came back—"

"Stop! Where had he been when he came back? "

"He said he felt a little lonely after you went out, and he thought it might cheer him up if he went to the club. I was to tell you where he had gone if you asked what had become of him. He said it kindly and pleasantly—quite like himself, sir. But, when he came back—if you'll excuse my saying so—I never saw a man in a worse temper. 'Tell my brother I am obliged to him for his hospitality, and I won't take advantage of it any longer. ' That was Mr. Herbert's message. I tried to say a word. He banged the door, and away he went. "

Even Randal's patient and gentle nature rose in revolt against his brother's treatment of him. He entered his sitting-room in silence. Malcolm followed, and pointed to a letter on the table. "I think you must have thrown it away by mistake, sir, " the old man explained; "I found it in the waste-paper basket. " He bowed with the unfailing respect of the old school, and withdrew.

Randal's first resolve was to dismiss his brother from further consideration. "Kindness is thrown away on Herbert, " he thought; "I shall treat him for the future as he has treated me. "

But his brother was still in his mind. He opened Mrs. Presty's letter—on the chance that it might turn the current of his thoughts in a new direction.

In spite of Mrs. Presty, in spite of himself, his heart softened toward the man who had behaved so badly to him. Instead of reading the letter, he was now trying to discover a connection between his brother's visit to the club and his brother's angry message. Had Herbert heard something said, among gossiping members in the smoking-room, which might account for his conduct? If Randal had belonged to the club he would have gone there to make inquiries. How could he get the information that he wanted, in some other way?

After considering it for a while, he remembered the dinner that he had given to his friend Sarrazin on his return from the United States, and the departure of the lawyer to his club, with a purpose in view which interested them both. It was the same club to which Herbert belonged. Randal wrote at once to Mr. Sarrazin, mentioning what had happened, and acknowledging the anxiety tha t weighed on his mind.

Having instructed Malcolm to take the letter to the lawyer's house, and, if he was not at home, to inquire where he might be found, Randal adopted the readiest means of composing himself, in the servant's absence, by lighting his pipe.

He was enveloped in clouds of tobacco-smoke—the only clouds which we can trust never to prove unworthy of our confidence in them—when Mrs. Presty's letter caught his attention. If the month had been January instead of July, he would have thrown it into the fire. Under present circumstances, he took it up and read it:

"I bear no malice, dear Randal, and I write to you as affectionately as if you had kept your temper on the occasion when we last met.

"You will be pleased to hear that Catherine was as thoroughly distressed as you could wish her to be, when it became my disagreeable duty to mention what had passed between us, by way of accounting for your absence. She was quite unable to rally her spirits, even with dear Captain Bennydeck present to encourage her.

"'I am not receiving you as I ought, ' she said to him, when we began dinner, 'but there is perhaps some excuse for me. I have lost the regard and esteem of an old friend, who has cruelly wronged me. ' From motives of delicacy (which I don't expect you to understand) she refrained from mentioning your name. The prettiest answer that I ever heard was the answer that the Captain returned. 'Let the true friend, ' he said, 'take the place in your heart which the false friend has lost. '

"He kissed her hand. If you had seen how he did it, and how she looked at him, you would have felt that you had done more toward persuading my daughter to marry the Captain than any other person about her, myself included. You had deserted her; you had thrown her back on the one true friend left. Thank you, Randal. In our best interests, thank you.

"It is needless to add that I got out of the way, and took Kitty with me, at the earliest opportunity—and left them by themselves.

"At bed-time I went into Catherine's room. Our interview began and ended in less than a minute. It was useless to ask if the Captain had proposed marriage; her agitation sufficiently informed me of what had happened. My one question was: 'Dearest Catherine, have you said Yes? ' She turned shockingly pale, and answered: 'I have not said No. ' Could anything be more encouraging? God bless you; we shall meet at the wedding. "

Randal laid down the letter and filled his pipe again. He was not in the least exasperated; he was only anxious to hear from Mr. Sarrazin. If Mrs. Presty had seen him at that moment, she would have said to herself: "I forgot the wretch was a smoker. "

In half an hour more the door was opened by Malcolm, and Mr. Sarrazin in person answered his friend.

"There are no such incorrigible gossips, " he said, "as men in the smoking-room of a club. Those popular newspapers began the mischief, and the editor of one of them completed it. How he got his information I am not able to say. The small-talk turned on that report about the charming widow; and the editor congratulated himself on the delicacy of his conduct. 'When the paragraph reached me, ' he said, 'the writer mentioned that Mrs. Norman was that well-known lady, the divorced Mrs. Herbert Linley. I thought this rather too bad, and I cut it out. ' Your brother appears to have been present—but he seldom goes to the club, and none of the members knew him even by sight. Shall I give you a light? Your pipe's out. "

Randal's feelings, at that moment, were not within reach of the comforting influence of tobacco.

"Do you think your brother has gone to Sydenham? " Mr. Sarrazin asked.

Randal answered: "I haven't a doubt of it now. "

Chapter XLIII.

Know Your Own Mind.

The garden of the hotel at Sydenham had originally belonged to a private house. Of great extent, it had been laid out in excellent taste. Flower-beds and lawns, a handsome fountain, seats shaded by groups of fine trees at their full growth, completed the pastoral charm of the place. A winding path led across the garden from the back of the house. It had been continued by the speculator who purchased the property, until it reached a road at the extremity of the grounds which communicated with the Crystal Palace. Visitors to the hotel had such pleasant associations with the garden that many of them returned at future opportunities instead of trying the attraction of some other place. Various tastes and different ages found their wishes equally consulted here. Children rejoiced in the finest playground they had ever seen. Remote walks, secluded among shrubberies, invited persons of reserved disposition who came as strangers, and as strangers desired to remain. The fountain and the lawn collected sociable visitors, who were always ready to make acquaintance with each other. Even the amateur artist could take liberties with Nature, and find the accommodating limits of the garden sufficient for his purpose. Trees in the foreground sat to him for likenesses that were never recognized; and hills submitted to unprovoked familiarities, on behalf of brushes which were not daunted by distance.

On the day after the dinner which had so deplorably failed, in respect of one of the guests invited, to fulfill Catherine's anticipations, there was a festival at the Palace. It had proved so generally attractive to the guests at the hotel that the grounds were almost deserted.

As the sun declined, on a lovely summer evening, the few invalids feebly wandering about the flower-beds, or resting under the trees, began to return to the house in dread of the dew. Catherine and her child, with the nursemaid in attendance, were left alone in the garden. Kitty found her mother, as she openly declared, "not such good company as usual. " Since the day when her grandmother had said the fatal words which checked all further allusion to her father, the child had shown a disposition to complain, if she was not constantly amused. She complained of Mrs. Presty now.

"I think grandmamma might have taken me to the Crystal Palace, " she said.

"My dear, your grandmamma has friends with her—ladies and gentlemen who don't care to be troubled with a child. "

Kitty received this information in a very unamiable spirit. "I hate ladies and gentlemen! " she said.

"Even Captain Bennydeck? " her mother asked.

"No; I like my nice Captain. And I like the waiters. They would take me to the Crystal Palace—only they're always busy. I wish it was bedtime; I don't know what to do with myself. "

"Take a little walk with Susan. "

"Where shall I go? "

Catherine looked toward the gate which opened on the road, and proposed a visit to the old man who kept the lodge.

Kitty shook her head. There was an objection to the old man. "He asks questions; he wants to know how I get on with my sums. He's proud of his summing; and he finds me out when I'm wrong. I don't like the lodge-keeper. "

Catherine looked the other way, toward the house. The pleasant fall of water in the basin of the distant fountain was just audible. "Go and feed the gold-fishes, " she suggested.

This was a prospect of amusement which at once raised Kitty's spirits. "That's the thing! " she cried, and ran off to the fountain, with the nursemaid after her.

Catherine seated herself under the trees, and watched in solitude the decline of the sun in a cloudless sky. The memory of the happy years of her marriage had never been so sadly and persistently present to her mind as at this time, when the choice of another married life waited her decision to become an accomplished fact. Remembrances of the past, which she had such bitter reason to regret, and forebodings of the future, in which she was more than half inclined to believe, oppressed her at one and the same moment. She thought of the different circumstances, so widely separated by time, under which Herbert (years ago) and Bennydeck (twenty-four hours since) had each owned his love, and pleaded for an indulgent hearing. Her mind contrasted the dissimilar results.

Pressed by the faithless man who had so cruelly wronged her in after-years, she only wondered why he had waited so long before h e asked her to marry him. Addressed with equal ardor by that other man, whose age, whose character, whose modest devotion offered her every assurance of happiness that a woman could desire, she had struggled against herself, and had begged him to give her a day to consider. That day was now drawing to an end. As she watched the setting sun, the phantom of her guilty husband darkened the heavenly light; imbittered the distrust of herself which made her afraid to say Yes; and left her helpless before the hesitation which prevented her from saying No.

The figure of a man appeared on the lonely path that led to the lodge gate.

Impulsively she rose from her seat as he advanced. She sat down again. After that first act of indecision, the flutter of her spirits abated; she was able to think.

To avoid him, after he had spared her at her own request, would have been an act of ingratitude: to receive him was to place herself once more in the false position of a woman too undecided to know her own mind. Forced to choose between these alternatives, her true regard for Bennydeck forbade her to think of herself, and encouraged her to wait for him. As he came nearer, she saw anxiety in his face and observed an open letter in his hand. He smiled as he approached her, and asked leave to take a chair at her side. At the same time, when he perceived that she had noticed his letter, he put it away hurriedly in his pocket.

"I hope nothing has happened to annoy you, " she said.

He smiled again; and asked if she was thinking of his letter. "It is only a report, " he added, "from my second in command, whom I have left in charge of my Home. He is an excellent man; but I am afraid his temper is not proof against the ingratitude which we sometimes meet with. He doesn't yet make allowances for what even the best natures suffer, under the deteriorating influence of self-distrust and despair. No, I am not anxious about the results of this case. I forget all my anxieties (except one) when I am with you. "

His eyes told her that he was about to return to the one subject that she dreaded. She tried—as women will try, in the little emergencies of their lives—to gain time.

"I am interested about your Home, " she said: "I want to know what sort of place it is. Is the discipline very severe? "

"There is no discipline, " he answered warmly. "My one object is to be a friend to my friendless fellow-creatures; and my one way of governing them is to follow the teaching of the Sermon on the Mount. Whatever else I may remind them of, when they come to me, I am determined not to remind them of a prison. For this reason— though I pity the hardened wanderers of the streets, I don't open my doors to them. Many a refuge, in which discipline is inevitable, is open to these poor sinners already. My welcome is offered to penitents and sufferers of another kind—who have fallen from positions in life, in which the sense of honor has been cultivated; whose despair is associated with remembrances which I may so encourage, with the New Testament to help me, as to lead them back to the religious influences under which their purer and happier lives may have been passed. Here and there I meet with disappointments. But I persist in my system of trusting them as freely as if they were my own children; and, for the most part, they justify my confidence in them. On the day—if it ever comes—when I find discipline necessary, I shall suffer my disappointment and close my doors. "

"Is your house open, " Catherine asked, "to men and women alike? "

He was eager to speak with her on a subject more interesting to him even than his Home. Answering her question, in this frame of mind, his thoughts wandered; he drew lines absently with his walking-stick on the soft earth under the trees.

"The means at my disposal, " he said, "are limited. I have been obliged to choose between the men and the women. "

"And you have chosen women? "

"Yes. "

"Why? "

"Because a lost woman is a more friendless creature than a lost man. "

"Do they come to you? or do you look for them? "

"They mostly come to me. There is one young woman, however, now waiting to see me, whom I have been looking for. I am deeply interested in her. "

"Is it her beauty that interests you? "

"I have not seen her since she was a child. She is the daughter of an old friend of mine, who died many years ago. "

"And with that claim on you, you keep her waiting? "

"Yes. "

He let his stick drop on the ground and looked at Catherine; but he offered no explanation of his strange conduct. She was a little disappointed. "You have been some time away from your Home, " she said; still searching for his reasons. "When do you go back? "

"I go back, " he answered, "when I know whether I may thank God for being the happiest man living. "

They were both silent.

Chapter XLIV.

Think of Consequences.

Catherine listened to the fall of water in the basin of the fountain. She was conscious of a faint hope—a hope unworthy of her—that Kitty might get weary of the gold-fishes, and might interrupt them. No such thing happened; no stranger appeared on the path which wound through the garden. She was alone with him. The influences of the still and fragrant summer evening were influences which breathed of love.

"Have you thought of me since yesterday? " he asked gently.

She owned that she had thought of him.

"Is there no hope that your heart will ever incline toward me? "

"I daren't consult my heart. If I had only to consider my own feelings—" She stopped.

"What else have you to consider? "

"My past life—how I have suffered, and what I have to repent of. "

"Has your married life not been a happy one? " he asked.

"Not a happy one—in the end, " she answered.

"Through no fault of yours, I am sure? "

"Through no fault of mine, certainly. "

"And yet you said just now that you had something to repent of? "

"I was not thinking of my husband, Captain Bennydeck, when I said that. If I have injured any person, the person is myself. "

She was thinking of that fatal concession to the advice of her mother, and to the interests of her child, which placed her in a false position toward the honest man who loved her and trusted her. If he had been less innocent in the ways of the world, and not so devotedly

265

fond of her, he might, little by little, have persuaded Catherine to run the risk of shocking him by a confession of the truth. As it was, his confidence in her raised him high above the reach of suspicions which might have occurred to other men. He saw her turn pale; he saw distress in her face, which he interpreted as a silent reproach to him for the questions he had asked.

"I hope you will forgive me? " he said simply.

She was astonished. "What have I to forgive? "

"My want of delicacy. "

"Oh, Captain Bennydeck, you speak of one of your great merits as if it were a fault! Over and over again I have noticed your delicacy, and admired it. "

He was too deeply in earnest to abandon his doubts of himself.

"I have ignorantly led you to think of your sorrows, " he said; "sorrows that I cannot console. I don't deserve to be forgiven. May I make the one excuse in my power? May I speak of myself? "

She told him by a gesture that he had made a needless request.

"The life I have led, " he resumed, "accounts, perhaps, in some degree, for what is deficient in me. At school, I was not a popular boy; I only made one friend, and he has long since been numbered with the dead. Of my life at college, and afterward in London, I dare not speak to you; I look back at it with horror. My school-friend decided my choice of a profession; he went into the navy. After a while, not knowing what else to do, I followed his example. I liked the life—I may say the sea saved me. For years, I was never on shore for more than a few weeks at a time. I saw nothing of society; I was hardly ever in the company of ladies. The next change in my life associated me with an Arctic expedition. God forbid I should tell you of what men go through who are lost in the regions of eternal ice! Let me only say I was preserved—miraculously preserved—to profit by that dreadful experience. It made a new man of me; it altered me (I hope for the better) into what I am now. Oh, I feel that I ought to have kept my secret yesterday—I mean my daring to love you. I should have waited till you knew more of me; till my conduct pleased you perhaps, and spoke for me. You won't laugh, I am sure, if I confess (at my age!) that I am inexperienced. Never till I met you have I known what true love is—and this at forty years old. How some people would laugh! I own it seems melancholy to me. "

"No; not melancholy. "

Her voice trembled. Agitation, which it was not a pain but a luxury to feel, was gently taking possession of her. Where another man might have seen that her tenderness was getting the better of her discretion, and might have presumed on the discovery, this man, innocently blind to his own interests, never even attempted to take advantage of her. No more certain way could have been devised, by the most artful lover, of touching the heart of a generous woman, and making it his own. The influence exerted over Catherine by the virtues of Bennydeck's character—his unaffected kindness, his manly sympathy, his religious convictions so deeply felt, so modestly restrained from claiming notice—had been steadily increasing in the intimacy of daily intercourse. Catherine had never felt his ascendancy over her as strongly as she felt it now. By fine degrees, the warning remembrances which had hitherto made her hesitate lost their hold on her memory. Hardly conscious herself of what she was doing, she began to search his feelings in his own presence. Such love as his had been unknown in her experience; the luxury of looking into it, and sounding it to its inmost depths, was more than the woman's nature could resist.

"I think you hardly do yourself justice, " she said. "Surely you don't regret having felt for me so truly, when I told you yesterday that my old friend had deserted me? "

"No, indeed! "

"Do you like to remember that you showed no jealous curiosity to know who my friend was? "

"I should have been ashamed of myself if I had asked the question. "

"And did you believe that I had a good motive—a motive which you might yourself have appreciated—for not telling you the name of that friend? "

"Is he some one whom I know? "

"Ought you to ask me that, after what I have just said? "

"Pray forgive me! I spoke without thinking. "

"I can hardly believe it, when I remember how you spoke to me yesterday. I could never have supposed, before we became acquainted with each other, that it was in the nature of a man to understand me so perfectly, to be so gentle and so considerate in feeling for my distress. You confused me a little, I must own, by what you said afterward. But I am not sure that ought to be severe in blaming you. Sympathy—I mean such sympathy as yours—sometimes says more than discretion can always approve. Have you not found it so yourself? "

"I have found it so with you. "

"And perhaps I have shown a little too plainly how dependent I am on you—how dreadful it would be to me if I lost you too as a friend? "

She blushed as she said it. When the words had escaped her, she felt that they might bear another meaning than the simple meaning which she had attached to them. He took her hand; his doubts of himself, his needless fear of offending her, restrained him no longer.

"You can never lose me, " he said, "if you will only let me be the nearest friend that a woman can have. Bear with me, dearest! I ask for so much; I have so little to offer in return. I dream of a life with you which is perhaps too perfectly happy to be enjoyed on earth. And yet, I cannot resign my delusion. Must my poor heart always long for happiness which is beyond my reach? If an overruling Providence guides our course through this world, may we not sometimes hope for happier ends than our mortal eyes can see? "

He waited a moment—and sighed—and dropped her hand. She hid her face; she knew what it would tell him: she was ashamed to let him see it.

"I didn't mean to distress you, " he said sadly.

She let him see her face. For a moment only, she looked at him—and then let silence tell him the rest.

His arms closed round her. Slowly, the glory of the sun faded from the heavens, and the soft summer twilight fell over the earth. "I can't speak, " he whispered; "my happiness is too much for me. "

"Are you sure of your happiness? " she asked.

"Could I think as I am thinking now, if I were not sure of it? "

"Are you thinking of *me?* "

"Of you—and of all that you will be to me in the future. Oh, my angel, if God grants us many years to come, what a perfect life I see! "

"Tell me—what do you see? "

"I see a husband and wife who are all in all to each other. If friends come to us, we are glad to bid them welcome; but we are always happiest by ourselves. "

"Do we live in retirement? "

"We live where you like best to live. Shall it be in the country? "

"Yes! yes! You have spoken of the sea as you might have spoken of your best friend—we will be near the sea. But I must not keep you selfishly all to myself. I must remember how good you have been to poor creatures who don't feel our happiness, and who need your kindness. Perhaps I might help you? Do you doubt it? "

"I only doubt whether I ought to let you see what I have seen; I am only afraid of the risk of making you unhappy. You tempt me to run the risk. The help of a woman—and of such a woman as you are—is the one thing I have wanted. Your influence would succeed where my influence has often failed. How good, how thoughtful you would be! "

"I only want to be worthy of you, " she said, humbly. "When may I see your Home? "

He drew her closer to him: tenderly and timidly he kissed her for the first time. "It rests with you, " he answered. "When will you be my wife? "

She hesitated; he felt her trembling. "Is there any obstacle? " he asked.

Before she could reply, Kitty's voice was heard calling to her mother—Kitty ran up to them.

Catherine turned cold as the child caught her by the hand, eagerly claiming her attention. All that she should have remembered, all that she had forgotten in a few bright moments of illusion, rose in judgment against her, and struck her mind prostrate in an instant, when she felt Kitty's touch.

Bennydeck saw the change. Was it possible that the child's sudden appearance had startled her? Kitty had something to say, and said it before he could speak.

"Mamma, I want to go where the other children are going. Susan's gone to her supper. You take me. "

Her mother was not even listening. Kitty turned impatiently to Bennydeck. "Why won't mamma speak to me? " she asked. He quieted her by a word. "You shall go with me. " His anxiety about Catherine was more than he could endure. "Pray let me take you back to the house, " he said. "I am afraid you are not well. "

"I shall be better directly. Do me a kindness—take the child! "

She spoke faintly and vacantly. Bennydeck hesitated. She lifted her trembling hands in entreaty. "I beg you will leave me! " Her voice, her manner, made it impossible to disobey. He turned resignedly to Kitty and asked which way she wanted to go. The child pointed down the path to one of the towers of the Crystal Palace, visible in the distance. "The governess has taken the others to see the company go away, " she said; "I want to go too. "

Bennydeck looked back before he lost sight of Catherine.

She remained seated, in the attitude in which he had left her. At the further end of the path which led to the hotel, he thought he saw a figure in the twilight, approaching from the house. There would be help near, if Catherine wanted it.

His uneasy mind was in some degree relieved, as he and Kitty left the garden together.

Chapter XLV.

Love Your Enemies.

She tried to think of Bennydeck.

Her eyes followed him as long as he was in sight, but her thoughts wandered. To look at him now was to look at the little companion walking by his side. Still, the child reminded her of the living father; still, the child innocently tortured her with the consciousness of deceit. The faithless man from whom the law had released her, possessed himself of her thoughts, in spite of the law. He, and he only, was the visionary companion of her solitude when she was left by herself.

Did he remind her of the sin that he had committed? —of the insult that he had inflicted on the woman whom he had vowed to love and cherish? No! he recalled to her the years of love that she had passed by his side; he upbraided her with the happiness which she had owed to him, in the prime and glory of her life. Woman! set *that* against the wrong which I have done to you. You have the right to condemn me, and Society has the right to condemn me—but I am your child's father still. Forget me if you can!

All thought will bear the test of solitude, excepting only the thought that finds its origin in hopeless self-reproach. The soft mystery of twilight, the solemn silence of the slowly-coming night, daunted Catherine in that lonely place. She rose to return to light and human beings. As she set her face toward the house, a discovery confronted her. She was not alone.

A woman was standing on the path, apparently looking at her.

In the dim light, and at the distance between them, recognition of the woman was impossible. She neither moved nor spoke. Strained to their utmost point of tension, Catherine's nerves quivered at the sight of that shadowy solitary figure. She dropped back on the seat. In tones that trembled she said: "Who are you? What do you want? "

The voice that answered was, like her own voice, faint with fear. It said: "I want a word with you. "

Moving slowly forward—stopping—moving onward again—hesitating again—the woman at last approached. There was light enough left to reveal her face, now that she was near. It was the face of Sydney Westerfield.

The survival of childhood, in the mature human being, betrays itself most readily in the sex that bears children. The chances and changes of life show the child's mobility of emotion constantly associating itself with the passions of the woman. At the moment of recognition the troubled mind of Catherine was instantly steadied, under the influence of that coarsest sense which levels us with the animals—the sense of anger.

"I am amazed at your audacity, " she said.

There was no resentment—there was only patient submission in Sydney's reply.

"Twice I have approached the house in which you are living; and twice my courage has failed me. I have gone away again—I have walked, I don't know where, I don't know how far. Shame and fear seemed to be insensible to fatigue. This is my third attempt. If I was a little nearer to you, I think you would see what the effort has cost me. I have not much to say. May I ask you to hear me? "

"You have taken me by surprise, Miss Westerfield. You have no right to do that; I refuse to hear you. "

"Try, madam, to bear in mind that no unhappy creature, in my place, would expose herself to your anger and contempt without a serious reason. Will you think again? "

"No! "

Sydney turned to go away—and suddenly stopped.

Another person was advancing from the hotel; an interruption, a trivial domestic interruption, presented itself. The nursemaid had missed the child, and had come into the garden to see if she was with her mother.

"Where is Miss Kitty, ma'am? " the girl asked.

The Evil Genius

Her mistress told her what had happened, and sent her to the Palace to relieve Captain Bennydeck of the charge that he had undertaken. Susan listened, looking at Sydney and recognizing the familiar face. As the girl moved away, Sydney spoke to her.

"I hope little Kitty is well and happy? "

The mother does not live who could have resisted the tone in which that question was put. The broken heart, the love for the child that still lived in it, spoke in accents that even touched the servant. She came back; remembering the happy days when the governess had won their hearts at Mount Morven, and, for a moment at least, remembering nothing else.

"Quite well and happy, miss, thank you, " Susan said.

As she hurried away on her errand, she saw her mistress beckon to Sydney to return, and place a chair for her. The nursemaid was not near enough to hear what followed.

"Miss Westerfield, will you forget what I said just now? " With those words, Catherine pointed to the chair. "I am ready to hear you, " she resumed—"but I have something to ask first. Does what you wish to say to me relate only to yourself? "

"It relates to another person, as well as to myself. "

That reply, and the inference to which it led, tried Catherine's resolution to preserve her self-control, as nothing had tried it yet.

"If that other person, " she began, "means Mr. Herbert Linley—"

Sydney interrupted her, in words which she was entirely unprepared to hear.

"I shall never see Mr. Herbert Linley again. "

"Has he deserted you? "

"No. It is *I* who have left *him*. "

"You! "

The emphasis laid on that one word forced Sydney to assert herself for the first time.

"If I had not left him of my own free will, " she said, "what else would excuse me for venturing to come here? "

Catherine's sense of justice felt the force of that reply. At the same time her sense of injury set its own construction on Sydney's motive. "Has his cruelty driven you away from him? " she asked.

"If he has been cruel to me, " Sydney answered, "do you think I should have come here to complain of it to You? Do me the justice to believe that I am not capable of such self-degradation as that. I have nothing to complain of. "

"And yet you have left him? "

"He has been all that is kind and considerate: he has done everything that a man in his unhappy position could do to set my mind at ease. And yet I have left him. Oh, I claim no merit for my repentance, bitterly as I feel it! I might not have had the courage to leave him—if he had loved me as he once loved you. "

"Miss Westerfield, you are the last person living who ought to allude to my married life. "

"You may perhaps pardon the allusion, madam, when you have heard what I have still to say. I owe it to Mr. Herbert Linley, if not to you, to confess that his life with me has *not* been a life of happiness. He has tried, compassionately tried, to keep his secret sorrow from discovery, and he has failed. I had long suspected the truth; but I only saw it in his face when he found the book you left behind you at the hotel. Your image has, from first to last, been the one living image in his guilty heart. I am the miserable victim of a man's passing fancy. You have been, you are still, the one object of a husband's love. Ask your own heart if the woman lives who can say to you what I have said—unless she knew it to be true. "

Catherine's head sank on her bosom; her helpless hands lay trembling on her lap. Overpowered by the confession which she had just heard—a confession which had followed closely on the thoughts inspired by the appearance of the child—her agitation was beyond control; her mind was unequal to the effort of decision. The woman who had been wronged—who had the right to judge for herself, and to speak for herself—was the silent woman of the two!

It was not quite dark yet. Sydney could see as well as hear.

For the first time since the beginning of the interview, she allowed the impulse of the moment to lead her astray. In her eagerness to complete the act of atonement, she failed to appreciate the severity of the struggle that was passing in Catherine's mind. She alluded again to Herbert Linley, and she spoke too soon.

"Will you let him ask your pardon? " she said. "He expects no more. "

Catherine's spirit was roused in an instant. "He expects too much! " she answered, sternly. "Is he here by your connivance? Is he, too, waiting to take me by surprise? "

"I am incapable, madam, of taking such a liberty with you as that; I may perhaps have hoped to be able to tell him, by writing, of a different reception—" She checked herself. "I beg your pardon, if I have ventured to hope. I dare not ask you to alter your opinion—"

"Do you dare to look the truth in the face? " Catherine interposed. "Do you remember what sacred ties that man has broken? what memories he has profaned? what years of faithful love he has cast from him? Must I tell you how he poisoned his wife's mind with doubts of his truth and despair of his honor, when he basely deserted her? You talk of your repentance. Does your repentance forget that he would still have been my blameless husband but for you? "

Sydney silently submitted to reproach, silently endured the shame that finds no excuse for itself.

Catherine looked at her and relented. The noble nature which could stoop to anger, but never sink to the lower depths of malice and persecution, restrained itself and made amends. "I say it in no unkindness to you, " she resumed. "But when you ask me to forgive, consider what you ask me to forget. It will only distress us both if we remain longer together, " she continued, rising as she spoke. "Perhaps you will believe that I mean well, when I ask if there is anything I can do for you? "

"Nothing! "

All the desolation of the lost woman told its terrible tale in that one word. Invited to rest herself in the hotel, she asked leave to remain where she was; the mere effort of rising was too much for her now. Catherine said the parting words kindly. "I believe in your good intentions; I believe in your repentance. "

"Believe in my punishment! " After that reply, no more was said.

Behind the trees that closed the view at the further extremity of the lawn the moon was rising. As the two women lost sight of each other, the new light, pure and beautiful, began to dawn over the garden.

Chapter XLVI.

Nil Desperandum.

No horror of her solitude, no melancholy recollections, no dread of the future disturbed Sydney's mind. The one sense left in her was the sense of fatigue. Vacantly, mechanically, the girl rested as a tired animal might have rested. She saw nothing, heard nothing; the one feeling of which she was conscious was a dull aching in every limb. The moon climbed the heavens, brightened the topmost leaves of the trees, found the gloom in which Sydney was hidden, and cheered it tenderly with radiant light. She was too weary to sleep, too weary even to shade her face when the moonbeams touched it. While the light still strengthened, while the slow minutes still followed each other unheeded, the one influence that could rouse Sydney found her at last—set her faint heart throbbing—called her prostrate spirit to life again. She heard a glad cry of recognition in a child's voice:

"Oh, Sydney, dear, is it you? "

In another instant her little pupil and playfellow of former days was in her arms.

"My darling, how did you come here? "

Susan answered the question. "We are on our way back from the Palace, miss. I am afraid, " she said, timidly, "that we ought to go in. "

Silently resigned, Sydney tried to release the child. Kitty clung to her and kissed her; Kitty set the nurse at defiance. "Do you think I am going to leave Syd now I have found her? Susan, I am astonished at you! "

Susan gave way. Where the nature is gentle, kindness and delicacy go hand-in-hand together, undisturbed by the social irregularities which beset the roadway of life. The nursemaid drew back out of hearing. Kitty's first questions followed each other in breathless succession. Some of them proved to be hard, indeed, to answer truly, and without reserve. She inquired if Sydney had seen her mother, and then she was eager to know why Sydney had been left in the garden alone.

"Why haven't you gone back to the house with mamma? " she asked.

"Don't ask me, dear, " was all that Sydney could say. Kitty drew the inevitable conclusion: "Have you and mamma quarreled? "

"Oh, no! "

"Then come indoors with me. "

"Wait a little, Kitty, and tell me something about yourself. How do you get on with your lessons? "

"You dear foolish governess, do you expect me to learn my lessons, when I haven't got you to teach me? Where have you been all this long while? *I* wouldn't have gone away and left *you!* " She paused; her eager eyes studied Sydney's face with the unrestrained curiosity of a child. "Is it the moonlight that makes you look pale and wretched? " she said. "Or are you really unhappy? Tell me, Syd, do you ever sing any of those songs that I taught you, when you first came to us? "

"Never, dear! "

"Have you anybody to go out walking with you and running races with you, as I did? "

"No, my sweet! Those days have gone by forever. "

Kitty laid her head sadly on Sydney's bosom. "It's not the moonlight, " she said; "shall I tell you a secret? Sometimes I am not happy either. Poor papa is dead. He always liked you—I'm sure you are sorry for him. "

Astonishment held Sydney speechless. Before she could ask who had so cruelly deceived the child, and for what purpose, the nursemaid, standing behind the chair, warned her to be silent by a touch.

"I think we are all unhappy now, " Kitty went on, still following her own little train of thought. "Mamma isn't like what she used to be. And even my nice Captain hasn't a word to say to me. He wouldn't come back with us; he said he would go back by himself. "

Another allusion which took Sydney by surprise! She asked who the Captain was. Kitty started as if the question shocked her. "Oh dear, dear, this is what comes of your going away and leaving us! You don't know Captain Bennydeck. "

The name of her father's correspondent! The name which she vaguely remembered to have heard in her childhood! "Where did you first meet with him? " she inquired.

"At the seaside, dear! "

"Do you mean at Sandyseal? "

"Yes. Mamma liked him—and grandmamma liked him (which is wonderful)—and I gave him a kiss. Promise me not to tell! My nice Captain is going to be my new papa. "

Was there any possible connection between what Kitty had just said, and what the poor child had been deluded into believing when she spoke of her father? Even Susan seemed to be in the secret of this strange second marriage! She interfered with a sharp reproof. "You mustn't talk in that way, Miss Kitty. Please put her off your lap, Miss Westerfield; we have been here too long already. "

Kitty proposed a compromise; "I'll go, " she said, "if Syd will come with me. "

"I'm sorry, my darling, to disappoint you. "

Kitty refused to believe it. "You couldn't disappoint me if you tried, " she said boldly.

"Indeed, indeed, I must go away. Oh, Kitty, try to bear it as I do! "

Entreaties were useless; the child refused to hear of another parting. "I want to make you and mamma friends again. Don't break my heart, Sydney! Come home with me, and teach me, and play with me, and love me! "

She pulled desperately at Sydney's dress; she called to Susan to help her. With tears in her eyes, the girl did her best to help them both. "Miss Westerfield will wait here, " she said to Kitty, "while you speak to your mamma. —Say Yes! " she whispered to Sydney; "it's our only chance. "

The child instantly exacted a promise. In the earnestness of her love she even dictated the words. "Say it after me, as I used to say my lessons, " she insisted. "Say, 'Kitty, I promise to wait for you. '"

Who that loved her could have refused to say it! In one form or another, the horrid necessity for deceit had followed, and was still following, that first, worst act of falsehood—the elopement from Mount Morven.

Kitty was now as eager to go as she had been hitherto resolute to remain. She called for Susan to follow her, and ran to the hotel.

"My mistress won't let her come back—you can leave the garden that way. " The maid pointed along the path to the left and hurried after the child.

They were gone—and Sydney was alone again.

At the parting with Kitty, the measure of her endurance was full. Not even the farewell at Mount Morven had tried her by an ordeal so cruel as this. No kind woman was willing to receive her and employ her, now. The one creature left who loved her was the faithful little friend whom she must never see again. "I am still innocent to that child, " she thought—"and I am parted from her forever! "

She rose to leave the garden.

A farewell look at the last place in which she had seen Kitty tempted her to indulge in a moment of delay. Her eyes rested on the turn in the path at which she had lost sight of the active little figure hastening away to plead her cause. Even in absence, the child was Sydney's good angel still. As she turned away to follow the path that had been shown to her, the relief of tears c ame at last. It cooled her burning head; it comforted her aching heart. She tried to walk on. The tears blinded her—she strayed from the path—she would have fallen but for a hand that caught her, and held her up. A man's voice, firm and deep and kind, quieted her first wild feeling of terror. "My child, you are not fit to be by yourself. Let me take care of you—let me comfort you, if I can. "

He carried her back to the seat that she had left, and waited by her in merciful silence.

"You are very young to feel such bitter sorrow, " he said, when she was composed again. "I don't ask what your sorrow is; I only want to know how I can help you. "

"Nobody can help me. "

"Can I take you back to your friends? "

"I have no friends. "

"Pardon me, you have one friend at least—you have me. "

"You? A stranger? "

"No human creature who needs my sympathy is a stranger. "

She turned toward him for the first time. In her new position, she was clearly visible in the light. He looked at her attentively. "I have seen you somewhere, " he said, "before now. "

She had not noticed him when they had passed each other at Sandyseal. "I think you must be mistaken, " she answered. "May I thank you for your kindness? and may I hope to be excused if I say good-night? "

He detained her. "Are you sure that you are well enough to go away by yourself? " he asked anxiously.

"I am quite sure! "

He still detained her. His memory of that first meeting at the seaside hotel reminded him that he had seen her in the company of a man. At their second meeting, she was alone, and in tears. Sad experience led him to form his own conclusions. "If you won't let me take care of you, " he said, "will you consider if I can be of any use to you, and will you call at that address? " He gave her his card. She took it without looking at it; she was confused; she hardly knew what to say. "Do you doubt me? " he asked—sadly, not angrily.

282

"Oh, how can I do that! I doubt myself; I am not worthy of the interest you feel in me. "

"That is a sad thing to say, " he answered. "Let me try to give you confidence in yourself. Do you go to London when you leave this place? "

"Yes. "

"To-morrow, " he resumed, "I am going to see another poor girl who is alone in the world like you. If I tell you where she lives, will you ask her if I am a person to be trusted? "

He had taken a letter from his pocket, while he was speaking; and he now tore off a part of the second leaf, and gave it to her. "I have only lately, " he said, "received the address from a friend. "

As he offered that explanation, the shrill sound of a child's voice, raised in anger and entreaty, reached their ears from the neighborhood of the hotel. Faithful little Kitty had made her escape, determined to return to Sydney had been overtaken by the maid — and had been carried back in Susan's arms to the house. Sydney imagined that she was not perhaps alone in recognizing the voice. The stranger who had been so kind to her did certainly start and look round.

The stillness of the night was disturbed no more. The man turned again to the person who had so strongly interested him. The person was gone.

In fear of being followed, Sydney hurried to the railway station. By the light in the carriage she looked for the first time at the fragment of the letter and the card.

The stranger had presented her with her own address! And, when she looked at the card, the name was Bennydeck!

Chapter XLVII.

Better Do It Than Wish It Done.

More than once, on one and the same day, the Captain had been guilty of a weakness which would have taken his oldest friends by surprise, if they had seen him at the moment. He hesitated.

A man who has commanded ships and has risked his life in the regions of the frozen deep, is a man formed by nature and taught by habit to meet emergency face to face, to see his course straight before him, and to take it, lead him where it may. But nature and habit, formidable forces as they are, find their master when they encounter the passion of Love.

At once perplexed and distressed by that startling change in Catherine which he had observed when her child approached her, Bennydeck's customary firmness failed him, when the course of conduct toward his betrothed wife which it might be most becoming to follow presented itself to him as a problem to be solved. When Kitty asked him to accompany her nursemaid and herself on their return to the hotel, he had refused because he felt reluctant to intrude himself on Catherine's notice, until she was ready to admit him to her confidence of her own free will. Left alone, he began to doubt whether delicacy did really require him to make the sacrifice which he had contemplated not five minutes since. It was surely possible that Catherine might be waiting to see him, and might then offer the explanation which would prove to be equally a relief on both sides. He was on his way to the hotel when he met with Sydney Westerfield.

To see a woman in the sorest need of all that kindness and consideration could offer, and to leave her as helpless as he had found her, would have been an act of brutal indifference revolting to any man possessed of even ordinary sensibility. The Captain had only followed his natural impulses, and had only said and done what, in nearly similar cases, he had said and done on other occasions.

Left by himself, he advanced a few steps mechanically on the way by which Sydney had escaped him—and then stopped. Was there any sufficient reason for his following her, and intruding himself on her notice? She had recovered, she was in possession of his address, she had been referred to a person who could answer for his good intentions; all that it was his duty to do, had been done already. He turned back again, in the direction of the hotel.

Hesitating once more, he paused half-way along the corridor which led to Catherine's sitting-room. Voices reached him from persons who had entered the house by the front door. He recognized Mrs. Presty's loud confident tones. She was taking leave of friends, and was standing with her back toward him. Bennydeck waited, unobserved, until he saw her enter the sitting-room. No such explanation as he was in search of could possibly take place in the presence of Catherine's mother. He returned to the garden.

Mrs. Presty was in high spirits. She had enjoyed the Festival; she had taken the lead among the friends who accompanied her to the Palace; she had ordered everything, and paid for nothing, at that worst of all bad public dinners in England, the dinner which pretends to be French. In a buoyant frame of mind, ready for more enjoyment if she could only find it, what did she see on opening the sitting-room door? To use the expressive language of the stage, Catherine was "discovered alone"—with her elbows on the table, and her face hidden in her hands—the picture of despair.

Mrs. Presty surveyed the spectacle before her with righteous indignation visible in every line of her face. The arrangement which bound her daughter to give Bennydeck his final reply on that day had been well known to her when she left the hotel in the morning. The conclusion at which she arrived, on returning at night, was expressed with Roman brevity and Roman eloquence in four words:

"Oh, the poor Captain! "

Catherine suddenly looked up.

"I knew it, " Mrs. Presty continued, with her sternest emphasis; "I see what you have done, in your face. You have refused Bennydeck. "

"God forgive me, I have been wicked enough to accept him! "

Hearing this, some mothers might have made apologies; and other mothers might have asked what that penitential reply could possibly mean. Mrs. Presty was no matron of the ordinary type. She welcomed the good news, without taking the smallest notice of the expression of self-reproach which had accompanied it.

"My dear child, accept the congratulations of your fond old mother. I have never been one of the kissing sort (I mean of course where women are concerned); but this is an occasion which justifies something quite out of the common way. Come and kiss me. "

Catherine took no notice of that outburst of maternal love.

"I have forgotten everything that I ought to have remembered, " she said. "In my vanity, in my weakness, in my selfish enjoyment of the passing moment, I have been too supremely happy even to think of the trials of my past life, and of the false position in which they have placed me toward a man, whom I ought to be ashamed to deceive. I have only been recalled to a sense of duty, I might almost say to a sense of decency, by my poor little child. If Kitty had not reminded me of her father—"

Mrs. Presty dropped into a chair: she was really frightened. Her fat cheeks trembled like a jelly on a dish that is suddenly moved.

"Has that man been here? " she asked.

"What man? "

"The man who may break off your marriage if he meets with the Captain. Has Herbert Linley been here? "

"Certainly not. The one person associated with my troubles whom I have seen to-day is Sydney Westerfield. "

Mrs. Presty bounced out of her chair. "You—have seen—Sydney Westerfield? " she repeated with emphatic pauses which expressed amazement tempered by unbelief.

"Yes; I have seen her. "

"Where? "

"In the garden. "

"And spoken to her? "

"Yes. "

Mrs. Presty raised her eyes to the ceiling. Whether she expected our old friend "the recording angel" to take down the questions and answers that had just passed, or whether she was only waiting to see the hotel that held her daughter collapse under a sense of moral responsibility, it is not possible to decide. After an awful pause, the old lady remembered that she had something more to say—and said it.

"I make no remark, Catherine; I don't even want to know what you and Miss Westerfield said to each other. At the same time, as a matter of convenience to myself, I wish to ascertain whether I must leave this hotel or not. The same house doesn't hold that woman and ME. Has she gone? "

"She has gone. "

Mrs. Presty looked round the room. "And taken Kitty with her? " she asked.

"Don't speak of Kitty! " Catherine cried in the greatest distress. "I have had to keep the poor innocent affectionate child apart from Miss Westerfield by force. My heart aches when I think of it. "

"I'm not surprised, Catherine. My granddaughter has been brought up on the modern system. Children are all little angels—no punishments—only gentle remonstrance—'Don't be naughty, dear, because you will make poor mamma unhappy. ' And then, mamma grieves over it and wonders over it, when she finds her little angel disobedient. What a fatal system of education! All my success in life; every quality that endeared me to your father and Mr. Presty; every social charm that has made me the idol of society, I attribute entirely to judicious correction in early life, applied freely with the open hand. We will change the subject. Where is dear Bennydeck? I want to congratulate him on his approaching marriage. " She looked hard at her daughter, and mentally added: "He'll live to regret it! "

Catherine knew nothing of the Captain's movements. "Like you, " she told her mother, "I have something to say to him, and I don't know where he is. "

Mrs. Presty still kept her eyes fixed on her daughter. Nobody, observing Catherine's face, and judging also by the tone of her voice, would have supposed that she was alluding to the man whose irresistible attractions had won her. She looked ill at ease, and she spoke sadly.

"You don't seem to be in good spirits, my dear, " Mrs. Presty gently suggested. "No lovers' quarrel already, I hope? "

"Nothing of the kind. "

"Can I be of any use to you? "

"You might be of the greatest use. But I know only too well, you would refuse. "

Thus far, Mrs. Presty had been animated by curiosity. She began now to feel vaguely alarmed. "After all that I have done for you, " she answered, "I don't think you ought to say that. Why should I refuse? "

Catherine hesitated.

Her mother persisted in pressing her. "Has it anything to do with Captain Bennydeck? "

"Yes. "

"What is it? "

Catherine roused her courage.

"You know what it is as well as I do, " she said. "Captain Bennydeck believes that I am free to marry him because I am a widow. You might help me to tell him the truth. "

"What!!! "

That exclamation of horror and astonishment was loud enough to have been heard in the garden. If Mrs. Presty's hair had been all her own, it must have been hair that stood on end.

Catherine quietly rose. "We won't discuss it, " she said, with resignation. "I knew you would refuse me. " She approached the door. Her mother got up and resolutely stood in the way. "Before you commit an act of downright madness, " Mrs. Presty said, "I mean to try if I can stop you. Go back to your chair. "

Catherine refused.

"I know how it will end, " she answered; "and the sooner it ends the better. You will find that I am quite as determined as you are. A man who loves me as *he* loves me, is a man whom I refuse to deceive. "

"Let's have it out plainly, " Mrs. Presty insisted. "He believes your first marriage has been dissolved by death. Do you mean to tell him that it has been dissolved by Divorce? "

"I do. "

"What right has he to know it? "

"A right that is not to be denied. A wife must have no secrets from her husband. "

Mrs. Presty hit back smartly.

"You're not his wife yet. Wait till you are married. "

"Never! Who but a wretch would marry an honest man under false pretenses? "

"I deny the false pretenses! You talk as if you were an impostor. Are you, or are you not, the accomplished lady who has charmed him? Are you, or are you not, the beautiful woman whom he loves? There isn't a stain on your reputation. In every respect you are the wife he wants and the wife who is worthy of him. And you are cruel enough to disturb the poor man about a matter that doesn't concern him! you are fool enough to raise doubts of you in his mind, and give him a reproach to cast in your teeth the first time you do anything that happens to offend him! Any woman—I don't care who she may be— might envy the home that's waiting for you and your child, if you're wise enough to hold your tongue. Upon my word, Catherine, I am ashamed of you. Have you no principles? "

She really meant it! The purely selfish considerations which she urged on her daughter were so many undeniable virtues in Mrs. Presty's estimation. She took the highest moral ground, and stood up and crowed on it, with a pride in her own principles which the Primate of all England might have envied.

But Catherine's rare resolution held as firm as ever. She got a little nearer to the door. "Good-night, mamma, " was the only reply she made.

"Is that all you have to say to me? "

"I am tired, and I must rest. Please let me go. "

Mrs. Presty threw open the door with a bang.

"You refuse to take my advice? " she said. "Oh, very well, have your own way! You are sure to prosper in the end. These are the days of exhibitions and gold medals. If there is ever an exhibition of idiots at large, I know who might win the prize. "

Catherine was accustomed to preserve her respect for her mother under difficulties; but this was far more than her sense of filial duty could successfully endure.

"I only wish I had never taken your advice, " she answered. "Many a miserable moment would have been spared me, if I had always done what I am doing now. You have been the evil genius of my life since Miss Westerfield first came into our house. "

She passed through the open doorway—stopped—and came back again. "I didn't mean to offend you, mamma—but you do say such irritating things. Good-night. "

Not a word of reply acknowledged that kindly-meant apology. Mrs. Presty—vivacious Mrs. Presty of the indomitable spirit and the ready tongue—was petrified. She, the guardian angel of the family, whose experience, devotion, and sound sense had steered Catherine through difficulties and dangers which must have otherwise ended in utter domestic shipwreck—she, the model mother—had been stigmatized as the evil genius of her daughter's life by no less a person than that daughter herself! What was to be said? What was to be done? What terrible and unexampled course of action should be taken after such an insult as this? Mrs. Presty stood helpless in the middle of the room, and asked herself these questions, and waited and wondered and found no answer.

An interval passed. There was a knock at the door. A waiter appeared. He said: "A gentleman to see Mrs. Norman. "

The gentleman entered the room and revealed himself.

Herbert Linley!

The Evil Genius

Chapter XLVIII.

Be Careful!

The divorced husband looked at his mother-in-law without making the slightest sacrifice to the claims of politeness. He neither offered his hand nor made his bow. His frowning eyebrows, his flushed face, betrayed the anger that was consuming him.

"I want to see Catherine, " he said.

This deliberate rudeness proved to be the very stimulant that was required to restore Mrs. Presty to herself. The smile that always meant mischief made its threatening appearance on the old lady's face.

"What sort of company have you been keeping since I last saw you? " she began.

"What have you got to do with the company I keep? "

"Nothing whatever, I am happy to say. I was merely wondering whether you have been traveling lately in the south part of Africa, and have lived exclusively in the society of Hottentots. The only other explanation of your behavior is that I have been so unfortunate as to offend you. But it seems improbable—I am not your wife. "

"Thank God for that! "

"Thank God, as you say. But I should really be glad (as a mere matter of curiosity) to know what your extraordinary conduct means. You present yourself in this room uninvited, you find a lady here, and you behave as if you had come into a shop and wanted to ask the price of something. Let me give you a lesson in good manners. Observe: I receive you with a bow, and I say: How do you do, Mr. Linley? Do you understand me? "

"I don't want to understand you—I want to see Catherine. "

"Who is Catherine? "

"You know as well as I do—your daughter. "

"My daughter, sir, is a stranger to you. We will speak of her, if you please, by the name—the illustrious name—which she inherited at her birth. You wish to see Mrs. Norman? "

"Call her what you like. I have a word to say to her, and I mean to say it. "

"No, Mr. Linley, you won't say it. "

"We'll see about that! Where is she? "

"My daughter is not well. "

"Well or ill, I shan't keep her long. "

"My daughter has retired to her room. "

"Where is her room? "

Mrs. Presty moved to the fireplace, and laid her hand on the bell.

"Are you aware that this house is a hotel? " she asked.

"It doesn't matter to me what it is. "

"Oh yes, it does. A hotel keeps waiters. A hotel, when it is as large as this, has a policeman in attendance. Must I ring? "

The choice between giving way to Mrs. Presty, or being disgracefully dismissed, was placed plainly before him. Herbert's life had been the life of a gentleman; he knew that he had forgotten himself; it was impossible that he could hesitate.

"I won't trouble you to ring, " he said; "and I will beg your pardon for having allowed my temper to get the better of me. At the same time it ought to be remembered, I think, in my favor, that I have had some provocation. "

"I don't agree with you, " Mrs. Presty answered. She was deaf to any appeal for mercy from Herbert Linley. "As to provocation, " she added, returning to her chair without asking him to be seated, "when you apply that word to yourself, you insult my daughter and me. *You* provoked? Oh, heavens! "

"You wouldn't say that, " he urged, speaking with marked restraint of tone and manner, "if you knew what I have had to endure—"

Mrs. Presty suddenly looked toward the door. "Wait a minute, " she said; "I think I hear somebody coming in. "

In the silence that followed, footsteps were audible outside—not approaching the door, however, but retiring from it. Mrs. Presty had apparently been mistaken. "Yes? " she said resignedly, permitting Herbert to proceed.

He really had something to say for himself, and he said it with sufficient moderation. That he had been guilty of serious offenses he made no attempt to deny; but he pleaded that he had not escaped without justly suffering for what he had done. He had been entirely in the wrong when he threatened to take the child away from her mother by force of law; but had he not been punished when his wife obtained her Divorce, and separated him from his little daughter as well as from herself? (No: Mrs. Presty failed to see it; if anybody had suffered by the Divorce, the victim was her injured daughter.) Still patient, Herbert did not deny the injury; he only submitted once more that he had suffered his punishment. Whether his life with Sydney Westerfield had or had not been a happy one, he must decline to say; he would only declare that it had come to an end. She had left him. Yes! she had left him forever. He had no wish to persuade her to return to their guilty life; they were both penitent, they were both ashamed of it. But she had gone away without the provision which he was bound in honor to offer to her.

"She is friendless; she may be in a state of poverty that I tremble to think of, " Herbert declared. "Is there nothing to plead for me in such anxiety as I am suffering now? " Mrs. Presty stopped him there; she had heard enough of Sydney already.

"I see nothing to be gained, " she said, "by dwelling on the past; and I should be glad to know why you have come to this place to-night. "

"I have come to see Kitty. "

"Quite out of the question. "

"Don't tell me that, Mrs. Presty! I'm one of the wretchedest men living, and I ask for the consolation of seeing my child. Kitty hasn't forgotten me yet, I know. Her mother can't be so cruel as to refuse. She shall fix her own time, and send me away when she likes; I'll submit to anything. Will you ask Catherine to let me see Kitty? "

"I can't do it. "

"Why not? "

"For private reasons. "

"What reasons? "

"For reasons into which you have no right to inquire. "

He got up from his chair. His face presented the same expression which Mrs. Presty had seen on it when he first entered the room.

"When I came in here, " he said, "I wished to be certain of one thing. Your prevarication has told me what I wanted to know. The newspapers had Catherine's own authority for it, Mrs. Presty, when they called her widow. I know now why my brother, who never deceived me before, has deceived me about this. I understand the part that your daughter has been playing—and I am as certain as if I had heard it, of the devilish lie that one of you—perhaps both of you—must have told my poor child. No, no; I had better not see Catherine. Many a man has killed his wife, and has not had such good reason for doing it as I have. You are quite right to keep me away from her. "

He stopped—and looked suddenly toward the door. "I hear her, " he cried, "She's coming in! "

The footsteps outside were audible once more. This time, they were approaching; they were close to the door. Herbert drew back from it. Looking round to see that he was out of the way, Mrs. Presty rushed forward—tore open the door in terror of what might happen—and admitted Captain Bennydeck.

Chapter XLIX.

Keep the Secret.

The Captain's attention was first attracted by the visitor whom he found in the room. He bowed to the stranger; but the first impression produced on him did not appear to have been of the favorable kind, when he turned next to Mrs. Presty.

Observing that she was agitated, he made the customary apologies, expressing his regret if he had been so unfortunate as to commit an intrusion. Trusting in the good sense and good breeding which distinguished him on other occasions, Mrs. Presty anticipated that he would see the propriety of leaving her alone again with the person whom he had found in her company. To her dismay he remained in the room; and, worse still, he noticed her daughter's absence, and asked if there was any serious cause for it.

For the moment, Mrs. Presty was unable to reply. Her presence of mind—or, to put it more correctly, her ready audacity—deserted her, when she saw Catherine's husband that had been, and Catherine's husband that was to be, meeting as strangers, and but too likely to discover each other.

In all her experience she had never been placed in such a position of embarrassment as the position in which she found herself now. The sense of honor which had prompted Catherine's resolution to make Bennydeck acquainted with the catastrophe of married life, might plead her excuse in the estimation of a man devotedly attached to her. But if the Captain was first informed that he had been deceived by a person who was a perfect stranger to him, what hope could be entertained of his still holding himself bound by his marriage engagement? It was even possible that distrust had been already excited in his mind. He must certainly have heard a man's voice raised in anger when he approached the door—and he was now observing that man with an air of curiosity which was already assuming the appearance of distrust. That Herbert, on his side, resented the Captain's critical examination of him was plainly visible in his face. After a glance at Bennydeck, he asked Mrs. Presty "who that gentleman was. "

"I may be mistaken, " he added; "but I thought your friend looked at me just now as if he knew me. "

"I have met you, sir, before this. " The Captain made the reply with a courteous composure of tone and manner which apparently reminded Herbert of the claims of politeness.

"May I ask where I had the honor of seeing you? " he inquired.

"We passed each other in the hall of the hotel at Sandyseal. You had a young woman with you. "

"Your memory is a better one than mine, sir. I fail to remember the circumstance to which you refer. "

Bennydeck let the matter rest there. Struck by the remarkable appearance of embarrassment in Mrs. Presty's manner—and feeling (in spite of Herbert's politeness of language) increased distrust of the man whom he had found visiting her—he thought it might not be amiss to hint that she could rely on him in case of necessity. "I am afraid I have interrupted a confidential interview, " he began; "and I ought perhaps to explain—"

Mrs. Presty listened absently; preoccupied by the fear that Herbert would provoke a dangerous disclosure, and by the difficulty of discovering a means of preventing it. She interrupted the Captain.

"Excuse me for one moment; I have a word to say to this gentleman. " Bennydeck immediately drew back, and Mrs. Presty lowered her voice. "If you wish to see Kitty, " she resumed, attacking Herbert on his weak side, "it depends entirely on your discretion. "

"What do you mean by discretion? "

"Be careful not to speak of our family troubles—and I promise you shall see Kitty. That is what I mean. "

Herbert declined to say whether he would be careful or not. He was determined to find out, first, with what purpose Bennydeck had entered the room. "The gentleman was about to explain himself to you, " he said to Mrs. Presty. "Why don't you give him the opportunity? "

She had no choice but to submit—in appearance at least. Never had she hated Herbert as she hated him at that moment. The Captain went on with his explanation. He had his reasons (he said) for hesitating, in the first instance, to present himself uninvited, and he accordingly retired. On second thoughts, however, he had returned, in the hope—

"In the hope, " Herbert interposed, "of seeing Mrs. Presty's daughter? "

"That was one of my motives, " Bennydeck answered.

"Is it indiscreet to inquire what the other motive was? "

"Not at all. I heard a stranger's voice, speaking in a tone which, to say the least of it, is not customary in a lady's room and I thought—"

Herbert interrupted him again. "And you thought your interference might be welcome to the lady! Am I right? "

"Quite right. "

"Am I making another lucky guess if I suppose myself to be speaking to Captain Bennydeck? "

"I shall be glad to hear, sir, how you have arrived at the knowledge of my name. "

"Shall we say, Captain, that I have arrived at it by instinct? "

His face, as he made that reply, alarmed Mrs. Presty. She cast a look at him, partly of entreaty, partly of warning. No effect was produced by the look. He continued, in a tone of ironical compliment: "You must pay the penalty of being a public character. Your marriage is announced in the newspapers. "

"I seldom read the newspapers. "

"Ah, indeed? Perhaps the report is not true? As you don't read the newspapers, allow me to repeat it. You are engaged to marry the 'beautiful widow, Mrs. Norman. ' I think I quote those last words correctly? "

Mrs. Presty suddenly got up. With an inscrutable face that told no tales, she advanced to the door. Herbert's insane jealousy of the man who was about to become Catherine's husband had led him into a serious error; he had driven Catherine's mother to desperation. In that state of mind she recovered her lost audacity, as a matter of course. Opening the door, she turned round to the two men, with a magnificent impudence of manner which in her happiest moments she had never surpassed.

"I am sorry to interrupt this interesting conversation, " she said; "but I have stupidly forgotten one of my domestic duties. You will allow me to return, and listen with renewed pleasure, when my household business is off my mind. I shall hope to find you both more polite to each other than ever when I come back. " She was in such a frenzy of suppressed rage that she actually kissed her hand to them as she left the room!

Bennydeck looked after her, convinced that some sinister purpose was concealed under Mrs. Presty's false excuses, and wholly unable to imagine what that purpose might be. Herbert still persisted in trying to force a quarrel on the Captain.

"As I remarked just now, " he proceeded, "newspaper reports are not always to be trusted. Do you seriously mean, my dear sir, to marry Mrs. Norman? "

"I look forward to that honor and that happiness. But I am at a loss to know how it interests you. "

"In that case allow me to enlighten you. My name is Herbert Linley. "

He had held his name in reserve, feeling certain of the effect which he would produce when he pronounced it. The result took him completely by surprise. Not the slightest appearance of agitation showed itself in Bennydeck's manner. On the contrary, he looked as if there was something that interested him in the discovery of the name.

"You are probably related to a friend of mine? " he said, quietly.

"Who is your friend? "

"Mr. Randal Linley. "

Herbert was entirely unprepared for this discovery. Once more, the Captain had got the best of it.

"Are you and Randal Linley intimate friends? " he inquired, as soon as he had recovered himself.

"Most intimate. "

"It's strange that he should never have mentioned me, on any occasion when you and he were together. "

"It does indeed seem strange. "

Herbert paused. His brother's keen sense of the disgrace that he had inflicted on the family recurred to his memory. He began to understand Randal's otherwise unaccountable silence.

"Are you nearly related to Mr. Randal Linley? " the Captain asked.

"I am his elder brother. "

Ignorant on his part of the family disgrace, Bennydeck heard that reply with amazement. From his point of view, it was impossible to account for Randal's silence.

"Will you think me very inquisitive, " Herbert resumed, "if I ask whether my brother approves of your marriage? "

There was a change in his tone, as he put that question which warned Bennydeck to be on his guard. "I have not yet consulted my friend's opinion, " he answered, shortly.

Herbert threw off the mask. "In the meantime, you shall have my opinion, " he said. "Your marriage is a crime—and I mean to prevent it. "

The Captain left his chair, and sternly faced the man who had spoken those insolent words.

"Are you mad? " he asked.

Herbert was on the point of declaring himself to have been Catherine's husband, until the law dissolved their marriage—when a waiter came in and approached him with a message. "You are wanted immediately, sir. "

"Who wants me? "

"A person outside, sir. It's a serious matter—there is not a moment to lose. "

Herbert turned to the Captain. "I must have your promise to wait for me, " he said, "or I don't leave the room. "

"Make your mind easy. I shall not stir from this place till you have explained yourself, " was the firm reply.

The servant led the way out. He crossed the passage, and opened the door of a waiting-room. Herbert passed in—and found himself face to face with his divorced wife.

Chapter L.

Forgiveness to the Injured Doth Belong.

Without one word of explanation, Catherine stepped up to him, and spoke first.

"Answer me this, " she said—"have you told Captain Bennydeck who I am? "

"Not yet. "

The shortest possible reply was the only reply that he could make, in the moment when he first looked at her.

She was not the same woman whom he had last seen at Sandyseal, returning for her lost book. The agitation produced by that unexpected meeting had turned her pale; the overpowering sense of injury had hardened and aged her face. This time, she was prepared to see him; this time, she was conscious of a resolution that raised her in her own estimation. Her clear blue eyes glittered as she looked at him, the bright color glowed in her cheeks; he was literally dazzled by her beauty.

"In the past time, which we both remember, " she resumed, "you once said that I was the most truthful woman you had ever known. Have I done anything to disturb that part of your old faith in me? "

"Nothing. "

She went on: "Before you entered this house, I had determined to tell Captain Bennydeck what you have not told him yet. When I say that, do you believe me? "

If he had been able to look away from her, he might have foreseen what was coming; and he would have remembered that his triumph over the Captain was still incomplete. But his eyes were riveted on her face; his tenderest memories of her were pleading with him. He answered as a docile child might have answered.

"I do believe you. "

She took a letter from her bosom; and, showing it, begged him to remark that it was not closed.

"I was in my bedroom writing, " she said, "When my mother came to me and told me that you and Captain Bennydeck had met in my sitting-room. She dreaded a quarrel and an exposure, and she urged me to go downstairs and insist on sending you away—or permit her to do so, if I could not prevail on myself to follow her advice. I refused to allow the shameful dismissal of a man who had once had his claim on my respect. The only alternative that I could see was to speak with you here, in private, as we are speaking now. My mother undertook to manage this for me; she saw the servant, and gave him the message which you received. Where is Captain Bennydeck now? "

"He is waiting in the sitting-room. "

"Waiting for you? "

"Yes. "

She considered a little before she said her next words.

"I have brought with me what I was writing in my own room, " she resumed, "wishing to show it to you. Will you read it? "

She offered the letter to him. He hesitated. "Is it addressed to me? " he asked.

"It is addressed to Captain Bennydeck, " she answered.

The jealousy that still rankled in his mind—jealousy that he had no more lawful or reasonable claim to feel than if he had been a stranger—urged him to assume an indifference which he was far from feeling. He begged that Catherine would accept his excuses.

She refused to excuse him.

"Before you decide, " she said, "you ought at least to know why I have written to Captain Bennydeck, instead of speaking to him as I had proposed. My heart failed me when I thought of the distress that he might feel—and, perhaps of the contempt of myself which, good and gentle as he is, he might not be able to disguise. My letter tells him the truth, without concealment. I am obliged to speak of the manner in which you have treated me, and of the circumstances which forced me into acts of deception that I now bitterly regret. I have tried not to misrepresent you; I have been anxious to do you no wrong. It is for you, not for me, to say if I have succeeded. Once more, will you read my letter? "

The sad self-possession, the quiet dignity with which she spoke, appealed to his memory of the pardon that she had so generously granted, while he and Sydney Westerfield were still guiltless of the injury inflicted on her at a later time. Silently he took the letter from her, and read it.

She kept her face turned away from him and from the light. The effort to be still calm and reasonable—to suffer the heart-ache, and not to let the suffering be seen—made cruel demands on the self-betraying nature of a woman possessed by strong emotion. There was a moment when she heard him sigh while he was reading. She looked round at him, and instantly looked away again.

He rose and approached her; he held out the letter in one hand, and pointed to it with the other. Twice he attempted to speak. Twice the influence of the letter unmanned him.

It was a hard struggle, but it was for her sake: he mastered his weakness, and forced his trembling voice to submit to his will.

"Is the man whom you are going to marry worthy of *this?* " he asked, still pointing to the letter.

She answered, firmly: "More than worthy of it. "

"Marry him, Catherine—and forget Me. "

The great heart that he had so sorely wounded pitied him, forgave him, answered him with a burst of tears. She held out one imploring hand.

His lips touched it—he was gone.

Chapter LI.

Dum Spiro, Spero.

Brisk and smiling, Mrs. Presty presented herself in the waiting-room. "We have got rid of our enemy! " she announced, "I looked out of the window and saw him leaving the hotel. " She paused, struck with the deep dejection expressed in her daughter's attitude. "Catherine! " she exclaimed, "I tell you Herbert has gone, and you look as if you regretted it! Is there anything wrong? Did my message fail to bring him here? "

"No. "

"He was bent on mischief when I saw him last. Has he told Bennydeck of the Divorce? "

"No. "

"Thank Heaven for that! There is no one to be afraid of now. Where is the Captain? "

"He is still in the sitting-room. "

"Why don't you go to him? "

"I daren't! "

"Shall I go? "

"Yes—and give him this. "

Mrs. Presty took the letter. "You mean, tear it up, " she said, "and quite right, too. "

"No; I mean what l say. "

"My dear child, if you have any regard for yourself, if you have any regard for me, don't ask me to give Bennydeck this mad letter! You won't hear reason? You still insist on it? "

"I do. "

"If Kitty ever behaves to you, Catherine, as you have behaved to me—you will have richly deserved it. Oh, if you were only a child again, I'd beat it out of you—I would! "

With that outburst of temper, she took the letter to Bennydeck. In less than a minute she returned, a tamed woman. "He frightens me, " she said.

"Is he angry? "

"No—and that is the worst of it. When men are angry, I am never afraid of them. He's quiet, too quiet. He said: 'I'm waiting for Mr. Herbert Linley; where is he? ' I said. 'He has left the hotel. ' He said: 'What does that mean? ' I handed the letter to him. 'Perhaps this will explain, ' I said. He looked at the address, and at once recognized your handwriting. 'Why does she write to me when we are both in the same house? Why doesn't she speak to me? ' I pointed to the letter. He wouldn't look at it; he looked straight at me. 'There's some mystery here, ' he said; 'I'm a plain man, I don't like mysteries. Mr. Linley had something to say to me, when the message interrupted him. Who sent the message? Do you know? ' If there is a woman living, Catherine, who would have told the truth, in such a position as mine was at that moment, I should like to have her photograph. I said I didn't know—and I saw he suspected me of deceiving him. Those kind eyes of his—you wouldn't believe it of them! —looked me through and through. 'I won't detain you any longer, ' he said. I'm not easily daunted, as you know—the relief it was to me to get away from him is not to be told in words. What do you think I heard when I got into the passage? I heard him turn the key of the door. He's locked in, my dear; he's locked in! We are too near him here. Come upstairs. "

Catherine refused. "I ought to be near him, " she said, hopefully; "he may wish to see me. "

Her mother reminded her that the waiting-room was a public room, and might be wanted.

"Let's go into the garden, " Mrs. Presty proposed. "We can tell the servant who waits on us where we may be found. "

Catherine yielded. Mrs. Presty's excitement found its overflow in talking perpetually. Her daughter had nothing to say, and cared nothing where they went; all outward manifestation of life in her seemed to be suspended at that terrible time of expectation. They wandered here and there, in the quietest part of the grounds. Half an hour passed—and no message was received. The hotel clock struck the hour—and still nothing happened.

"I can walk no longer, " Catherine said. She dropped on one of the garden-chairs, holding by her mother's hand. "Go to him, for God's sake! " she entreated. "I can endure it no longer. "

Mrs. Presty—even bold Mrs. Presty—was afraid to face him again. "He's fond of the child, " she suggested; "let's send Kitty. "

Some little girls were at play close by who knew where Kitty was to be found. In a few minutes more they brought her back with them. Mrs. Presty gave the child her instructions, and sent her away proud of her errand, and delighted at the prospect of visiting the Captain by herself, as if she "was a grown-up lady. "

This time the period of suspense was soon at an end. Kitty came running back. "It's lucky you sent me, " she declared. "He wouldn't have opened the door to anybody else—he said so himself. "

"Did you knock softly, as I told you? " Mrs. Presty asked.

"No, grandmamma, I forgot that. I tried to open the door. He called out not to disturb him. I said, 'It's only me, ' and he opened the door directly. What makes him look so pale, mamma? Is he ill? "

"Perhaps he feels the heat, " Mrs. Presty suggested, judiciously.

"He said, 'Dear little Kitty, ' and he caught me up in his arms and kissed me. When he sat down again he took me on his knee, and he asked if I was fond of him, and I said, 'Yes, I am, ' and he kissed me again, and he asked if I had come to stay with him and keep him company. I forgot what you wanted me to say, " Kitty acknowledged, addressing Mrs. Presty; "so I made it up out of my own head. "

"What did you tell him? "

"I told him, mamma was as fond of him as I was, and I said, 'We will both keep you company. ' He put me down on the floor, and he got up and went to the window and looked out. I told him that wasn't the way to find her, and I said, 'I know where she is; I'll go and fetch her. ' He's an obstinate man, our nice Captain. He wouldn't come away from the window. I said, 'You wish to see mamma, don't you? ' And he said 'Yes. ' 'You mustn't lock the door again, ' I told him, 'she won't like that'; and what do you think he said? He said 'Good-by, Kitty! ' Wasn't it funny? He didn't seem to know what he was talking about. If you ask my opinion, mamma, I think the sooner you go to him the better. " Catherine hesitated. Mrs. Presty on one side, and Kitty on the other, led her between them into the house.

Chapter LII.

L'homme propose, et Dieu dispose.

Captain Bennydeck met Catherine and her child at the open door of the room. Mrs. Presty, stopping a few paces behind them, waited in the passage; eager to see what the Captain's face might tell her. It told her nothing.

But Catherine saw a change in him. There was something in his manner unnaturally passive and subdued. It suggested the idea of a man whose mind had been forced into an effort of self-control which had exhausted its power, and had allowed the signs of depression and fatigue to find their way to the surface. The Captain was quiet, the Captain was kind; neither by word nor look did he warn Catherine that the continuity of their intimacy was in danger of being broken—and yet, her spirits sank, when they met at the open door.

He led her to a chair, and said she had come to him at a time when he especially wished to speak with her. Kitty asked if she might remain with them. He put his hand caressingly on her head; "No, my dear, not now. "

The child eyed him for a moment, conscious of something which she had never noticed in him before, and puzzled by the discovery. She walked back, cowed and silent, to the door. He followed her and spoke to Mrs. Presty.

"Take your grandchild into the garden; we will join you there in a little while. Good-by for the present, Kitty. "

Kitty said good-by mechanically—like a dull child repeating a lesson. Her grandmother led her away in silence.

Bennydeck closed the door and seated himself by Catherine.

"I thank you for your letter, " he said. "If such a thing is possible, it has given me a higher opinion of you than any opinion that I have held yet. "

She looked at him with a feeling of surprise, so sudden and so overwhelming that she was at a loss how to reply. The last words which she expected to hear from him, when he alluded to her confession, were the words that had just passed his lips.

"You have owned to faults that you have committed, and deceptions that you have sanctioned, " he went on—"with nothing to gain, and everything to lose, by telling the truth. Who but a good woman would have done that? "

There was a deeper feeling in him than he had ventured to express. It betrayed itself by a momentary trembling in his voice. Catherine drew a little closer to him.

"You don't know how you surprise me, how you relieve me, " she said, warmly—and pressed his hand. In the eagerness of her gratitude, in the gladness that had revived her sinking heart, she failed to feel that the pressure was not returned.

"What have I said to surprise you? " he asked. "What anxiety have I relieved, without knowing it? "

"I was afraid you would despise me. "

"Why should I despise you? "

"Have I not gained your good opinion under false pretenses? Have I not allowed you to admire me and to love me without telling you that there was anything in my past life which I have reason to regret? Even now, I can hardly realize that you excuse and forgive me; you, who have read the confession of my worst faults; you, who know the shocking inconsistencies of my character—"

"Say at once, " he answered, "that I know you to be a mortal creature. Is there any human character, even the noblest, that is always consistently good? "

"One reads of them sometimes, " she suggested, "in books. "

"Yes, " he said. "In the worst books you could possibly read—the only really immoral books written in our time. "

"Why are they immoral? "

"For this plain reason, that they deliberately pervert the truth. Claptrap, you innocent creature, to catch foolish readers! When do these consistently good people appear in the life around us, the life that we all see? Never! Are the best mortals that ever lived above the reach of temptation to do ill, and are they always too good to yield to it? How does the Lord's Prayer instruct humanity? It commands us all, without exception, to pray that we may not be led into temptation. You have been led into temptation. In other words, you are a human being. All that a human being could do you have done—you have repented and confessed. Don't I know how you have suffered and how you have been tried! Why, what a mean Pharisee I should be if I presumed to despise you! "

She looked at him proudly and gratefully; she lifted her arm as if to thank him by an embrace, and suddenly let it drop again at her side.

"Am I tormenting myself without cause? " she said. "Or is there something that looks like sorrow, showing itself to me in your face? "

"You see the bitterest sorrow that I have felt in all my sad life. "

"Is it sorrow for me? "

"No. Sorrow for myself. "

"Has it come to you through me? Is it my fault? "

"It is more your misfortune than your fault. "

"Then you can feel for me? "

"I can and do. "

He had not yet set her at ease.

"I am afraid your sympathy stops somewhere, " she said. "Where does it stop? "

For the first time, he shrank from directly answering her. "I begin to wish I had followed your example, " he owned. "It might have been better for both of us if I had answered your letter in writing. "

"Tell me plainly, " she cried, "is there something you can't forgive? "

"There is something I can't forget. "

"What is it? Oh, what is it! When my mother told poor little Kitty that her father was dead, are you even more sorry than I am that I allowed it? Are you even more ashamed of me than I am of myself? "

"No. I regret that you allowed it; but I understand how you were led into that error. Your husband's infidelity had shaken his hold on your respect for him and your sympathy with him, and had so left you without your natural safeguard against Mrs. Presty's sophistical reasoning and bad example. But for *that* wrong-doing, there is a remedy left. Enlighten your child as you have enlightened me; and then—I have no personal motive for pleading Mr. Herbert Linley's cause, after what I have seen of him—and then, acknowledge the father's claim on the child. "

"Do you mean his claim to see her? "

"What else can I mean? Yes! let him see her. Do (God help me, now when it's too late!)—do what you ought to have done, on that accursed day which will be the blackest day in my calendar, to the end of my life. "

"What day do you mean? "

"The day when you remembered the law of man, and forgot the law of God; the day when you broke the marriage tie, the sacred tie, by a Divorce! "

She listened—not conscious now of suspense or fear; she listened, with her whole heart in revolt against him.

"You are too cruel! " she declared. "You can feel for me, you can understand me, you can pardon me in everything else that I have done. But you judge without mercy of the one blameless act of my life, since my husband left me—the act that protected a mother in the exercise of her rights. Oh, can it be you? Can it be you? "

"It can be, " he said, sighing bitterly; "and it is. "

"What horrible delusion possesses you? Why do you curse the happy day, the blessed day, which saw me safe in the possession of my child? "

"For the worst and meanest of reasons, " he answered—"a selfish reason. Don't suppose that I have spoken of Divorce as one who has had occasion to think of it. I have had no occasion to think of it; I don't think of it even now. I abhor it because it stands between you and me. I loathe it, I curse it because it separates us for life. "

"Separates us for life? How? "

"Can you ask me? "

"Yes, I do ask you! "

He looked round him. A society of religious persons had visited the hotel, and had obtained permission to place a copy of the Bible in every room. One of those copies lay on the chimney-piece in Catherine's room. Bennydeck brought it to her, and placed it on the table near which she was sitting. He turned to the New Testament, and opened it at the Gospel of Saint Matthew. With his hand on the page, he said:

"I have done my best rightly to understand the duties of a Christian. One of those duties, as I interpret them, is to let what I believe show itself in what I do. You have seen enough of me, I hope, to know (though I have not been forward in speaking of it) that I am, to the best of my poor ability, a faithful follower of the teachings of Christ. I dare not set my own interests and my own happiness above His laws. If I suffer in obeying them as I suffer now, I must still submit. They are the laws of my life. "

"Is it through me that you suffer? "

"It is through you. "

"Will you tell me how? "

He had already found the chapter. His tears dropped on it as he pointed to the verse.

"Read, " he answered, "what the most compassionate of all Teachers has said, in the Sermon on the Mount. "

She read: "Whosoever shall marry her that is divorced committeth adultery. "

Another innocent woman, in her place, might have pointed to that first part of the verse, which pre-supposes the infidelity of the divorced wife, and might have asked if those words applied to *her*. This woman, knowing that she had lost him, knew also what she owed to herself. She rose in silence, and held out her hand at parting.

He paused before he took her hand. "Can you forgive me? " he asked.

She said: "I can pity you. "

"Can you look back to the day of your marriage? Can you remember the words which declared the union between you and your husband to be separable only by death? Has he treated you with brutal cruelty? "

"Never! "

"Has he repented of his sin? "

"Yes. "

"Ask your own conscience if there is not a worthier life for you and your child than the life that you are leading now. " He waited, after that appeal to her. The silence remained unbroken. "Do not mistake me, " he resumed gently. "I am not thinking of the calamity that has fallen on me in a spirit of selfish despair—I am looking to *your* future, and I am trying to show you the way which leads to hope. Catherine! have you no word more to say to me? "

In faint trembling tones she answered him at last:

"You have left me but one word to say. Farewell! "

He drew her to him gently, and kissed her on the forehead. The agony in his face was more than she could support; she recoiled from it in horror. His last act was devoted to the tranquillity of the one woman whom he had loved. He signed to her to leave him.

Chapter LIII.

The Largest Nature, the Longest Love.

Mrs. Presty waited in the garden to be joined by her daughter and Captain Bennydeck, and waited in vain. It was past her grandchild's bedtime; she decided on returning to the house.

"Suppose we look for them in the sitting-room? " Kitty proposed.

"Suppose we wait a moment, before we go in? " her wise grandmother advised. "If I hear them talking I shall take you upstairs to bed. "

"Why? "

Mrs. Presty favored Kitty with a hint relating to the management of inquisitive children which might prove useful to her in after-life. "When you grow up to be a woman, my dear, beware of making the mistake that I have just committed. Never be foolish enough to mention your reasons when a child asks, Why? "

"Was that how they treated *you*, grandmamma, when you were a child yourself? "

"Of course it was! "

"Why? "

They had reached the sitting-room door by this time. Kitty opened it without ceremony and looked in. The room was empty.

Having confided her granddaughter to the nursemaid's care, Mrs. Presty knocked at Catherine's bedroom door. "May I come in? "

"Come in directly! Where is Kitty? "

"Susan is putting her to bed. "

"Stop it! Kitty mustn't go to bed. No questions. I'll explain myself when you come back. " There was a wildness in her eyes, and a tone of stern command in her voice, which warned her mother to set dignity aside, and submit.

"I don't ask what has happened, " Mrs. Presty resumed on her return. "That letter, that fatal letter to the Captain, has justified my worst fears. What in Heaven's name are we to do now? "

"We are to leave this hotel, " was the instant reply.

"When? "

"To-night. "

"Catherine! do you know what time it is? "

"Time enough to catch the last train to London. Don't raise objections! If I stay at this place, with associations in every part of it which remind me of that unhappy man, I shall go mad! The shock I have suffered, the misery, the humiliation—I tell you it's more than I can bear. Stay here by yourself if you like; I mean to go. "

She paced with frantic rapidity up and down the room. Mrs. Presty took the only way by which it was possible to calm her. "Compose yourself, Catherine, and all that you wish shall be done. I'll settle everything with the landlord, and give the maid her orders. Sit down by the open window; let the wind blow over you. "

The railway service from Sydenham to London is a late service. At a few minutes before midnight they were in time for the last train. When they left the station, Catherine was calm enough to communicate her plans for the future. The nearest hotel to the terminus would offer them accommodation for that night. On the next day they could find some quiet place in the country—no matter where, so long as they were not disturbed. "Give me rest and peace, and my mind will be easier, " Catherine said. "Let nobody know where to find me. "

These conditions were strictly observed—with an exception in favor of Mr. Sarrazin. While his client's pecuniary affairs were still unsettled, the lawyer had his claim to be taken into her confidence.

* * * * * * * * * * * * * * * * * *

The next morning found Captain Bennydeck still keeping his rooms at Sydenham. The state of his mind presented a complete contrast to the state of Catherine's mind. So far from sharing her aversion to the personal associations which were connected with the hotel, he found his one consolation in visiting the scenes which reminded him of the beloved woman whom he had lost. The reason for this was not far to seek. His was the largest nature, and his had been the most devoted love.

As usual, his letters were forwarded to him from his place of residence in London. Those addressed in handwritings that he knew were the first that he read. The others he took out with him to that sequestered part of the garden in which he had passed the happiest hours of his life by Catherine's side.

He had been thinking of her all the morning; he was thinking of her now.

His better judgment protested; his accusing conscience warned him that he was committing, not only an act of folly but (with his religious convictions) an act of sin—and still she held her place in his thoughts. The manager had told him of her sudden departure from the hotel, and had declared with perfect truth that the place of her destination had not been communicated to him. Asked if she had left no directions relating to her correspondence, he had replied that his instructions were to forward all letters to her lawyer. On the point of inquiring next for the name and address, Bennydeck's sense of duty and sense of shame (roused at last) filled him with a timely contempt for himself. In feeling tempted to write to Catherine—in encouraging fond thoughts of her among scenes which kept her in his memory— he had been false to the very principles to which he had appealed at their farewell interview. She had set him the right example, the example which he was determined to follow, in leaving the place. Before he could falter in his resolution, he gave notice of his departure. The one hope for him now was to find a refuge from himself in acts of mercy. Consolation was perhaps waiting for him in his Home.

His unopened correspondence offered a harmless occupation to his thoughts, in the meanwhile. One after another he read the letters, with an attention constantly wandering and constantly recalled, until he opened the last of them that remained. In a moment more his interest was absorbed. The first sentences in the letter told him that the deserted creature whom he had met in the garden—the stranger to whom he had offered help and consolation in the present and in the future—was no other than the lost girl of whom he had been so long in search; the daughter of Roderick Westerfield, once his dearest and oldest friend.

In the pages that followed, the writer confided to him her sad story; leaving it to her father's friend to decide whether she was worthy of the sympathy which he had offered to her, when he thought she was a stranger.

This part of her letter was necessarily a repetition of what Bennydeck had read, in the confession which Catherine had addressed to him. That generous woman had been guilty of one, and but one, concealment of the truth. In relating the circumstances under which the elopement from Mount Morven had taken place, she had abstained, in justice to the sincerity of Sydney's repentance, from mentioning Sydney's name. "Another instance, " the Captain thought bitterly, as he closed the letter, "of the virtues which might have made the happiness of my life! "

But he was bound to remember—and he did remember—that there was now a new interest, tenderly associating itself with his life to come. The one best way of telling Sydney how dear she was to him already, for her father's sake, would be to answer her in person. He hurried away to London by the first train, and drove at once to Randal's place of abode to ask for Sydney's address.

Wondering what had become of the postscript to his letter, which had given Bennydeck the information of which he was now in search, Randal complied with his friend's request, and then ventured to allude to the report of the Captain's marriage engagement.

"Am I to congratulate you? " he asked.

"Congratulate me on having discovered Roderick Westerfield's daughter. "

That reply, and the tone in which it was given, led Randal to ask if the engagement had been prematurely announced.

"There is no engagement at all, " Bennydeck answered, with a look which suggested that it might be wise not to dwell on the subject.

But the discovery was welcome to Randal, for his brother's sake. He ran the risk of consequences, and inquired if Catherine was still to be found at the hotel.

The Captain answered by a sign in the negative.

Randal persisted. "Do you know where she has gone? "

"Nobody knows but her lawyer. "

"In that case, " Randal concluded, "I shall get the information that I want. " Noticing that Bennydeck looked surprised, he mentioned his motive. "Herbert is pining to see Kitty, " h continued; "and I mean to help him. He has done all that a man could do to atone for the past. As things are, I believe I shall not offend Catherine, if I arrange for a meeting between father and child. What do you say? "

Bennydeck answered, earnestly and eagerly: "Do it at once! "

They left the house together—one to go to Sydney's lodgings, the other on his way to Mr. Sarrazin's office.

Chapter LIV.

Let Bygones Be Bygones.

When the servant at the lodgings announced a visitor, and mentioned his name, Sydney's memory (instead of dwelling on the recollection of the Captain's kindness) perversely recalled the letter that she had addressed to him, and reminded her that she stood in need of indulgence, which even so good a man might hesitate to grant. Bennydeck's first words told the friendless girl that her fears had wronged him.

"My dear, how like your father you are! You have his eyes and his smile; I can't tell you how pleasantly you remind me of my dear old friend. " He took her hand, and kissed her as he might have kissed a daughter of his own. "Do you remember me at home, Sydney, when you were a child? No: you must have been too young for that. "

She was deeply touched. In faint trembling tones she said; "I remember your name; my poor father often spoke of you. "

A man who feels true sympathy is never in danger of mistaking his way to a woman's heart, when that woman has suffered. Bennydeck consoled, interested, charmed Sydney, by still speaking of the bygone days at home.

"I well remember how fond your father was of you, and what a bright little girl you were, " the Captain went on. "You have forgotten, I dare say, the old-fashioned sea-songs that he used to be so fond of teaching you. It was the strangest and prettiest contrast, to hear your small piping child's voice singing of storms and shipwrecks, and thunder and lightning, and reefing sails in cold and darkness, without the least idea of what it all meant. Your mother was strict in those days; you never amused her as you used to amuse your father and me. When she caught you searching my pockets for sweetmeats, she accused me of destroying your digestion before you were five years old. I went on spoiling it, for all that. The last time I saw you, my child, your father was singing 'The Mariners of England, ' and you were on his knee trying to sing with him. You must have often wondered why you never saw anything more of me. Did you think I had forgotten you? "

The Evil Genius

"I am quite sure I never thought that! "

"You see I was in the Navy at the time, " the Captain resumed; "and we were ordered away to a foreign station. When I got back to England, miserable news was waiting for me. I heard of your father's death and of that shameful Trial. Poor fellow! He was as innocent, Sydney, as you are of the offense which he was accused of committing. The first thing I did was to set inquiries on foot after your mother and her children. It was some consolation to me to feel that I was rich enough to make your lives easy and agreeable to you. I thought money could do anything. A serious mistake, my dear— money couldn't find the widow and her children. We supposed you were somewhere in London; and there, to my great grief, it ended. From time to time—long afterward, when we thought we had got the clew in our hands—I continued my inquiries, still without success. A poor woman and her little family are so easily engulfed in the big city! Years passed (more of them than I like to reckon up) before I heard of you at last by name. The person from whom I got my information told me how you were employed, and where. "

"Oh, Captain Bennydeck, who could the person have been? "

"A poor old broken-down actor, Sydney. You were his favorite pupil. Do you remember him? "

"I should be ungrateful indeed if I could forget him. He was the only person in the school who was kind to me. Is the good old man still living? "

"No; he rests at last. I am glad to say I was able to make his last days on earth the happiest days of his life. "

"I wonder, " Sydney confessed, "how you met with him. "

"There was nothing at all romantic in my first discovery of him. I was reading the police reports in a newspaper. The poor wretch was brought before a magistrate, charged with breaking a window. His one last chance of escaping starvation in the streets was to get sent to prison. The magistrate questioned him, and brought to light a really heart-breaking account of misfortune, imbittered by neglect on the part of people in authority who were bound to help him. He was remanded, so that inquiries might be made. I attended the court on the day when he appeared there again, and heard his statement

321

confirmed. I paid his fine, and contrived to put him in a way of earning a little money. He was very grateful, and came now and then to thank me. In that way I heard how his troubles had begun. He had asked for a small advance on the wretched wages that he received. Can you guess how the schoolmistress answered him? "

"I know but too well how she answered him, " Sydney said; "I was turned out of the house, too. "

"And I heard of it, " the Captain replied, "from the woman herself. Everything that could distress me she was ready to mention. She told me of your mother's second marriage, of her miserable death, of the poor boy, your brother, missing, and never heard of since. But when I asked where you had gone she had nothing more to say. She knew nothing, and cared nothing, about you. If I had not become acquainted with Mr. Randal Linley, I might never have heard of you again. We will say no more of that, and no more of anything that has happened in the past time. From to-day, my dear, we begin a new life, and (please God) a happier life. Have you any plans of your own for the future? "

"Perhaps, if I could find help, " Sydney said resignedly, "I might emigrate. Pride wouldn't stand in my way; no honest employment would be beneath my notice. Besides, if I went to America, I might meet with my brother. "

"My dear child, after the time that has passed, there is no imaginable chance of your meeting with your brother—and you wouldn't know each other again if you did meet. Give up that vain hope and stay here with me. Be useful and be happy in your own country. "

"Useful? " Sydney repeated sadly. "Your own kind heart, Captain Bennydeck, is deceiving you. To be useful means, I suppose, to help others. Who will accept help from me? "

"I will, for one, " the Captain answered.

"You! "

"Yes. You can be of the greatest use to me—you shall hear how. "

He told her of the founding of his Home and of the good it had done. "You are the very person, " he resumed, "to be the good sister-friend that I want for my poor girls: *you* can say for them what they cannot always say to me for themselves. "

The tears rose in Sydney's eyes. "It is hard to see such a prospect as that, " she said, "and to give it up as soon as it is seen. "

"Why give it up? "

"Because I am not fit for it. You are as good as a father to those lost daughters of yours. If you give them a sister-friend she ought to have set them a good example. Have I done that? Will they listen to a girl who is no better than themselves? "

"Gladly! *Your* sympathy will find its way to their hearts, because it is animated by something that they can all feel in common—something nearer and dearer to them than a sense of duty. You won't consent, Sydney, for their sakes? Will you do what I ask of you, for my sake? "

She looked at him, hardly able to understand—or, as it might have been, perhaps afraid to understand him. He spoke to her more plainly.

"I have kept it concealed from you, " he continued—"for why should I lay my load of suffering on a friend so young as you are, so cruelly tried already? Let me only say that I am in great distress. If you were with me, my child, I might be better able to bear it. "

He held out his hand. Even a happy woman could hardly have found it in her heart to resist him. In silent sympathy and respect, Sydney kissed the hand that he had offered to her. It was the one way in which she could trust herself to answer him.

Still encouraging her to see new hopes and new interests in the future, the good Captain spoke of the share which she might take in the management of the Home, if she would like to be his secretary. With this view he showed her some written reports, relating to the institution, which had been sent to him during the time of his residence at Sydenham. She read them with an interest and attention which amply justified his confidence in her capacity.

"These reports, " he explained to her, "are kept for reference; but as a means of saving time, the substance of them is entered in the daily journal of our proceedings. Come, Sydney! venture on a first experiment in your new character. I see pen, ink, and paper on the table; try if you can shorten one of the reports, without leaving out anything which it is important to know. For instance, the writer gives reasons for making his statement. Very well expressed, no doubt, but we don't want reasons. Then, again, he offers his own opinion on the right course to take. Very creditable to him, but I don't want his opinion—I want his facts. Take the pen, my secretary, and set down his facts. Never mind his reflections. "

Proud and pleased, Sydney obeyed him. She had made her little abstract, and was reading it to him at his request, while he compared it with the report, when they were interrupted by a visitor. Randal Linley came in, and noticed the papers on the table with surprise. "Is it possible that I am interrupting business? " he asked.

Bennydeck answered with the assumed air of importance which was in itself a compliment to Sydney: "You find me engaged on the business of the Home with my new secretary. "

Randal at once understood what had happened. He took his friend's arm, and led him to the other end of the room.

"You good fellow! " he said. "Add to your kindness by excusing me if I ask for a word with you in private. "

Sydney rose to retire. After having encouraged her by a word of praise, the Captain proposed that she should get ready to go out, and should accompany him on a visit to the Home. He opened the door for her as respectfully as if the poor girl had been one of the highest ladies in the land.

"I have seen my friend Sarrazin, " Randal began, "and I have persuaded him to trust me with Catherine's present address. I can send Herbert there immediately, if you will only help me. "

"How can I help you? "

"Will you allow me to tell my brother that your engagement is broken off? "

Bennydeck shrank from the painful allusion, and showed it.

Randal explained. "I am grieved, " he said, "to distress you by referring to this subject again. But if my brother is left under the false impression that your engagement will be followed by your marriage, he will refuse to intrude himself on the lady who was once his wife. "

The Captain understood. "Say what you please about me, " he replied. "Unite the father and child—and you may reconcile the husband and wife. "

"Have you forgotten, " Randal asked, "that the marriage has been dissolved? "

Bennydeck's answer ignored the law. "I remember, " he said, "that the marriage has been profaned. "

Chapter LV.

Leave It to the Child.

The front windows of Brightwater Cottage look out on a quiet green lane in Middlesex, which joins the highroad within a few miles of the market town of Uxbridge. Through the pretty garden at the back runs a little brook, winding its merry way to a distant river. The few rooms in this pleasant place of residence are well (too well) furnished, having regard to the limits of a building which is a cottage in the strictest sense of the word. Water-color drawings by the old English masters of the art ornament the dining-room. The parlor has been transformed into a library. From floor to ceiling all four of its walls are covered with books. Their old and well-chosen bindings, seen in the mass, present nothing less than a feast of color to the eye. The library and the works of art are described as heirlooms, which have passed into the possession of the present proprietor—one more among the hundreds of Englishmen who are ruined every year by betting on the Turf.

So sorely in need of a little ready money was this victim of gambling—tacitly permitted or conveniently ignored by the audacious hypocrisy of a country which rejoiced in the extinction of Baden, and which still shudders at the name of Monaco—that he was ready to let his pretty cottage for no longer a term than one month certain; and he even allowed the elderly lady, who drove the hardest of hard bargains with him, to lessen by one guinea the house-rent paid for each week. He took his revenge by means of an ironical compliment, addressed to Mrs. Presty. "What a saving it would be to the country, ma'am, if you were Chancellor of the Exchequer! " With perfect gravity Mrs. Presty accepted that well-earned tribute of praise. "You are quite right, sir; I should be the first official person known to the history of England who took proper care of the public money. "

Within two days of the time when they had left the hotel at Sydenham, Catherine and her little family circle had taken possession of the cottage.

The two ladies were sitting in the library each occupied with a book chosen from the well-stocked shelves. Catherine's reading appeared to be more than once interrupted by Catherine's thoughts. Noticing this circumstance, Mrs. Presty asked if some remarkable event had happened, and if it was weighing heavily on her daughter's mind.

Catherine answered that she was thinking of Kitty, and that anxiety connected with the child did weigh heavily on her mind.

Some days had passed (she reminded Mrs. Presty) since the interview at which Herbert Linley had bidden her farewell. On that occasion he had referred to her proposed marriage (never to be a marriage now!) in terms of forbearance and generosity which claimed her sincerest admiration. It might be possible for her to show a grateful appreciation of his conduct. Devotedly fond of his little daughter, he must have felt acutely his long separation from her; and it was quite likely that he might ask to see Kitty. But there was an obstacle in the way of her willing compliance with that request, which it was impossible to think of without remorse, and which it was imperatively necessary to remove. Mrs. Presty would understand that she alluded to the shameful falsehood which had led the child to suppose that her father was dead.

Strongly disapproving of the language in which her daughter had done justice to the conduct of the divorced husband, Mrs. Presty merely replied: "You are Kitty's mother; I leave it to you"—and returned to her reading.

Catherine could not feel that she had deserved such an answer as this. "Did I plan the deception? " she asked. "Did I tell the lie? "

Mrs. Presty was not in the least offended. "You are comparatively innocent, my dear, " she admitted, with an air of satirical indulgence. "You only consented to the deception, and profited by the lie. Suppose we own the truth? You are afraid. "

Catherine owned the truth in the plainest terms:

"Yes, I *am* afraid. "

"And you leave it to me? "

"I leave it to you. "

Mrs. Presty complacently closed her book. "I was quite prepared to hear it, " she said; "all the unpleasant complications since your

Divorce—and Heaven only knows how many of them have presented themselves—have been left for me to unravel. It so happens—though I was too modest to mention it prematurely—that I have unraveled *this* complication. If one only has eyes to see it, there is a way out of every difficulty that can possibly happen. " She pushed the book that she had been reading across the table to Catherine. "Turn to page two hundred and forty, " she said. "There is the way out. "

The title of the book was "Disasters at Sea"; and the page contained the narrative of a shipwreck. On evidence apparently irresistible, the drowning of every soul on board the lost vessel had been taken for granted—when a remnant of the passengers and crew had been discovered on a desert island, and had been safely restored to their friends. Having read this record of suffering and suspense, Catherine looked at her mother, and waited for an explanation.

"Don't you see it? " Mrs. Presty asked.

"I can't say that I do. "

The old lady's excellent temper was not in the least ruffled, even by this.

"Quite inexcusable on my part, " she acknowledged; "I ought to have remembered that you don't inherit your mother's vivid imagination. Age has left me in full possession of those powers of invention which used to amaze your poor father. He wondered how it was that I never wrote a novel. Mr. Presty's appreciation of my intellect was equally sincere; but he took a different view. 'Beware, my dear, ' he said, 'of trifling with the distinction which you now enjoy: you are one of the most remarkable women in England—you have never written a novel. ' Pardon me; I am wandering into the region of literary anecdote, when I ought to explain myself. Now pray attend to this: —I propose to tell Kitty that I have found a book which is sure to interest her; and I shall direct her attention to the lamentable story which you have just read. She is quite sharp enough (there are sparks of my intellectual fire in Kitty) to ask if the friends of the poor shipwrecked people were not very much surprised to see them again. To this I shall answer: 'Very much, indeed, for their friends thought they were dead. ' Ah, you dear dull child, you see it now! "

Catherine saw it so plainly that she was eager to put the first part of the experiment to an immediate trial.

Kitty was sent for, and made her appearance with a fishing-rod over her shoulder. "I'm going to the brook, " she announced; "expect some fish for dinner to-day. "

A wary old hand stopped Catherine, in the act of presenting "Disasters at Sea, " to Kitty's notice; and a voice, distinguished by insinuating kindness, said to the child: "When you have done fishing, my dear, come to me; I have got a nice book for you to read. —How very absurd of you, Catherine, " Mrs. Presty continued, when they were alone again, "to expect the child to read, and draw her own conclusions, while her head is full of fishing! If there are any fish in the brook, *she* won't catch them. When she comes back disappointed and says: 'What am I to do now? ' the 'Disasters at Sea' will have a chance. I make it a rule never to boast; but if there is a thing that I understand, it's the management of children. Why didn't I have a large family? "

Attended by the faithful Susan, Kitty baited her hook, and began to fish where the waters of the brook were overshadowed by trees.

A little arbor covered by a thatched roof, and having walls of wooden lattice-work, hidden by creepers climbing over them inside and out, offered an attractive place of rest on this sheltered side of the garden. Having brought her work with her, the nursemaid retired to the summer-house and diligently plied her needle, looking at Kitty from time to time through the open door. The air was delightfully cool, the pleasant rippling of the brook fell soothingly on the ear, the seat in the summer-house received a sitter with the softly-yielding submission of elastic wires. Susan had just finished her early dinner: in mind and body alike, this good girl was entirely and deservedly at her ease. By finely succeeding degrees, her eyelids began to show a tendency downward; her truant needle-work escaped from her fingers, and lay lazily on her lap. She snatched it up with a start, and sewed with severe resolution until her thread was exhausted. The reel was ready at her side; she took it up for a fresh supply, and innocently rested her head against the leafy and flowery wall of the arbor. Was it thought that gradually closed her eyes again? or was it sleep? In either case, Susan was lost to all sense of passing events; and Susan's breathing became musically regular, emulous of the musical regularity of the brook.

As a lesson in patience, the art of angling pursued in a shallow brook has its moral uses. Kitty fished, and waited, and renewed the bait and tried again, with a command of temper which would have been a novelty in Susan's experience, if Susan had been awake. But the end which comes to all things came also to Kitty's patience. Leaving her rod on the bank, she let the line and hook take care of themselves, and wandered away in search of some new amusement.

Lingering here and there to gather flowers from the beds as she passed them, Kitty was stopped by a shrubbery, with a rustic seat placed near it, which marked the limits of the garden on that side. The path that she had been following led her further and further away from the brook, but still left it well in view. She could see, on her right hand, the clumsy old wooden bridge which crossed the stream, and served as a means of communication for the servants and the tradespeople, between the cottage and the village on the lower ground a mile away.

The child felt hot and tired. She rested herself on the bench, and, spreading the flowers by her side, began to arrange them in the form of a nosegay. Still true to her love for Sydney, she had planned to present the nosegay to her mother, offering the gift as an excuse for returning to the forbidden subject of her governess, and for asking when they might hope to see each other again.

Choosing flowers and then rejecting them, trying other colors and wondering whether she had accomplished a change for the better, Kitty was startled by the sound of a voice calling to her from the direction of the brook.

She looked round, and saw a gentleman crossing the bridge. He asked the way to Brightwater Cottage.

There was something in his voice that attracted her—how or why, at her age, she never thought of inquiring. Eager and excited, she ran across the lawn which lay between her and the brook, before she answered the gentleman's question.

As they approached each other, his eyes sparkled, his face flushed; he cried out joyfully, "Here she is! "—and then changed again in an instant. A horrid pallor overspread his face as the child stood looking at him with innocent curiosity. He startled Kitty, not because he seemed to be shocked and distressed, she hardly noticed that; but because he was so like—although he was thinner and paler and older—oh, so like her lost father!

"This is the cottage, sir, " she said faintly.

His sorrowful eyes rested kindly on her. And yet, it seemed as if she had in some way disappointed him. The child ventured to say: "Do you know me, sir? "

He answered in the saddest voice that Kitty had ever heard: "My little girl, what makes you think I know you? "

She was at a loss how to reply, fearing to distress him. She could only say: "You are so like my poor papa. "

He shook and shuddered, as if she had said something to frighten him. He took her hand. On that hot day, his fingers felt as cold as if it had been winter time. He led her back to the seat that she had left. "I'm tired, my dear, " he said. "Shall we sit down? " It was surely true that he was tired. He seemed hardly able to lift one foot after the other; Kitty pitied him. "I think you must be ill; " she said, as they took their places, side by side, on the bench.

"No; not ill. Only weary, and perhaps a little afraid of frightening you. " He kept her hand in his hand, and patted it from time to time. "My dear, why did you say 'poor papa, ' when you spoke of your father just now? "

"My father is dead, sir. "

He turned his face away from her, and pressed both hands on his breast, as if he had felt some dreadful pain there, and was trying to hide it. But he mastered the pain; and he said a strange thing to her—very gently, but still it was strange. He wished to know who had told her that her father was dead.

"Grandmamma told me. "

"Do you remember what grandmamma said? "

"Yes—she told me papa was drowned at sea. "

He said something to himself, and said it twice over. "Not her mother! Thank God, not her mother! " What did he mean?

Kitty looked and looked at him, and wondered and wondered. He put his arm round her. "Come near to me, " he said. "Don't be afraid of me, my dear. " She moved nearer and showed him that she was not afraid. The poor man seemed hardly to understand her. His eyes grew dim; he sighed like a person in distress; he said: "Your father would have kissed you, little one, if he had been alive. You say I am like your father. May I kiss you? "

She put her hands on his shoulder and lifted her face to him. In the instant when he kissed her, the child knew him. Her heart beat suddenly with an overpowering delight; she started back from his embrace. "That's how papa used to kiss me! " she cried. "Oh! you *are* papa! Not drowned! not drowned! " She flung her arms round his neck, and held him as if she would never let him go again. "Dear papa! Poor lost papa! " His tears fell on her face; he sobbed over her. "My sweet darling! my own little Kitty! "

The hysterical passion that had overcome her father filled her with piteous surprise. How strange, how dreadful that he should cry— that he should be so sorry when she was so glad! She took her little handkerchief out of the pocket of her pinafore, and dried his eyes. "Are you thinking of the cruel sea, papa? No! the good sea, the kind, bright, beautiful sea that has given you back to me, and to mamma—! "

They had forgotten her mother! —and Kitty only discovered it now. She caught at one of her father's hands hanging helpless at his side, and pulled at it as if her little strength could force him to his feet. "Come, " she cried, "and make mamma as happy as I am! "

He hesitated. She sprang on his knee; she pressed her cheek against his cheek with the caressing tenderness, familiar to him in the first happy days when she was an infant. "Oh, papa, are you going to be unkind to me for the first time in your life? "

His momentary resistance was at an end. He was as weak in her hands now as if he had been the child and she had been the man.

Laughing and singing and dancing round him, Kitty led the way to the window of the room that opened on the garden. Some one had closed it on the inner side. She tapped impatiently at the glass. Her mother heard the tapping; her mother came to the window; her mother ran out to meet them. Since the miserable time when they left Mount Morven, since the long unnatural separation of the parents and the child, those three were together once more!

AFTER THE STORY

1. —The Lawyer's Apology.

That a woman of my wife's mature years should be jealous of one of the most exemplary husbands that the records of matrimony can produce is, to say the least of it, a discouraging circumstance. A man forgets that virtue is its own reward, and asks, What is the use of conjugal fidelity?

However, the motto of married life is (or ought to be): Peace at any price. I have been this day relieved from the condition of secrecy that has been imposed on me. You insisted on an explanation some time since. Here it is at last.

For the ten-thousandth time, my dear, in our joint lives, you are again right. That letter, marked private, which I received at the domestic tea-table, was what you positively declared it to be, a letter from a lady—a charming lady, plunged in the deepest perplexity. We had been well known to each other for many years, as lawyer and client. She wanted advice on this occasion also—and wanted it in the strictest confidence. Was it consistent with my professional duty to show her letter to my wife? Mrs. Sarrazin says Yes; Mrs. Sarrazin's husband says No.

Let me add that the lady was a person of unblemished reputation, and that she was placed in a false position through no fault of her own. In plain English, she was divorced. Ah, my dear (to speak in the vivid language of the people), do you smell a rat?

Yes: my client was Mrs. Norman; and to her pretty cottage in the country I betook myself the next day. There I found my excellent friend Randal Linley, present by special invitation.

Stop a minute. Why do I write all this, instead of explaining myself by word of mouth? My love, you are a member of an old and illustrious family; you honored me when you married me; and you have (as your father told me on our wedding day) the high and haughty temper of your race. I foresee an explosion of this temper, and I would rather have my writing-paper blown up than be blown up myself.

Is this a cowardly confession on my part? All courage, Mrs. Sarrazin, is relative; the bravest man living has a cowardly side to his character, though it may not always be found out. Some years ago, at a public dinner, I sat next to an officer in the British army. At one time in his life he had led a forlorn hope. At another time, he had picked up a wounded soldier, and had carried him to the care of the surgeons through a hail-storm of the enemy's bullets. Hot courage and cool courage, this true hero possessed both. *I* saw the cowardly side of his character. He lost his color; perspiration broke out on his forehead; he trembled; he talked nonsense; he was frightened out of his wits. And all for what? Because he had to get on his legs and make a speech!

Well: Mrs. Norman, and Randal Linley, and I, sat down to our consultation at the cottage.

What did my fair client want?

She contemplated marrying for the second time, and she wanted my advice as a lawyer, and my encouragement as an old friend. I was quite ready; I only waited for particulars. Mrs. Norman became dreadfully embarrassed, and said: "I refer you to my brother-in-law. "

I looked at Randal. "Once her brother-in-law, no doubt, " I said; "but after the Divorce—" My friend stopped me there. "After the Divorce, " he remarked, "I may be her brother-in-law again. "

If this meant anything, it meant that she was actually going to marry Herbert Linley again. This was too ridiculous. "If it's a joke, " I said, "I have heard better fun in my time. If it's only an assertion, I don't believe it. "

"Why not? " Randal asked.

"Saying I do want you, in one breath—and I don't want you, in another—seems to be a little hard on Divorce, " I ventured to suggest.

"Don't expect *me* to sympathize with Divorce, " Randal said.

I answered that smartly. "No; I'll wait till you are married. "

He took it seriously. "Don't misunderstand me, " he replied. "Where there is absolute cruelty, or where there is deliberate desertion, on the husband's part, I see the use and the reason for Divorce. If the unhappy wife can find an honorable man who will protect her, or an honorable man who will offer her a home, Society and Law, which are responsible for the institution of marriage, are bound to allow a woman outraged under the shelter of their institution to marry again. But, where the husband's fault is sexual frailty, I say the English law which refuses Divorce on that ground alone is right, and the Scotch law which grants it is wrong. Religion, which rightly condemns the sin, pardons it on the condition of true penitence. Why is a wife not to pardon it for the same reason? Why are the lives of a father, a mother, and a child to be wrecked, when those lives may be saved by the exercise of the first of Christian virtues—forgiveness of injuries? In such a case as this I regret that Divorce exists; and I rejoice when husband and wife and child are one flesh again, re-united by the law of Nature, which is the law of God. "

I might have disputed with him; but I thought he was right. I also wanted to make sure of the facts. "Am I really to understand, " I asked, "that Mr. Herbert Linley is to be this lady's husband for the second time? "

"If there is no lawful objection to it, " Randal said—"decidedly Yes. "

My good wife, in all your experience you never saw your husband stare as he stared at that moment. Here was a lady divorced by her own lawful desire and at her own personal expense, thinking better of it after no very long interval, and proposing to marry the man again. Was there ever anything so grossly improbable? Where is the novelist who would be bold enough to invent such an incident as this?

Never mind the novelist. How did it end?

Of course it could only end in one way, so far as I was concerned. The case being without precedent in my experience, I dropped my professional character at the outset. Speaking next as a friend, I had only to say to Mrs. Norman: "The Law has declared you and Mr. Herbert Linley to be single people. Do what other single people do. Buy a license, and give notice at a church—and by all means send wedding cards to the judge who divorced you. "

Said; and, in another fortnight, done. Mr. and Mrs. Herbert Linley were married again this morning; and Randal and I were the only witnesses present at the ceremony, which was strictly private.

2. —The Lawyer's Defense.

I wonder whether the foregoing pages of my writing-paper have been torn to pieces and thrown into the waste-paper basket? You wouldn't litter the carpet. No. I may be torn in pieces, but I do you justice for all that.

What are the objections to the divorced husband and wife becoming husband and wife again? Mrs. Presty has stated them in the following order. Am I wrong in assuming that, on this occasion at least, you will agree with Mrs. Presty?

First Objection: Nobody has ever done such a thing before.

Second Objection: Penitent or not penitent, Mr. Herbert Linley doesn't deserve it.

Third Objection: No respectable person will visit them.

First Reply: The question is not whether the thing has been done before, but whether the doing of the thing is right in itself There is no clause in the marriage service forbidding a wife to forgive her husband; but there is a direct prohibition to any separation between them. It is, therefore, not wrong to forgive Mr. Herbert Linley, and it is absolutely right to marry him again.

Second Reply: When their child brings him home, and takes it for granted that her father and mother should live together, *because* they are her father and mother, innocent Kitty has appealed from the Law of Divorce to the Law of Nature. Whether Herbert Linley has deserved it or whether he has not, there he is in the only fit place for him—and there is an end of the second objection.

Third Reply: A flat contradiction to the assertion that no respectable person will visit her. Mrs. Sarrazin will visit her. Yes, you will, my dear! Not because I insist upon it—Do I ever insist on anything? No; you will act on your own responsibility, out of compassion for a misguided old woman. Judge for yourself when you read what follows, if Mrs. Presty is not sadly in need of the good example of an ornament to her sex.

The Evil Genius of the family joined us in the cottage parlor when our consultations had come to an end. I had the honor of communicating the decision at which we had arrived. Mrs. Presty marched to the door; and, from that commanding position, addressed a few farewell remarks to her daughter.

"I have done with you, Catherine. You have reached the limits of my maternal endurance at last. I shall set up my own establishment, and live again—in memory—with Mr. Norman and Mr. Presty. May you be happy. I don't anticipate it. "

She left the room—and came back again for a last word, addressed this time to Randal Linley.

"When you next see your friend, Captain Bennydeck, give him my compliments, Mr. Randal, and say I congratulate him on having been jilted by my daughter. It would have been a sad thing, indeed, if such a sensible man had married an idiot. Good-morning. "

She left the room again, and came back again for another last word, addressed on this occasion to me. Her better nature made an effort to express itself, not altogether without success.

"I think it is quite likely, Mr. Sarrazin, that some dreadful misfortune will fall on my daughter, as the punishment of her undutiful disregard of her mother's objections. In that case, I shall feel it my duty to return and administer maternal consolation. When you write, address me at my banker's. I make allowances for a lawyer, sir; I don't blame You. "

She opened the door for the third time—stepped out, and stepped back again into the room—suddenly gave her daughter a fierce kiss—returned to the door—shook her fist at Mrs. Linley with a theatrically-threatening gesture—said, "Unnatural child! "—and, after this exhibition of her better nature, and her worse, left us at last. When you visit the remarried pair on their return from their second honeymoon, take Mrs. Presty with you.

3. —The Lawyer's Last Word.

"When you force this ridiculous and regrettable affair on my attention" (I think I hear Mrs. Sarrazin say), "the least you can do is to make your narrative complete. But perhaps you propose to tell me personally what has become of Kitty, and what well-deserved retribution has overtaken Miss Westerfield."

No: I propose in this case also to communicate my information in writing—at the safe distance from home of Lincoln's Inn Fields.

Kitty accompanies her father and mother to the Continent, of course. But she insisted on first saying good-by to the dear friend, once the dear governess, whom she loves. Randal and I volunteered to take her (with her mother's ready permission) to see Miss Westerfield. Try not to be angry. Try not to tear me up.

We found Captain Bennydeck and his pretty secretary enjoying a little rest and refreshment, after a long morning's work for the good of the Home. The Captain was carving the chicken; and Sydney, by his side, was making the salad. The house-cat occupied a third chair, with her eyes immovably fixed on the movements of the knife and fork. Perhaps I was thinking of sad past days. Anyway, it seemed to me to be as pretty a domestic scene as a man could wish to look at. The arrival of Kitty made the picture complete.

Our visit was necessarily limited by a due remembrance of the hour of departure, by an early tidal train. Kitty's last words to Sydney bade her bear their next meeting in mind, and not be melancholy at only saying good-by for a time. Like all children, she asks strange questions. When we were out in the street again, she said to her uncle: "Do you think my nice Captain will marry Syd?"

Randal had noticed, in Captain Bennydeck's face, signs which betrayed that the bitterest disappointment of his life was far from being a forgotten disappointment yet. If it had been put by any other person, poor Kitty's absurd question might have met with a bitter reply. As it was, her uncle only said: "My dear child, that is no business of yours or mine."

Not in the least discouraged, Kitty turned to me. "What do *you* think, Samuel?"

I followed Randal's lead, and answered, "How should I know? "

The child looked from one to the other of us. "Shall I tell you what I think? " she said, "I think you are both of you humbugs. "

CPSIA information can be obtained
at www.ICGtesting.com
Printed in the USA
FSHW012302121221
86871FS

9 781406 582901